SCRAPS

A GROTESQUE ANTHOLOGY OF NEW AND EXCITING
EXTREME HORROR AND SPLATTERPUNK STORIES

CURATED BY JUDITH SONNET

EDITED BY
DANIELLE YEAGER
AND JUDITH SONNET

Copyright @ 2024 Judith Sonnet

Publication date: 2/1/2024

ISBN: 979-8-89342-994-7

Imprint: Independently published

Cover design A. A. Medina (Fabled Beast Design)

Edited by Danielle Yeager (Hack & Slash Editing) and Judith Sonnet.

Formatted by Ruth Anna Evans

WARNING:

This is an extreme and disturbing anthology.

If you don't like extreme horror, don't read it!

Dedicated to John Skipp.
You're an inspiration to us all.

Contents

...	1
Oral Fixations Judith Sonnet	2
...	25
The Book of Revenge Cassandra Daucus	27
...	49
Filth RE Shambrook	51
...	67
Sober Chaz Williams	69
...	95

Rita	97
Ruth Anna Evans	
...	113
FF	115
Brian G Berry	
...	145
Wet Hair	146
Jayson Dawn	
...	179
Bonemeal	181
Harrison Phillips	
...	207
Regurgitating Menstrual Seepage at The Spittoon Saloon	209
Otis Bateman	
...	255
Amateur Surgery	257
Mique Watson	
...	289
Putrefying Malediction	291
Stephanie E Jensen	
...	309
FETAL BACKWASH	310
A Novella by Judith Sonnet	

...	451
ABOUT THE WRITERS	453
...	458

***

We are, all of us, sitting in a place I like to call The Scrapyard. Out of sight and out of mind, it is a place where only true denizens of the dark and macabre thrive. We gather here, slinking out of our shadows like snakes through tall grass. Each of us has been digging, and each of us has a treasure we'd like to share with our friends. Gathered around the bonfire, which illuminates our haggard, grinning faces, we all reveal the scraps we found.

My name is Judith Sonnet, and I'm the opener and closer of tonight's festivities.

I start by sharing a treasure that I discovered underneath a pile of dirty magazines. It is small in the palm of my hand, and I have to pass it around so everyone can see it properly.

SCRAPS

It's a gleaming, rotted, broken fragment. But I know exactly what it is.

It's a tooth . . .

Oral Fixations

Judith Sonnet

I couldn't remember what had happened to us when I woke up in the basement.

The only sense I had left was sight, but there wasn't much to look at.

There was a small arrow of light coming through the floorboards above us. Every now and then, it would flicker when my captor walked over it.

I shook my head, trying to get the weariness out. Like I was beating a near-empty ketchup bottle.

I tested the ropes wrapped around my wrists holding me upright. My shoulders were bruised—I could imagine purple lumps rising beneath my skin—and my wrists were skittered with burns.

At least I was feeling *something* in my arms. I was more worried about my lower extremities.

I could feel a cold achiness in my thighs. Everything below that was empty and lifeless. I couldn't even wiggle my toes.

"Hullo?" I asked the darkness and was answered by my girlfriend, "Paul? Paul, is that you? Oh my God!"

"Kat! Are you okay?" Dumb question.

Kat paused before answering. "I'm all right, Paul."

"What happened?" The moment I asked, I remembered. I had been driving. We were swerving through the hills headed to Max Sheen's house. He was hosting a graduation party. We were racing to get there before the other kids.

Sheen and Rebecca were sitting in the back seat, trying not to smoke the quarter of weed sitting between them. They distracted themselves with kisses and heavy fondling.

I kept watching through the rearview mirror. Kat knew I was feeling horny, and she reached over to touch my inner thigh. I thought, *This is perfect. I'm out of high-school . . . I'm getting blazed and laid tonight . . . I'm hanging with my best friend . . .*

And here is where God becomes cruel.

I couldn't even finish my thoughts before a truck came barreling through the woods and smacked into us.

My memory faded after that . . . until I woke up.
In the basement.

My name is Paul Baylor. I'm a graduate of the class of 2015. I'm not handsome, but I'm fairly popular. I played basketball with Max Sheen, and that's how we became best friends. He's my opposite, with dashing looks, good grades, and a rich family. I'm homely, average, and poor as hell. But there is no animosity between us. Sheen was never one to gloat over what he had and I'm not an envious person, so we got along fine despite our different upbringings. Sheen and Rebecca started seeing each other only a few weeks ago. As with most of Sheen's girlfriends, he was love blind. I liked Rebecca, but what they had wasn't meant to last. It was all chemistry and no substance. Kat and I have been together for about a year now. I was treating it pretty seriously. She was part of the drama club and a real overachiever. Again, it's strange that she and I are so close.

"What happened after the crash?" I asked.

Kat whimpered.

"I'll tell you," Sheen spoke up. I couldn't tell where his voice was coming from. "We rolled down the hill and stopped once we hit a tree. You were knocked unconscious. Kat tried to get out, but her legs were all busted. So was her arm. I started screaming . .

. and *he* came running down the hill. I thought he was coming to help, but he immediately took out a smelly rag and pressed it against Kat's face. Knocked her out. I think it was chloroform."

Jesus. God.

"I woke Rebecca up while he was taking care of you both. She wasn't too hurt. So I threw a punch when he came to me and knocked his head back. He took it like it was nothing and he . . . took my hand and broke it."

I couldn't believe this. Sheen sounded so detached.

"He broke it just like that. Then Rebecca scrambled away. He chased after—"

Sheen broke. I heard a gurgle building in the back of his throat. I could imagine tears dripping down his cheeks.

"Is she okay?" I asked. "Did he catch her?"

"He brought her body back for me to see. Paul, he broke her neck so far back, her head was between her shoulder blades."

"Oh my God." It was all I could say.

I could feel cold sweat crawling down my spine, running between my balls, pooling in my pits, and lapping my brow.

"Then he put that rag against me—"

"How long has it been?"

"I don't know. I only woke up a few hours ago."

I didn't know what to say. Rebecca had been cool. She was a beautiful, innocent-looking girl. Petite and feisty, with long red hair and green eyes. Everyone treated her like a little sister. Now, whenever I thought of her, I imagined her head upside down, like how Sheen had described it.

I started to feel angry.

Angry that Kat was here and that this animal had put his hands on her.

Then I felt *fear*. It was quick and harsh.

I could only imagine what he had in store for us.

"Can you describe him?" Maybe we know him," I suggested.

"I didn't recognize him. He's big, Paul," Kat stated. "He's the tallest, strongest man I think I've ever seen. I've never seen anyone his size at Oak Hill."

"What about the party? Will they be looking for us?"

"Yeah . . . but where are we? If he doesn't live in town, we can only assume he took us away . . . maybe far away. Who knows how long we were out and what time of day it is."

Kat was more collected than me. I could tell she had already gone through all of this mentally before I had woken up. I wanted to hug her and hold her close. I wanted to run my hand through her curly hair, cup her soft cheek, and kiss her. But she was probably hanging by her wrists like I was.

"Sheen . . . I'm sorry," I said. "Maybe if I had been paying more attention—"

"No. Don't." He wasn't mad . . . he was tired. I could only imagine what he was going through. What would happen to me if it had been Kat who had gotten killed? I would be losing my shit. I'd be crying and cursing God.

But Sheen was still and quiet. Maybe it hadn't hit him yet. Maybe some small part of him was arguing that this was just a bad dream, and he was going to wake up in a few seconds and forget about it.

But it was all too real for me. I could smell the dampness of the basement. I could smell my own blood and piss. I knew that the rope around my wrists was too tight to be made of dreams.

I knew I was dying.

The basement door opened and slammed shut. We waited, expectantly. Our killer was standing in the darkness on top of the stairs.

"Hello?" Kat ventured, bravely.

The man didn't respond.

"Hello?" she repeated.

"Hi." His voice was small and childish. A flutter of giggles followed. "Nice to meet you. Hi." More laughter.

"Hey, man! Listen! You don't have to do this. We ain't seen anything. We don't know where we are or even what you look like!"

There was a long silence.

"We didn't see you. We can't identify you. Even if we told the police, what could they do? Just let us go!"

"You don't know who I am?" he asked.

"No." Kat returned.

The lights came on.

He was just as Kat described him . . . the biggest man I've ever seen. He stood nearly seven feet, and his body was rolling with fat. His cheeks seemed to slide down his face and neck. There were hairy moles poking out from the undersides of his rolls. He was naked, glistening with sweat and grease. I could tell, even from this distance, that he hadn't brushed his teeth after his last meal. There was ketchup fringing the corners of his mouth and bits of seasoned beef falling from his tongue with every word he spoke.

"My name is Owen Deerling. I was born in 1983. You're in my house, 134 Acorn Lane . . . Melody, Missouri. I live far away from anyone else, so if you scream, no one will hear." He said it matter-of-factly, but I could tell he was holding back laughter. "Yer two hours away from Oak Hill. I never collect anyone from my town. They'd notice in a heartbeat, they would."

"Owen."

"I done this before . . . and I'll do it again. I'm making a name for myself. You know what they call me?"

"Owen, please!" My girlfriend was naked. I just noticed it. The goddamn bastard had stripped her with his disgusting fingers. My rage was becoming hot. I wanted to cover her up, but all I could do was look away from the body I had touched, kissed, and loved for so long. I turned my head in shame. When I glanced at Owen, I saw that his cock was getting harder.

"They got a nickname for me in the papers . . . you read the papers? I don't get internet—don't want it—but a kid brings Mama the paper every Sunday morning and I've read about me in there." He touched his palm against his cock, knocking it up and down. "They call me the Missouri Tooth Fairy. Ain't that a hoot?"

I felt my heart drop. I recognized the name.

The Missouri Tooth Fairy was almost as infamous as The Phantom Killer of Texarkana or Jack the Ripper.

He was a nameless legend that had been plaguing us on and off for about a decade now.

Everyone had all but given up hope of finding him.

Bodies turned up every few years horribly mutilated and raped . . . and worse.

The nickname had been used by a local tabloid after the first three bodies were found with their teeth bashed in with hammers in the summer of 2001.

Ever since then, the police had stopped releasing the graphic information, but people had a way of finding out which corpses belonged to the Missouri Tooth Fairy and which ones didn't.

A woman and her child were found raped and murdered. The woman's teeth had all been replaced by bamboo shoots, and the child had been tied to a tree with a wire threaded through her braces and attached to the back of the killer's car. When he drove off, it pulled her braces and gums apart. He had gone back to shoot her. At least . . . that's how rumor had it.

A fisherman was found with all the contents of his tackle box speared through his gums and lips, and his neck was sawed open.

A basketball player and his girlfriend had been curb-stomped after being raped.

All gossip, of course.

Everything I knew, I had gleaned from drunken conversation or hushed whispers in the school's hallway. So far, he hadn't struck near Oak Hill, so none of us had been concerned.

We should've been.

Owen started down the stairs.

"They ain't gonna catch me . . . I don't exist. I'm a secret. So, don't think they gonna get me after what I do ta y'all. Don't think yer families is gonna get justice. They ain't never gonna find me. I'm a ghost."

He stumbled toward Kat and slapped her breast. She yelped and tried to jump back but only managed to swing from her bonds. This made Owen giggle. He put a hand between her legs. She went still and white. I saw her eyes get large and wet as he plucked at her clit.

Kat began to piss, she was so frightened.

This excited Owen.

Giddily, he slapped her vagina, spattering urine like water from a sprinkler.

"Get your goddamn hands off her, motherfucker!" I shouted with a rage I had never before been able to muster.

Owen spun around and smiled. He brandished his pee-coated hand for me to see.

"Imma do you last," he said. "Imma make her *scream* so loud it'll break yer heart . . . and then . . . Imma kill you *real bad*."

From upstairs, I heard another set of footsteps and a shrill voice. "Owen! Owen! Turn off the light!"

With urgency, the large man dashed up the stairs, his whole body shaking. He stopped just before getting to the light and snapped his fingers. He lumbered back down the stairs.

"Hurry!" the voice wailed. "They're a-coming!"

"I got it, Mama! I got it!" Owen began to rifle through the toolboxes in the corner. I took this opportunity to scan my surroundings. The walls were made of cold cement. The floor was dirt. The ceiling was wood. It creaked with every footstep Owen's mama took. Dust sprinkled down as she paced. My ropes were tied to an iron ring secured to the ceiling. The wood looked sturdy. Still, there was a chance that I could pull my ring out with some effort.

There were some tools lying around like discarded playthings.

A clunky pressure washer . . . a pair of hedge trimmers . . . a dirty mattress . . . and a stack of porno magazines.

Bondage and fetish shit.

There was something else. A piece of furniture. But it was covered by a black cloth. It looked like a table.

Then, Owen was in front of me, and he was securing a ball gag into my mouth, despite my protesting.

He did the same to Kat and Sheen. He started back up the stairs to turn off the light. His mama was urging him hectically.

In the moment before shadows entombed us, I looked down at my legs and saw that they were missing just below my knees.

They had been amputated neatly.

The shock was overwhelming.

I didn't even feel pain or discomfort.

Merely terrified.

Darkness fell.

Owen hid with us.

We could hear Mama talking to a gruff-sounding man. I tried screaming around my ball gag. I heard Kat and Sheen doing the same, but our cries were muffled, and Mama spoke so loudly there was no way for us to be heard.

Owen was good at hiding.

I could only guess how well-practiced he was at sitting still and holding his breath. We had only gotten snippets of their story, but I knew enough. Owen was Mama's shame. No one knew about him. Like us, he was kept under the floorboards.

Upstairs, Mama was talking to the man about church. He was helping construct a new wing to the building for the children's nursery. Mama was willing to donate and said she would also be bringing her famous chicken potpie to the silent fundraising auction.

He offered to help her with her garden, and she said she'd pay him to come back in a few days when the tomatoes had ripened.

Then they were out of earshot.

We waited in tense silence.

Sheen was still attempting to scream, but he was losing the strength he once had. It sounded like air escaping a vent.

Owen spoke through the darkness, "I want you. I want all of you so bad it hurts."

I felt like pissing myself.

In some alternate world, I'm at a party with my best friends.

We are drinking and being stupid, but no one is getting hurt.

Sheen and Rebecca are slobbering over each other, and Kat keeps making promises we don't know if we can keep.

We watch a movie together—something scary but not too real or heady—and everyone jumps and laughs at all the right moments.

We talk about our plans for the future.

Most of us are going to college.

I'm taking a gap year, while Sheen is headed straight for St. John's. He got a scholarship that pays for his room and board for four years! He's on a full meal plan. He has been chatting with his roommate on Facebook.

Kat wants to go to law school but needs to make some extra money first. Unlike me, she's going to attend online courses at the local community college.

Rebecca said she's going to study art in San Francisco, her favorite city.

Kat and I go to her place since her parents are never home.

We try to make love, but we are so drunk we fall asleep before either of us can finish.

We don't care.

We're happy.

But Owen Deerling tied me up and cut off my legs.

And stripped my girlfriend, preparing her for molestation.

And more likely than not, Sheen isn't going to St. John's.

And Rebecca is dead.

Owen turned on the lights when he was absolutely sure that the man had left. Mama was pacing upstairs nervously. Dust fluttered down from where her feet fell. Owen removed my gag, and I started yelling again. A quick slap stopped me.

"You! Quit it!" he scolded.

I didn't have any choice. I closed my mouth and shut my eyes, waiting for more abuse. It didn't come. Owen turned his attention to my girlfriend. He wandered toward her, took a handful of her hair, and pulled her head back. He sniffed her neck, tongued her ear, and gripped her breast tightly. The skin wrinkled around her nipple, and I could imagine bruises forming beneath his tight hold. He didn't release her, even when she started whimpering.

"Stop it," Sheen muttered. "Please . . . stop it."

Owen turned toward him and pointed a greasy finger. "Imma do you first. Imma kill you now."

Sheen looked ready to struggle, then fell limp against his bonds. He had no fight left.

Sheen and I had been best friends for so long . . . I'd never seen him lose a fight. But the fights he had been in were not life-and-death situations. And none of the men he had been up against were like Owen.

I didn't blame him for giving in.

Owen came over to Sheen and took him by the cheeks. He looked at his face for the longest time before making his decision. He waddled to the toolbox and rifled through it. We waited in fearful anticipation.

Owen pulled out a chisel and a hammer. He set both on the ground and then wandered to the black cloth. He pulled it away, revealing a table with a thick hole sawed into the middle. He wiped a hand over it and then investigated all four legs. There were thick ropes tied to each of them.

He smiled at Sheen.

"Here, pig... Here, baby pig!" He charged forward with surprising speed. Every layer of fat and muscle rippled wildly and energetically.

Owen tore Sheen's ropes loose and tossed him to the ground.

Sheen started to scramble away on his hands, dragging his legs behind him. I could see that his knees had been broken. Whether by the crash or by Owen, I at first couldn't tell. But then, I decided that Owen must have hobbled him, albeit to a lesser degree than he had me.

Owen straddled Sheen as if he were a hog and held his head back by the hair.

"Nope! You stay still! You stay still, little pig!" Owen punched Sheen directly in the back of his skull, knocking his head onto the wet ground. Sheen quivered but put up no further resistance. Owen dragged him to the table and sat him upright beneath it. He fit Sheen's head through the hole in the table's center and tied his hands taut with the ropes. Sheen looked around groggily, mouthing words I could not decipher.

"Sheen, we're gonna kill this bastard! Sheen! We're gonna fucking kill him! We're gonna kill him and cut off his legs and make him bleed out slow!" I said, hoping to encourage my friend in his final moments.

Owen laughed and went back to the toolbox.

He pulled out something I recognized from an S&M fetish video I had watched when I was a freshman.

It's called an O-ring mouth gag. It's like a ball gag, only there is a metal ring in the center that holds the mouth wide open for easier access to the oral cavity. Four spider legs come out and peel the lips backward. The band was tar-black, and the metal ring and spider legs were rusted and stained.

Aggressively, Owen fit the O-ring into my best friend's mouth. By the time he was finished, Sheen looked lipless and scared.

I could see his teeth attempting to chatter, but the gag gave no relief.

I could see his tongue frisking the metal.

I could see his throat flexing.

In fact, his mouth was open so wide I could see his uvula.

Owen put a foot on the table and shoved his hardened prick into Sheen's mouth.

Sheen screamed through Owen's member. I saw his head bucking back. I could imagine he was trying to bite down against his restraints. I could see his hands clench into fists and fight against the tightened ropes. He tried falling backward and slipping his head out from the hole, but Owen took him by the hair and held him in place.

Owen speared him so hard that I could hear Sheen gag. I could hear my best friend vomiting . .

. and then Owen was shouting with joy and pulling away. A fresh load of sperm dropped and dribbled from Sheen's mouth.

He was crying.

He was crying so hard his muscles all stood up and danced. His eyes had gone red. Vomit had pulsed from his throat and lay in a thick smattering on the table.

"We're gonna kill him," I said weakly.

Owen picked up the chisel and unceremoniously placed it on the line between gum and incisor on the top row of Sheen's mouth. His eyes popped out of his skull. Owen relished the sound of the chisel scraping against the hard teeth. He tested the weight of the hammer.

"We won't kill him . . . we can't." Kat laughed feverishly.

Owen swung the hammer.

Sheen's throat broke with screams. Blood gushed from the places where teeth had been broken from the gums. Owen didn't hesitate but started breaking more of them. Soon, blood, vomit, and sperm coated the table and Sheen's chin. His squeals and screams turned into hyperventilating. Quick, terrified gasps burst out of his blood-soaked mouth in bubbles. After Owen got tired of the teeth, he began to hammer on his jaw. He took Sheen by the back of the head and held him steady, so his hammer hit true with each and every strike. The blows landed on the mouth and jaw.

Owen flipped over to the claw end and began to scrape out the inside of Sheen's cavity. The tongue became a pink mess of pulp and tissue being dragged out between the claws. The gums were shredded. The cheeks were torn and tattered.

The killing blow knocked his jaw so far inward that it broke and caved in his face.

Then Owen let Sheen's head drop into the pool of gore.

It was over almost as soon as it had started.

Owen sat down and began to masturbate frantically, using a handful of blood as lubrication. His prick was slickened with red. No matter how much his palm fought it, it stayed soft. It seemed Owen was spent. He gave up on his endeavor and charged upstairs.

After a few minutes, we heard the shower run and their water heater scream.

Mama was still pacing. Her footsteps sounded nervous.

"Paul?" Kat squeaked. "Paul . . ."

"Kat, I'm so sorry. I'm so fucking sorry." I was crying hard. My face was wet with snot and hot tears.

"We can't get out of this," she reaffirmed. "We are as good as dead."

"I'm sorry." It was all I could say.

If this had been a movie, I would have found some way to slip out of my restraints.

I'd have crawled across the room and grabbed a weapon—maybe the hammer that Owen had used to kill Sheen.

That would be poetic.

I'd lay in wait for Owen to come back for me or my girlfriend, and I'd dig the claw end into his heel and tear him down. Of course, we would struggle for an extended period of time and things would look dire . . . but inevitably, I would gain the upper hand. I would smash his face in with the hammer or force him to eat the handle. He would die screaming. Mama may come down to help, but she was old and frail. I would barely have to bother with her.

But . . . if this was a movie, Kat would be jumping and holding my arm in a darkened theater.

Rebecca and Sheen would be too distracted to pay attention.

There would be transitions and we would see what our parents were up to while all of this went down.

Where were they searching?

Would they find our bodies?

What would we see of Sheen's parents? Would they be full of unrepressed sorrow, as if they already knew their son had been killed?

If this was a movie . . . we could forget about it all when we left the theater.

Kat had to go to the bathroom. She screamed, maybe hoping that Owen would bring a bucket. After a while, the screams for help became humiliated whimpers.

She tried to squat as best she could against her bonds.

I looked away.

When she was done, Owen came down, undid her ropes, and forced her nose into the pile she'd left on the dirt.

She stopped crying after that.

I think she saw no point to it anymore.

Owen tied her up again and left. Only an hour later, I had to go too. I made no sound. I just allowed my bowels to move and waited for Owen to give me my punishment.

Another hour.

Both of us had stopped screaming for help. Both of us knew that we were dead. Both of us avoided looking at Sheen's mess. It wasn't even Sheen anymore, it was just . . . a mess. Like the stains Kat and I had left on the ground.

She broke the silence. "Paul, do you love me?"

"Yes."

"Tell me."

"I've loved you since I took you to eat sushi, and you couldn't figure out how to use the chopsticks, so you used both of your hands."

"More."

"I've been in love with you since the day you came over to my house at two in the morning, drunk, just to kiss me and throw up on my sofa."

"We weren't even dating then."

"I know."

She giggled. "I've had a crush on you since we were kids."

"Why?" I closed my eyes.

"I don't know. You were nice and gentle."

"You were so much smarter than me."

"No. No. You're smart . . . but it doesn't matter. I never loved you for what you knew or didn't know. I loved you because you were real and solid, and you were never mean to anyone. Everyone else was full of hatefulness, but even when you were angry, you never let it control you."

I almost started crying again.

"I really love you," Kat said. "Would we have gotten married?"

"I think so."

"Would we have had children?"

"Yes."

"Describe them."

"I don't know—"

"We'd have two girls and a boy, wouldn't we? They'd be just like you . . . they wouldn't be full of anger . . . they would be kind."

"Yes . . . They'd be like you too. They'd have it all figured out. They would have as much fun as they possibly could and still outsmart everyone else in the room."

"Do you think they'd play sports or—"

"The girls would definitely be like their mom. Volleyball, softball, track and field."

"And the boy?"

"I see him being a choir kid."

Kat said nothing. I kept my eyes sealed and let myself wander through fantasies.

"We would live modestly. Hell, I'd be happy in a trailer park. We'd spend as much time enjoying ourselves before having kids. Focusing on us and only us. A dinner party every Friday night . . . Sheen and Rebecca always invited."

I had run out of tears. I was feeling woozy. My joints were all bruised and my muscles were strained from supporting my own weight. My stomach ached and my head was flaring. "I think we'll homeschool the kids until middle school. I'd like them to be social. That's what my folks did. I think it worked."

I talked on and on.

Kat mumbled agreement every few seconds, but I don't remember if she actually added to the conversation.

I kept my eyes shut as I imagined the life we were meant to have lived.

I opened my eyes right when Owen started the pressure washer. I had been so lost in my own reverie that I didn't even realize he had set it up. He had a long tube leading from the washer up the stairs. Water was running through it loudly and squealing out of a small rip in its seam. The sound of the engine was an overpowering roar that filled the basement. I looked for Kat and saw her tied beneath the table with her head through the hole. Sheen's body lay against the wall, all mashed and battered.

Kat had an O-ring gag secured in her beautiful mouth.

I wanted to kiss her tears away.

The water sprayed out in a hard blast that seared through her cheek. I could only imagine how sharp the pain must have been. He stuck the nozzle down her throat and pressed down on the handle, blowing water through the most sensitive parts of her skin. Blood and water sputtered out of her, and her eyes rolled back into her head. Owen held the sprayer down and rotated the nozzle in mean circles, as if he was brushing her teeth.

She died quickly.

Then he raped her body.

He spoke to it like a lover.

---

*I can't feel anything.
 I'm ready to die.*

The next day, Owen dragged me to the table. He tied my hands to the legs and set my head upright in the hole. I made no arguments. He spoke to himself as he brought out a brand-new gag for me to wear. It pried my mouth open and held it there. I had gone without food for so long my stomach was almost begging for death to alleviate its burden.

Owen stroked his cock and talked to me about how much he wanted me.

"Did you see what I did to your girl? You watched, didn't you? I bet you liked seeing her naked. Had you seen her naked before? She was real pretty . . . she still is."

Kill me.

"First girl I ever saw naked was Mama, an' she yelled at me fer a week fer peekin'."

Kill me.

"I wanna take your girl again. How's that make you feel, boy? Want my prick up her shitter?"

Kill me.

He stuck his fingers into my mouth and frisked my tongue. I instinctively jumped, then gave in to his molestations. He pulled my tongue as far as it could go, then pushed a pin through it. I saw the yellow bulb on its top and felt hot blood course into my mouth. He pulled out another pin and screwed it between my two front teeth and into my gums.

More blood.

More pain.

I was screaming through it all.

"I ain't even started, boy. It's gonna get a helluva lot worse from here!"

He took a lighter and began to burn the tip of the next pin, which he pushed through my lip and into the gum. It burned hot and slid through the skin like butter. He burned each pin before sticking me with them. By the end, my entire mouth was a pin cushion. He had them on the roof of my mouth, through my lips, between my teeth, and all along my tongue. Blood was slipping in rivulets from my shaking orifice.

Then he removed each pin, one by one. My mouth was pockmarked and irritated afterward.

Owen smiled and kissed my gaping, bloody hole.

"Feels good, don't it? Feels rich . . . feels powerful."

Owen went back to the toolbox and came back with the chisel and the hammer.

I was still screaming.

"You all gonna be my fucktoys . . . they gonna find you ruined!"

That was when a shot rang out from the top of the stairs and half of Owen's head exploded. Chunks of greasy meat and chips of skull rained down on me. His hands fell and what was left of his head turned sideways. Then his entire body slumped down and died . . . painlessly and silently.

I heard footsteps coming toward me.

It was Mama.

She had a double-barreled shotgun cupped in her frail arms.

Her lips and limbs were quivering, and her eyes were bloodshot.

The woman was older than I had imagined.

The weight of Owen's crimes must have been heavy on her, and it was my shit luck that just when I was ready to die, Mama had gained some balls.

Why couldn't she have done this when she figured out what her son was?

Why wait so long?

Fear?

Sympathy?

Love?

I never got an answer. Mama sighed, put the gun beneath her chin, and said her last words, "I'm sorry, there's only one shell left. I thought he had finished with you already. My mistake. I hate leavin' you like this, but maybe someone will come an' find ya. Maybe."

Then the top of her head did a backflip and her body landed on her son's.

I barely heard the thunderclap of gunfire.

I think a day has gone by since my killer died.

I'm not sure if I'm alive or dead. I've been going through my story over and over again. Maybe I'll write it down if someone—anyone—finds me. I'm not ready to die.

Even without Sheen and Kat, there is so much to live for.

In the moment, death seemed good, but that was a relatively quick death. It was painful, yes, but Owen allotted us a clear end to his torture.

Starvation is far worse than anything Owen could have done. It is slow . . . it is burning . . . it gives one time to reflect.

I could have recovered.

I could have gone to therapy.

I could have made new friends.

I could have loved again.

I could have learned how to function without my legs.

Please, God, let someone find me!

•••

After I finish spinning my yarn, Cassandra Daucus steps into the firelight. She's smiling wide enough to split her skull, and I see that she holds a leather tome. Faded, aged, and crumbling. I worry, as she opens it and flips through the pages, that the paper will deteriorate in her hands, leaving her scrap as nothing more than a pile of weeping dust . . .

The Book of Revenge

Cassandra Daucus

France, thirteenth century

"You don't have to do it."

The monk ignored the oblate–just a child—who pattered after him. His black robe billowed out behind him as he strode down the hallway that led from the scriptorium to the abbot's private office.

"Brother Adso. Adso." The boy grabbed the monk's sleeve and pulled him behind a pillar. "Adso. Please." He took a watery breath. "Don't do it."

"Michael." Adso looked down at him. Adso had never been blessed with a younger brother—a *real* brother—but if he had, he thought that brother would have been like Michael. Curious and clever as a fox. He took in the bruise on the boy's cheek from where the abbot had struck him for talking out of turn and thought about the scars on his back that remained after one of the abbot's more violent beatings. That had happened when Adso was assigned to the infirmary, and he'd helped Malachi all night tending to Michael's tender flesh. He'd nearly bitten through his own tongue while the infirmarian went on and on about how blessed and godly the abbot was, and how Michael must have deserved it for the abbot to treat him so harshly.

That's when Adso decided he needed to do something because nobody else would.

The abbot insisted the beatings were for the spiritual well-being of those who received them, but Adso knew it was no more than base cruelty. And for some reason, young Michael had become the focus of his savagery.

"Brother Adso, you know I'm *puer oblatus*. I only have to stay until my voice changes, then I can choose to leave."

Brother Adso leaned close. "I'm afraid you won't survive here until your voice changes." He thought of the abbot, how the man *laughed* when doling out punishments, particularly Michael's. *He doesn't even pretend not to enjoy it.*

"I can run away. I can go to the nunnery, the abbess—"

Adso scoffed. "That fine lady will send you back. There's no other choice, Michael."

"Please." Michael reached for the book, but Adso tucked it away in his sleeve. Michael's lower lip and voice both trembled as he whispered, "Murder is a sin. Burn the page."

"It is not murder. Now, go to the dormitory and bide your time there."

Without waiting for a reply, Adso resumed his march toward the abbot's office, listening as Michael scurried away behind him. When he reached the heavy oak door, he paused and pulled the book out from the sleeve of his robe one more time. The brief conversation with Michael had shaken him, although he was sure that he was in the right. He couldn't bear to have that man's hands on innocent Michael, or any of the other *pueri obtulerunt*, one more time. He had the power to stop him, and he intended to use it.

Despite the evils of the abbot, Adso had faith in God. He took the time to silently recite the Pater Noster while turning the book over and around in his hands. When he ran out of words he took a long, shuddering breath and knocked on the door.

"Enter," a deep voice said immediately. Adso stepped through and pushed the door closed behind him. Late afternoon sun shined through the open window, bringing a warm breeze and the distant shouts of the gardener along with it. The abbot, gray-faced and clad in black, crouched like a spider behind his desk, which was piled with stacks of parchment. Quarterly payments were due from the peasants who farmed the monastery's land, and the abbot wasn't about to miss a single coin owed. Yet another way the abbot took advantage. Adso's gut twisted in disgust.

After a pause that was too long to be comfortable, the abbot said, "Brother Adso. You may speak."

"Abbot Nicholas." Adso lowered his head, avoiding his gaze.

"You finished it? The copy of *De obedientia*?"

Adso clutched the book. It was small, not much more than a handful. The new leather, which had just been attached the day before, slid against his sweaty palm.

"Yes."

"Show me."

Adso set the book on the edge of the abbot's desk, ignoring his outstretched hand. The abbot frowned as he picked it up. "Your hands are shaking."

Adso stuck his hands back under the cover of his sleeves and pulled them to his chest. "I'm just a little cold."

The abbot chuckled unkindly.

"If you weren't disobedient I wouldn't have to constantly reprimand you. You and that oblate." His lips twisted nastily. "I have been hoping that separating you and assigning you to the scriptorium

THE BOOK OF REVENGE

would provide the structure that you so desperately need. Saint Benedict's treatise on the importance of obedience is the perfect first book for you. Brother William speaks well of your work, but this will serve as proof of your success." He tapped the cover. "If it satisfies me."

Adso swallowed around the lump in his throat. "I hope it satisfies you, Father."

The abbot made a production of examining the binding before he set the book on the tabletop and lifted the front board. His eyebrows pulled together as he squinted at the scrawl that marred the creamy parchment of the first leaf. Something brownish-red had been smeared across it, and at the sight of it, Adso shifted his eyes to stare at the square of blue sky visible outside the window and pulled his still-sore thumb into his fist.

"What's this?" the abbot grumbled. "A stain? In a *brand-new book*? And a scribble? Unacceptable! I should—" His shouting was cut short by a hideous crunch. Adso screamed in shock as something hot and wet gushed over him.

The abbot had been reduced to a glistening pile of red and gray, flesh and viscera piled in his chair and splattered across the desk. Adso had spent some time gutting pigs in the monastery's abattoir, so the coppery foulness of blood and feces was familiar, but knowing this was a human and not an animal disgusted him in a way that was new.

His body prepared to retch. But he kept down the sourness that threatened to come up and looked around the room. Whatever had happened to the abbot had sent pieces of his body to the farthest corners of his room. Crimson mixed with something darker splashed the floor around the desk and dripped from the ceiling. Gray chunks and shards of bone were sprinkled across the plaster wall. Larger chunks of the abbot decorated the small pile of books on the shelf. Something shiny slid down the door and landed with a *splat*.

It was like nothing Adso could have imagined in his wildest dreams.

He wiped a sleeve across his face, and it came back wet and smeared with gray flecks. He imagined how vivid it would be if, instead of the black of the Benedictines he was clad in the cream robe of the Cistercians. At the thought, a giggle bubbled up and overflowed into a laugh. He drew a hand across his freshly-tonsured crown; a clump of muscle and bone dropped onto the ground, and he laughed even louder.

A crimson-smeared stump rested on the still-open book. Adso pushed it aside and slammed the book shut before the cursed sigil could find his eyes.

A bang against the door brought him up short.

"Abbot Nicholas! What is happening in there?" It was Brother Jakob, the monastery's prior and the abbot's right-hand man and enabler of his worst appetites. Jakob hated joy, and Adso chuckled as he tore open the door and stepped aside to allow the prior access.

"Brother Adso! What— Dear God!" The older monk touched his own forehead and chest, but distracted by the bloody mess he didn't finish making the sign of the cross. He took a few tentative steps into the room, gazing around as though he couldn't quite believe what he was seeing. His foot squelched as it hit the floor, and he audibly groaned but seemed unable to move otherwise. He pressed his arm against his face, but it was too much for him; he doubled over and expelled that morning's stew all over the desk— lamb and carrots acrid with bile. When he caught sight of what remained of the abbot in the chair, he did it again—more stomach acid than food. Alas, the parchments were beyond saving. No payments would be made that month.

Adso laughed so hard his belly hurt.

"Brother Adso!" Jakob stared at Adso, blood-smeared and cackling, with an expression of horror.

Adso opened the cover of the book and shoved it into Jakob's face.

As soon as he focused on the scribbled smudge of a sigil, Jakob's eyes bugged from his head, and his cheeks puffed out like he'd been running (not a thing Jakob had ever done in his soft and cozy monastic life). A second later, his head and torso exploded, the gore splatting against the ceiling and raining down over Adso, who slammed the book shut and ran out the door shrieking with laughter as he skipped down the hallway.

Adso had known the sigil, sealed with his blood, would kill anyone who looked at it, but he had no idea it would do *that*.

It was the long summer hours between nones and vespers, so most of the monks were hard at work—preparing dinner, gardening, studying in the library, or writing in the scriptorium—so Adso didn't run into anyone else before he reached the dormitory. Michael was waiting for him at the top of the stairs, and his eyes widened as he took in Adso's approach—laughing and covered with blood.

"What happened?" He flinched in horror as Adso skipped up the stairs and leaned in close.

"It worked. It *worked!*" Adso hopped from foot to foot. "First the abbot, then Jakob."

"But what did it do?" Michael brought his sleeve to his nose and took a step back.

By answer, Adso held up a fist, then opened it, accompanying the movement by blowing across his tongue. He laughed.

"It made a mess."

"Brother Adso?" A deep, familiar voice came from the hallway, and Michael grabbed Adso and pulled him into the room behind him. But he wasn't quick

THE BOOK OF REVENGE

enough to escape Aldhelm, the chamberlain; Aldhelm had very long legs. "What happened to you? You're dripping blood. Let me take you to the infirmary."

"Brother Aldhelm," Michael said quickly, trying desperately to push Adso behind the door. "Brother Adso is fine, he just—"

"Brother Adso *is* fine!" Shoving the boy aside, Adso jumped into the doorway and opened the book in the face of Aldhelm. In a moment, his innards spattered the stairs and into the dormitory like blackberries smashed underfoot. Michael screamed so loudly it could have raised Christ himself.

"Hush." Adso clamped his bloodied hand over Michael's mouth and dragged him into the dormitory, slamming the door behind him. He moved them away from the worst of the muck that had been Aldhelm, which was steaming gently in the doorway. Luckily, given the time of day, the room was empty aside from them. "Everyone is going to hear you. Is that what you want? Everyone coming here?"

"He just . . . he just—" Michael blubbered through tears that ran down blood-spattered cheeks.

"He did, didn't he?"

"He was kind!" Michael turned on Adso, fists raised. "He didn't like the abbot! He even gave me an extra blanket last winter! And you just . . . turned him inside out!"

"But he's one of them. It's not the people, it's the monastery. The church ignores the true word of God, his kindness and generosity. They allow the cruelty to continue. Don't you see?"

"What does that mean?"

"It means they all have to die."

On the other side of the door there was a shout followed by a clamber, and then more shouts. The two stood quietly for a few minutes while movement carried on at the top of the stairs. Michael shook with tears, Adso from excitement. Eventually, there was a tap on the door.

"Brother Adso? Michael? May I come in? Just to talk."

Michael gasped. "Brother William! Don't come in!" He threw himself against the door, feet tripping over the ropes of Aldhelm's intestines, with Adso close behind. "Brother William is good!" he yelled, struggling to keep the door closed. "Don't do it to him!"

"He's one of them," Adso insisted through clenched teeth. But he was so intent on opening the door that he lost his grip on the book. It slipped from his hand and before it could hit the floor, Michael had it and took off in a run toward the night stairs on the other end of the dormitory, leaving crimson footprints in his wake.

Adso followed, which allowed William through the door. Michael ran straight through the room, with

THE BOOK OF REVENGE

Adso and William close behind. They ran down the night stairs and out into the church. Michael stumbled on his way through the great wooden screen that divided the space where the monks prayed from the main part of the church, and as he hit the ground he lost hold of the book. It slid across the stones and came to rest at the base of a pillar, where Adso leapt upon it. But Michael was quick and scrambled over. He managed to wrestle it out of Adso's hands before William reached them.

Michael opened the book.

"Yes!" Adso yelled. "Show it to William! Show him my work!"

With a sinking heart, Adso realized that Michael was lifting the book to his own face.

"No!" With a scream, Adso grabbed the book out of Michael's hands at the same time William reached for it, and the book turned toward him. He found himself facing the sigil, his own bloody thumbprint slapped across it like a perfect bruise.

His final thought was that it really was a very fine sigil indeed. He hoped the abbot had been satisfied.

Three days later, everything had been cleaned up and Michael was calm enough to share what he knew.

"He found the curse in a book in the library. I didn't even think it would work, but if it did, I didn't know—"

"That's all right, Michael," Brother William interrupted gently. "We understand that it was his idea and not yours. I hadn't believed the abbot when he warned that Brother Adso was a bad influence on you, but now, I know it's true."

Adso had been the only person willing to protect him, but Michael held his tongue on that matter. "You need to burn it," he said instead. "At least burn the cursed page."

Brother William smiled. "It's been taken care of. No one else will get hurt, I promise you."

"It's gone?"

"All gone. Now, why don't you get back to the garden? I know Brother Severinus has missed your smiling face."

Brother William watched Michael leave, and he thought about the book, locked away in the strong room along with the coin. It would be safe there, he was sure.

University Town, USA, Today

"You don't want to go to the police, but can't you complain to the provost?" Rachel asked, following the curator into her office.

Charlotte scoffed and hung her coat on the hook behind the door. "Turner's next in line for provost. He's been a dean for a decade and besides, they're best friends. Fucking old boys club, they won't do anything no matter who complains."

"But you're on staff! You're highly respected in the field, not just some random student. Somebody should do *something*."

Their conversation was interrupted by a knock on the door. "Package for you!"

"Thanks, Ed."

"Sure thing." Ed set the box on the side table and bid them adieu.

Rachel looked it over while Charlotte tracked down the utility knife. The box was wrapped in brown paper and had a packet of import papers attached to it. The return address was an auction house in Germany.

"Do you want me to get the phone? Instagram loves a good unboxing."

"Nah, that's okay." Charlotte started to cut. "I got this at a serious discount. 'Mystery manuscript found in a medieval monastery' is all I know. Could be a total dud. If it's not, we can wrap it up again and make a video!"

Once dug out of its tomb of foam peanuts and released from its bubble wrap shroud, the book was interesting. It was small, with a heavily stained leather binding.

"This is very cool," Charlotte said.

"It looks almost new." Rachel took it from her and turned it over. "Aside from the staining."

"But what's up with this?" Charlotte tugged at the chain that had been wrapped around the book, looped around both vertically and horizontally and sealed with an ancient padlock. "I've never seen anything like it."

"Maybe it's cursed, and they don't want us opening it."

Charlotte rolled her eyes. "Ha ha. Good thing I keep bolt cutters in my office."

"What?"

She winked. "I never know when I might need them."

Rachel held the book steady while Charlotte snipped through the chain—carefully, to avoid slicing the leather that encased the wooden cover. A few minutes later, the chain was off, and Charlotte was opening the book. She cracked the middle first. "Oh wow. This is the cleanest book I've ever seen. As if nobody's ever touched it."

Rachel peeked over her shoulder. "That parchment is flawless. No dirt on those pages at all."

"Just that." Charlotte ran her finger along the edge, where a brown stain leaked in. "Like it was soaked in something."

There was a knock on the door, and Emily went to check. It was Ed again, holding a letter.

THE BOOK OF REVENGE

"Here. I forgot to give her that too."

"Thanks so much."

"Anytime." Ed saluted her awkwardly and she closed the door behind him.

As she turned back, Charlotte said, "Hey, the front flyleaf is a mess, there's a lot more staining and a weird mark, maybe an owner's sig—"

And then she exploded. The top of her head hit the ceiling and one of her arms flew across to the bookshelf, where it got stuck. The rest of her was everywhere, including, Rachel realized, on her.

Too shocked to scream, Rachel stood, blinded by the salty ichor dripping in her eyes. The raw meat scent that permeated the room made her stomach turn upside down; she was glad Charlotte kept her wastepaper basket next to the door. It took a few minutes before she thought she could move without passing out. She took a step and then another one. She really should call the police. Shouldn't she? Yes, of course.

She was impressed by how calm she sounded explaining the situation to the dispatcher. Once that was done and the police were on their way, she called Ed and asked him to come back—just in case she needed a witness. As she waited for him, she eyed the book, which was sitting closed on the desk, in front of the horror that had been Charlotte.

It must have been the book that did it; the mess on the front flyleaf that Charlotte mentioned right before she—before it happened. What else could it have been? Rachel wasn't a believer. The library had an occult collection, so Rachel had read a lot of spells and looked at a lot of sigils. She assumed it was bullshit. She *knew* it. But Charlotte had seen something on the flyleaf and then she'd blown to bits.

She hadn't deserved to have her insides sprayed all over her office. She was funny and so clever that sometimes Rachel was irritated by it, but Rachel only wanted the best for her. Rachel considered her a friend. That's why the thing with Turner had bothered her so much; Charlotte was a little naive for dating a married man, but he'd led Charlotte on and then turned around and hurt her.

Rachel's gut twisted, but not in revulsion this time. She couldn't help Charlotte now, couldn't bring her back to life, but maybe she could use the book that killed her to make the world a better place for everyone else. Would that help make things equal?

She picked up the book, wiped it on the back of her shirt and stuck it in her bag.

She just had to wait—for the police to finish questioning her, for the EMTs to give her the okay to leave, for the director of the library and the director of facilities to ask their own questions, and for her next-door neighbor to come with a change of clothes and to escort her home. Thank goodness the library had a shower.

That night, she finalized a plan. She checked a few group chats she was part of and came up with a list of names.

"Brock Caldwell?"

Rachel's friend Marcia had met Brock through an app. She'd gone out with him to dinner and awakened in the morning in his bed with no memory of what had happened after the entree. He had insisted that she'd gotten "wasted" and "begged" him to take her home, that he hadn't done anything she didn't want him to do. Their friend group knew better, even if Marcia couldn't prove it and the police did nothing to help.

"Hey, yeah." He leered at her over his cup of coffee, still dressed in his pajamas. He checked her out like a brother from a shitty frat rather than the advanced graduate student she knew he was. "Is it raining?"

She glanced down at her brand-new, shiny red rain slicker, complete with raised hood and matching boots. "I just like to be prepared. Here."

He had the decency to set down his mug before he took the book and turned it over dubiously. "What's this? Looks old."

"It is. Eight hundred years old, maybe."

"Whoa. That's older than Shakespeare."

"Why don't you open it?"

His forehead scrunched up. "You're just, what? Bringing old books door-to-door and asking people to look at them?"

Rachel grinned. "Yeah, I'm with the library's special collections department. It's a new form of outreach we're experimenting with. Are your hands clean?"

"Ma'am," Brock said with a crooked grin as he lifted the front cover of the book, "my hands are always clean."

He looked down, and she pulled the door closed just in time.

Brock was piled behind the door, and she had to push through it to get the door open. It was a lot of work and left a long and nasty smudge across the floor, but it was worth it to not have her slicker sullied so early in the day. It took her a while to find the book; it was buried under warm intestines that were kind of okay until she punctured something that released a vile miasma. That had her on the verge of throwing up, but she'd skipped breakfast in anticipation of her day and managed to keep anything that was in there, down.

Thankfully, the book had landed closed. She wiped it down at the kitchen sink, grabbed a pair of yellow kitchen gloves, and headed to the next address on her list.

THE BOOK OF REVENGE

Rachel's friend, Imogen, enjoyed clubbing, and that's how she met Allen Kim. He cornered her on the dance floor and then cornered her later in the toilets. She reported him to the police, but it was her word against his, and he insisted the sex was consensual. She had been drunk and was wearing a short dress, so really, what could they be expected to do?

Allen had a roommate, so Rachel waited across the street for the roommate to leave. She knocked on his door a few minutes before ten a.m.

"Allen Kim?"

"Yeah?"

"Sorry to interrupt," Rachel said, holding the book out. "Have you ever wanted to hold an old book?"

He frowned at her and rubbed sweat out of his eyes. An exercise video featuring a sweaty, muscle-bound grunter boomed out of the massive TV behind him.

"Is this some kind of religious thing?"

"Nope. Just library outreach."

"That's original, I guess."

Rachel thrust the book at him again. He chuckled.

"Can I keep it?"

"Sure. We have more."

"This is worth a lot of money, right? Ugh, it's sticky." He'd finally accepted the book and was examining the binding. "It's kind of gross." He tried to hand it back.

"I spilled maple syrup on it at breakfast." She took a step back into the hallway. "Go on. Take a look inside."

"You're freaking me out, lady, just take the book and go. I need to finish my workout."

He tried again to get her to take the book, but she just stood there, hands folded demurely in front of her. Allen shrugged.

"It's your book."

He dropped it. Rachel growled and started for it, tensing her muscles for a fight, but it landed with the front cover open. Having experienced two explosions recently plus however many others in the past, the front flyleaf was a mess, covered with smears of varying shades of reddish-brown.

Rachel quickly looked away.

"Whoa!" Allen crouched down like he was kneeling before a religious icon. "This is blood, right? That's so fucking—"

Rachel turned her back on him just in time. Allen popped like a very large and meaty grape, and since his apartment was open concept, his guts had room to fly. Something that Rachel guessed was a partial rib cage soared past her and hit the door on the other side of the hallway with a meaty *splat*.

"Shit!" Rachel came in, allowing the door to swing shut, and said a prayer to whatever goddess was listening that whoever lived there was already at work. Then she found the remote and turned off the fucking TV.

The book was still open on the floor and the opening was coated with gore. She scraped off what she could, but some gray flecks had found their way into the gutter, and she couldn't immediately get them out. The yellow gloves had seemed like a good idea earlier, but now they just seemed silly. She washed her hands at the tap and stood under the shower to rinse off her slicker.

She had picked her way through the puddles of blood and muck and was just about to walk out the front door when it opened in her face.

"Hey, Allen, there's something funky in the hall—Fuck!"

It was the roommate, holding a bag of fast-food takeout. He stood there, door open, mouth agape, staring at the gore splattered all over everything, his face growing paler and paler.

This was not planned for, and Rachel had no patience. She acted on instinct, dragging the roommate into the room and opening the book in his face. It took him a few seconds for the sigil to find his eyes, marred as it was by the new, heavy stains on the page. His shock didn't help. But eventually, he focused.

Rachel had no choice but to bear the brunt of it. She was careful to keep her mouth and eyes closed, but she still had to scrape off the raw juice and viscera that coated her face and shiny new slicker. It was unpleasant, but there was one more predator to visit, and she was going to do whatever she needed to make her appointment with him.

She cleaned up again and on her way out the door, she tried not to wonder too much about who the roommate was and whether or not he deserved to have his insides spread all over his living room floor.

Rachel had been aggressively checking her phone all morning. The sudden death of a librarian was being discussed everywhere, but not in any kind of detail. Charlotte's name wasn't mentioned. Apparently, the police were being very hush-hush about it, and Rachel couldn't blame them. Every time she thought about poor Charlotte, she teared up. But she hoped that what she was doing could make up for it, somehow. In any case, there was no chatter about other deaths, so Brock, Allen, and Allen's roommate appeared to be still undiscovered.

Hopefully, they would stay that way, just for a couple more hours.

Rachel's appointment with Dr. Turner was at noon; she'd called his office first thing that morning and taken the only time available. She barely had time to get home and give her rainwear a good rinse with the hose before she had to get back to campus, although she did take a minute to wipe all the blood off the book's leather binding with a damp cloth and dry it thoroughly. Her heart beat like a running bull and her hands shook, but by the time she got done cleaning it the leather was shining like new.

She turned on her favorite self-improvement podcast for the ride back to campus and followed the host's instruction to breathe as deeply as she could. Just one more. She could do this.

"How can I help you?"

Dr. Turner's office had windows on two walls and a desk made of real wood. He sat behind it comfortably, leaning back in his chair, one hand toying with a pen that probably cost as much as Rachel made in a week. He had dimples and gray at his temples, and he oozed that particular kind of charm exuded by men who knew they were handsome and expected it to count. Rachel had to hold back a sneer. Instead, she did her best to channel Cher Horowitz.

"I'm a cataloger in special collections, and I've been working on this one but I'm having trouble." She placed it on the edge of the desk. "Can you take a look and tell me what you think?"

He leaned forward and grinned like a man who was thrilled to be asked for his opinion.

"I've been out of the academic side of things for so long I'm surprised anyone even remembers that medieval manuscripts are my specialty."

"Oh, Charlotte told me all about you," Rachel said mildly, with a smile. She was taking a chance. Did Turner know that Charlotte was dead? She liked the way he froze, his fingers a hair's breadth from the book. His eyes shifted, and when Rachel followed his gaze, she found a framed family photo on the bookshelf. Turner, along with a handsome woman about his age and two smiling teens—a boy and a girl. They were joined by an elderly woman seated in the middle, who looked so much like Turner that she must be his mother. Rachel wondered if it was taken at church or as a holiday package down at the mall.

His Adam's apple bobbed once.

"Charlotte." Unfrozen, he stroked the leather gently, and the intimate touch sent a burst of anger through Rachel's veins. Had he touched Charlotte like that before he raped her? How she wanted to pull the book out of his reach and open it up in his face.

But it would be so much more satisfying to get him to do it himself. So she waited.

"I haven't heard from Charlotte in a while. How is she doing?"

His eyes were back on the book and not on Rachel. She wasn't sure if he was playing her or what, so she went along with it.

"She's been under the weather, but I think she'll be feeling better soon."

"That's good. Tell her I send her my best."

"I will." Rachel relaxed as Turner finally picked up the book, then tensed up in preparation to throw herself to the floor . . . but instead of opening the front cover, he opened the book to the middle. Turning a few pages, he hummed.

"Thirteenth century, I think. The hand is Northern French, but not very well done. Text is some kind of theological treatise. Aquinas, maybe? Although he may be too late for the hand. The parchment is very well preserved."

"That's what I thought, too," Rachel said. "About the parchment, I mean. It looks untouched."

"Yes, it— Oh, here's a bad stain." He'd reached a page that had managed to get splattered. "What's the provenance?"

"We purchased it from a bookseller in Germany. Apparently, it was found in a monastery." Rachel's heart beat as if it might hop right out of her chest. "There's an owner's signature at the front. Maybe you can decipher it?"

That did it. He flipped the pages eagerly until he reached the flyleaf. He leaned over, his nose almost touching the parchment.

"It's ripe," he said with a chuckle. "I'd forgotten how bad old books can smell. And the stains, *whew*. There, I can see the signature, just need to focus—"

Rachel ducked behind the desk just as that now-familiar crunching noise filled the room, and the scent of Turner's insides filled her nose.

"I am *not* going to miss that," she grumbled. She was pleased to find that her plan had worked, and there was no gore in her hair or elsewhere on her person.

Most of Turner's head had been blown onto the page. She scraped the pages along the edge of the office's fancy wooden wastebasket, removing as much of the muck as she could. Then she wrapped it in a scarf that was hanging on the back of the door. The rain slicker she considered, then she simply turned it inside out.

Nobody stopped Rachel on her way out of the building.

She went home.

Rachel tried not to worry. Even if she was caught on camera near each of the death scenes, what could they do? A woman in a rain slicker carrying a medieval manuscript? There's nothing dangerous about that.

A coincidence, surely.

That afternoon, Rachel took a nap. She was exhausted from her day, and once the excitement was over she just wanted to crash. She turned down her phone's volume. Around six, she finally dragged herself out of bed. There were a handful of calls from numbers she didn't recognize, but that was a problem for future Rachel. Present Rachel had other things to do.

Present Rachel heated up a frozen pizza and opened a bottle of Syrah she'd been saving for a special occasion. She lit a few candles, just to make the whole event a bit more festive.

Sated and tipsy, with half a bottle left, Rachel pulled out the book. For several long minutes she turned it over and around in her hands. It was such a powerful weapon and could do a lot of good in the world. It *had*, already. Rachel was sure everyone was better off without Brock or Allen or Turner in the world. But the method was very messy and also uncertain. What if the sigil got completely covered, and it could no longer be seen? What if she tried to clean off the blood and ended up ruining it instead?

There was the other thing, too, the one she didn't want to think about that much. She'd dreamed about the smiling faces of Turner's children and Allen's roommate, whose only crime as far as she knew was sharing an apartment with a shitty rapist. The temptation to keep the book was strong, but in the end, Rachel knew it was time to let it go.

She dug around in the junk drawer of her kitchen and came out with a utility knife similar to the one Charlotte had used to open the package just the day before. Cracking the book to the second page, to avoid any accidental focusing on the sigil, she pressed the tip of the razor blade into the book's gutter and tugged down in one smooth move. The flyleaf lifted away, and Rachel took a deep breath. Normally, she would find such an egregious act of biblioclasm unconscionable, but this was almost enjoyable. When else would she have a good reason to cut a leaf out of a medieval manuscript?

Before she could change her mind and tuck the sheet into a drawer, she held the upside-down page over the closest candle, about where she thought the sigil would be. It took a moment for a black spot to appear on the clean side of the parchment, and then the edges caught fire, and along with it, the scent of burning flesh.

"Ugh."

It was gross but not the worst thing she'd smelled that day. She held on as the flame licked through and turned the creamy parchment black. It burned more slowly than paper, which just gave her more time to enjoy it.

After a few minutes, the fire threatened her fingers, and she took it to the kitchen to drop it into the sink. She let it burn and returned to the table, filling her glass again before she picked up the book.

She hadn't really had a chance to look at it. She'd been afraid, but now with the sigil gone she could enjoy it as a book, the same way she enjoyed all the other books she got to experience as part of her work. She hated to discover that Turner had been right about the hand. It was untrained. Amateurish. Not bad, just . . . not very good.

When Rachel finally flipped to the end, she was surprised to find a colophon. A note from the scribe was always a treat, so she leaned in close to decipher the Latin.

"I am the book of revenge," she read. "Adso made me. His first book. He hopes the abbot will find it satisfactory."

Rachel raised her glass to the flame. "Thank you for this book, Adso. And I do hope your abbot appreciated it."

•••

The second Cassandra finishes her tale, RE Shambrook leaps toward us, startling everyone in our sordid circle. He shows his teeth, and his eyes are taunting. He holds what he found in both of his hands, cupping it like a kitten. I'm mortified, and I'm not alone. RE Shambrook is presenting, gladly, a pile of oozing muck littered with pieces of corn. When he dashes it into the fire, he laughs giddily, watching it sizzle and burn . . .

Filth

RE Shambrook

The man entered The Warehouse, a kinky BDSM club in Graves, Illinois. He knew what he wanted. This club was new and promised to facilitate all kinks and fetishes. His needs were sick, but a promise is a promise.

There had to be a whore whose sexual desires were just as fucked up as his were. There had to be! He couldn't be the only one whose appetite was difficult to sate. Besides, whores would do *anything* for money, right? Even if she wasn't *into* it, he hoped he'd find one that was willing to *go along* with it.

There was a man sitting in an overstuffed chair. He was dressed immaculately in a suit and tie. Bald and with a jet-black goatee, his look came across as evil as opposed to classy . . . or even kinky. It was the facial hair that made the man appear this way. He looked a lot like a wannabe devil worshipper. Perhaps, though, he was reading the man wrong, and he was just a pretentious edgelord.

He saw a woman standing behind the bar. He decided to talk to her instead of the man. He didn't want to give the wrong impression. Besides, he didn't know if the man seated in the chair was an employee or a customer.

He approached the woman. She was dressed in a black latex catsuit. Only her eyes and mouth were visible. He explained in short detail what he wanted. The woman nodded toward the back of the club with a grin.

He followed her nod and found a woman sitting at a back table watching a live sex show featuring two women and five men.

The man was surprised at what he witnessed. For being early in the afternoon, they were really into their performance. There were only a handful of patrons scattered among the tables. A cloud of rank cigarette smoke hung above the room like a foreboding cloud. While the sparse crowd seemed to be watching, no one seemed to be enjoying it.

He watched for a moment. The women were bound, nude, and covered in red stripes and welts. Some of the wounds were bleeding. Bruises of all stages were evident.

The women did not seem to be enjoying their time in the spotlight. He wondered if they were even willing participants. As the men used them violently, they cried out. To the man, it sounded more like pain and fear than enjoyment.

Finally, she acknowledged his presence.

She was a professional. She gave his appearance a quick once over. She didn't turn her nose up at his sloppy appearance. He was balding with a bad comb-over and his face had more grease than the top of a pepperoni pizza. He was overweight but not exactly fat. He wore a black Twisted Cricket T-shirt and khaki pants, both stained with only the Devil knew what.

His shoes were untied, and he smelled rancid. The combination of body odor, unwashed feet, and ass that had recently shit without wiping assaulted her nostrils.

He, too, took an unnecessary moment and evaluated what was in front of him.

This woman was way too attractive to be willing to meet his needs. She was slim and blonde and wearing a bright pink lingerie set with lacy black trim. That was all. Her breasts were of average size and well-proportioned to her body. Natural. No silicone in those airbags. But it wasn't her tits that he wanted. Every woman had tits. He wanted something more risqué than breasts of any size.

He was used to extremely overweight women with sagging tits who weren't keen on personal hygiene. He knew that he himself fell into that category, which was why he didn't openly complain about the slim pickings in partners.

The man hesitantly leaned down to explain his needs into her ear. He hoped that she could hear him correctly over the bass-driven music. He stood and waited for the laughter. The kink shaming. The rejection.

The woman looked at him with a raised eyebrow and a smirk.

The man pulled out a large wad of cash to show her he was serious.

She stubbed out her cigarette and swallowed the remainder of her drink before standing. She took him by the hand and led him to an all-but-empty room.

The walls were painted a flat sanitarium white. Matching white tiles covered the floor. In the center, butted up against the wall, was a bed. A sparse metal frame held a single mattress covered with a rubber sheet. He took in the bleak interior, considering what it would look like when they finished their session.

After she closed the door behind them, she hesitated before flipping the switch. She peered through the window, curious if anyone noticed. She didn't really want to turn the switch on. Not this time.

The switch turned on a light outside the door. The light was green, signaling to any patrons so inclined that they were welcome to watch. It also turned on the cameras in the room and began their recording.

There was more than one way to make money. Eight cameras would film the tryst. Their footage would be edited down and posted on a dedicated website. There was no consent form for the customer to sign, and the working girls didn't have a choice. The act was more than illegal, but it was a solid and steady stream of revenue.

The man rucked his shirt over his head as the woman ordered him to lie down on the bed.

He obeyed.

She removed his pants and dingy, yellowed briefs. He was a chubby fellow with a pudgy stomach and a less-than-average-sized pecker.

Again, she remained professional and didn't snicker at the inch of mushroom cap poking out of his black, unruly and matted forest of pubic hair. She hoped he was a grower and not a shower, or else this endeavor would be less than satisfying.

She removed her pink and black lace bra, exposing him to her all-natural and still-firm breasts. Her areolae were not too large and not too small. Her nipples were like gumdrops. The pink circles were an alluring contrast to the tanned skin.

She caressed and gently pinched her nipples. She was giving him a show and yet his inch of manhood stayed where it was. Not showing any signs of life or excitement. She continued. She knew what he wanted, but still, a naked woman baring her flesh to him should get *some* sort of reaction.

The woman slid her thumbs into the lace waistband and dropped her pink panties to the floor, letting him take in her full body. She moved her hands across her breasts, down her stomach, and to the neatly maintained triangle of dark hair. It wasn't mowed down, just trimmed. The hair was thick and soft. Her hand slid between her legs and lingered as she massaged her sex.

She knew there was no way this man could get a woman like her without him having to pay for it. She wanted to make sure that he could see every inch of her perfection. Still, the man and his tiny pecker showed no signs of arousal.

She climbed onto the bed and stood over him, facing the door. His view from below caused the south to rise in full force. She squatted over him and looked down. To her amazement, that one inch that was all head turned into at least seven inches of thick, throbbing man meat. He held his firm cock to her waiting hole and began stroking.

Her perfect globes of flesh hovered over his groin. He followed her split with lustful eyes. He realized that she didn't sport one tan line. Her cute little pucker of an asshole had apparently been bleached as it matched her perfectly colored body. Kissed by the sun to a beautiful bronze. The only change in color was the rose-red of her open sex peeking out through the black veil of her bush.

He wanted to be turned on by the pink maw that was apparently hungry for his cock. He knew he *should* be. But it was that cute little star just above that got him going. It was like an eye that stared into his soul.

He stared back at it.

He would never violate that hole. Never poke that eye with his prick. It was too sacred.

It took her a moment, but her tight pucker finally began to wink at him. His hand was moving dryly yet fervently up and down his length. He watched intently until the brown started to crown.

This was it. This was the fuel to his lust.

She grunted as she let out a blast of rancid air. The long dark brown cylinder slowly began to emerge from her back passage. His hand moved faster, and he was afraid that if it didn't fall soon, he was going to jerk himself raw. Her aim was on point as it landed directly over his cock and hand.

He mushed the semisolid fecal matter around his stiffness and used it to continue pleasuring himself. He let out an ecstatic moan as the scat lubricated his stroking. Up and down, he smeared her shit with one hand while the other massaged his balls.

He almost squealed in joy when his eyes caught the second log beginning to work its way out. He was panting with enthusiastic anticipation. He was slowly running out of breath through his exertion. If he died of a heart attack now, he didn't care. This was the greatest moment of his life. The most beautiful woman he had ever seen was shitting on his cock. He would die a truly happy man.

Unbeknownst to the man, the woman who squatted over and defecated on him was making eyes at the camera. She also blew kisses to Charlotte, the woman in the catsuit, who was watching through the window of the door.

Once evacuated, she stood and turned around to unleash a hot stream of asparagus-scented piss onto his dick and stomach. He moaned in sick pleasure at the added bonus. He didn't care if she charged him extra for that. It wasn't as much of a turn-on as the bowel movement had been, but he still enjoyed the filthiness of it.

He nodded at her to imply she had done well, and he was now going to jerk himself into euphoric bliss.

The woman turned and got on all fours between his legs. Without hesitation, the woman pushed his filthy hand away from his cock. She scooped up some of her droppings and smeared them onto his shaft.

She then opened her mouth and began sucking the shit off of his dick. She collected it and mixed it with her saliva before spitting it back onto his raging erection. She continued the process of sucking and spitting.

The man's head was about to explode. This beautiful goddess was sucking his shitty cock. *She was sucking her own shit off of his cock.* This was a new advancement to his fantasy, and he was enjoying it.

She mashed the foul substance with her tongue to the roof of her mouth and showed him so he could watch it ooze out between her teeth. He was getting close. The man used his shit-smeared hand to grab a handful of her hair and force her head down. He wanted to hear her choke and gag on his cock as her fecal matter ran down her throat.

Her nose planted into his shit-laced pubic hair. When he let her up for air, her face was covered in waste. Liquid shit drooled out of her mouth. The brown-tinted saliva dropped onto his groin and ran down between his legs. He let out a sigh of ecstasy as the slime reached his balls. He was sent into a sexual high as it reached his taint and formed a puddle. Shifting caused the puddle to work its way between the cleft of his buttocks and tease his asshole.

The sight of her mixed with the sensation of leaking fluids was too much. He forced her head back down. He bucked into her face, grinding it further into his shit-covered groin. He held her tight as he launched his genetic goo deep into her throat.

The woman was a trouper and didn't gag once as her airway was blocked. She continued to suck, sending aftershocks of euphoria through his body. When he had spent all of his seed, she lifted her head and showed him the tie-dye white, yellow, and brown swirl on her tongue.

Inspired, he quickly formulated a second round of awful activity while she swallowed down the unholy concoction and showed him her empty mouth.

Shit caked her teeth, and she ran her tongue across them, licking the foul substance and smearing it further. She blew him a kiss and climbed down off the bed.

The man stood and pointed to the spot he had just occupied. This was going to be new for him as well. He was eager for the adventure.

The woman got onto the bed and laid on her back. She spread her legs and bent her knees, waiting for a good hard fuck. This man had just shot his load down her throat, but his cock still raged in a full erection. The man climbed onto the bed, positioning himself between her splayed legs. It took some effort on his part, but in the end, he stood in the same position that she had at the beginning of their session.

The man's ass was flat, pale, and hairy. Ingrown hairs and zits peppered the milk-white plane. His stomach fell in front of him and dangled down between his knees. He spread his cheeks, giving her a clear view of the festering boils and the wild forest of hair circling his asshole.

It didn't take him long before he ripped out a long, wet fart. The odor emitted smelled of old, used grease. It was quickly followed by an eruption of liquid shit. The fecal substance sprayed up the woman's already sewage-slicked body.

Ever the professional, she didn't wince or gag. Instead, she began to massage it into her skin.

When she could sense the second explosion coming, she reached down and spread her labia open. The vile liquid dribbled out of his anus and onto the woman's displayed canal. She began to rub her clit with his diarrheal lubricant.

The second blast finally came in another explosion of runny, lumpy, malodorous filth. She continued to use his offering to stimulate her fuck button as he got off the table.

He grabbed her legs and pulled her to the edge of the bed. She threw her legs over his shoulders. He inhaled the scent of their combined feces on her body.

She wondered if he could smell the congestion of yeast that clumped inside of her vagina like cottage cheese. She assumed he couldn't through the overwhelming scent of fecal matter. Also, his mind was so preoccupied with his lust for shit that he wasn't paying attention to any other details.

The man didn't think twice as he buried his face into her feces-filled snatch. His tongue probed deep inside her. The whore's ripe and sour scent—mixed with the smell of shit—was making his cock *throb* in lewd anticipation.

He lapped at her pussy and sucked on her clit. He drooled rectal-flavored saliva back onto her. He sucked the flavor out of her thick bush and spat it inside her cunt. His tongue worked the spit further into her, coating her walls with their bodies' waste.

The man's back was to the door. He didn't see that Mo, the bald man with the goatee in the suit, had joined Charlotte in the window. Her jaw was hanging open and Mo's face wore a sinister grin.

The piggish client's hands roamed the prostitute's body, further smearing his and her dirt onto her. He kneaded her natural C-cup breasts and held her hips. He put his hands under her ass to lift her muff up to his mouth and his tongue danced around her clit. She squirmed and rolled her hips as he electrified her sensitive nerve endings.

As he did so, a straggling nugget fell from her back door. He laid her back down, picked up the fresh feces, and slathered it into his raging cock.

She grabbed his hair and held his face in place as he worked her sensitive button with his tongue. The man slid two shit-caked fingers into her shit-coated snatch. Angling his digits upward and giving the "come here" motion got the woman squirming with more enthusiasm.

He worked her spot and sucked her clit until she let out a gush of girl juice onto his face and chest. He was shocked that it had worked. He had seen it done in the movies but didn't know that it was truly possible.

He was relentless and didn't let up, sending her into a second fountain. He backed away, catching as much as he could in his mouth. Moving to her head, he watched as she panted. Her face was covered in shit, cum, piss, drool, and a look of euphoric bliss.

He spat her juices onto her face, shocking her back to reality. She saw he was ready to go again and slid off the bed. She couldn't stand and dropped to her knees. It had been a long time since a man had made her cum like that.

On her knees on the floor, she gobbled up his throbbing manhood. She hoped to suck thick ropes of semen from it.

She sucked and slurped the excrement-covered organ. Rather than an orgasmic moan, he let out a rumbling, oily fart.

She heard his bowels begin to churn once more and spit his cock out of her mouth. He began to squat as another stream of foul feculence ripped out of his bowels with wet, ass-cheek-clapping flatulence.

She caught as much as she could in her hands and began squishing the lumpy stool on his cock and balls. She slathered him in the greasy filth and used two hands to work his cock, each hand turning in a different direction as she slid them methodically up and down.

The man grabbed her hair, forcing his dung-covered dong down her throat. She bobbed up and down a few times before she pulled away and scraped up more filth from the floor. She began shoving as much of his excretion into her already waste-coated gash as would fit.

The woman stood and bent over the bed, resting on her forearms. The man got behind her and slipped his filthy cock into her warm, shit-stuffed love tunnel. As he pushed in, he watched as the overflow of shit oozed out and mashed into his crotch hair all the way up to his navel.

The woman let out a low, sultry moan as he pumped in and out of her. The sound of the mucky filth smooshing between them and the *drip-drop* sound as it overflowed onto the floor sent them both into an exhilarated spiral.

He held her hips and groped her tits, smearing the brown stuff all over her in the process. She moaned and screamed until they both reached their climax.

The man backed out of her, and she once more went to her knees for a final taste of their coupling.

He reached down and tilted her chin up, forcing her to look at him.

"Can I see you again?" he asked as he picked up his pants.

She raised an eyebrow.

He pulled the wad of cash out of his pocket and began peeling off bills until she nodded.

The woman scrunched up her face and wriggled her hips slightly. She reached down and slipped a digit up her shit-slicked slot. She fished around, sending a flood of shit, spunk, spit, and who knows what else onto the floor between her feet.

She stood up and held a single kernel of corn in her hand. The man peeled off another bill and the woman placed the befouled morsel on her tongue. He leaned down and sucked the kernel out of her mouth.

He smiled.

●●●

When RE Shambrook has concluded his disgusting, dirty story, Chaz Williams is next. He holds his scrap behind his back while he looks meaningfully at his audience. Slowly, steadily, he reveals what he found. A half-empty bottle of whiskey. He swirls it around, and in the firelight, it seems to sparkle . . .

Sober

Chaz Williams

Kris looks at her Fitbit for the third time in the past hour. It read 12:58 a.m. The regret of offering to cover the closing shift at SONIC weighs heavily on her as she struggles to stay awake for one last minute. Kris didn't have the luxury of taking summers off like some of her classmates attending Stanford who came from wealth. She got in on an academic scholarship and had to work odd jobs during the semester and summer to pay for the roof over her head and the food in her stomach. She knows this is all temporary. One more year and she'll have her Bachelor of Business Administration degree and–hopefully–with a Google internship she'll be offered a job as soon as she graduates.

The alarm on her phone goes off, signaling that it's officially one a.m. Time for her to close up and leave. The smell of well-done burgers and French fries had become her permanent perfume. Although this summer had been hard on her, at least she didn't have to skate around like the car hops. Plus, free SONIC Blasts and milkshakes are always nice, so things could be much worse. Stepping outside–with the blast of fresh air on her face like a tidal wave of freedom–she locks the door and makes her way toward her 2011 black Toyota Corolla. Black Betty was a high school graduation present from her parents. They had paid $750 for the car at a public auction. Money was tight for them, but her folks wanted her to have a reliable form of transportation when making the drive home from Palo Alto to Fresno.

That car had been by her side through thick and thin, from her first heartbreak to her first music festival. Kris took good care of Black Betty, so she never had to worry about getting stuck somewhere.

As she turns the key in the ignition and the engine roars to life, the sounds of Hayley Williams's voice booms out of the speakers and fills up the car.

"Ain't It Fun" by Paramore had been her favorite song since its release back in 2013. It always reminded her that even as she ventured into the cold and frightening real world that she had to appreciate each day and have fun with her life.

BANG! BANG! BANG!

The loud knocks on her window pull Kris out of her head and back to the present. The sweet serenade dissolves around her as she focuses on the intruder. A man, dark and haggard, holding something in his hand, is motioning for her to roll her window down. Immediately panic sets in as she worries that she's being carjacked—something her mother had warned her about endlessly; especially since Kris was working such late shifts, she begged for her to stay vigilant at all times.

Kris's fight-or-flight instincts take over. She immediately shifts into reverse to pull out of the SONIC parking lot before the man has the opportunity to use what's in his hand. As the car speeds away from him, he yells out, "Hey lady, you dropped your wallet!"

But the adrenaline coursing through her veins and the volume of the music didn't allow Kris to hear anything the man had to say. She's laser focused on getting out of Dodge and on the road to her apartment.

Going through the green light, she breathes a sigh of relief for avoiding the first real encounter of danger she's ever experienced in life. As she approaches the next traffic light, it turns green. She laughs to herself, thinking, *Wow, I can't wait to tell Mom and Dad about this*!

The impact is immediate and unforgiving.

Metal on metal creates an orchestra of destruction.

Kris's body is split in half, like she's been cut through by a swinging, bladed pendulum. The jaws of life are used to retrieve what's left of her body.

The drunk driver was traveling at a speed of 140 miles per hour. Although, after the impact, their car veered off the road and crashed into a massive redwood, they only sustained a broken arm, broken collar bone, a concussion, and some scrapes and bruises. Lucky outcome for someone who was two times over the legal limit for alcohol.

Kris would never get that degree or internship with Google.

"And to you all, my loyal and amazing fans and subscribers, I just want to say that you are the reason I am still here today. You lift me up and give me the strength to keep fighting and never fall back into bad habits . . . the habits that almost cost me everything. We are Liz strong! *Wooooo!* Please make sure to bookmark my upcoming scheduled live shows and I will keep you all in my thoughts until we meet again, my love bugs!"

The live stream ends as Liz Fuller sets her phone down and takes a sip from her cup—a mixture of vodka and cranberry juice coats her throat as she lets the alcohol do its work on her. It's been two years since the fateful night when she ran a red light and killed a young woman on her way home from work.

She never spent a night in jail. The perks of having a judge for a father and a state senator for a mother. Things seem to work their way out with privilege. On her social media accounts to the outside world, Liz has been two years sober since the accident, but in reality . . . she has never stopped drinking. She just doesn't drive anymore and has a personal chauffeur to take her wherever she needs to go. She doesn't drink when she knows she has to make public appearances or go live for her fans. But since the accident, she has hit the booze harder than ever.

In the influencer circles, she's known as Good Time Liz—because after a few drinks she will fuck and suck anybody if you're cute or famous enough.

Tonight's post-live rendezvous is with Sebastian Walcott. A pretty boy surfer and extreme sports influencer who has just as big a following as Liz and the good looks to draw in a loyal female audience.

"Margaret, can you bring me a fresh bottle of Weller? It's Sebastian's favorite and I want him happy when he gets here," Liz says as she applies red lipstick to her pert mouth.

"Very well, Ms. Fuller. I took the liberty of pouring two fingers for both of you. Mr. Walcott has just arrived," Margaret, the new personal assistant, says as she sets down a tray of two glasses and a bottle of bourbon.

Sebastian rolls in without even acknowledging the presence of anyone but Liz. He kisses her like she is his lost love. Like they have been reunited after years apart.

"Calm down, boy, I don't let the help watch," Liz says while motioning toward Margaret.

"Sorry, bae, I just couldn't help myself. You look so fucking good! And I've been *dying* to see you all day," Sebastian says with the excitement of a high schooler about to get laid for the first time.

"That'll be all, Margaret. You are free to go for the night. I'll see you tomorrow," Liz says while making a motion with her hand indicating Margaret to leave. "Now, let's make a toast to our shared success on this new business venture with Under Armour!"

They clink their glasses together as they finish their drinks in one gulp. Falling to the bed, they begin making out. After a minute or so, they are both passed out as Margaret walks back into the room with the new chauffeur. The Rohypnol she snuck into their glasses had done its job and devilish smiles spread on their faces. One at a time, the two of them carry the lifeless bodies to the SUV waiting outside. A much easier job in theory, but now as they struggle to get the dead weight down these stairs, they realize this probably should have been planned out better.

The smell of bleach awakens Liz from her restful sleep. Groggily, she sits up and wipes the crust from her eyes. Still not realizing what type of situation she is in until she notices she's not in her bedroom and not on her bed. In fact, she's sitting on a cot straight from the set of *M*A*S*H*.

She also notices Sebastian is knocked out, lying on a cot across from her. She stands on shaky legs like a newborn fawn. Liz makes her way over to Sebastian. She shakes him awake.

"What the fuck? Let me sleep in a bit. Shit!" he says, annoyed, but Liz immediately slaps him awake. "Why the fuck did you do that, bitch?" he screams.

"Can you shut up for a second and let me look around? Where the fuck are we?" a panicked Liz asks, as she notices that they are in a room with no windows, two cots, one steel door, and a bucket in the corner.

"Clearly someone is fucking with us because there's no way we got here on our own," Sebastian replies in his cocky tone. He makes his way to the door and begins banging on it. "Okay! Joke's over! You've had your fun, guys! Let us out! I've gotta piss like a racehorse." Nothing but silence fills the room. He turns to look at Liz who is less composed than he is at the moment. Turning back toward the door, striking it even harder, he says, "Hey! Open this fucking door before I *really* get mad!"

The door suddenly bursts open, and Sebastian is hit with a stun gun that makes him immediately drop to the ground and he pisses his pants. His entire body seizing from the electric current flowing through him.

Entering the room are two familiar faces. A woman ahead of a man who holds some type of black handheld object in his massive hands.

"Margaret! Robert! What the fuck is going on?" she asks with a sudden sliver of relief after seeing her assistant and driver.

"Actually, Ms. Fuller, our names are *not* Margaret and Robert, but Susan and Richard. Susan and Richard Holmes," the woman says.

"I don't understand what's going on right now. Where are we?" Liz asks in a confused state.

"It's quite simple, darling, we are here to give you the *real* help you need to become clean and sober. You have so much life ahead of you and you've been given a second chance. Something not every person is afforded. You mustn't squander it!" Susan replies in her most caring and motherly voice.

Sebastian dazedly interjects from the floor, saying, "Yeah, that's fine and dandy . . . but why am *I* here?"

For the first time, the tall man speaks and says, "We'd like to offer you the same opportunity to earn your sobriety and turn your life around. Consider this . . . a charitable outreach program."

Laughing in the most condescending manner, Sebastian threatens, "You two are fucking out of your minds and you'll go straight to fuckin' jail for this! Do you know who my father is? Do you know the influence we have?"

Richard replies in a calculated tone, "We are very aware of who both your and Liz's parents are. You'll see them very soon, actually, so long as you accept this gift and kick your bad habits cold turkey. But, if you refuse, I'm afraid you'll never see them again."

Liz's demeanor immediately goes sour, as if she was punched in the gut and the air has all but escaped her body. Sebastian, on the other hand, rushes the man.

He has no plans of being a part of whatever sick and twisted games these two have in store. Unfortunately for him, as he approaches Richard, Sebastian receives a shot to the head that leaves him stunned.

Richard stands before him. His thick salt and pepper beard gives a look of sophistication, but his cold dead eyes show that he is a broken man with only revenge on his mind. "Have you ever heard of a blackjack, son? That's the old-school name, I think it's called a sap now. It's quite handy in close proximity altercations. Packs one hell of a punch, perfect for bludgeoning someone to death." Sebastian tries to steady and brace himself, but it makes no difference as Richard strikes the young man over and over across the face. In a complete daze, Sebastian tries to crawl away as he lays on the ground. Before he can, Richard is on him in seconds, and he pins him to the ground. Once more, he begins slapping Sebastian over and over in the face with the weapon.

"This is the problem with your generation! You take, take, take and never accept a good thing when it's right in front of you." Richard stands over Sebastian's body. "But that's okay. I will give you what you deserve . . . right . . . now!"

In an instant, Richard's size fourteen boot is stomping on Sebastian's face. The crack of bones and blood and cartilage spewing up from his face is like a volcanic eruption of pain and suffering. By the time Richard is done with what used to be Sebastian's face, there is nothing left but a hollow pool of blood. His lifeless body lays there as Liz begins hyperventilating.

She's on the verge of passing out.

Susan runs over to her and grabs her face. "Look at me, Liz! I know that was hard to see but in the end, you will understand our purpose here! I need you to slow your breathing. Can you do that for me? Nice slow, deep breaths for me, honey."

As Liz's breathing starts to calm down, Richard picks up the dead body and carries it out of the room.

"We start your detox tomorrow, Liz. For now, try and stay calm. Everything will be all right. This will be a life-changing experience for you. You will never appreciate what you have more than when you give up your vices and accept a clean life. Get some rest. We will bring you lunch in a couple of hours."

Susan kisses Liz on the forehead and exits the room.

Liz sits there on the ground, staring at the bloodstains smeared across the floor like a grotesque Norman Rockwell painting. The cruel and horrific reminder of seeing his face caved in like that makes her puke up the bile and traces of alcohol that are still in her stomach. She cries herself to sleep on the cot, afraid of what will come next.

For the next seventy-two hours Liz experiences what can only be described as Hell on Earth. A small price to pay for ridding the body of all the toxins alcohol had poisoned her with. The sweating was only a little annoying at first, mix that with the body pains and the chills from the fever she had, and it was almost like she was ten years old again, staying home from school to fight out a sinus infection that turned into the flu. Unfortunately, alcohol is a vengeful bitch and does not like being expelled from the body—especially after having been with Liz since the age of fourteen.

Those sweats and pains turned into seizures.

Her body was betraying her.

Every hour or so, the room would start to spin like a Tilt-A-Whirl from one of the local carnivals that would roll into town. Smells of cotton candy and popcorn filled her nose as one minute she laughed with friends while the ride spun round and round without a care in the world. Next, she's back to reality, her body violently shaking like she was hit with a jolt of electricity. Something she welcomes with open arms at this point in time as the withdrawal symptoms bring her closer and closer to her breaking point. Just as things seemed like they would get a little better . . . the vomiting started.

The bile of her empty stomach expelled the remaining alcohol and acid that still sat inside of her. Praying to the porcelain god—or in her case, the bucket god—on her knees like she's at Sunday service, waiting to receive the body of Christ.

But there is no salvation here. Only hurt and memories of a life wasted and an existence given a second chance.

SOBER

They say the first forty-eight hours are the worst . . . but for those unlucky few, once you make it past that timestamp, you begin to see things.

Impossible things.

Things that will haunt you for the rest of your life.

Liz could only focus on one memory as the hallucinations started. It was that fateful night when she took a life.

Images of her body being pulled from her G-Wagon, cuts and scrapes all over her body, the throbbing sensation of pain radiating from her arm that couldn't move an inch without a sudden burst of pain. All in all, not too bad for a person who just ran a red light and crashed into another car. Lying there in bed, she got to replay that moment endlessly, always focusing on the message from her mother advising her not to be out all night drinking like she had become accustomed to. Except this time, she doesn't crawl out of her totaled vehicle. No, on this occasion, the wreckage is all around her in the middle of that empty room. Fire and metal blazing like she's in the aftermath of a war zone. The smell of gasoline and burning flesh fills her nostrils. From the wreckage, an angel approaches–her guardian angel, here to protect her.

Only, this is no guardian angel. Its mouth is filled with razor-sharp teeth.

The angel straddles Liz and rips a chunk of flesh from her throat. Blood sprays like a water sprinkler and releases an endless mist all over the angel.

The angel—a perfect mix of a Greek goddess with long curly hair and a demon straight out of your worst nightmare with large claws that could rip a grizzly bear to shreds—looks down at Liz. Soaked in the blood of her victim, the angel raises its claws, which reveal a set of sharpened talons glittery, curved, and steely . . . the claws would put an eagle to shame. She rips apart Liz's midsection.

Guts and intestines spread across the room, like a feast for a hungry family of wild boars.

The angel grabs Liz by the face and looks deeply into her eyes. A full smile splits open the celestial menace's face.

"This is not true suffering, not yet."

She gauges out Liz's eyeballs. The pressure of the talons ripping into the optic nerves leaves Liz to give the most sickening scream the human body can produce before she's back in the room, her body intact, and must go through the torture once again. She experiences these hallucinations for a day and a half. How her mind did not break only proves that she was worthy of earning this gift that was being bestowed upon her. Sobriety is something that is a battle every single day for the rest of your life, and getting through the withdrawal is the first test of truly being reborn.

With the worst of the withdrawal symptoms behind her, Liz goes through extensive therapy sessions with Susan.

She spills her soul about the wrongs she has done and the people she has hurt due to alcohol. Admitting that drinking had ruled her life was no easy task, but doing so made Liz feel as if the world had been lifted from her shoulders. She was never a religious person at all, but thanks to the guidance of Susan and Richard, she learned that there is a higher power, a singular God who will strengthen her to continue to fight every single day. To never give in to the temptations of the world. She is but a humble servant who only wishes to serve and give her life to His will.

After two months of intense prayer and begging for forgiveness, she asks that the Lord remove the shortcomings in her character that made her choose alcohol in the first place.

Making amends with those she has hurt by writing letters to anyone she has wronged gives her a euphoric feeling. For the first time, she understands what those people who say they are high on life must feel like.

The energy of the Holy Spirit within her gives her the strength to write the most important letter she will ever write in her life.

To Whom It May Concern,

The fact that I even have to start this letter this way just shows how horrible a person I am. I took your only child away from you, and I didn't even learn her name till months later when my father helped get the case against me dropped. I am a flawed woman who doesn't deserve your pity or your forgiveness. But in order for me to truly move on to the next step in my sobriety, I need to tell you how incredibly sorry I am for what I did to your family and your daughter. There's nothing I can do or say that will ever make up for it, but I promise from this day forth to honor her memory in the best way I possibly can. I hope one day I can meet you in person and give you this letter, so you can see the sincerity in my face and know that I am truly a changed person.

Liz Fuller

Never in a million years did Liz think she would get to this point. She's now been sober for three months, a length of time without alcohol she hasn't experienced since she was a teen.

She is writing in her journal when Susan comes to her with some exciting news. "Liz, I wanted to let you know that with you coming up on ninety days sober, you will be able to see your parents for the first time since we brought you here. They are so excited to see their baby girl again and cannot wait to hear about all the progress you have made!"

Liz could not contain the amount of pure joy she had hearing that. She jumped up, ran over to Susan, and gave her a big hug.

"You and your husband literally saved my life. There will never be a way for me to repay you for this . . . but I promise to stay clean. Forever! I promise! I'll do it . . . to honor you!" Liz had tears in her eyes as Susan comforted her.

"Every day you take a breath, you honor us, sweetheart. Let's get preparations together for your parents to come visit! Gotta make sure you look presentable, and this room is squeaky clean." Susan looks lovingly at Liz.

She hands Liz a fresh bottle of water. "Make sure you're staying hydrated. It can get pretty warm down here once you start cleaning."

Liz takes a few gulps of the refreshing spring water and sets off to straighten up her cot . . . but before she can even get started, she collapses on the bed.

An inaudible voice is speaking as the cobwebs clear from her fragile mind. Once again Liz awakes in that room that was once her prison but has become her salvation.

Her arms are zip-tied behind her back and each leg is zip-tied to the legs of the chair she's seated in.

Once her vision clears, the nature of her current situation becomes even more dire and nauseating. She finds her mother and father both sitting across from her, their mouths covered with duct tape and limbs also secured to their seats. The look of panic on their faces is so haunted and defeated, as if they know this is the end of a long road. There is no salvation in sight. Only the terrors of a fate so hopeless that not even an optimist could look at the glass half full.

The voice that woke her is one she's heard millions of times. Bewildered as to why at such a high-stakes moment, a Paramore song is playing, she allows herself to get lost in the lyrics to calm her mind.

A slap across her face jolts her out of the daydream she conjured up so as not to face her sickening and disturbing reality. The sensation is like being stung by a million wasps at once; all her pain feels so real without the numbing effects of alcohol to dull her senses.

"In these past ninety days, not once did you connect the dots as to who we are and why we were doing this." Susan stands in front of Liz with a determined expression on her face as she speaks with such calm and purpose. "Sure, we could just be some religious zealots who wanna see you turn your life around, but truth be told . . . I lost all hope in God when my daughter was killed and the person responsible for it never even spent a night in jail." Susan says with anger bubbling up as she looks Liz dead in her eyes. "I can't even fault you for that because you don't have the connections and political pull to make that happen, but these two, on the other hand . . ." Susan motions toward her parents. She pulls a knee from the small of her back as she walks toward them. "They made sure their precious daughter was well taken care of. But what about my daughter? Who was gonna make sure she was served justice, so her death wasn't in vain and forgotten!" Susan screams, gripping the knife, begging for it to find its mark.

Richard steps forward to console his wife. He has been her rock these past two years and hasn't allowed himself to properly grieve because he must stay strong for her.

"Elizabeth Marie Fuller, you killed my daughter. Her name was Kristine Love Holmes. She was the most important thing in our lives and our greatest accomplishment. You snuffed out her life in an instant and never even thought about her once after it happened, did you? A normal person would feel remorse—most couldn't live with the fact that they got away with murder—but not you. You are a special breed. And you became this way because of your environment and the way you were raised," Richard says, still holding his wife. "The time for justice is here. We are taking matters into our own hands . . . and these hands have a great need for retribution."

Liz, a sobbing mess, sat there helplessly.

"You are good people; you spent the last three months getting me sober. That has to count for something. You say you lost faith in God, but you've been teaching me His ways, helping me become the best version of myself I've ever been. Why would you do that just to have my parents and me here now, and you ready to hurt us?"

Susan approaches Liz and kneels before her so they are eye to eye. "Faith is a cancer that gives you false hope. It spreads to every inch of your life, giving you that security you need to go on with your existence. If God were real, the suffering would not be like this. The wounds would not reopen every morning. The torture of knowing I could not protect my baby girl wouldn't haunt me every single day. We wanted to get you of sound mind and judgment because you can never fully appreciate the pain, grief, and guilt of losing a loved one until you feel it . . . *sober*."

Richard pulls out his phone to turn the volume of the music up. The guitar riffs and the vocals drown out the muffled screams that come out of the covered mouths of Liz's parents.

Susan gets down on her knees and starts to undo Mr. Fuller's slacks. She exposes his tiny excuse of a penis. She takes him into her mouth and begins sucking his micro-penis until it swells to a full erection.

"You better savor that, old boy, because it will be the last time you ever get your dick wet," Richard says as he watches his wife perform the act.

Liz is stunned by their vulgarity. These two saved her life and are now two completely different people—monsters, more accurately.

Susan feels Mr. Fuller start to squirm. His penis throbs in her mouth and as he is on the cusp of ejaculation, she pulls away. Quickly grabbing a scalpel hidden in her pocket and with one precise slash along the shaft of his penis, he begins to bleed out.

The screams coming out of him are animalistic and primal.

He begins to thrash back and forth in an attempt to break free from the chair. A loud thud encompasses the room as Richard delivers a bone-shattering blow to the back of Mr. Fuller's skull. His body shakes uncontrollably as he starts to have a seizure and with another blow to the side of the skull, his body all at once slumps over.

Susan takes the scalpel and begins cutting into his penis little by little, like she is cutting through a brick of cheese.

She wants him to feel the pain her daughter felt but even more so for helping cover it up. The sensation of having his manhood cut off brings Mr. Fuller back to the land of the conscious. He begins to vomit in his mouth. With nowhere for it to go, he begins to gag and choke on the bile and acid within.

Susan, like the Iron Chef of mutilation, cuts through his penis completely. She tosses the tiny organ onto Liz's lap. The girl begins to scream uncontrollably.

Richard kicks the man in the chest and his body slams to the ground. With the rage of a million men, he hammers the man's face until all that is left is a Picasso level of artwork that used to be Mr. Fuller.

Mrs. Fuller pees herself watching everything that happened to her husband. Sobbing, she knows that she is next. She closes her eyes and accepts her fate.

Susan leans close to her and quietly whispers into her ear, "Oh, don't turn a blind eye now! The fun is just getting started."

With the swift swing of a bat, Mrs. Fuller's knee is shattered upon impact. The sound is reminiscent of a mirror being violently thrown to the ground. Like shards of glass scattering all over the pavement.

The screams coming from her mouth mimic the sounds of an animal on the verge of death.

There will be no sweet release for Mrs. Fuller on this day.

Susan takes a scalpel and starts to cut into her flesh. Blood covers her hands as she makes deep lacerations into her breast. After successfully cutting her left breast off, Susan walks over to Mr. Fuller's dead body and leans down on top of him. With a staple gun in hand, she punctures the filleted piece of flesh onto what used to be his face.

Richard cuts the restraints from her body and throws her to the ground. Mrs. Fuller lays there unconscious, a hollowed-out shell of the woman she once was.

"I was a pretty good baseball player in my heyday. Even played in college. Never thought I'd have an opportunity to swing the bat like this again. But I gotta tell you, it feels so *fucking* good."

With a downward motion, as if he were swinging an ax into an oak tree, the baseball bat makes a loud and audible *pop* as her skull is immediately crushed under the force of the swing.

Brains and fluid leak on the ground around her head while Richard takes swing after swing after swing after swing after—

When her husband was done, Susan approached Mrs. Fuller's body, carrying a handsaw with her.

"This room is so dead; we'll need to brighten it up some!" With that, Susan takes the saw to Mrs. Fuller's neck as she begins to remove the pulverized head from the rest of her body.

Next, the removal of each limb made Liz sick to her stomach. Her throat had become hoarse from the nonstop screaming while witnessing the two people who had changed her life suddenly turn into monsters. It was more than she could bear to watch. Unfortunately, every time she tried to look away, Richard was there to snap her back to reality and make her watch the carnage before her.

When the job was done, Mrs. Fuller's body was cut into pieces and scraps, her flesh discarded all over the room. Liz was wrapped in her mother's intestines. They hung around her like a sadistic Christmas tree decoration—like snotty, gory, bloody tinsel.

The bodies and pieces of what used to be her parents lay at her feet like gifts waiting to be opened.

After their masterpiece of blood and bones was complete, Susan and Richard hugged and kissed each other.

Richard went to the corner of the room to retrieve more tools of torture. Liz couldn't tell what it was he was holding . . . until he turned around. Her heart dropped in an instant at the sight before her.

Holding two revolvers, he began walking toward her.

Liz sobbed uncontrollably. "Please, you've done enough. My parents are dead. You don't have to kill me too!"

Susan once again dropped to her knees to look Liz in the eyes. "Oh, sweet angel, you still don't get it, do you? We're not *killing* you. We want you to live forever with the knowledge that you ruined two families because of your addiction. Through your sobriety, you get to sit here. Forever. And you'll think about what life could have been." Richard hands one of the revolvers to his wife. They stare lovingly into each other's eyes.

"Let's reunite with our baby girl."

Two loud bangs ring out in unison. Their bodies drop to the floor.

Liz screams out in panic. The two people who put her here are dead, and she is stuck tied to the chair with only her thoughts and the carcasses of her loved ones to keep her company.

They gave her the gift of sobriety . . . and the curse of living with it.

∙∙∙

Chaz Williams bows, then returns to his seat. Slowly, he opens the bottle and takes a sip. While he does this, Ruth Anna Evans approaches the bonfire. I see that her cheeks are streaked with tears. She sniffles before displaying her scrap. It's a dog collar and hanging from it is a tag. In the orange glow of the fire, I see that the dog was named . . .

Rita

Ruth Anna Evans

"Sweetie, I'm so sorry, but we have to get rid of Rita." Stef took her hand off the steering wheel and gave Drake's thigh a squeeze. This was the second time she had said something about it. He knew she wasn't going to let it go.

"No chance. I've had her since she was six weeks old. She's a good dog."

In the back seat, Dewey blew a raspberry and giggled. Drake reached back and wiped his face with the cloth.

"Babe, she isn't good around Dewey. You know this."

"We'll keep them apart until he learns."

Stef didn't answer at first. Then, softly, "You know he's not going to learn."

Drake didn't answer. She was right. Even at five, it was clear that there was a lot Dewey was never going to learn. He didn't walk until he was three. Still only had about four words. Words that didn't sound like much, really, but at least he finally said "Mama" in that sweet high-pitched voice of his. For Stef's sake, Drake was glad of that. He wondered if "Daddy" would ever come. He could only pray. He had been praying since the day his son had been born, so brutally, his little head bruised and misshapen from the forceps. He felt like he never stopped asking God to make it right.

But giving up his dog was something he couldn't do. Not Rita. She was his girl. He'd found her abandoned in a parking lot, a scrawny, flea-bitten, wiggling little pup of murky heritage, and it was instant love. She was silver, sleek, with the coat of a pittie but the face of a boxer.

"We'll have to figure something out," he said.

Stef took her hand away and gripped the steering wheel. Dewey kicked the back of Drake's seat and sang in his wordless way, loudly.

"He's going to get hurt," she said under the noise, her voice carefully controlled. "She's a big dog. He's so tiny."

"She's never bitten him, never put a scratch on him," he answered, his voice also controlled.

"You've seen the way she looks at him. She growls, bares her teeth. It's dangerous!"

"She's warning him. He stares her in the eyes. She's a dog."

"This is your son! It is your JOB to keep him safe!"

Dewey echoed her shout and laughed again.

Drake took a deep breath and tried not to yell. He loved his son. He loved his son so much it hurt to breathe sometimes. But he loved Rita too. Her heart would break if he abandoned her. She'd never be the same. He'd seen those dogs at the shelter with their half-lit eyes, just watching people walk past, just watching for that one person who would never come. He couldn't do that to her. He'd be broken too. And if he was honest with himself, it would make him love Dewey just a little bit less. He couldn't risk that.

They pulled into the driveway of Stef's parents' house.

"Please, Drake. Please think about it."

"I'll get her some training." He felt like he was begging.

Stef slammed the car into park and whipped her head to glare at him.

"You. Are. Not. Listening."

"I am. I'll take care of it."

She said nothing.

"I promise. I won't let anything happen."

Stef threw off her seat belt and grabbed her purse from the floorboard, marching into the house and leaving Drake in the car.

Drake sighed as he got out of the car. He unbuckled Dewey's seat belt, then wiped the boy's face carefully. He lifted him out of his car seat and set him down gently, letting him get his footing on the uneven drive. His son smiled at him. He took the child's small hand in his, so he didn't stumble going up the steps.

Drake prepared himself for a long afternoon of everyone pretending to be nice, of trying to help Dewey behave as normally as possible. Even if his son was as good as gold, though, Drake would feel the judgment of Stef's parents. Somehow, as little sense as it made, they blamed Drake for the fact that their grandson was disabled. As if there was something he could have done to get the baby out of the birth canal without crushing part of his brain. If there had been, he would have done it. He would have ripped apart Heaven and Earth to bring his son safely into the world.

Rita was wiggling in joy at the door when they got home, her stuffed frog hanging from her mouth as she grinned at Drake. She politely waited for him to deposit the sleeping Dewey into his crib so he could play tug with her.

See? Drake wanted to say. *She's a good girl.* But he held his tongue and took his boy to his room.

Stef followed him and together they settled Dewey into his bed. They had both commented so many times about how "normal" he looked when he was sleeping that it was now just an unspoken exchange. It hurt exactly the same amount each time it passed between them.

Drake shut Dewey's door softly behind him and caught Stef giving Rita a little stroke on her silver ears, the way she liked.

He couldn't help himself. "You like her too."

"I love her," Stef said. "But I love our son more." She turned and walked into the bathroom, shutting the door behind her.

They didn't speak for the rest of the evening, not even when they were brushing their teeth, side by side, taking turns spitting in the single sink. Normally when they went to bed, before turning off the light, no matter what, he'd lean over for a quick kiss. Tonight, his feelings were too bruised. He lay in the dark, fuming, refusing to fight. Not if she was willing to be so cruel. He didn't know what he would say. He lay awake a long time, wondering whether he was in the right marriage. At some point Rita pulled herself up on the bed and curled around his feet, just as she had since she was a puppy. Her gentle snores finally lulled him to sleep.

He heard the snarling and thought he was dreaming; thought he was having a nightmare prompted by Stef's worries. Then he heard the screaming.

"DRAKE! DRAKE! OH MY GOD, DRAKE! RITA! NO! RITA! LET GO! STOP! DEWEY, MY BABY, MY BABY! RITA PLEASE STOP! NO! NO!"

Drake was out of bed before his eyes were open, running in the direction of his wife's screaming. Dewey's garbled cries were choked. He sprinted to his son's room and horror met his eyes. He froze. His wife was straddling Rita, prying her jaws open with her bare hands. The dog's mouth was clamped on his son's neck, and she was shaking him like a captured rabbit. Blood was spurting . . . spraying . . . soaking. His wife's face was dripping with her child's blood. His son's mouth was opening and closing, but his eyes were glazed and placid. In the time since Drake had sprung out of bed, Dewey's ability to make noise had been cut off.

"Stef, oh my God!"

"FUCKING HELP ME!" she screamed.

He ran to the dog and started kicking her in the head with his heel, hard. She twisted and yelped and dropped the boy, then ran from the room.

RITA

Stef and Drake both fell to their knees, scrambling to put pressure on the wounds, which they couldn't find through the gushing blood.

"Go! Go! Call 911!" Stef cried.

Drake scrambled to the bedroom, found his phone, and dialed. Rita was cowering in the corner of the bedroom, tail between her legs.

"What have you done?" he whispered to her as the phone rang in his ear. He slammed the door behind him and ran back to his mauled boy. Stef was bent over his body, keening.

My only son. My only son. My only son. His brain was buzzing with adrenaline and fear and horror.

"Nine-one-one, what is your location?" A professionally calm woman listened while he rushed through his address.

"My dog attacked my son and he's bleeding." Drake realized his hands were shaking. Hell, his whole body was shaking.

"He's unconscious!" Stef said loudly enough that the woman could hear her.

"We have someone on the way. You'll need to put pressure on the wounds."

"It's his throat! She's torn out his FUCKING THROAT!" Stef screamed. The look in her eyes was of a crazed monster. Underneath the fear for Dewey, Drake felt afraid of his wife, of what she would do to him. She would never forgive him. Never.

Drake looked at his son, completely helpless. Dewey was limp on the floor. If he hadn't been so pale under all of the blood, it would have looked like he was sleeping.

The saddest moment wasn't the funeral, with the soft blue blanket pulled up tight under Dewey's chin, cocooning him. The saddest moment wasn't when Drake and Stef trickled dirt through their fingers down on top of the small cream-colored coffin that enclosed their only child.

The saddest moment, somehow, was watching Stef scrub the blood out of the carpet, her shoulders square and her arms strong. Dewey's birth had ripped her insides apart. There would never be another baby.

"You need to leave," she said without looking at him. "I just can't. You have to go."

"Where should I go?"

"Go to a hotel, go to Adam's, go to the cabin. I don't care. I don't want to look at you." She kept scrubbing. "Take her with you and don't come back until she's gone."

"And then?"

"We'll see."

RITA

The police had said they would be picking Rita up but they hadn't shown yet, and it had been five days. Stef had been on the phone with animal control, but they said they had to wait for the police. She was going to drive the dog to the shelter herself . . . but Stef was frightened of the animal. She didn't bother asking Drake to do it. She knew if he was going to do it, he would have already.

"It's not her fault, you know," he said to her back as she scrubbed the carpet.

"I know," she said. "It's yours."

He loaded Rita into his truck. She was smiling at him, bouncing up and down, happy for a ride. He checked the glove compartment, and his gun was still there. He had only shot it once, when he bought it. He wasn't a hunter and only bought the gun because Stef was worried about a home invasion. He was always more worried about Dewey somehow getting it and blowing his brains out. *At least that would have been quicker,* he thought, slammed with the vision of his child lying on the floor choking on his own blood—a vision that would now never go away.

He pulled out the gun and held it, cold and heavy, in his hand. If Rita was going to be put down, he'd do it himself. But as much as he told himself it was the right thing to do—he couldn't keep a dog around that had killed someone, had killed his son—he knew he didn't have the strength.

Maybe he just wouldn't come home. Their marriage was shot, and they both knew it. He put the gun back in the glove box and started his engine.

On his way out of town, Drake went by the bank and emptied out his personal account, then got on the road toward the cabin. Rita snuggled into his lap. Normally he'd stroke her soft ears and tell her what a good girl she was. Today, though, he remembered when he had sprayed her down with the hose and the water had come away red with his son's blood. He pushed her away. She rumbled at him and licked his hand on the steering wheel, then nudged her way back under his arm and laid her head on his lap. Her touch was tentative, as though she knew she was in trouble but loved him anyway.

That was the hard part. His heart was ripped into shreds and the little bits and pieces of it still loved his dog. Without realizing he was doing it, he let his hand fall to her head as it always had.

"I'm sorry, sweet girl," he said. "It was my fault. I'm sorry."

The cabin was about two hours away and Drake realized it had been a mistake to allow himself that much time to be alone with his thoughts. He thought of the gun in the glove box and what he could do with it.

He pulled out his phone and called his brother, who answered on the first ring.

RITA

"Hey bro," Adam said in a surprised voice. The two hadn't talked since Dewey died. Drake's parents had taken care of getting everyone to the funeral, and Drake hadn't spoken to anyone there. Adam had shaken his hand and hugged him and that was all—which Drake had appreciated. "How are you?"

"I'm hanging in there," Drake said. "Headed to the cabin."

"Is Stef with you?"

"Stef kicked me and the dog out."

Adam didn't answer.

"You still there?"

"You still have the dog?" His voice had lost all jollity.

"Yes."

"Are you taking her out there to shoot her?"

"That's what Stef wants me to do."

"It's what you should do."

"It wasn't her fault. She's a dog. Stef warned me."

"She's dangerous. You should have listened to Stef then and you should listen to me now. Put her down."

Drake didn't know what to say. He couldn't.

"Do you need me to come do it?"

"No." He couldn't think of anything worse at this point in his life than letting his brother kill his dog. It would be the ultimate betrayal. His heart settled on the matter. "I'll take care of it. Sorry I bothered you."

"You can do this, little bro."

"Thanks, man."

The truck hugged the curves for the next half hour as Drake drove up the mountain to the cabin. Drake stopped at the guard shack for the keys, flashing his ID. He and Stef had started leasing this place a year after Dewey was born. A friend had recommended that they get away together regularly to retain some normalcy between them. It had been working. Things were pretty good, actually. They talked to each other. They loved each other. Together, they were tackling the challenge of raising a seriously disabled child, something neither of them could imagine doing alone. Now, he didn't know how they'd ever look at each other the same way again.

He clipped Rita's leash onto her collar as he let her out of the truck. She looked at him, confused at the pull. He never leashed her. But he thought of the guilt he would feel if she attacked someone else. Not to mention the liability.

In a dark moment, he flipped open the glove box and got the gun. He made sure the safety was on and tucked it in his waistband, in the back because he wasn't an idiot, and he liked his dick more than his ass cheeks in case the thing went off.

He led Rita into the cabin. The place was filled with dust and a few spiders but was otherwise clean. Family pictures were everywhere—he had forgotten. Stef always missed Dewey terribly while they were here, so she'd bring a new picture every time they came. He had always kind of liked them, himself. Though he was always relieved at the break, part of him would half-wish they had brought the kid with them, as high-maintenance as he would have been outside of his normal routine.

Now, the pictures stared at him accusingly.

He had destroyed this. He had destroyed everything.

The fridge was stocked with beer and wine—beer for him, wine for her. They always did a grocery trip right before they left for home so that they would be able to just show up and relax the next time. He put the gun on the table and started drinking. Rita sniffed around the cabin and then lay with a satisfied huff at his feet, watching him with liquid eyes the way good dogs do, just making sure he was doing okay.

He wasn't doing okay. His son was dead. He was going to get good and drunk, and he was not going to shoot his dog, and so he was not going to be married for much longer.

Before he could finish his third beer—he was chugging them as fast as he could, waiting for the numbness to set in—Rita got up and whined at the door, then barked and started pawing. He realized he hadn't let her pee when they got out of the truck.

A little buzzed, he got to his feet with a small stumble. He forgot to clip the leash on her, and when he opened the door, she shot out with an aggressive bark.

He heard a child's yell. Then a snarl. Then shouting. There were other campers. They must be at the playground. With a child.

Drake moved quickly; buzz forgotten. He snatched the gun off of the table and stepped onto the porch. He knew the family; they'd gotten to know each other over the years of camping. Their daughter was about the same age as Dewey. The little girl's father was standing between Rita and his child, shouting at the dog to *"GET BACK!"*

Rita was bobbing and weaving, trying to get past him to the little girl.

Drake, with long strides, walked to his dog. He raised his arm and sighted along the top of the gun. As he did, she jumped, jaws wide, past the man and toward his crying, curly-haired daughter. The gun cracked.

Rita's body fell to the ground with a *thump*.

The sudden silence was loud in Drake's ears.

"I'm sorry," he said to the man, who had swept his child up in his arms.

"Your dog almost killed my kid!"

"I'm sorry."

Drake scooped Rita's body up and carried her back into the cabin. He laid her on the bed, which was soon soaked with her blood. It was a slow seeping; her heart wasn't pumping to make it spurt or gush. He had aimed true.

He picked up his phone and dialed his wife.

"It's me," she said.

"I did it," he said.

"I'm sorry," she said.

"Bye."

"Bye."

Drake hung up the phone. His fingers lingered on the soft ears of his good girl, now sticky with blood. He wanted to tell her he was sorry, but he had said those words so many times now that they were empty of meaning. There was nothing he could say, so he said nothing. He just put the gun in his mouth, and he pulled the trigger.

***

Ruth Anna Evans takes her seat. She holds the dog collar close to her chest and continues to weep. There's no consolation or comfort in The Scrapyard, and so we listen to her cry as our own tears stain our faces. When all of us finish crying, Brian G Berry's turn has come. He looks uncomfortable, as if the thing he is holding is burning his hands. As if he wants to drop it right away.

When I see what it is, I understand why.

He's holding a baby's skull. As soft and as delicate as a newly hatched sparrow, it sits in his hands, staring at the fire with wide-eyed wonder . . .

FF

Brian G Berry

Rain was pissing on the windshield as Mark slowed his speed and pulled up to a checkpoint in the road.

"Wonder what's going on," he said, narrowing a glare, spotting the shape of a man. It was more of a pixelated distortion than a human shape. He had a flashlight and wore a dark rain slicker. He approached the hood, waving the beam of the light from side to side.

"Is it a cop?" Debra asked in a sleepy, exhausted voice, tired from the drive, from the hospital—from everything.

"Yeah, it looks like it. I wonder if there was an accident or something."

Mark moved his hand to roll the window down when the windshield in front of him was hit with a cracking spiderweb. A force slammed into him, knocking his head back with a strangled cry and a spray of blood from his mouth.

It happened so fast; Debra wasn't even sure what the hell caused it.

That is until she saw Mark—or his *head*, and the gruesome, smoking hole in his face. His right cheek had been blown out, stuffed with wet red meat and chips of bone. His eyes flickered and rolled over as his body spasmed, locked in place by the seat belt. Dark blood ran down his neck, sluicing over his shoulders and chest, pooling in his lap.

The door was flung back, and the wind came blowing in. The man in the rain slicker was standing there like a cardboard cutout. She cried and screamed when his hand came inside the car and popped the belt on Mark, dragging him out in the rain. Mark's body kicked with rippling spasms as he was dropped to the pavement.

The man held a silenced pistol in his hand. The muzzle jetted a beam of smoke, smacking Mark in the temple. His head broke open, deflating as mulched brain matter and blood formed into a thick red creek, spreading with the rain.

Debra pulled at her belt, working to free herself. But it was hard—hard with a belly swollen and her body sore, her strength all but depleted. She managed to thumb the catch free and was tugging at the door. It opened and a squall of rain and wind hit her face, soaking her through the gown.

The man was there too. He was staring down at her with that black, shadowy face and pistol raised, the muzzle pressed against her right orbit.

She went to scream when a thick blunt tool crashed into her temple, dropping her senselessly back into her seat.

She awoke, not in the agreeable or comfortable way she would from a happy dream. But in a terrible, embarrassing position of heaving breath and sweat and tense nerves—like the aftermath of a nightmare.

She was stripped, lying naked on a cold metal table, her legs spread open and locked tightly at the ankles. Her arms had been pulled—strained—overhead, both wrists secured with a heavy rope. Any attempt to scream was cut off as a seam of adhesive gummed her lips shut. Her eyes rolled, searching.

But there was not much to see.

Just a small workshop of sorts, a single light bulb hanging from a wire and aluminum cone-shield overhead. She couldn't make out what lay past six feet, as everything had been consumed by shadow. The place smelled of a machine shop, like a mechanic's bay: oily, musty, dank, with a sharp odor she couldn't place. If there had been a way to identify its source with a verbal take, she would have to say that it smelled—well, it smelled like blood. Only this blood had been super-heated in a kettle, brought to a fine red soup, the odor of it heavy and nauseating to the senses.

Footsteps.

She heard these and stopped fighting with her restraints. They were coming from behind her. Slowly, almost *purposefully,* so as to destabilize her mind and build it up all over again.

It was working.

Her heart nearly leapt from her chest when the footsteps stopped, and the sound of breathing took its place. A face leaned over her, blotting out the light. They had a paper medical mask on. It covered everything but the eyes. He was wearing a blue surgeon's smock. The sight of him upped the rate of her heart, spiking her blood level to dangerous heights.

"Mmmm . . . aahhm . . . mmghhh . . ."

That's what she said, but of course, none of it was intelligible.

If anyone had heard, she would have said, *Who are you—what do you want with me?*

The man moved to her side, his finger uncurling from a tight fist and lowering the tip to touch her face, dragging it down the dip of her neck, tracing the valley of her cleavage, rolling over the mound of her belly, and finally terminating at her vulva. He teased her dry, hairy lips, finding her clit and flicking it violently.

She kicked and grumbled, shaking him away like a bad case of fleas.

No sound was heard from the man. He might as well have been imaginary—this whole thing might have been an illusion of sorts—a bad trip maybe. She was hoping that's all it was. It had to be, right? Nothing like this happened to good, decent people without a smudge on their records. This kind of thing happened only to people kidnapped in the shit holes of the world, or to those mean, evil crowds of criminals. The ones deserving of such dark and grisly tortures.

Or horror movies.

Yes, they happened in horror movies. The same films Debra could never handle because of the blood and hideous, frightening creatures in rubber suits that looked too real.

She heard the sound of metal scraping stone, of chains clinking, of water leaking in somewhere.

He appeared at her side after having disappeared a moment before.

He had something in his hand that made her body tremble. A scalpel. The sight alone started her resistance, and the first thing that happened was sickness. It came up her throat and boiled in her mouth until the seam gave and burst out in a jet of milky-yellow, splashing over her face. She choked and fought to breathe, dislodging chunks of food.

None of this had any effect on the man. He acted as though this had all been normal from the start, which made Debra wonder how many other women he had done this to, in this very room, on this very table.

No time was wasted. Everything was clockwork.

The small blade incised her from the top of the dome to just below the navel. The pain of it worked to blow a scream from her throat and thrash her head from side to side. Blood washed down her belly from the seam, then gushed in red hot waves as his hands peeled both sides back, cracking rib bones to widen the gap. Agony whipped through her nerves, driving spasms through her. She stuttered in an imbecilic diction.

He grabbed a pair of forceps, hovering over the top of her with the delicacy and focus of a specialist, a professional. The forceps went in, digging around, and with a sudden clamp, they came out dripping blood and held a lump of shrieking meat. He held the fetal ball up to the lamp, turning it this way and that, appraising it like a jewel. He nodded, satisfied by his observations.

Debra watched him as he walked away with her baby, wanting to scream, but unable to force it out. Inside her head, she was crying, reaching, panicking and jumping off the table, and biting her way through the man's throat to get her baby back.

But outside, where the blood splattered below the table like a leaking rain gutter, where the cavity of her stomach steamed from the coolness of the basement, where her eyes glazed with a film of finality, she simply went limp, shivered, and died.

Tyler was your average dirtbag, piece of shit, loser, fucking deviant-looking mess. He was the man you see down the street and wonder about. The one whose hygiene held a suspicion. Like maybe he didn't shower as much as your ordinary person or didn't find it prudent enough to wipe his asshole after filling the toilet with a day's worth of frozen burritos, peanut butter, and fast food. Maybe he looked at you funny or eyed your children the wrong way when they were in their bathing suits. Could be he preferred to look at your kids like a man ogles a centerfold, with his pants down.

Yeah, that was Tyler Foster. A heavy, slouching body with a face round and white as the moon, a hairline somewhere far back from his brow, his skin dotted with strange lesions and shellacked with an oily sheen. A cloud of flies followed him wherever he went. His lifestyle often invited insects into his pad who had a taste for death and rot, things spoiling and cooking in the summer sun.

His house was the worst one on the block. A beat-up clapboard on the way of needing a wrecking ball or a Molotov. He was the one with the yard waste piling, weeds overgrown and enveloping the sides of the house. His windows were smoky, his roof flaking, the paint chipped and washed away in spots. He had the old rust bucket of a Chevy in the driveway, yet it never seemed to move, and cobwebs anchored it to the pavement—the dust sitting on its body thick enough to finger a mural into.

He was always seen wearing the same shit. No matter the weather, that nasty oaf of fucking degeneracy and sweat had the yellow-stained wifebeater and a pair of shorts with dark spots hanging around the crotch and up his ass. He routinely picked his nose and tasted the prize, scratched his balls and gave a whiff.

Tyler Foster, in effect, was the man you had to watch out for, and secretly wanted something very bad to happen to.

Right about the time the man in the cellar was packing Debra into individual garbage bags for deposit in the Jones River, Tyler was a naked travesty of sweaty, stinking meat, shoving his cock into the narrow channel hollowed out in the fetus. It was an Asian baby—his request—and its body was on its way to going to rot. Even with the formaldehyde, the fetus fleshlight was losing its consistency.

It happened, of course.

This was the third one now. When they got warped and stretched out from his abuse, they were no good to him anymore. Manipulating them back like clay to something able to give pleasure never worked out. He would have to dip into his inheritance and get himself another one. With the old, stressed out, and purpling ones, he would often hurl them down the storm drain or toss in the field behind his house for the coyotes and vultures to pick apart. So you could say Tyler was something of an environmentalist, in a way.

And if you agreed, then you might as well fix the rope to your neck and swing from the highest limb. Because Tyler—yeah, he was fucking nasty and deserving of the grave.

Just a month back, when the fetus wasn't delivered on time, he made his way to a neighboring city and snatched himself a kid. No, not a kid—a fucking baby. He beat the mother with a bat until her brains sprayed from her skull, then snatched her bundle of joy from the stroller and went home.

But it wasn't the same.

Sure, it felt good to Tyler, and he would sink his pecker into that sluggish, bloated form until he hollowed it out and was left with a rag of a body dripping off his cock.

Still, it didn't feel as good as the fetus fleshlight.

With those works of art, he could fill out the chamber with delicacies such as honey or flavored lube, barbecue sauce even.

Once he would work himself up into a fervor, he'd pull his cock out and go down to his back, lay the fetus on the ground while he rolled his legs up and dangled his penis over his mouth. He would pull on it until hot gouts of semen landed on his tongue and squirmed down his throat.

After, he'd wipe himself off, clean up the fetus, and prepare it for next time—which was always no more than a few hours or less.

In fact, the last time he chucked his load through the hollow in the skull of a fetus was no more than an hour before. Now, he was close to busting again, holding on to the tiny arms of the fetus, drilling it wider with heavy strokes. He slid it up past his glans and down to his bush, over and over, speeding up and slowing down as the load ejected from the crown of the fetus and sprayed the faces on the photograph tacked to the wall above his bed—the faces of the neighbors' kids.

Throwing aside the fetus to the pillow, Tyler got up, however shaky his stance, and walked to the bathroom. He looked at himself, his erection wet and withering. There was no shame in those eyes. Nothing but a blank, emotionless stare—the empty glare of a zombie. Something undead and needing only one thing to survive. He was an evil, vile, wicked abomination.

The reports said he'd lost both his parents brutally to a home invasion when he was ten years old.

The truth was another thing altogether.

The part about the invasion was true. But what wasn't reported—or discovered—was how Tyler was the one who killed his folks, blaming it on two male intruders, who, to this day, had never been found. His mother and father were badly mutilated in their bed. But it was Tyler who butchered and raped them, laid them open with an axe.

Since that time long ago, Tyler, nearly seventy now, had been living his days at home, surviving on his parents' inheritance. His hobbies included sitting outside of schools and pulling on his pecker, getting sweaty-faced when little girls and boys found out what he was doing. He had to move school locations so much it was getting to be a hassle. His other hobbies had him fucking fetuses, and the abduction and murder and rape of children on rare occasions.

To slap a term on him: he was a ruthless *monster*.

Shaking himself after the piss, he flushed the toilet and was back in his room. He saw the fetus, a distended purple tube warped with an arch at the spine and widened around the mouth and anus, a literal blown-out thing. He got angry looking at it because it wasn't doing the job anymore. He needed a new one. Something plump.

He would have to call *The Man*.

He picked his phone up, dialed the number, and the voice spoke with a digitized, heavy staccato, "What flavor?"

"Vanilla this time. Extra scoops."

"Consider it done. I'll contact you within the week."

"No. Tonight."

"The ice cream won't have time to settle properly by then."

"I don't give a shit. I'm paying you good money for this! Deliver it tonight."

"But—"

"Look, do you want my money? Or do I have to go out there and find one myself?"

There was a pause of heavy breathing. "It will be done. Tonight. You remember the location?"

"Of course I do, you fucking asshole."

"Be there."

"Fuck you."

The phone clicked off.

The Man had a target.

A fat woman. Huge, really. Somewhere in the 450-500 range. She was pregnant, and her swollen belly had to weigh more than the load carried by a dump truck at the end of the day.

He had to be careful here. Essentially, he was behind enemy lines, inside the hospital, scoping things out, under the scrutiny of many eyes.

Situations such as these presented difficulties as opposed to the women he caught outdoors. Most of whom he either intercepted when they were out for a walk or taking their groceries back to the car.

This one he spotted lumbering out of the Dairy Queen and followed—straight to the hospital. Fitting into the workforce of medical centers had its issues but was quickly solved when he grabbed a white smock hanging on a hook, masked his face, and traveled the halls until he found his quarry.

Sticking around for too long in a place like this would lead to exposure and small talk from the workers, something he couldn't afford, so he couldn't dally. He just had to confirm a couple of things before he could make his exit.

One: was she giving birth?

Two: was this some sort of routine checkup?

He smiled after learning this was all just a simple appointment and nothing more.

It wouldn't be long now that she would waddle her ass out the door and be back in her car. The surprising thing, in this case, was that she was *alone*. You would think with a heap of bones like that, you'd need the support of a wench or a partner—someone to encourage you physically back into your vehicle.

But as it was, she was plenty capable of just about anything.

She came out of the hospital like any other person, albeit with a more atypical gait. He followed her with his eyes as she reached her car. It was one of those huge family vans, painted brown and flecked with spots of rust. The van wobbled and lowered as she got behind the wheel.

She was out of the parking lot and down the street when The Man picked up her trail, cruising at a law-abiding clip as the wind picked at the branches of trees lined along the road.

As he kept his pace in line with her, pulling into wherever she pulled in, he had time to glance over the charts he snatched from the clipboard on his way out. The target's name was Penelope Johnson. Age 35. Brunette. Green eyes. She had a baby cooking in her that would shame a prized ham: *14.5 lbs*. An absolute porker of a child, slowly roasting in a bed of fluids.

That sick fuck will enjoy this one.

The problem was, there was no sign of her slowing down, and every place she ran an errand was crowded. He had to time his moment carefully. One fuck up could spell disaster, and that would lead to a loss of money. Or worse.

He got lucky when she hit Arby's and rolled up the road a mile to a well-treed park, pulled into a space, killed the engine, and let the windows down.

A quick search showed him the park was empty. It was like this was all meant to be for him—a perfect situation.

Still, he had to be cautious. Any daylight grab could go south fast. He could wait it out until the sun fully sank, but an opportunity like this was too rare to pass up. Leaving his pistol behind, he took the baton and slapped it into his palm.

"Make it quick," he told himself.

He was out the door and over to her car.

Not wanting to scare her, he waved at her like a nervous old man needing help with directions. She wasn't pleased to have to put her half-eaten turkey BLT on the seat next to her. She spoke over the half-open window.

"Can I help you?" she asked, the annoyance thick with every word, crumbs on her chin.

"Yeah, I was actually lost and thought maybe you could point me the right way. If it's not too much trouble." He showed her the smile of a clueless man desperate for help.

Rolling her puckered eyes, she lowered the window fully, not bothering to wipe away the ranch dressing on her lips. "What is it you're looking for?"

He thought of a place quickly. "Adam's Bookstore."

"*Bookstore?*" She crunched down on that a moment. "I don't know of any bookstores around here. Sorry I can't help."

She was rolling the window back up when The Man stepped forward, swinging the baton and catching her on the jaw. It deflected, bouncing off her cheek and widening out her eyes, not with the pain you'd expect of a person just slapped with a cudgel, but with anger—seething, red-hot anger.

He went to smack her again when the door flew open and out came a big fucking gun in her hand. A revolver six inches long and gleaming with a blue barrel. She cranked off a round that sent her wrist bucking and the pistol jerking in her hand. She followed this through with another shot. The Man, wild-eyed and fearing to feel the power sitting in the cylinder of that fucking magnum, made his move quick. He brought the club down on her wrist and the blow snapped the bone. She dropped the gun with a squealing, cheated cry, leaning down after it.

The Man hit her again, this time a direct shot to the melon. She sagged a bit with a groan but was still reaching. He hit her again and again, clubbing the ever-loving piss right out of her skull, until finally, she moaned like a struck cow, breathing heavily and hoarse.

Seizing this convenience, he grabbed the magnum, stuck it in one of the many folds beneath her large left breast, and *BAM! BAM! BAM!*

She mumbled something sharp and spit out blood. It was running from her nose and mouth like water from a faucet. More of it was puddling the ground from the holes in her chest.

He dropped the gun, shaking from the adrenaline, not even thinking about what he had done.

He fucked up. He never should have reacted so rashly, but it was instinct that carried his actions. It was ego. He couldn't let this bitch get one up on him. He needed to show her he was a real man, so he did what any other egocentric lunatic would do at a time like this.

Now, his whole mission had gone to the gutter.

Fifteen thousand dollars gone! Because of how you handled this!

No, there was still time to do what he must. First, he had to make sure nobody had heard the opening shot. He was positive nobody heard the last three because each one was about as quiet as the silenced .32 caliber pistol waiting for him in the car. If it wasn't for all the fat piled on her body, those heavy .44 slugs would have woken a fucking corpse from its casket.

Finding it difficult to breathe, he was happy to see the park undisturbed. Nothing but a slight breeze in the trees, the sun on a fast decline to the west. Just an easy silence.

But . . . one problem persisted.

Now that a good amount of blood had formed a lake that was rolling under her car, he still had to get the baby. His initial plan was to back up, crack her head, and heap her unconscious ass into his trunk. But that would be impossible with all the blood now.

He had to do this the hard way. A field surgery.

Hurrying to secure his gear from the car, he made fast work. He opened her belly with a ragged incision that proved difficult on account there was so much fat he figured he might need a chainsaw. After folding back mats of rubbery flesh, thick as fiberglass insulation, the baby was there. Alive. Screeching like a newborn bird hatched from an egg. Sickened by it, he brought his club down onto the head.

Surprisingly, the damn thing was still kicking and screeching, stubborn as its mother.

He hit it again, this time with a blow that split its skull open to the neck. The brain shot out in a pink, slimy ribbon. It hung from its head like a ball of pink yarn.

Snapping out the heavy Ziploc bag, he grabbed the fetus with his hand and shoved it inside, sealing the top, then twisting it securely with a rubber band. He was back in his car, boxing it up, tossing it in his trunk, and was gone, leaving behind a scene of blood-spattered death.

The kid was stupid as shit if you asked Tyler.

So gullible and dumb nowadays. He was happy about it. He saw the kid walking up the road, seemingly in his own head. The boy was whistling. He strode along the curb as though he were balancing on a high rope.

"Hey, kid," Tyler said softly from his house, ensuring nobody was peeking at him. "You like candy? Cake?"

The kid's eyes brightened like any child at the call of sugar. The kid had to be ten, maybe a year younger. He liked them somewhere just above five but below ten, so this kid would work out just fine.

He beckoned the kid to his yard by waving around a brownie with a thick coat of vanilla icing. "Fresh out of the oven!"

The kid actually licked his lips like he hadn't had a meal in a week. And maybe he hadn't. The kid did look funny, dirty even. Tyler didn't recognize him at all, and he was well aware of every child on the block. This kid didn't belong. His clothes were ragged like he'd been wearing them for a month. His hair was black and knotted and his skin had been thoroughly baked by the sun.

"What's your name?" Tyler asked the kid.

"Jason."

"Nice to meet you, Jay. You don't mind if I call you Jay, now, do you?"

The kid smiled.

"Come on in, you can help me eat all of my brownies. Fresh out of the oven they are."

That was five minutes ago. And now Jason was seated at Tyler's table, and Tyler was seated across from him, sharing and munching on a plate of brownies. Unbeknown to the kid, the old man had his penis out in his hand, pulling on it as he ate and stared at him.

"You like toys, Jason?"

Immediately the kid's eyes lifted as if he had forgotten what they were.

"I haven't played with toys in a long time," he said with a broken, almost stunted way of speaking.

"And why is that?"

"My parents no more."

"Ah, I'm sorry to hear. But you know what? My parents are no more too. They died a long time ago, Jason. Horribly so."

There was a bond forming here, Jason was feeling. He went to say something, maybe ask the old fat guy what happened to his parents, but Tyler cut him off with a wave of his hand.

"Say, you want to play with some of my toys? I think you might like my toys."

Tyler was thinking of taking the kid down into the basement where he had taken a few others in the past. There was a bed down there, some toys, drawings on the wall, and pictures—hundreds of

Polaroids taped to the ceiling—all of them showing things that would land him a lifetime in prison.

Jason stared over the brownie for what felt like the longest time before answering with a mouthful of chocolate and saliva. "I'd love it. *To*, I mean. I'd love *to*."

Tyler smiled and shook his head. "Oh, that's okay, Jay, you don't have to correct yourself around me. I get it. You haven't been to school or had anyone looking out for you, have you?"

Jason nodded. "No friends, no school."

If Tyler had been anyone else, he would have felt bad for this kid. He would have scraped together some money and bought the kid some new clothes and gotten him something to eat before promptly reporting him to the police and child services.

But Tyler wasn't the caring sort. He didn't have that much sympathy for anyone except himself. What he did have was a penis full of blood and a rising need to shoot his load.

"I'm sorry to hear that, Jay, but I'll be your friend!"

Jason liked that. "Thank you, Ty—*Tylar*."

"It's Tyler, but you'll catch on."

He led the boy downstairs into the murk of the basement. Sunlight beams full of motes sliced open just enough to see with. Jason hadn't noticed the pictures, and even if he had, there were so many up there—most of which were curled inward from the heat—he wouldn't be able to figure out what was going on in them.

"So many toys," Jason said with all the wonder of a child on Christmas day.

"Yes, and now they are yours."

Jason went unabashed into the pile of toys, digging in and smiling, even giggling. What he didn't know is that when Jason was munching on some brownies, Tyler had hidden a special prize within that pile of toys.

"What's this?" Jason asked after a time, pulling a toy out from the pile and holding it out like something you really didn't want to hold for long.

"Oh, that? That's a *special* toy."

Jason's scrunched-up face was proof enough that he wasn't understanding what he was looking at. "It looks like a . . . doll, but . . ."

"It *is* a doll," Tyler told him. "Sorry about the coloring—the purple and green spots—that's just old paint." He wasn't sure if the kid would buy it, but at that point, it didn't really matter. The kid was not going anywhere. Tyler could take his clothes off and not worry about how the kid would react. Jason was still holding it out from him, turning it around as though it fascinated him, repulsed him maybe. He brought the hole at the bottom of its body to his eye and was staring down its length like you would a telescope.

"It smells weird," he said, plugging his nose.

Tyler laughed. "Let me show you how it works."

When Tyler dropped his shorts and let his penis fling out there, the kid went to stone. He couldn't take his eyes off Tyler and what he seemed to be doing. "You grab the doll in your hands like this." He grabbed it like a football with both hands. "Then you slide your penis down here." He worked his cock into the channel. "It's better if you have lube, like spit or syrup or chocolate sauce." Tyler was shaking, piss going down his leg, a trembling moan rolling off his lips. "Since I have it firmly on me, Jay, do you mind leaning over and spitting in that hole for me? You are my friend, right?"

That's when Jason found his footing and ran. He ran right past Tyler heading for the stairs, screaming. But Tyler stepped out and caught the kid's foot with an ankle. He went crashing into the stairs face-first, his mouth busting against a board, teeth flying from his gums. The blood came fast and poured plenty. Jason was crying and screaming on his back, holding his mouth.

Tyler was on him, even with the fetus sheathed on his penis, he grabbed the back of Jason's head, jerked it back with a snap, spit in his eyes, then bashed it over and over and over again until Jason's face literally caved in, forming to the edge of the step.

After the kid bled out and Tyler had his fun with the fetus for the last time. He checked his watch. "If

The Man doesn't meet me tonight, at least I have some fresh meat." Which got him thinking. "Well, might as well have an appetizer while I'm waiting for dinner."

"Time to go," The Man said, punching the clock.

He left his work for a two-hour lunch. He figured it would be plenty of time to get to his place and meet up with the molester and get his money.

He was edgy, though. So far, no reports had been made on the news of the woman's death in the parking lot. Maybe he had gotten lucky. On the other hand, it could be the police found out he was the culprit and were on their way to apprehend him. They would want the media to keep it quiet until that time.

"Stop it, you're going to drive yourself crazy."

And he was.

But here was the part that was getting his blood pumping.

He'd been killing women and stealing their babies for a few years now, and so far, he had evaded the police. During that time, he had been careful, never allowing himself to get sloppy. Until now. The woman at the park changed all that. And the missing baby in her womb was the cherry on the shit cake this time around.

Here's the thing you have to know: *The Man* was known in the media as the *Womb Slayer*. This moniker, penned by the police department, had been held accountable for over eight murders—fifteen now. And at each scene, he thoroughly sterilized traces of his presence. The only thing leading them to a connection, of course, was the bodies he had left behind in the past. Now, the bodies would never be discovered, because instead of dumping them in some random spot, he would chop them up, bag them tight, and toss their remains in a river, somewhere the current would carry them to the bottom and fish would pick them clean.

But now . . . now he left a body—one Penelope Johnson, thirty-five, with brown hair and green eyes, spilling blood in the parking lot of Oak Park, her stomach ripped open and missing something vital.

"You really fucked up, you know that? Now the police will be scouring the town looking for you."

It never stopped them before. Pregnant women would still go missing. The only problem in this instance was, he fucked up when leaving Penelope behind without so much as a proper covering-up. In his haste, he could have left evidence in place that would garner them a lead. He had acted foolishly. He should have just—

"It doesn't matter now. She's dead. And you killed her."

He was pulling to a stop at a streetlight, the red of it pushing through his windshield. He bit his nail as he waited. Once it turned green, he eased on the accelerator and about had a fucking stroke when the police lights flashed behind him and the siren wailed for him to stop.

"Shit! Shit! Shit!"

Should he run? Should he hop out of the car with his pistol and shoot the cop dead as he approached?

No, be cool. Maybe it was something traffic-related. Why else would they pull you over? If it was because of the woman, they would have pulled a gun out already and had you on the ground.

This much was true, but he was nervous—more nervous than he had ever been.

He took the pistol and put it under his leg for easy reach, just in case. He wouldn't be taken alive. If it came to it, there was no way he could be thrown into the spotlight for the media to blast. He would do what he had to do to get himself out of it. And if that meant shooting his way to freedom or his death, then so be it.

"Evening, sir," the cop said, putting a flashlight beam in The Man's face. "The reason I pulled you over is because you were under the limit back on Broadmoore Avenue. Just making sure you're okay."

Fucking dumb sonofabitch! You need to keep your head about you! This is about a speed violation. Just take it easy and stay in control.

So he did. He followed protocol and the cop let him go with a warning.

Making sure this time around he was keeping to the posted speed limit, he went to his house.

There, he let out a sigh. "You almost fucked that up."

He scolded himself all the way down to the basement. He grabbed the fetus. It wasn't ready, but it would have to do. Tyler wouldn't give a shit anyway. The borehole was perfect, so it would work either way.

Back in his car, he made the five-mile drive to the spot.

Tyler was there, smiling like a fucking goblin in the early moonlight.

"You have it?" he asked, once The Man was outside the car.

"You have the money?"

"As always. Now, give me my toy."

The exchange was fast. Tyler was gone, and the whole time The Man wanted to shoot him in the face. Maybe he would next time. Carry his work to a better city. Shit was getting out of control now.

He was back at work, walking to the building, getting into character before going through the door. The moment he came through the sliding glass entrance, three cops were waiting for him, hands resting on the butts of the guns in their belts.

"Doctor Luis Robertson?" one of them asked sternly.

Luis felt his pulse quicken. This was it. They had him. He fucked up and they fucking had him belted. There was no way out of this. "Yes?" he answered timidly, knowing he was only buying time.

"We need you to come with us. We have reason—"

The gun was in his hand before he knew it. Screams started from the nurses. Luis raised his piece and the slide winked back several times as five rounds left the barrel, finding two of the officers who were down on their backs, squirming, bleeding from holes in their faces.

The remaining cop opened fire, striking Luis in the belly and knee.

Luis, still holding on, capped off three more rounds. *Pff, pff, pff!*

Each one missed their mark.

The surviving cop found some cover and returned fire, chipping out the floor around Luis, who was struggling to stand.

It's over, old boy. You are the Womb Slayer no more. You have retired from pediatrics. If you survive this, they'll parade you for the rest of your days in front of cameras and you can hear how much of a monster you are.

That sealed it.

He put the gun to his temple and squeezed. The bullet bounced around in his skull before exiting with an explosion of brains and blood on the wall to his side.

He sank, his eyes dropping into their sockets like warm wax, then jolted with a final heave before shuddering and lying still.

Tyler was sweating on the couch, his legs open wide, using the stiff arms of the fetus to guide it up and down his penis. It was like a spit-roasted hog, that fetus, plump and positively ripe, the channel perfectly formed to his penis. He was close to busting when a *Breaking News* bulletin interrupted his show on the television.

"Doctor Luis Robertson, the supposed *Womb Slayer*, has been gunned down at his place of employment tonight after a shootout at Saint Mary's Hospital that left two officers in critical condition."

Tyler slowed his pace, recognizing the face of *The Man* whose picture was a smiling Doctor Luis Robertson in a pressed blazer.

"What the fuck . . ."

He started to breathe faster as he pumped the fetus up and down, stroking through it rapidly until it became a blur. Before he could ejaculate, he grunted like a caveman and shot off gouts of hot semen onto his coffee table. He left the fetus there while he reached for a smoke, his belly heaving with the exertion.

"Fucking shit," he said about it. "Now what am I going to do? *Fuck!*"

He brainstormed this, pulling off his cigarette, coughing, and sweating. Then he remembered the dead kid sitting next to him. Jason, the kid with a dented face crusted in dried blood and gummy brains.

"At least I have you," he said as he pulled the fetus off and tossed it. As he rolled over to Jason's corpse for a second round, pain shot right up his left arm, crawling into his scalp and causing his right hand to clutch at his chest. He was sucking, wheezing, but it didn't last.

His heart burst not a second later.

He lay there with his pants off, a dead fetus at his side. Crumpled over the body of a boy whose rot would set in long before being discovered.

...

After he's spoken his last word, Brian G Berry heads back into The Scrapyard. We can hear him digging a hole and then refilling it. When he returns, the skull is no longer on his person, and his fingers are dirty. It's the closest thing to a proper burial anyone can expect in The Scrapyard.

Jayson Dawn has waited patiently, and he is rewarded with our full attention. Clearing his throat, he holds his scrap above his head like a sword in the hands of a brave warrior. It's a hairbrush, knotted and crusty with dried hairs, long torn from a sensitive scalp. Patches of skin dangle like rotating snowflakes from the strands . . .

Wet Hair

Jayson Dawn

The empty conditioner bottle smashed to the floor beside the trash can, spiked like a post-touchdown football. Already running behind for her date, Marjorie didn't have the time to clean the bathroom, but she also couldn't leave the room in this level of disarray. Bad enough that her two teenage children made it so that, yet again, her own hygiene had to go to the back burner, but leaving the bathroom like this would be neglect.

"So, nobody was going to tell me that we were out of conditioner?" Marjorie screamed in the steam-filled bathroom. "What the hell do you two even do when you get home?" Turning off the water, she ripped her towel off the overburdened wall bar. She wrapped the towel around her body like a strapless dress and stepped from the tub. "God forbid you two go to the store and pick up something for the house. Lord KNOWS that's asking too much. But at least throw the goddamn containers out when you finish them!"

The only response either of the teenage children gave was the angry screeching of her son, Andre, yelling at his online friends during their *CoD* match. That boy couldn't hear a thing with his headset on, making him somehow even more useless than normal. Marjorie would have long ago tossed that damned brain-melting box out the window if it hadn't cost so much.

Those kids didn't realize how good they had it. A single mom providing them each with their own bedroom in today's economy?

They never knew a day without food. The bills always got paid. She made it to every game. Marjorie had been working double shifts for as long as she could remember, making sure her kids lived a good life. How many moms didn't even work but still couldn't remember to feed their kids, much less go to their parent-teacher conferences? And fathers?

Meanwhile, Marjorie's ungrateful little shits couldn't even clean up after themselves. Dirty clothes in clumps on the floor. Toilet paper overflowing from the trash can. A sink covered in all kinds of various half-empty containers.

Up until the past year, Hilary and Andre didn't even buy any of their crap themselves. Now they both had jobs, but Lord knows, they never showed anything for it. They wasted all their money on irresponsible bullshit, grew tired of it, then left it as trash for their mother to pick up. Wouldn't want to overtax their frail teenage bodies by washing a dish.

Marjorie looked at her haggard reflection and released a sigh. Deep-set bags framed her sunken eyes. Her once attractive features, marred by over a decade's worth of stress, frozen in a perpetual scowl. She wondered how many years those children had stolen from her. Her hair, showing horrifying signs of thinning, drooped toward her neckline like grease-coated straw.

"Hilary! When I get back, I'm going to have some words for you! Because I know it's you who used the conditioner. If you blew this date for me—"

Marjorie swallowed her words before they escaped. Ben asked her on a second date, and she didn't need anything to jinx it. How a man who looked that good in uniform saw anything in a past-her-prime hostess was anyone's guess.

Marjorie reached for the faucet, knocking a haphazard arrangement of shaving paraphernalia into the sink. She nearly cut her arm along the blade of a rusted disposable razor clogged with a glob of shaving cream and fine hairs. She pelted it at the wall. It rebounded back into the ever-growing pile of garbage spilling from the trash can. For good measure, she disposed of the rusted can of shaving cream and overpriced aftershave as well.

Andre's face barely grew hair yet. The thick, wiry hair collected in the blade didn't come from a beard and the thought of what she might have been touching made Marjorie gag.

Splashing water into the sink, she willed the black coils down the drain. They clung to the sides of the porcelain, glued on by congealed shaving cream. They looked like a swarm of squirming insects, and try as she might, Marjorie's mind gave no alternative explanation for the hair.

"Clean up your goddamn pubes! What the hell is wrong with you, leaving that shit by the sink?"

Pulling open the vanity's uppermost drawer, Marjorie reached in blindly and pulled out one of the rags. She focused her attention away from the pubes and scrubbed at the stains of toothpaste matted along the faucet. She followed the slime trail up the aluminum toward the mirror, dabbing away at the rock-solid spittle. She scrubbed for several seconds before she noticed the rag's color.

Blue.

Blue for body.

Marjorie's scrubbing slowed as she acknowledged the cloth draping over her freshly painted nails. The damned thing was still wet, and not the kind of wet that came from the condensation on the mirror, but wet as if the rag had been used and never dried. Specs of old soap, flakes of skin, and, of course, even more body hair wove into the fibers, confirming her worst suspicions.

One of the disgusting gremlins she called children put their body washcloth into the drawer with the bathroom cleaning rags.

Used.

Stinking.

Festering.

And now Marjorie held the putrid thing in her hand unable to let go.

Blue for body, kept in the bath.

Fuchsia for face, next to the faucet.

White is right for everything else.

Rules simple enough for a five-year-old who just learned their colors to follow, but her nearly adult children failed to grasp even these most basic instructions. She pictured the washcloth, which festered inside the vanity long enough to grow a camouflage pattern of mildew, sliding around her children's naked bodies. Working its way into every crevice of their privates, sopping up their germs and filth, creating a cocktail of hazardous bodily waste. Waste now collecting in Marjorie's palm.

Like a video on replay, Marjorie saw the rag plunging between her son's ass cheeks as he washed away his after-football practice grime. The rag slid below her daughter's breasts collecting the cottage cheese buildup of dead skin. It dabbed at her daughter's menstrual blood. Wiped piss from her son's Johnson. Every substance, from every known and unknown orifice on her children's bodies, coated Marjorie's hand.

With no additional thought, she reached into the cabinet, scooped up all of the towels, and chucked them to the floor. Swiping her arm across the counter, a never-ending mountain of hygiene products smashed into the sink.

"Goddamn, you fucking filthy-ass kids! I raised you better than this. You wanna live like animals? I'll treat you like animals! This room had better be clean when I get back!"

It might have been in her head, but it sounded like one of the ungrateful shits said something under their breath. Something that sounded dangerously close to "Whatever."

Marjorie pulled open every drawer and dumped their contents. Nail files, clippers, makeup, electric razors—everything clattered to the floor. She yanked the towels from the rack so hard that the bracket on the wall mount came loose. She kicked over the overfilled trash can and chucked a roll of toilet paper at the mirror. She even considered ripping the drawers from their flimsy aluminum runners but had a moment's clarity where she considered her security deposit and stopped.

She stood silently inside a ring of junk. Spilled lotion seeped out of exploded bottles. Fractured bits of plastic rested among unpackaged Q-tips and dried-out makeup. Combs and brushes lay in the brown stains near the rim of the toilet and somehow one of the toothbrushes wound up resting on a crumpled ball of snot-filled toilet paper.

Marjorie inhaled through her nose, filling her lungs with cool air as her vision began to waver around the edges. Her jaw muscles ached, and her limbs felt like she had put them through an arduous workout. She worked her hands open, her joints like rusted hinges, slowly closing them again, distracting herself from the building pressure behind her eyes.

A soft tap on the other side of the door gave pause to Marjorie's breakdown.

"Mom?" Marjorie's sixteen-year-old daughter, Hilary, called. She sounded on the verge of tears herself. "Mom, are you okay? I . . . I just want to make sure everything is okay in there. Do you need help?"

Marjorie looked around at the aftermath of her explosion, wondering if she didn't need help. The kind of help one paid for. She struggled to remember how to swallow, and a wave of embarrassment struck her with the force of a runaway train. Despite the barrier of a closed door, she felt exposed. When she spoke, her throat ached as if she had gargled sand.

"No, honey... It's okay. I'm okay." The waterworks began to flow, an unstoppable flood that no amount of stiff upper lips could hold back. "I didn't mean to scare you... I was upset. You kids need to learn to clean up after yourselves. That's all." Marjorie slumped onto the edge of the tub. "I'm sorry. Don't worry. I'm going to clean this up, then I'll call Ben. I don't think I'm really in the right headspace tonight. Why don't you and your brother order Chinese or something?"

Hilary's voice faded somewhat as she stepped away from the door. "Mom. I just want you to know ... you're right. We should help out more. I'll get Andre off the game, and we can sweep up a little. Then let's rent a movie. Have a family night."

Marjorie nodded to herself, using her towel to wipe away her tears. "Yeah, hon. That would be nice. You go do what you gotta do. I'll be out in a minute. I love you guys."

Like a distant memory, Hilary's voice replied, "We love you too."

Marjorie reminded herself that, despite her children being sewage creatures born of pure filth, she *did* love them. She rubbed her fingers together, sliding them along the greasy film of soap grime still coating her palm and swallowed the disgust bubbling in her gut. She loved them more than the air she breathed. She loved them enough to ignore the curly half-inch hair stuck to her palm.

As Hilary began pounding on her brother's door, Marjorie turned on the bathtub's hot water faucet and looked out across the mess. She loved her children more than life itself, and she would do anything for them.

Running her hand below the lukewarm water, Marjorie's chest began to float. She could even forgive them for the clump of wet hair sticking out of the drain.

The hairs shimmered in a slick film of residue and a thick coating of conditioner. Possibly weeks old, Marjorie had no doubt her children never even considered cleaning the drain of their hair after showering. The long strands of oil-black hair climbed out of the drain and lay over the tub in the shape of a lizard's tongue. Rolling her eyes, Marjorie grabbed the coils and began to pull.

The greasy slop slipped through her fingers, coating her digits in a clear slime. The sharp smell of raw sewage burped up from the drain with every tug. Her expression turned dire as the drain burped again, releasing a stronger wave of the awful smell.

The hair continued endlessly.

Inch by inch, coil after coil, she pulled and pulled, but even after extracting a whole head's worth of hair, the hair showed no signs of stopping.

WET HAIR

Like a spoiled batch of horse hoof glue, the hair's mucus coating collected on Marjorie's arms, exuding its foul odor. The more she smelled the horrendous stench, the more alien it felt. The odor clung to her sinuses and burned her soft tissues. It smelled like roasted shit mixed with spoiled soup left in a sink full of dishes, and the rank scent forced her to gag.

Releasing the rope of hair that now extended halfway across the tub's length, Marjorie cupped her hand over her mouth to keep from vomiting.

The action was miscalculated.

Majorie felt the cold kiss of the congealed slime transfer from her hand onto her nose. Immediately, she emptied the contents of her stomach.

After covering the bath in a fresh coat of steaming bile, Marjorie eyed the rancid tangle with a scowl. In all her years, she had never witnessed a clog so stubborn or hair so putrid. Clumps of mysterious filth clung to the hair as it rested in her puddle of sick. Capillaries of fungi wove throughout the strands like a cardiovascular structure made of dryer lint.

Simply looking at the mass made Marjorie feel sick. So sick, in fact, that her eyes played tricks on her. The hair appeared to be moving. Each individual strand wriggled and waved. The more she focused on the ropes, the more it looked like a river flowing away from the steaming waterfall running from the tap.

She extended her hand, pushing back the ridiculous fears telling her to run from the room. Wet hair might be gross, but there was no reason for her heart to race. She forced herself to laugh, resisting the building urge to scream. She grabbed the hair again.

This time, it grabbed her back.

The hair shot up her arm like the branching proboscis of a ribbon worm. Shooting off an expanding network of vines, the hairs climbed up her arm before Marjorie's brain could even process what was happening. She jumped back, yanking her arm away, but the hair clung to her, pulling back with double the force. She smashed into the tub, coating her face in cooled vomit, painfully aware of her proximity to the hairball's main body.

On closer inspection, the amorphous blob of black strings wasn't just moving, but it slithered like a snake, pulsing its way out of the drain. The colony of worms worked in tandem, creating a sentient mass of gyrating creatures. They wrapped around Marjorie's arm, constricting and pulling her into their body. With a massive burst of effort, Marjorie shoved herself out of the tub.

"Hel—"

Before she finished her cry for help, the cord of hair along Marjorie's arm split off into another branch and slammed into her face. A fist-sized mass burrowed into her mouth, choking off any further attempt to make a sound.

She stumbled onto her feet, grabbing the shaft of the swirling, ever-growing column of serpents. Stomping down, Marjorie barely noticed the discarded scissors that punched through her foot. Falling to the side, she smashed into the wall, the towel rack slicing a gash in her side.

The sentient hairs overpowered her, tunneling deeper into her esophagus. A taste like raw fish marinated in the pus from an anal abscess coated every square inch of her mouth. She inhaled through her nose, becoming engulfed in the smell of the oozing, rotten thing digging inside her body.

Marjorie tried to bite down, but the hair flexed like a muscle, and the striations grew stiff and rigid. As her teeth came into contact with the surface of the thing, its body spun like a drill bit, catching and ripping out her incisors. Instinctually, Marjorie opened her throat to scream, and the invader plunged in deeper.

It sank into Marjorie's chest. Her insides erupted in flames as if she had swallowed a pitcher of molten steel. The strands pumped and pulsed into her, the coating of slime easing their passage. Her lungs filled to bursting and refused to exhale. She tried to breathe through her nose, ignoring the smell, desperate for any release from the unbearable pressure. Instead of air, long, thin tendrils coated in shimmering layers of blood escaped her nasal cavity.

The hairs continued to enter her while expanding inside her body. Nerves she never knew she possessed screamed out as the invaders occupied her organs, filling every available cavity. They filled her intestines and wormed their way through her veins. Wrapping around her spinal column, she took some solace that if this nightmare was real, soon it would all be over. The hairs squeezed on every nerve and flooded every synapse with a sensation of pain. As Marjorie lost control over her motor functions and her arms went limp, she made peace with her exit from this mortal coil.

The hairs climbed along her brain, breaking and replacing even her smallest capillaries. As tears of ruby blood ran from her eyes, she mourned never seeing her children again. Never seeing them grow old. Her vision grew dark as a branching pattern of black strings wove before her eyes.

But she didn't die.

Gradually, the blackness in front of her vision lightened until she saw the world from behind a tinted lens. She couldn't move. She couldn't breathe. She remained trapped behind the walls of her physical body, imprisoned, neither alive nor dead, existing in a hellscape of never-ceasing agony. She heard the sounds of her children down the hall

WET HAIR

and watched as some unknown entity took control of her body.

Her consciousness screamed as she felt the muscles of her body snap and twist and move without her volition. Her body shambled toward the exit and her face pulled itself into a deranged excuse for a smile.

"Come on, you asshole, get up," Hilary said, kicking her brother's bean bag chair. "We gotta help Mom."

Andre rolled his eyes and scooted closer to the TV. "Shut up. Mom's just having one of her fits. You clean up. She's just gonna wear herself out yelling about something stupid, like a pair of socks I didn't pick up. I'll pick the socks up and an hour after that, she'll be crying, saying how sorry she is, yadda, yadda, yadda . . . Same as always."

Hilary smacked the back of her brother's head hard enough to knock off his headset. Even at two years her senior, Andre had the maturity level of an edgelord tween. "Quit being a jerk. You know if we actually cleaned up after ourselves, Mom might stay calm." Hilary thought of how her mom acted whenever their father brought his newest girlfriend over for visitations. "Well . . . *calmer*."

Andre raised his thigh and pushed out a blast of noxious fumes strong enough to make his bean bag chair vibrate. The putrid smell of protein powder farts only added to the rich aroma of teenage boy musk. Hilary fanned her face and staggered into Andre's laundry basket spilling a mountain of XXL football jerseys to the floor.

"This is what mom's talking about!" Hilary said, ripping a spoon from a bowl of curdled cereal milk on the dresser. She chucked the utensil at Andre's head, clocking him squarely in the temple. The spoon left an Elmer's glue-colored imprint in his hair. "You're a fucking slob and don't do anything to help. It all falls on us!"

Andre paused his game and brought his hand to the milk splatter sticking to his hair. In disbelief, he studied his fingers as he slowly began to rise. Standing a good foot taller and easily three times wider than his sister, Andre cast an intimidating shadow across the room.

He dropped the controller and rolled his head from side to side. His knuckles sounded like bubble wrap as he mashed them into his hand.

"You know what's gonna happen now? I'm gonna murder you," Andre said, looking toward the ground, bathing his face in shadow. "I'll make it quick. 'Cuz you are my sister, after all." He threw his headset at Hilary and charged.

Hilary did the only thing that came to mind. She grabbed the bowl of milk—at least a week old based on the thickness of its congealed contents—and flung it at Andre's face. The cheese splattered across his features, splashing into his mouth and nose.

"Now I'm really going to kill you!" Andre dove blindly as Hilary slipped out of the door.

"MooOOoom!" Hilary sprinted down the hall, nearly tripping on the bunching carpet. "Mooom! Andre's threatening me! Tell him to stop!"

The bathroom door slammed open in a cloud of steam. The doorknob connected with the wall so hard the drywall cracked, and the door swung back to a nearly closed position.

"Mom?"

Greenish-gray fingers crept around the crack in the door. They wrapped around the frame, moving unnervingly reminiscent of a spider's legs. The fingernails sank into the wood, revealing a dark network of what appeared to be mold clinging to the underside of the nail. It climbed out from below, making the fingertips look like they were covered in fur. The door eased open, squealing along its dried-out hinges, releasing a sound like a teakettle past the boiling point.

"Mom . . . is that you?" Hilary asked whoever stood on the other side of the door. "What happened? Is everything all right?"

Hilary stepped back, her skin feeling like ice as her blood pulled away from her extremities. A massive force from behind sent her crashing onto the floor.

Andre's meaty hands wrapped around her head as he mashed her face into the carpet.

"Say you're sorry, and I'll stop," Andre teased as he pulled her hair to lift her face and let her breathe. "Say I'm a bitch, and my brother is awesome." His laughter and brutish movements shielded him from acknowledging the evolving situation. "You're *so* lucky I love you enough to not really hurt you."

Hilary punched Andre in the thigh, getting him to release his grip as a charley horse ignited his nerves. He wrapped his hands around his leg, freeing Hilary to point toward the still-opening door.

"There's something wrong with mom. Quit being an asshole for like two minutes and help—"

The door opened, revealing the haphazard silhouette of a broken woman. Every joint popped and clicked as she lumbered forwards with a gait like a newborn calf suffering from severe cerebral palsy. Stepping through the cloud of steam into the hallway, Marjorie grinned down at her children, completely nude.

"Jesus Christ, Mom!"

Hilary gawked at her mother's body, barely noticing her nudity but transfixed by her skin. It fluctuated through shades of deep purples and greens under a layer of almost black mottling. It pulsed in undulating waves. Each limb expanded and contracted at its own tempo, making it look as if her meat itself breathed. The bloated flesh swelled close to bursting. Infected boils leaked yellow ooze down her limbs with every movement. Black veins below the surface of the skin ripped fissures along her bone structure, making her appear gaunt despite her face being swollen to twice its normal size.

An inky black substance clouded her eyes. It swirled toward the point where one might expect a pupil, but instead, her eyes were yellow pupilless orbs resting in beds of bloodied pus. Small cracks ran across the eyes' dried-out surfaces as she scanned the teenagers' faces.

Marjorie's lips peeled open in an abstract interpretation of a grin. Her voice echoed through her throat creating a harmony with itself in a singsong delivery.

"Don't use the Lord's name in vain, honey." Marjorie's head snapped to her shoulder. "Sinners go to Hell, and you're Mommy's little angel, right?"

Andre grabbed the back of his sister's sweater, his mouth hanging agape. "Hill? What's wrong with Mom? She doesn't look right."

Hilary flinched back as her mother took a step forward on a leg so twisted it had to be broken. "Mom is just . . . sick. We need to get her to the hospital."

Marjorie collapsed into another step like a marionette with a broken string. She pulled her lips back into a snarl and a multitude of hairs sliced through her gums, floating several inches away from her face. Tar-thick, black sludge dribbled from her mouth as she spoke.

"I'm not sick." Marjorie raised her arm in a horrifying display of jerking motions. Holes erupted along her palm as a mass swelled her hand to the size of a volleyball. "This is the real me, is all. I'm so tired of holding everything back. So now I'm finally letting it all out."

Ropes of tangled hair shot through Marjorie's palm, tearing her forearm into the bloom of a five-petaled flower. Covered in miscellaneous chunks of gore, the slicked ropes of hair made a twisting beeline directly toward the siblings.

"Fucking move!" Andre yanked his sister from the living room into the kitchen. A column of spinning hair blasted into the wall, spraying gypsum and shattered tiles across the floor. "Stay low. If we can make it outside, we'll be able to run for it."

"Dre . . . What the fuck happened to Mom? What's going on?"

Marjorie's twisted, malformed shadow lurched forward, growing along the floor. A musical cackle cut through the apartment like a wolf's mating call in an empty forest. Another pillar of hair whistled through the air, stopping in the kitchen entryway. The hair branched out, becoming a hand with far

WET HAIR

too many excessively spindly digits. The black fingers shot out and gripped onto the moldings and door frames.

"You children and your filthy mouths," Marjorie called, her body's shadow rising into the air as it climbed toward the kitchen. "You need to clean your mouths out. Open wide and take your medicine."

The teens pressed their backs against the lower kitchen cabinets, cowering below the approaching shadows. Andre reached behind his head and knocked the knife block off the counter. Steel clattered to the floor and a four-inch band of hair dropped from the black mass above the door. The branch of swirling hairs periscoped in like a sentry.

The band edged closer, floating above the kitchen's small island toward where the two kids hid. Andre shoved the handle of a chef's knife to Hilary and took another for himself. He rose into a crouch. Releasing a roar, he charged, driving all of his strength into his weapon. The knife punched through the tentacle, pinning it to the island. The banshee cackled and sped toward the door.

"There you two are." Marjorie swung into view, hanging from the rope extending out of her exploded arm. Black liquid charcoal dribbled from between her teeth. "My filthy little yeast infections. I thought I'd never find you!" Her hair climbed deeper into the kitchen, spreading like mildew seen in time-lapse footage.

Hilary raised her chef's knife up to chest level and her skin lost all color. Tears splashed down her chin in never-ending waterfalls.

"Please, Mom . . . D-d-d-don't come closer." Hilary's blubbering turned her words into a mishmash of incomprehensible sounds. "We love you. You're scaring us, Mommy. Please."

"Oh, little girl, why are you worried?" Marjorie's voice held all the comfort of a rusted bag of nails. As she spoke, strands of hair fell from the door head like a beaded curtain. They wove around each other, creating a dense net blocking the children's only avenue for escape. "I would never hurt something I love. Too bad no one could ever love a filthy, bloody slut such as yourself."

Marjorie pointed her remaining arm at Hilary. Bones creaked before her tissues made a sound like a paper bag being ripped. Her arm exploded into ribbons as a sentient rope fired from her annihilated limb.

Shoving Hilary from the trajectory, Andre dodged low and scooped up another sizeable knife.

"Run!"

Andre slammed into the hair. He sawed and hacked, cutting a few strands before the main mass split and punched him in the solar plexus. Andre dropped his knife and stumbled into the Formica counter.

Majorie kept her sickening smile latched onto Hilary as she retracted her extended tentacle and shot it into the ceiling. Her tendrils spread out and expanded, slowly engulfing the room. Even as Marjorie rode up her hair and contorted until her feet pressed into the ceiling, her eyes remained glued on Hilary. Scurrying like an insect, Marjorie scuttled above Andre and abruptly came to a halt. Finally, with enough force to break bone, she snapped her head down.

Hilary bolted to the door. She tugged on the netting, unable to break a strand. She slammed the cheap kitchen knife into the hairs, but the slime-slicked strands flexed out of the way of the dull blade.

Marjorie used the ropes from her arms to free rappel to the ground. Hovering over Andre, she swiveled her head to look over her back. "Where do you think you are off to, young lady? You wait right there, and when I finish with your brother, it's your turn."

Sticky strands of noxious goo clung to the countless strands of hair that detached from the ceiling. They shuddered and split into forearm-width tentacles before descending to the floor. Skittering like electrified snakes, they wrapped around anything in range—primarily, the knives.

Andre shook his head, freeing himself from his stunned stupor. He looked from side to side at the flopping black worms. His face froze in a kind of determination he only showed on the field. "Mom . . . whatever is going on, we can find you help. You need a doctor."

"Oh, honey," Marjorie cooed, the tendrils of hair steadily dragging the various knives into the air. "Your concern is soooo sweet! But a doctor can't fix my problem. It's too late for them to give me an abortion."

The knives all sliced through the air in wild arcs and Andre tumbled and rolled. Ducking below one of the black tentacles, Andre escaped behind his mother. He charged toward his sister like he was gunning for the game-winning touchdown. Had any football player—even at pro level— been following him, he'd have been untouchable.

But a floor coated in sentient hair isn't something athletes train to sprint over. A band of hair shot up from the ground and grabbed his descending foot. With a single twist, Andre's athletic career came to an abrupt end. Bones cracked and meat popped as he plummeted to the ground. His face smashed into the tile with a *splat*.

Shrieking with laughter, Marjorie collapsed forward. A tumorous growth expanded between her shoulders until her upper back looked nine months pregnant with quadruplets. Across her shoulders and down the remaining tissues of her arms, the flesh split, then exploded in a steaming mist of gore.

An insurmountable number of serpentine protrusions shot into the air, becoming a tornado of black whips. In an instant, they shot up, rigid as steel beams, then snapped into dozens of multi-segmented dagger-pointed legs. They struck the walls and windows, creating a hailstorm of broken glass.

Marjorie scuttled over Andre at the speed of a pouncing lion. She whipped her face from side to side, spraying tar from her mouth onto his crippled body. In an instant she ceased all movement.

"Someone's been a bad boy," Marjorie teased with the cadence of a young child. "A very naughty troublemaker."

"Fuck you," Andre snarled. "You broke my goddamn leg. I don't know what you are, but you're not my mom."

"Well, you're a filthy little piggy. Wee, wee, wee, all the way to the market with you." One of the knife-wielding tentacles sank a paring knife into the palm Andre used to shield his face. In a flash of motion, the knife slid from palm to elbow releasing a curtain of blood. "Even filthy on the inside, huh, my little piglet? Oink oink."

The remnants of Hilary's sanity shattered under the weight of Andre's cries of pain. She collapsed to the floor covering her ears, her eyes incapable of looking away from the vision of her brother.

Marjorie's larger knives impaled Andre's limbs, pinning him to the floor. She ran her tentacles across his body, pulling hyperventilated pleas from his throat.

"I don't. I-I-I don't. Want to . . . die."

"You *never* want to do anything!" Marjorie taunted as a band of hair used a bread knife to saw through Andre's pant leg, exposing his broken ankle. "Be a good little piglet and stop fighting. It'll all be over soon."

"Please. Mom . . . stop. Don't hurt me. Please don't hurt me. I have so much to do . . . I'm too young—"

With an almost sensual slowness, Marjorie brought one of the tentacles to his lips like a finger. She shook her head, shushing him.

"You *HAD* so much more to do. Proper grammar, my little failure. Besides. You need not fear death. Death is too good for you."

Without any warning, several tentacles descended onto Andre's exposed leg, twisting and pulling on it until a geyser of blood gushed into the air. Tendrils pounded into the open wound and climbed under his flesh. More hair forced its way into his nearly bifurcated forearm, paralyzing Andre in a frozen scream of agony.

Marjorie's jaw descended beyond the point any joint could withstand. Popping and cracking, the skin around her mouth tore as her throat birthed a blackened tongue of throbbing parasites. Andre barely blinked, enraptured in the throes of shock as waterfalls of thick alien spittle coated his face.

Marjorie vomited her newly formed tongue into her son's mouth, her eyes rolling back in apparent ecstasy.

The tendrils invaded Andre's mouth with a sound like a toothless dog choking on soup. A chunky torrent of vomit gushed out of his mouth and then got sucked back in as the hair penetrated deeper into his throat. Bubbles of mucus poured from his nose in bloody streams and his eyes turned white as he looked toward the back of his head.

Then, as if a switch were flipped, the hairs stopped. Marjorie made a gurgling noise before she released a fountain of blood down the black tongue directly into Andres's mouth. Consciousness smashed into Andre like a brick through a window. He yanked his arms up hard enough to dislodge the knives. With an explosive burst of effort, he pulled the black cord of rope from his esophagus. A flood of yellow bile coated his chest as he heaved for air.

Marjorie blinked twice, her eyes pointing up toward the center of her head as if trying to look at the chef's knife impaled in her skull. Hilary backed away, trembling, her hands coated in her mother's blood. She attempted to make words, only able to stutter I'm sorrys in a voice no louder than air escaping a pinhole in a tire.

Like an actor in a harness, Marjorie rose into the air, propped up on her endless spider legs. Floating before her daughter, something about her face began to change. Began to become familiar. For a second, the eyes regained life, and an immense sorrow leaked out.

"Hilary. My baby girl," Majorie cried. Her torn-open smile drooping into something almost human as she struggled to mouth the words, "I live only for you both." She raised her foot—still impaled with scissors—and ran it along her daughter's cheek. Hilary's mind tore at its edges. Her mother's smile oozed a river of jet-black poison, and yet the feel of her skin, the scarce amount that remained, still felt like home.

"Now run."

Marjorie slammed her foot into Hilary's chest. Hilary reached out, clawing for something to stabilize herself, catching the handle of the scissors. She tore them through her mother's foot, releasing a torrent of viscera-soaked hair.

Marjorie reared back, extending all her knife-wielding tendrils to the side. One wrapped around the handle to the knife in her forehead.

"I love you both so much," Marjorie said, before all of the tentacles plunged down in a synchronized descent. They pounded into her skull as she cranked the handle embedded in her forehead. She ripped it down.

Her face split open like a worm-infested watermelon. Chunks of liquefied gore bathed Marjorie's naked chest as a pressurized blast of hair sprayed

WET HAIR

from her neck. Internal tissues caught in the tangles of hair flooded out of her cavity as bones and organs splashed the ceiling.

After only a few seconds, all that remained were a few twitching piles of muscle, an empty jumpsuit of gore-caked skin, and a walrus-sized clump of matted, blood-drenched hairs.

"We have to go!" Andre panted, as he limped toward the net impeding their exit. Using the strength he had left, he fell into the barrier, but like the knife before, he made no progress. "We have to get out of here. Mom isn't— She's— We just have to go. Now!"

He slammed into the net again and again, making no progress. Behind them, the massive blob of hair rose in a synchronized wave before splashing down again. Each slap released a shockwave of spores into the shattered floor tiles and dragged the parasite closer.

Hilary shoved her brother aside and tore open the blood-bathed scissors. She slammed them closed, and the hair, unable to dodge an attack on both ends, was finally cut.

She continued cutting until she tore a hole large enough for her brother to limp through. Hilary mostly carried him into the next room, his foot slowing him down tremendously.

Andre forced a smile that did nothing to mask his agony.

"You saved me. You did what you had to do." He fell into the couch's arm, shaking his head. Taking a deep breath, he absentmindedly dug his fingers into the still-bleeding wound on his arm. "That wasn't Mom in there. That was something else."

Hilary took Andre's hand, stopping him from scratching. He snapped his head to the side, releasing a loud pop as he hopped onto his good foot. He nodded to her, and they continued shuffling toward the door, the slurping sound of the slug growing quieter, filling with bass as it worked its way onto the carpet.

"You can't blame yourself," Andre continued. "Mom was already dead, Hil. Just like you will be soon. Then we'll have two stuck-up bitches rotting in Hell together."

"You fucking asshole!" Hilary shouted, shoving her brother off of her arm. "Are you out of your goddamn—"

Andre's broken leg vibrated with rippling flesh. Blood pumped out of his torn skin and waves of black meat trembled below the surface.

"Just because I ain't got time to be cleaning up all day, I'm the asshole? Well, I'm getting tired of it." Andre stepped forward, standing more upright as he cracked his neck from side to side. "You know what has to happen now, right?"

Hilary's heart pounded in her throat, and her vision became glassy. Her stomach flooded with acid as Andre's putrid scent clogged her sinuses. He stood before her spilling black bile from his crooked smile.

"Don't play dumb with me, Hil. We both know you're the smarter one between us. You know what's gonna happen now. I'm gonna murder you."

Andre contorted at an inhuman speed. His fingers snapped backward, bending until they became talons. His ribs cracked and pulled, expanding his back to twice its original size.

Hilary slammed the scissors into her brother's abdomen. A waterfall of hot blood cascaded onto the floor in a deafening roar. She pulled back and stabbed again, plunging her wrist deep into her brother's soft tissues before she allowed herself time to think. Steaming viscera splashed onto the floor as she drew back the blades.

Andre's fingers clung to Hilary's shirt, pulling her close, making it easier for her to carve into the muscles holding his vital organs in place. She pistoned into his abdomen, soaking herself in her brother's fluids. His molten stomach melted over her hands. She struggled to slice under the ceaseless flow of blood, resorting to more ripping than cutting.

Andre coughed a stream of black blood onto Hilary's shoulder. His raspy breath shuddered into her ear.

"I'm scared." Andre's voice rattled with thick clots of congealed blood. "The darkness is coming, and I can feel everything. Hilary, I don't want to go. I'm not ready." Tears ran down her face as Hilary punched the scissors in deeper, slicing into the cartilage on the tip of his sternum. "It hurts so bad. Please, Hil . . . make it stop. Make it stop. It's too much. Please . . . MAKE IT STOP!"

Andre's chest exploded. His sternum blasted open, flinging his rib cage apart like a Venus flytrap ready to be fed. Several black anacondas whipped out, slapping in the air, missing Hilary by inches as she ran for the door. She charged it, smashing it from two of its hinges. She swung it open, receiving a hot blast of early evening sunshine.

A balding man with a once-strong jawline and a stiff gait hurried up the parking lot toward their door. His comically thick but well-groomed mustache matched the contours of his beige uniform. Ben, the police officer Marjorie had been seeing.

Hilary ran toward him. Her ears rang and a heartbeat pounded in her head. Adrenaline blasted through her body, and her vision flashed in hot bursts.

She grabbed Ben's arm, tugging him toward the house. The words the nearly retired police officer shouted refused to process in Hilary's frazzled mind. Shrieking in unbelievable octaves, Hilary's relief couldn't be contained as she pulled his wrist.

Ben slammed his shoulder into Hilary's jaw. She spun around, her vision fuzzy. The confusion only became worse when she saw the rivers of tears pouring down Ben's face. Her blood turned to ice when she looked down and into the barrel of the gun in his hand. The hand she had been pulling on.

Hilary's shell-shocked body involuntarily leapt forward at the sound of a small rodent scurrying up a tree behind her. She brandished her scissors, having no time to explain.

A *pop* like a car's muffler exploded nearby. Every nerve on the left side of Hilary's face screamed under a blanket of fire. She fell to her knees, looking at the world through the lens of her one remaining blood-soaked eyeballs.

Ben hurried to the apartment door. He managed to peer inside for a matter of seconds before falling forward and vomiting all over his loafers.

Hilary's body collapsed onto the asphalt. Her vision grew distant, as if she were watching the world through a backward telescope. The only sound she heard was the slowing blood pumping through her veins.

A strand of her well-conditioned hair fell into the pool of warm fluids spilling from her head.

Wet hair.

Hilary loved a good wet hair look.

***

Harrison Phillips steps in after Jayson Dawn has finished speaking. He is proud of what he's found. He walks around the fire, not handing it to his listeners—it's precious cargo—but displaying it for them to see. He comes to me last, and my eyes sparkle with wonder. The Scrapyard is filled with death, but this simple seed with a green sprout is proof that it isn't devoid of life . . .

Bonemeal

Harrison Phillips

Despite the fact that four weeks had passed since they'd first arrived at Lakeview Pines, Jennifer still couldn't believe just how lucky they'd been. Even as Rob leaned out the driver's side window and punched the code into the numerical keypad. Even as the iron gates slowly swung open, granting them passage into the beautifully manicured estate. Even as they drove slowly along the street, the motor of their brand-new Tesla purring gently, those neighbours currently tending to their gardens waving as they passed by. Even as they pulled into the driveway of the five-bedroom townhouse they now called home, none of it seemed real. Jennifer occasionally had to pinch herself just to be sure she wasn't dreaming.

But, of course, this wasn't a dream. Nor was any of it truly down to any kind of luck. This was all the result of Rob's hard work, his passion, and his dedication to the business he had spent the past three years nurturing, until it had finally blossomed into the company it was today. He had developed a smartphone app that allowed the user to track their incoming and outgoing payments from all of their accounts in one safe and secure place. It was a huge success. Investors were practically begging him to come on board. In the end, he had sold the business for $127 million.

And Jennifer had been there with him every step of the way. While Rob had spent countless hours sitting at his computer, tirelessly stringing together one line of code after another, programming and debugging algorithm after algorithm, Jennifer had worked at their local supermarket. She had just about scraped together enough money to cover her half of the bills, plus a little extra for those occasions when Rob's freelance work would dry up.

But those days were long gone now, little more than a distant memory.

Now, they were rich.

It had been Rob's idea to move to Lakeview Pines—an idea Jennifer had been more than happy to agree to. It was beautiful, exactly the type of place Jennifer had always dreamed she would one day live. Only those with exceptional wealth could afford to live at Lakeview Pines. This was an exclusive gated community established back in 1996, just a few short years after Jennifer herself was born. It was a quiet and peaceful community, where each of the houses was practically identical, and their respective owners kept them looking immaculate. Tall pines lined each side of the wide road that snaked through the estate. Each house was set back behind a luscious green lawn, every blade of grass trimmed to a uniform length.

The house they had purchased cost them $2.6 million, but as far as Jennifer was concerned, it was worth every penny. There were five bedrooms and three bathrooms. The master bathroom was her favourite room in the house; a huge room with both a walk-in shower *and* a Jacuzzi bath big enough for four people, alongside the twin vanity unit, where she and Rob could brush their teeth together. There were two living rooms. The kitchen had granite worktops and a range cooker. There was a twin garage and a conservatory that stretched out to the rear, where Jennifer could enjoy her evenings with a glass of wine and a good book, the stars twinkling above her.

This was, in Jennifer's opinion, the perfect place to raise a child. Despite this, she and Rob had agreed that they weren't quite ready.

"Hey there, Dex," said Jennifer as she entered the house, the brown and white terrier sprinting to greet her at the door, his tail wagging furiously back and forth. "How's it going, boy? Did you miss us?"

"He always misses us," said Rob, following Jennifer inside. "We could be gone for five minutes, and he'd *still* act as though we'd abandoned him for a year."

"That's true." Jennifer laughed, bending to stroke the dog. "But he can't help it, he just loves us *soooo* much." Dexter hopped up so his front paws rested on Jennifer's bent thigh, then he licked and nibbled at her ear. Giggling, Jennifer pushed him away. She straightened herself up and headed into the kitchen, where she proceeded to put all of the groceries away into their rightful place.

That evening, Jennifer cooked spinach and ricotta cannelloni. With it, she and Rob shared a bottle of rosé. Once they had finished their dinner, Rob offered to wash the dishes while she walked the dog around the block. And so she clipped the collar around Dexter's neck and headed out.

It was dark by then, but Sandra Thomas—a woman in her fifties who lived with her husband four doors down—was still out, watering her lawn. "Evening," she said, smiling and waving as Jennifer walked by. "Nice night, isn't it?"

Jennifer smiled in return. "It sure is," she said, looking upward, only just now noticing there wasn't a single cloud in the sky. Above her, the moon was full, and the blackness of space was littered with stars. It still amazed her just how clear the sky was out here, away from the hazy pollution of the city. "Isn't it a bit late for gardening?" she asked, turning her attention back to Sandra.

Sandra raised her eyebrows. "Perhaps," she scoffed. "But in this sort of weather, you'll find that your lawn can get incredibly thirsty."

Jennifer smiled and nodded, unsure of how she ought to respond. "Well, I best get going."

"Of course. See you around."

Jennifer continued along the road until Dexter stopped to sniff at a tree, then finally did his business. She then circled back around, the dog following dutifully along, and returned home.

She and Rob made love that night. Happy and content, she fell asleep wrapped in Rob's arms, her smooth skin pressed against his muscular chest.

Rob had always been a light sleeper. Even the slightest of sounds could wake him. Jennifer wasn't anything like him in that regard; she could sleep through an earthquake without even stirring. Right now, she was lying beside him on the bed, naked, her slender body nuzzled into his chest, snoring softly.

But something had woken Rob. There was a noise, he was sure of it. It had come from the rear of the house. He had been (somewhat) asleep when he'd heard it, so there was no way for him to identify just *what* it was. But he had almost certainly heard *something*.

And then he heard it again. It was so quiet, for a brief moment he thought maybe he'd just imagined it. But there it was *again,* a soft, scraping sound. It baffled him how such a slight noise could rouse him. Still, rouse him it did, and Jennifer didn't even stir.

He checked the time. The digital alarm clock on the bedside table told him it was 2:13 a.m.

Whatever that sound was, it seemed to have no intention of stopping. Gently, Rob pulled at his arm, slowly teasing it out from under Jennifer's body. She grunted a minor complaint before pulling the sheet up over her shoulders and snoring once again.

With his arm now free, Rob climbed out of bed and pulled on his boxer shorts. He then crept over to the window, doing his utmost not to wake Jennifer (as if there were any chance of *that* happening). The cool blue light of the moon poured in through the gaps between the wooden slats of the Venetian blinds. Rob poked his fingers between those slats and pulled them downward a quarter of an inch, just enough so he could look out.

The sound was coming from next door. Norma Wallace was outside, wrapped up in her fluffy pink dressing gown. The moonlight illuminated her silver hair, causing it to glow bright white.

She was holding a yellow plastic bucket in one hand and a short, wooden-handled shovel in the other. The bucket was filled with what appeared to be some kind of white powder, which Norma was scooping out and sprinkling all over her lawn.

Rob watched for what felt like an hour, as Norma shuffled back and forth, scooping and sprinkling until her entire lawn was mottled gray and black. As she turned back toward the house, she seemed to sense that she was being watched. Quickly, Rob pulled away, releasing the blinds, just as Norma looked up toward his window. He waited a moment, his heart pounding in his throat, an irrational sense of guilt swamping him. After what felt like another hour had passed, he once again looked out through the blinds.

Norma was gone.

Confused as to what he'd just witnessed, Rob went back to bed. He hardly slept for the rest of the night, finally drifting off sometime after five a.m.

Fresh milk was delivered daily to Lakeview Pines. At first, Rob had been reluctant to have their milk delivered; he was quite capable of going to the store to buy it himself. But Jennifer had insisted—*everybody else* had their milk delivered, so *they* should too. And now, Rob had to admit, he quite liked getting his milk fresh every morning. At around seven a.m., he stepped out of his front door to collect the two bottles of milk that had been left on his doorstep.

Next door, Ed Wallace—Norma's husband—was out collecting his milk too. When he spotted Rob, he offered a wave. "Morning, neighbour," he said, his wide smile showing off his pearly white dentures.

"Good morning," said Rob, scooping the bottles into the crook of his arm. "Looks like it's going to be another nice day."

"Oh yeah." Ed nodded in agreement.

"Hey . . ." said Rob, an uneasy sense of guilt once again twisting in his stomach. "I saw your wife outside last night. She looked like she was spreading something over the grass."

Ed raised his eyebrows. He looked surprised, as if Rob had discovered some deep, dark secret. But then his face relaxed. He nodded his head. "That's right, she was feeding the lawn. Bonemeal. It really keeps the lawn looking healthy."

Rob could feel himself frowning. "But . . . in the middle of the night?"

Ed laughed. "Call it a *midnight feast*! Ha! No, in all seriousness, the grass here in Lakeview Pines doesn't do well in the heat. It's best to feed it during the night when the temperature drops."

Rob nodded, pretending he understood. The truth was, that didn't make a whole lot of sense to him. But then again, he wasn't a gardener, so what did he know?

"Well," said Ed, offering another wave. "I've got to get going. You have a good day now, okay?"

"Yeah. You too."

The two men returned to their respective homes. Rob made himself a bowl of cereal, drowning it in milk from a freshly opened bottle. When Jennifer finally woke, he told her about what he'd seen last night and what Ed had told him that morning. "That's really weird," she said, laughing dismissively. "Do you think *we'll* be crazy when we're that old?"

"Oh Jesus. I really hope not!" said Rob, joining in with Jennifer's laughter.

"Oh my God..." muttered Jennifer, transfixed by the grotesque sight before her.

"It's okay," said Angie, in a reassuring tone, as she wiped her bloody palms on the apron she was wearing. "I know what this *looks* like, but believe me, it's really nothing to worry about."

Angie lived on the other side of the road, in the house directly opposite. She lived with her husband and their two children. Frank—Angie's husband—had made his fortune selling imported animal feeds in the agricultural sector. For a time, Angie had worked alongside her husband, running the business with him. When the children were born, she quit work so she could raise them herself. Now, both the kids were of school age, but she had yet to return to work. She seemed to be quite happy at home, using her mornings to do whatever housework needed doing, so she could spend her afternoons drinking white wine spritzers.

But Angie was nice. She had been the first person to welcome Jennifer and Rob to Lakeview Pines. The very day they had moved in, Angie had knocked on their door and informed them that if they should ever need anything—*anything at all*—they were always more than welcome to give her a shout.

Jennifer had yet to have cause to take Angie up on the offer, but that morning, she had spilled cranberry tea on her sheepskin rug, and she was certain it would stain if she didn't clean it quickly. The trouble was, she didn't know what to clean it with *or* how.

Then it occurred to her. *Angie would know what to do.*

Jennifer tried knocking at the front door but had gotten no answer. As she stood there, contemplating what she ought to do next, she realized she could hear a noise coming from the back of the house. It was a dull thump, over and over. She knew Angie wouldn't mind—she had said as much herself—so Jennifer decided to head around to the back of the house to see if she could find her there.

Angie had a utility room in her back garden, separate from the house. Jennifer felt sure this was where she would find Angie, perhaps folding laundry. Not that this would explain the noise . . .

A pair of large glass doors opened up from the patio into the utility room. Angie was there. She stood behind a large steel vat, the sides of which were plastered in coagulated blood, thick and sticky, almost black. Inside the vat were dozens of bones, stringy bits of flesh still clinging to them. They clacked and clunked against each other as Angie smashed away at them with a heavy-looking lump hammer, crunching them down into almost nothing. Blood coated her hands and wrists and splattered onto her face.

Despite this, she was smiling.

She almost looked deranged.

"What *is* all this?" asked Jennifer. She could feel herself grimacing. She dreaded to think what she must've looked like from Angie's point of view.

"I'm making bonemeal," said Angie. "To fertilize the lawn. I make it fresh myself. It's far more nutritious than the stuff you can buy in the shops."

"B-but," Jennifer stuttered, still in shock. "You . . . you're covered in blood."

"Oh . . . Yes, I know." Angie shrugged her shoulders. She raised her arms and looked herself over. "Yep, that's definitely one of the downsides. But I promise you, the mess is all worth it. And don't panic, these are lamb bones."

Jennifer took a step forward and looked into the vat. Splintered fragments of bone sat in a puddle of thick, congealed blood. "You put *this* on the grass?"

Angie nodded. "Well, I need to dry it out first, then run it through the blender. I don't like my bonemeal to be too coarse; the lawn prefers a much finer consistency." Angie wiped the sweat from her brow with the back of her hand, smearing blood across her forehead.

Jennifer did her best to ignore this. "And this helps it to grow?"

"That's right. Grass needs to be fed, just like people do. And don't forget, keeping your lawns healthy *is* a part of the RCs."

Jennifer didn't quite understand what Angie was saying. It took her a moment to realize that she was referring to the "Restrictive Covenants"—the list of rules one had to follow when taking up residence in Lakeview Pines. They stated that you couldn't run a business from your home. They stated that you weren't allowed to erect or extend any buildings on the property. They also stated the exact shade of white your facias should be and the precise number of rose bushes you were permitted to grow out front. Some of the rules were silly, but still, Jennifer could understand why many of them had to be strictly adhered to. But the look on her face must've betrayed the fact that she hadn't really read them, and she certainly couldn't recall seeing anything about lawn maintenance. "You *did* read the RCs," said Angie. "Didn't you?"

"I *did* read them," Jennifer lied. "I just don't remember all the details."

Angie shook her head. "You should really know them like the back of your hand." She sighed, sounding almost disappointed. "Section four, paragraph seven states, 'It is the homeowner's responsibility to maintain a proper lawn, befitting Lakeview Pines.'"

Jennifer didn't know how to respond. It seemed silly to her. Did it really matter what each lawn looked like?

Before she could respond, Jennifer was being ushered out of the utility room by Angie. "I'll tell you what, when this batch is done, I'll bring you some over," said Angie, waving the backs of her bloody hands toward Jennifer, urging her out through the door. "We'll make sure your lawn is up to scratch."

"Yeah. That's great. Okay. Thank you."

Before she knew it, Jennifer was heading back across the road, Angie waving from her own doorstep with one blood-soaked hand.

Back home, Jennifer took a glass from the cupboard above the sink and poured herself some water. She drank it quickly, hoping to stifle the sickening feeling brewing inside her.

And she still didn't know how she was supposed to clean the rug.

It was late, almost midnight. Dexter was sniffing around at the back door, his claws click-clacking on the tiled floor of the kitchen. Jennifer had already walked him, but for some reason, he still wanted to be let out.

"Go on then, boy," said Rob as he opened the back door. Dexter hopped out and immediately went to sniff at the rolled-up rug Rob had put there earlier. Jennifer had spilled tea on it, and now it was ruined. Clearly Dexter didn't think much of it either; he cocked his leg and urinated on it, then disappeared off into the darkness.

Rob closed the door, shutting out the coolness of the night. It had been another warm day, but once again, as the sun went down, the temperature had dropped.

As Rob fixed himself a glass of apple juice, Jennifer joined him in the kitchen. She approached him from behind, wrapping her arms around his waist. Rob turned in her grasp so they were face-to-face. He kissed her forehead. "You okay?" he asked her.

Jennifer smiled, although Rob thought it looked forced. "Yeah." Jennifer sighed. "I just can't get that thought out of my head. I can still picture Angie breaking up those bones, all covered in blood."

Rob nodded. He could only imagine what Angie must've looked like. "It's bizarre. I don't care if homemade bonemeal *is* best, grinding animal bones in your own home is just weird."

Jennifer tiptoed up and kissed Rob on the lips. "Well," she said, "I'm ready for bed. You coming?"

Rob nodded once again. "I'll just get the dog in, then meet you up there."

"Okay. Don't be too long." Jennifer flipped her hair over her shoulder and left the kitchen, heading along the hallway and up the stairs.

Rob opened the back door once again. "Come on, Dex," he called into the darkness. "Come and get a treat."

Normally, at the sound of the word "treat," the dog would come running as if his life depended on it. But not tonight. Tonight, he was a no-show.

"Dexter?"

Rob stepped outside. The sky was thick with clouds blocking out most of the moonlight. "Dexter? What are you doing, boy? Get inside."

Still, the dog refused to reappear.

Rob returned to the kitchen and retrieved the flashlight from the drawer beside the microwave. He then stepped back out into the garden and clicked the flashlight on. The beam of light sliced through the darkness.

"Dex?"

He stepped off the patio onto the lawn. The soft grass felt cool on the soles of his bare feet, the soil compressing and massaging his toes. A few steps forward, Rob spotted something a few feet ahead: a shapeless lump lying on the grass.

Then something moved.

Rob couldn't be sure what it was. In fact, it may well have been nothing. But the grass seemed to undulate and the shrubs that flanked the lawn shifted, their leaves rattling as if something had just pushed its way through.

He quickened his pace, crossing the garden in just a few steps.

Whatever it was, it was gone. But the shape Rob had first seen was still there. He stood over it, his flashlight aimed down.

Suddenly, he wanted to puke.

It was the carcass of some animal, slick with blood. All of the skin had been removed, leaving only the flesh and the bones behind. Some of the bones had been stripped, too, the meat having been peeled away. Those bones that remained were twisted unnaturally, the legs wrenched backward and slung over the rib cage, the skull dragged back along the spine, toward the pelvis. The internal organs had spilled out of the chest cavity and lay in a steaming pile in the middle of the lawn.

That skull—it belonged to a dog.

It belonged to a *small* dog.

It belonged to Dexter.

Rob decided to bury him right then; the last thing he wanted was for Jennifer to see what had happened to him. He knew she'd be devastated when he told her, but he thought it would be for the best. He used a towel to scoop up the remains. He then dug a hole in the back corner of the garden, between two lavender shrubs, and buried Dexter there.

Jennifer *had* been distraught, but when Rob explained how Dexter had died—or at least how he *thought* he had died—and what state the carcass had been in (toning down the gory details as much as possible), she seemed to be somewhat grateful.

The following day, as Rob was about to head out, he bumped into Ed, who was just returning from a trip to the supermarket. He wasn't sure why, but something compelled him to tell Ed what had happened. "Ed," said Rob, waving his hands in an effort to draw his attention. "You got a second?"

"Of course," said Ed. "Anything for you, neighbour. What can I do for you?"

"Erm," mumbled Rob, unsure of how best to start. He decided it would be best just to come out with it. "Our dog . . . he . . . erm . . . he died last night."

"Oh." Ed rubbed the side of his face, clearly caught off guard. "What a shame."

"I think he was attacked by another animal. He was torn to pieces, and his skin was peeled from his body."

"Did you *see* this *other animal?*"

Rob shook his head. "No. But the grass and bushes were moving as if something had just been there. I don't know what it was, but *something* killed my dog."

"I'm sorry. I don't know what that could have been. We have foxes around here. Perhaps that was it."

"Yeah. Maybe."

Ed changed the subject then, seemingly unconcerned about the possibility of some wild animal roaming the neighbourhood. "I heard your better half was asking Angie about lawn care yesterday. Don't forget, strict adherence to the RCs is extremely important. Keeping a healthy lawn should be your top priority."

"Right," said Rob, feeling himself sinking into a stupor. "We'll bear that in mind."

"Yes, I would if I were you. You never know what might happen if you don't."

Rob shook his head, confused as to where this conversation was going. "Sorry, but my dog just died. Taking care of my lawn is pretty much at the bottom of my list of priorities right now."

Ed's face dropped as if his feelings had been hurt. "Well, it really shouldn't be," he said defensively. "The RCs must be—"

"I couldn't give a *fuck* about the RCs!" Rob could feel his blood beginning to boil. Dexter was dead! Was he *really* supposed to give a shit about these supposed *rules*?

"Well, then," said Ed, clearly perturbed, his teeth gritted, "perhaps Lakeview Pines isn't for you." And with that, he strutted into his house, slamming the door closed behind him.

Rob stood in his driveway for nearly half an hour, trying to catch his breath.

It had been a month since they had moved to Lakeview Pines, and during that time Jennifer had been *so* happy. But then she had found Angie crushing bloody lamb bones and Dexter had been killed, both in a single day. The truth was, Jennifer no longer felt safe at home. She felt more anxious with every passing second.

She couldn't tell Rob this, though. He'd spent a small fortune to move them out there. He'd worked so hard. Where would they go? What would they do?

But the more she thought about it, the more she knew she had to say something. Jennifer was just about to speak to Rob when there was a knock at the door.

The couple answered the door together. It was Ed. "Hi there," he said, offering a smile. "Would it be possible for you to join us over at Sandra's place? We're all getting together in the back garden to discuss something *very* important. We think you should be there."

"Who's '*we*'?" said Rob, asking the exact question that had crossed Jennifer's mind also.

"The residents. You two *are* residents now, aren't you?"

"*When* is this happening?" asked Jennifer, stepping out from behind Rob, just in case Ed hadn't realized she was there.

"Right now, actually." Ed was still smiling. He stepped aside, waving his arm to usher them along. "If you don't mind."

Rob looked into Jennifer's waiting eyes. Subconsciously, she was trying to beg him not to agree to this. But there was something reassuring in his eyes. He looked nervous, but he also looked as though he were in control. Jennifer trusted Rob wholeheartedly; whatever he decided to do, she would follow.

Rob nodded reassuringly. Jennifer nodded in return, letting him know that it was okay.

"All right," said Rob, returning his gaze to Ed. "Lead the way."

Ed escorted Jennifer and Rob along the street. Nobody spoke as they went, not even as Ed paused at the bottom of Sandra's driveway and urged them along with one outstretched arm. Terrified—although she didn't quite know why—Jennifer took ahold of Rob's hand and laced her fingers between his.

The side gate was ajar. Rob pushed it open and led Jennifer through. A narrow corridor, pitch-black, ran from the front of the house to the back, brick on one side, thick hedge on the other. And then they were in the rear garden.

At least two dozen people were there, standing on the lawn. Their hands were linked, forming a circle, swaying from side to side. Each of them wore a white robe with the hood pulled up over their heads. They were chanting, their voices low, the words unintelligible. With their faces shrouded in shadow, it was hard to tell who these people were. But Jennifer felt sure that she recognized some of the faces. Sandra was there, of course, as was her husband, Mike. Angie and Frank were there. Norma was there too. Jennifer seemed to recall having seen some of the other faces around Lakeview Pines, although she couldn't place their names.

A sudden and urgent sense of fear slammed through every inch of her body, and her heart began to race at a million beats per minute.

"What the fuck is this?" muttered Rob, almost to himself.

Jennifer wanted to run. She *had* to run. They needed to get the *fuck* out of there. She turned, only to find the path blocked by Ed. He had followed them into the garden, and he, too, was now wearing a robe, just like the others.

The residents turned to look at Jennifer and Rob. They were all smiling, wide-eyed. They looked deranged, almost as if their souls no longer inhabited their bodies.

Jennifer tried to push past Ed, but he stretched his arms out, blocking her path. "Please," he said, "I'd really like you to stay." He then grabbed hold of her arm.

Rob spun on the spot. "Hey!" he yelled. "What the fuck are you doing? Let go of her!" He grabbed Ed by the scruff of his robe and tried to drag him away. But then the other residents were on him, pulling him back into the middle of the lawn.

Jennifer screamed, on the verge of hysteria.

"That's it," said Ed, directing the other residents. "We'll start with him. Get him into position."

Jennifer could only watch as the residents forced Rob down onto his back and dropped their weight onto his outstretched limbs, pinning him to the ground. "No!" screamed Rob, his voice cracked and ragged. "Get off me!"

Ed dragged Jennifer forward. He stood behind her, hooking her arms behind her back with one hand and pointing at Rob with the other. "Watch," he said. "Watch as the goddess consumes."

Jennifer clamped her teeth together with such ferocity that she thought the enamel might crack.

Then she felt the blood drain from her face as the lawn beneath Rob began to shift.

The grass undulated as thousands of stringy roots began to slither out of the soil and wrap themselves around Rob's wrists and ankles. As soon as the roots had taken hold and tied him down, the residents released their grip and stood, heads tipped back, hands raised to the sky in prayer. They were chanting once again.

Rob had been wearing a plain white T-shirt. Where his forearms were bare, Jennifer could see the roots pulling tight against the skin, pressing deep into his flesh. Rob's teeth were clenched, the pain coursing through his body undoubtedly excruciating. Soon, his skin began to split as the roots dug their way in. Blood spilled from the ragged lacerations, splattering the soil beneath, his T-shirt saturated to a dark shade of crimson. Rob screamed as the roots pushed in under his skin and began to claw their way through his body. His mouth wide, the roots slithered in and down his throat, choking him, pushing in past his eyelids, deep into the sockets beyond.

Jennifer sobbed. "Please," she begged. "Don't do this. Make it stop. Please, just make it stop!"

Rob could no longer scream, his larynx clogged with this seemingly sentient plant life. The roots peeled the skin from his muscles, exposing the raw, bloody meat beneath, and dragged his epidermis down into the dirt. But he was still alive. He fought against the organic bindings that held him in place, struggling as his muscles were stripped from the bone. Those roots that had forced their way down his throat pushed out through the abdominal wall, separating his ribs as they writhed between the bones. His eyeballs were plucked from their sockets. His innards were dragged across the lawn, the roots digging into the soft flesh and shredding it like paper.

"Oh my God," moaned Jennifer, unable to look away from the horrifying scene unfolding before her. She pulled her arms free from Ed's grip and dropped to her knees, tears streaming down her face.

Thankfully, Rob was dead now, no longer suffering. Every scrap of meat had been stripped from his carcass. Now he was no more than a skeleton, stringy bits of flesh still clinging to the bones.

Just like the lamb bones that Angie had been grinding. No, thought Jennifer, trying desperately to bring her heaving sobs under control. *They weren't lamb bones. They were* human *bones.*

With Rob's corpse entirely decimated, the roots slithered their way back into the earth and the residents stopped chanting. "I'm sorry," said Ed, crouching beside Jennifer so he could look her in the eye. "We really wanted the both of you to join us. But then you started asking too many questions. You disregarded the RCs, as if they were nothing."

Jennifer turned her head so she and Ed were face-to-face. She sniffed back her tears, her own eyes stinging.

Ed continued, "The Goddess Cōātlīcue *needs* to be fed. She was here long before us, long before these houses were ever built. It is only right that *we* provide for *Her*, just as *She* provides for *us*."

Ed stood. He offered Jennifer a hand and helped her back up to her feet. "Perhaps it's not too late for you," he said. "Perhaps you can still be one of us. You've seen what She can do. Now, we'll grind Rob's remains into bonemeal, which will be enough to satiate Her appetite until the next feeding."

Jennifer swallowed back a ball of phlegm, clearing her throat. She took a deep breath. "A-a-and . . ." she stuttered, "then what happens?"

"Then, we will find another body with which to feed Her. In return, She allows us to prosper. My dearest Norma, she is already one hundred and fifty-six years old. I myself am one hundred and two. With the blessing of Cōātlīcue, we can live forever. Please, we don't want *you* to have to die too. Tell me you will join us. Please, tell me you'll dedicate your life in servitude to the great Goddess Cōātlīcue."

Jennifer couldn't quite wrap her head around what she was hearing. She looked to Norma, the woman Ed had just claimed was more than one hundred and fifty years old. She didn't look a day over seventy. Norma smiled. All the residents were smiling. It crossed Jennifer's mind that perhaps they were all insane. But then, she had seen the earth come alive and consume Rob with her very own eyes. That *had* happened.

Or perhaps it hadn't. Perhaps *she* was insane too.

She didn't know what it was, but a sense of belonging suddenly filled her entire being. She wanted to be there. She wanted to live forever. She looked into Ed's eyes and nodded.

Ed smiled. He directed Jennifer toward the others, who gathered around her. They hugged her and kissed her cheeks, welcoming her, making her feel as though she truly were one of them.

Ed draped a white robe over her shoulders. Smiling, Jennifer pulled the hood up over her head. Ed then took her left hand while Norma took her right. They stood in a circle on the lawn and began to chant as the tendrils of whatever creature this was that dwelled below the earth slithered out once again, and once again began to devour the remaining scraps of meat that clung precariously to Rob's carcass.

"All hail Cōātlīcue!"

...

Harrison Phillips sits down and cradles his find. Otis Bateman, who sits next to him, gets up and shows us a sneering grin. One that sends shivers down our spines. He stands as close to the edge of our roaring fire as he can get. I can hear his eyebrows singeing.

He shows his scrap briefly before eating it.
It's a cockroach . . .

Regurgitating Menstrual Seepage at The Spittoon Saloon

Otis Bateman

The final vestiges of sunlight were dwindling quickly as Rufus and Ezekiel made their way to the Spittoon Saloon on two worthless, busted-ass mares that their boss had thankfully allowed them to borrow for the night. Both fellers had a bad case of cabin fever and were ready to burst at the seams! The two young men were cattle herders. They'd spent the better part of a month ensuring the expansive lot of cows weren't endangered or stolen by no-good, thieving cattle rustlers. They loved being cowboys with all their hearts, but the work could be tedious and lonesome. The two of them had become quick friends. It was hard not to feel close when their job required them to depend on each other.

Rufus and Ezekiel had quickly gotten sick of canned beans—which was all they would eat if they didn't have any luck hunting or fishing. Every night, both men would blast noxious farts around the campfire, giggle like schoolchildren, and sing, "Beans, beans, the magical fruit, the more you eat, the more you toot!" The joke quickly wore off after about a week. It had become apparent neither man was the best hunter or angler. The dadgum beans became their main source of sustenance, which quickly put a damper on their spirits.

The other dilemma was the lack of pussy.

Both men were young and virile, so it didn't take long for the fellas to whack their weasels in their respective sleeping bags after it was time for shut-eye. The luster of bopping the bologna lasted a few days before the young men began lusting for some genuine, honest-to-goodness female company. Eventually, that was all the two friends thought or talked about. If it wasn't cattle herding or trying to secure some actual protein to eat, it was coochie.

Rufus and Ezekiel were low men on the totem pole, so their time off was dead last. The lascivious lads heavily discussed going to a whorehouse the first chance that was presented to them. They had seriously considered fucking one of the cows if they were forced to go on much longer! They had decided to fornicate with one they had selected, named Bessie, the next night, but their boss had finally approved their time off. Pussy was now within their grasp! Their dicks and spirits bulged in excitement!

The cowboys were now nearing the saloon. As their languid mares neighed in complete exhaustion, it was obvious the old bitches needed to be put out to pasture for good. Still, the beasts had gotten them to their destination, so the boys were eternally grateful for the haggard horses.

"I'm so excited to get my dick wet tonight! Yee-haw!" Rufus crowed.

"I hope they have some ginger quim for me to bust a nut in; you know how I love redheads!" Ezekiel spat.

"I heard they got every flavor of cunt you could ever dream of," Rufus said.

"Sheeeiiittt! You are going to make all the blood go straight to my pecker and stay there!" Ezekiel laughed.

Both men chuckled heartily as they arrived at the hitching post in front of the establishment. They looked up at the newly painted sign for the Spittoon Saloon. Some truly artistic bastards had drawn two clinking beer mugs and a set of fat titties that could choke a horse!

"Looks like we have died and gone to Heaven, Ezekiel. Two of our favorite things in one place!" Rufus remarked.

"Yessir, tonight is going to be the best night ever!" Ezekiel said.

They dismounted their exhausted horses, cinched them to the pole, and walked through the batwing doors into the saloon. A smattering of drinking and poker-playing customers casually looked up at the young men before going back to their activities. The bartender gave the newcomers a perfunctory glance before furiously polishing an array of shot glasses with a filthy rag. Without looking up again, the barkeep cleared his phlegmy throat loudly, startling the two young men.

"What'll it be, boys?" the barkeep barked.

"We— Uh . . . Well, sir, we're lookin' to partake in the company of a painted lady tonight, sir," Rufus said.

The bartender looked up keenly, now interested in the two drab men. He beamed broadly, revealing a smile on par with a jack-o'-lantern.

"Well, why didn't you say so sooner, boys? Take a seat and have a drink. I've got the best beer around! Plus, I have an icehouse down in the basement here. Coolest drinks for miles! This here ain't no flophouse, no siree. I've got premium amenities to go with my premium pussy, fellers!"

Rufus and Ezekiel were flabbergasted. They had never been to such a fancy place! They felt like a couple of high rollers in hog heaven.

"Great, sir! We'd love to take a gander at your sexy ladies!" Rufus said.

"Yeah, I hope you got a redhead!" Ezekiel gushed.

"Boys, we got every pussy under the rainbow! I'll call all my ladies down . . . the minute you show me you can pay for their company, of course."

"Great! We just got *paid*, so it's time to get *laid*! How much for two gals of our choice?" Rufus asked.

"Well, I got the cleanest ladies for as far as the eyes can see. Clean as a whistle! No clappy bitches in my roster, boys. So, rest assured, your waterworks will remain in tip-top shape! The price is steep, but you'll never have a piece of pussy this incredible ever again, unless, of course, you come back to my establishment!"

The young men felt their mouths dry with chalky doubt. A steep price? The last whorehouse they'd visited had charged five bucks a gal.

"What do your gals cost, sir?" Rufus asked.

"Don't call me sir, boy. The name's John. I work for a livin'!"

"How much is your whores, John?" Ezekiel inquired.

"For the paltry sum of fifty dollars per gal, you can both have the night of your young lives!" John said.

Rufus and Ezekiel immediately stared at one another in misery. They had nowhere near a hundred bucks. Shit, they didn't have more than thirty between them both. It felt like their dreams had immediately been dashed against a boulder. They both wanted to cry, but it wouldn't behoove them to start wailing like a couple of little girls with skinned knees. Rufus wondered if he could talk the barkeep down at all. It was worth a shot! Otherwise, he and Ezekiel would be sticking their stingers in Bessie later, and if a calf could easily slide out of her cunt, then the feeling wouldn't do too much for their five-inch cocks.

Sir, we've only got around thirty between the both of us." Rufus lamented.

John's face went from jovial to stern in an instant.

"Why the fuck are you wastin' my time jawflappin' then? Only an idiot doesn't know my prices. You want pauper pussy? Go three towns over. You'll probably get syphilis from those beat-ass whores, though. Now, you can drink here till your money runs out but don't even *think* 'bout tryin' to lower my pussy prices because it ain't happenin', boys!"

"C'mon, mister! There ain't nuthin' you can do? Me and my friend here have been without the company of a woman for months! We are fixin' to fill our britches with semen snot! We would do anything for a piece of ass!" Rufus pleaded.

The bartender stared at the two cringey cowboys and thought long and hard about what he was going to say next. He knew exactly what she would say to him for hesitating right now. He also knew the repercussions would be severe. There was only one viable option for John.

"Well, young fellers, you are in luck. My most beautiful whore, Aphrodite, is having a contest tonight. And to the victor go the spoils, which would be her delectable pussy for free!"

Rufus and Ezekiel immediately perked up and stared at the bartender in absorbed attention.

"Hot damn, John! What does Aphrodite look like, and what do we need to do?" Rufus asked.

"She is one of the most beautiful creatures on the planet, boys. Blonde hair, blue eyes, tall and slender with a bronze complexion! A blonde thatch of pubic hair to boot! A real blonde, yessir!"

"Wow, she sounds heavenly!" Ezekiel said.

"Don't it now?" John affirmed.

He smiled sourly in response to the boy's statement and spat into a nearby spittoon.

"What's the contest you were talking about?" Rufus asked.

"Well, fellers, my Aphrodite doesn't like to give her bewitching cunt to just anyone off the street. But from time to time, when the mood strikes her, she has been known to host a contest called *The Gauntlet*. Our beautiful Aphrodite is sexually wanton and likes men who aren't afraid to get a little—how should I put this—kinky, I suppose you'd say. If you do as she says and accomplish all the sexual tasks she requests of you, then you get her pussy as the grand prize, boys!"

Both young men stared at the liquor merchant, dumbfounded. Ezekiel had a head jam-packed full of cow manure, but even he knew this was too good to be true!

"What's the catch? Does she got a rotten snatch?" Ezekiel asked.

"Yeah, and how kinky we talkin'?" Rufus wondered.

"I can't tell you how kinky because I jus' don't know. All I do know is the men who did accomplish her tasks said it was the best goddamned pussy they had ever had! Said her pussy was so tight and wet that it milked their peckers dry, it did!"

The two weary travelers lit up with monumental mirth. They both were so horny they couldn't stand it! They'd fuck a beehive right about now if they could!

They quickly turned to each other and began whispering in a huddled stance like they were planning a bank robbery. After a few beats, they turned back to John, ever so anxious.

"We'll do it!" both said in unison.

John shot them a lecherous grin and rubbed his hands together.

"Excellent, boys! Truly excellent! Aphrodite's room is upstairs. It will be the last room on the left. Knock four times—that way she knows you both are going to run The Gauntlet—and wait for a response. Best of luck to you, young fellers!"

"Yeehaw!" Rufus crowed.

"Can't wait to see this beauty! Never seen a blonde snatch before!" Ezekiel brayed.

"Well, what are you still doing down here, pardners? Times a wastin'! Get on up there and get your dicks wet already!" John spat.

"YES, SIR!" Rufus and Ezekiel said in unison.

The young men began happily climbing the staircase.

John shot a knowing glance at the other customers who sat in the saloon. They all smiled at the ramifications of the two young cattle herders' decision.

Their fate was sealed.

"It has begun," John intoned.

When Rufus and Ezekiel arrived at Aphrodite's door, they both felt an overwhelming wave of nervousness. Both were filled with trepidation regarding the kink factor. If truth be told, neither youngster was all that well-versed in the act of lovemaking. They both had had sex with prostitutes, of course, but the sex act was extremely short-lived and vanilla. Neither knew much about being kinky; just stickin' their peckers in a wet hole and fillin' it up with cock cream was good enough for them!

"I'm nervous, Rufus!"

"Me, too, friend. I reckon we're going to learn a lot tonight!" Rufus gulped.

"Yessir! It's going to be a night we will never forget, I betcha!" Ezekiel agreed.

"I'm gonna knock now," Rufus said.

"Okay!"

Rufus's hand nervously knocked four times on the thick, ornate wooden door and waited for a response. After a minute, a muffled but alluring voice intoned from behind the door seductively.

"Come on in, boys!" Aphrodite said.

Rufus grabbed ahold of the knob and slowly opened the door. It made an eerie, screeching sound like the hinges were in desperate need of oiling. As soon as Rufus and Ezekiel saw Aphrodite, any unease quickly evaporated. She was stunning, but not like a typical gorgeous woman, she was exotic. She was more than that. She was like a work of art. Rufus, and especially Ezekiel, didn't have the vocabulary to describe it. There were simply no words for her. She sat on her king-sized bed in a see-through white negligee that revealed her amazingly perfect breasts and her blonde thatch of pubic curls. Aphrodite tittered as she visibly watched their arousal pump ample supplies of blood to their stiffening rods. Rufus had never felt so strongly for a woman before. She exuded a raw sexuality that almost surpassed her remarkable beauty. It felt like a carnal fog was billowing in the room that had enveloped both youths. They could only fixate on the act of fornication with the exceptional woman.

"Nice to meet you, fellers! The name is Aphrodite!"

"I'm Rufus!"

"I'm Ezekiel!"

"Pleased as punch to meet you both! I reckon if you did the *secret* knock, then that means you boys want to try and run The Gauntlet to get a free taste of my delectable, blonde pussy."

She deftly got up from her bed and was next to the boys before they even knew it. She dipped her fingers into her glistening honey pot, brought her gleaming fingers up, and placed them in Rufus's mouth first, then Ezekiel's. She assessed them as their faces lit up in erogenous pleasure. It was superior to any drug or drink they had imbibed.

"That's about the best thing I ever tasted!" Rufus squealed.

"Nectar of the gods!" Ezekiel agreed.

"Sugar, you don't know how right you are!" Aphrodite winked.

Both men were now sure they would do anything to get with this glorious goddess. They were ready to tackle The Gauntlet. How bad could it be, after all?

"All right, boys, here's how The Gauntlet works. I have four increasingly peculiar fetishes you have to complete in order to win the prize, which is my pretty little pussy!"

Just the mere mention of her delicious cunt caused Rufus and Ezekiel to slobber uncontrollably in delirious desire.

"To get the prize you must complete every task, no half-assing is allowed! You tap out and yer done, buster! No poontang for a loser is what I say! My creamy cunny only goes to the iron-willed! I mean, who doesn't want a slice of this here cherry pie?"

To prove her point, Aphrodite pinned her legs behind the back of her head like an expert contortionist, so her lovely pussy was on full display. Using her exercise-enhanced pelvic muscles, she clenched her clam like a powerful fist, relaxing and flexing her talented twat repeatedly.

REGURGITATING MENSTRUAL SEEPAGE... 235

"My little pussy will milk those juicy peckers of yours till they are bone dry of dong juice and you're begging me to stop!" Aphrodite teased.

"We'd do anything for a crack at your snatch, ma'am!" Rufus exclaimed.

"Yessum, we want to snack on your slit somethin' fierce! We can do The Gauntlet! We won't let you down!" Ezekiel added.

"Talk is cheap. Put your money where your mouth is. And speaking of mouths, my first kink for The Gauntlet is called snowballing!"

Rufus and Ezekiel looked at one another and shrugged. They had no idea what that meant. It sounded pleasant!

"Well, there *ain't* no snow out, Miss Aphrodite. That might be a tough one!" Ezekiel said.

"Oh no, silly! It's got nothing to do with snow. You see, boys, snowballing is a sexual game! After someone has had sperm ejaculated into their mouth, they hold it in rather than spitting or swallowing, then French-kiss their partner and exchange the spunk between one another via the mouth. Rufus, I'll start with you." Aphrodite said.

Rufus tried to wrap his head around this sex act. He wasn't so keen on having a mouthful of cum sloshing around in there, but he supposed it would be all right since it was his.

"I reckon that don't sound too bad," Rufus admitted.

"Great! Then let's get this show on the road! You have no idea how much I hunger for the both of you!" Aphrodite snarled.

Instantaneously, she was on her knees jerking down Rufus's faded, stain-speckled Wranglers with determined ferocity. She freed his imprisoned cock from the tight restriction of his pants. Rufus's dick sprung to attention against Aphrodite's pursed lips. Like the expert cocksmith she was touted to be, she devoured his dong like a gulping catfish, inhaling his penis deep within her mouth and down her esophagus.

She began to suck his schlong with authority, slobbering his knob with her sloppy slurping. And just like that, he could feel the need to shoot his load at once. He had never had to cum so quickly in his life. Rufus was mildly embarrassed that he could hardly last, but he reminded himself that she was a pro. Just then, he was rocketed by one of the most intense orgasms of his life. He shot thick ropes of hot, tacky semen against her uvula like the blast from a shotgun. Rope after rope of his baby butter barfed from his balls and filled Aphrodite's mouth to the brim with jizz. She arose from her feet, grabbed Rufus's face, and planted a hellacious French kiss on the young man, emptying her cum-filled mouth into his vacant maw. The consistency of the splooge was akin to room-temperature mucus or slime from a slug's trail.

It was truly gag-inducing, but Rufus knew he needed to not upchuck, or The Gauntlet would be over as soon as it had begun. So, he tried to cast out the thought of what he was housing in his mouth even though the sloshing gruel was puffing his cheeks out plumper than a squirrel foraging nuts. Aphrodite moseyed up to Ezekiel and took his skin sword into her warm, inviting mouth. It took even less time for Ezekiel to blast off into her vacuuming, proficient kisser. Once again, she repeated the process by depositing Ezekiel's man mayonnaise into his reluctant gob. Ezekiel was barely able to hold onto his composure, gagging repeatedly from the egg yolk consistency of the lukewarm cum jutting out his cheeks. Aphrodite stared at the young men approvingly before speaking again.

"Very good, fellas! Now here comes the kicker! I want you to French-kiss one another and swap semen between you both. After you have done so, swallow that seminal spunk and that's kink one completed!"

The men looked worriedly at one another as her ask sunk into their brains. This just went from grotesque to appalling. It was one thing to have their own semen in their respective mouths, but each other's. Things were beginning to feel pretty damned rotten in Denmark. But in the end, their horniness won out. They felt under a spell for that magnificent snatch of hers. Both men thought they might kill their own mothers to obtain access to Aphrodite's orifice. Shrugging at one another, they both placed their mouths together, allowing the slimy, congealing concoction to pass between the two of them. By now the consistency had become thick and gritty, mimicking spoiled tapioca pudding left out in the sun to spoil and fester. Rufus's gag reflex strongly advised him to evacuate this filth, but his brain persevered in the end, and he kept from regurgitating all over Aphrodite's bedroom floor. Ezekiel had even less of a cast-iron stomach than his counterpart but somehow managed to keep his rising gorge at bay. Aphrodite smiled wickedly at the green-gilled cowpokes, relishing the sickness she was causing them.

"Fantastic! Swallow it all and let's get on to challenge number two!"

Rufus and Ezekiel stared at one another in dismay, a steady stream of tears poured from their wincing eyes at the depravity they had just endured.

If this was challenge one, how much worse could it get? Rufus thought dismally.

Both cowhands shut off their brains for a moment and swallowed the gelatinous gunk. They felt the goo spread down their esophagus as it slowly chugged south into the pit of their stomachs. In unison, both boys' stomachs gurgled in a sick form of protest from the penile protein shake they had ingested. Aphrodite smiled perversely, taking pleasure from their debasement and desperation.

"Okay, fellas, on to challenge number two, where the stakes get *higher* to obtain the prize you both *desire*, which—lemme remind ya—is this tasty twat!"

She spread her glistening labia seductively. Her thumb played with her clit, eliciting a guttural moan from her pursed lips." Both men stared at the beautiful pink bud that bloomed in color right before their eyes, and both abruptly forgot all about sucking down one another's sickening semen for the time being.

"We're ready, Miss Aphrodite. We will do whatever it takes to win The Gauntlet!" Rufus exclaimed.

"We're in it to win it!" Ezekiel agreed.

"Wonderful news! I knew you both were special the moment I set my sights on you! Next up is a personal favorite of mine: menophilia!"

Both men looked at each other cluelessly before setting their gazes back on Aphrodite.

"What's that?" Rufus asked.

"That, my horny young friends, is the fetish for blood, specifically . . . period blood!"

"Period blood?!" Both men yelled in unison.

"You heard me right, boys! I am going to fill this spittoon on the ground with my menstruation and then you'll drink half, and your nitwit chum will guzzle the rest. Easy-peasy!"

Rufus took a long, hard look at the rusted, archaic spittoon and saw that it was partially filled with ancient chewing tobacco and old cigarette butts. He visibly retched in response to the grim sight.

"But, Miss Aphrodite, it's jam-packed with chaw spit and old cigarettes already. Can't we dump that out first?"

"Nope. My rules, sonny. Sorry. Now you can forfeit if you'd like, or you can man the fuck up and keep your eyes on the prize!"

To hammer her point home, she brought her steaming cunt right over to Rufus and forcefully placed his hand against her frothing box. Rufus couldn't believe how warm and inviting it felt. He *had* to have his dick buried to the hilt in that love canal of hers!

"I *ain't* no quitter!" Rufus announced.

"What about you, dummy? You a quitter?" Aphrodite asked.

"Only thing I ever quit was school!" Ezekiel said proudly.

Aphrodite smiled at the simpleton's response. This was going better than she ever could have dreamed of.

She quickly removed her negligee, allowing an unobstructed view of her pendulous breasts and shapely rump. The sight of her heavenly curves caused both boys to whistle appreciatively. Aphrodite assumed the position at the end of the bed, wrapping her taut, shapely legs behind her head, exposing her unparalleled cunt to the full view of the bedeviled boys. With one bloodred lacquered fingernail, she beckoned Rufus to bring the spittoon and place it beneath her taint to catch her crimson flow.

"Assume the position and prepare for challenge number two, Rufus, my sweet."

Like an enchanted patient, he quickly knelt below her orifice and prepared for the next part of The Gauntlet. He had seen a girl on the rag before and it didn't seem to account for too much blood, in his humble opinion. Rufus was sure this challenge would be a cakewalk. It would be gross, for sure, because of the other ingredients in the spittoon. Rufus's face blanched in shock when Aphrodite's plump pussy first started gurgling in distress and then began to blast a massive gush of period blood into the receptacle. Blood, almost black in hue, garnished with massive clots, channeled from her ruby-tinted cunt hole. Rufus stared in discomfort as the coppery smell assaulted his nostrils, and still, the blood poured out of her axe wound like an obliterating shotgun blast to the gut. Finally, the last remnants of her menstrual flow pissed out of her pussy hole until only a trickle of scarlet liquid remained streaming out, almost surpassing the brim of the dented spittoon. Aphrodite squealed like a pig as one last thunderous orgasm rocked her frame, causing one more gelatinous burst of pussy blood from her crimson cooch that landed directly in Rufus's left eye.

"UGH! It fuckin' burns! Shit fire and save the matches!" Rufus moaned.

"DANG! I never seen so much blood in my life. I think I'm traumatized!" Ezekiel spat.

Rufus grabbed a sheet off of Aphrodite's bed and began furiously wiping the fabric against his inflamed eye. She watched them like one would watch a comedic stage show and couldn't get over how dumb both young men were. But they were also stubborn and horny, which was a good thing. Aphrodite wondered how far these two assholes would make it in The Gauntlet.

"Okay. Since Rufus went first last time, it is only fair that you get the first crack at my syrupy, menstrual seepage surprise, Ezekiel! Share and share alike!

"I reckon that's fair, Miss Aphrodite," Ezekiel agreed.

He picked up the heavy spittoon and cringed at the congealing blood as it sloshed languidly in the brass cup. A lone cockroach used a partially smoked cigarette as a flotation device so it wouldn't drown in the vaginal cruor.

"There's a dadgum roach in there!" Ezekiel said.

Then you had best make sure and eat it too. Everything inside that spittoon counts. It all needs to be gone, no exceptions, or you forfeit your chance to fornicate with me *and* I'll have you both kicked out of here . . . but not before you get your asses whooped by those tough customers down in the saloon, you hear me?"

"Yessum!" Ezekiel sobbed.

Rufus could only watch in abject horror as Ezekiel slowly brought the caustic concoction to his trembling lips. He was about to start drinking the abhorrent brew when Aphrodite decided to throw a wrench into things.

"Now, Rufus, if Ezekiel throws up, the vomit will be added to your turn. Do you understand?"

Rufus's eyes grew to the size of saucer plates. He felt his dander rise at this. It just didn't seem fair to him.

"What if I refuse?"

"Then it's the end of the line for both of you and you can get right the fuck out of here! I was getting all hot and bothered thinking I had two guys with an actual chance of winning this thing. And I would fuck you both till your dicks fell off . . . but if you're going to be a coward, then it's probably just best to skedaddle now and quit wastin' my precious damn time."

Rufus thought long and hard about it and chose his words extremely carefully before he spoke. He had to be with her. He felt like he was bewitched and spellbound by her. Rufus would rather cornhole Jesse James himself than give up this chance to fuck this blonde goddess. Nothing was going to dissuade him tonight. He'd drown his pa in a bucket of piss to be with Aphrodite!

"I ain't quitting. I'll do whatever it takes to be with you!"

"You just made my pussy squirt for you, Rufus, my sweet!" Aphrodite chirped.

He beamed in obvious pride as his cock swelled in his pants and dribbled a dollop of pre-cum out of his piss slit from her amorous response.

Yes, this was happening tonight!

"Ezekiel, drink as much as you can, and I'll handle the rest! We are getting laid tonight, even if it's over our dead bodies!"

Ezekiel gave his cohort a strained, pale gaze before looking at the spittoon of doom. He could feel his gorge rise at once. He thought he would try and block the mental image of what he was about to do and think of pleasant things he liked to drink to hopefully trick his mind and taste buds.

"Here goes nuthin'!"

Ezekiel tipped the mammoth spit jar and began to ingest the foul liquid. The blood had cooled significantly and begun to coagulate, mimicking the consistency of a thick milkshake as it slowly oozed down his gullet like a slime trail from an oversized slug. Ezekiel felt the cockroach cling to his uvula with a hooked limb. It was struck by a wave of chunky pussy clots, causing the critter to tumble down into Ezekiel's belly.

There were so many clots, in fact, that Ezekiel had to chew them up as quickly as possible and swallow them in order not to choke to death on the cornucopia of chunks. They reminded him of giant ticks popping tiny geysers of blood as he gnawed them apart with his incisors. Their consistency reminded him of canned beets that his mother used to make him eat as a little boy. He would not be permitted to leave the table until he ate every single one.

The coppery taste of blood permeated his mouth, and a bevy of pubic hairs became lodged between his teeth, tickling his throat in the process. Ezekiel let loose a mammoth belch, causing a resurrection of some partially devoured clots from his gurgling, undulating belly. He promised Rufus he wouldn't barf, but by throwing up in his mouth just that tiny bit, it set into motion something that could not be staved off. A gallon of blood, bile, partially ingested clots, and that afternoon's lunch ejaculated from Ezekiel's stomach and then back into the partially empty spittoon until the cup had runneth over with a profuse amount of reeking vomitus. He took one look at Rufus's pained face. Ezekiel felt so terrible for his friend. Aphrodite had warned them that if someone threw up, the other participant would have to eat it as well! Ezekiel was flummoxed by how his buddy was going to accomplish this entirely heinous task. He wished they had just remained at the ranch and fucked a sow or a young ewe. He had been told by some of the older cowhands that lamb pussy was the closest thing to a woman's snatch you could get when whores were sparse. Anything would be preferable to this house of sexual perversions.

"I'm so sorry, pardner. I didn't mean to spew chunks," Ezekiel moaned.

"I know you didn't mean to, but you fucked me nonetheless, dickhead!" Rufus raged.

Aphrodite slunk over to Rufus and massaged his chest seductively before groping his rump affectionately.

"You got this, cowboy. Just keep your eyes on the prize, okay?"

To hammer the point home, she bit his lower lip playfully before sashaying away temptingly. Rufus's eyes felt like they were affixed to her ample curves. With a deep breath, he steeled his jangled nerves and placed the spittoon to his lips. Not only did it reek of thickened coppery menstrual blood, but now it stunk of partially consumed bacon, sausage, and eggs mixed with bile and coffee. Add to that stale tobacco leaves and you have a repugnant concoction. But his mind was made up. He cast away the thoughts from his mind and began chugging the gloopy gruel. He kept repeating a mental mantra as the puke and blood brew surged down his esophagus and into his churning, reproachful stomach. He said it over and over in his mind as he battled his mounting gorge.

Aphrodite will be mine. Aphrodite will be mine. Aphrodite will be mine.

The mantra was working as Rufus slowly but surely chugged the plasma-puke drink. For the first time tonight, Rufus was certain he'd be balls deep in Aphrodite's quim by the dawn's early light. With one final gargantuan gulp, he downed the last remnants of the beverage and turned the spittoon over, showing everyone that it was now bone dry.

"Challenge completed!" Rufus brayed.

"That's my sexy cowboy! I knew you wouldn't let me down like your dim-witted pal," Aphrodite sneered.

Ezekiel dropped his head in shame. He had let two people down and was feeling like a loser. Aphrodite glared at the nitwit harshly before turning her full attention to Rufus with a wry smile, then glided up beside him and began to whisper in his ear, "You know, if it was me, I think I would try and eliminate your pal from the competition. I mean, he has been *nothing* but a dead weight throughout The Gauntlet. Do you really want him to get a piece of my hair-pie for basically doing nothing more than making you eat his vomit? I sure wouldn't want to be the one to partake of Ezekiel's sloppy seconds!"

The mere idea of maybe having to go after his friend, even after Rufus had done all the hard parts of the challenge, was a sobering proposal. Aphrodite was right, it didn't seem fair that Ezekiel would get the same reward as Rufus. He never thought about killin' a feller before, let alone his best friend, but the gal had a way of implanting her will into a feller's noggin.

"Don't seem right!" Rufus squawked. "Don't seem right at all!"

"No, it doesn't, sugar! I'll tell you what, since you had to scarf up a bunch of barf as well as my putrid pussy plasma, I have decided to cut you a break and bypass challenge three and fast-track you to the final section of The Gauntlet. If you can't tell, I want you to win! I could just eat you right up! But I will hold off till the end. Rest assured, I believe in you, baby!"

Rufus's chest puffed in pride from her multiple platitudes. He felt like a hog wallowing in slop, and nothing could bring him down. At least, that's what he thought for the time being.

"All right, boys, it's time for the final challenge in The Gauntlet. You're in the home stretch but this

REGURGITATING MENSTRUAL SEEPAGE... 249

one is a doozy. Let me ask you both something. Have you ever heard of the term munging before?"

Both youths looked at Aphrodite blankly before shaking their heads in unison.

"Well, let me tell you, it isn't a walk in the park, fellas, it's a walk into the graveyard! The three of us are going to hike to the local cemetery and dig up a freshly buried corpse. Don't worry about having to pick it yourselves because I've already done that part for you. A week ago, one of the whores here, Jezebel, died from some crazed cowboy slittin' her throat after repeatedly raping her with his fist. I saw her battered, bruised body afterward and believe me when I say she was ghastly to behold. He had even cut off her tiny titties and stuffed them deep inside her neck slit to add insult to injury! He cut them into manageable strips and carefully pushed them through her ragged, gaping wound.

Both Rufus and Ezekiel physically blanched from Aphrodite's uncensored play-by-play of the prostitute's ugly, violent death. Rufus thought he caught a wistful twinkle in Aphrodite's eyes as she relayed the graphic, gory details to the two of them.

"Anyway, where was I? Oh yes, munging and what it means! The three of us will go to the gravesite of poor, dead Jezebel and dig her body out of her pauper's grave. After we have her rotting corpse on the ground and ready to defile, one of you will place your mouth over her pussy and anus while the other climbs atop the tombstone, howls like a rabid wolf, and performs a devastating elbow drop onto Jezebel's bloated, corpse-gas-filled stomach. Which forces out a rich, fetid blend of gangrenous body fluids and any kind of critters that had made their home inside her cadaver, shooting it directly into the other person's waiting mouth and face. The malodorous blend is called mung. The act of getting this mixture on your face and in your mouth is called *munging*. Nothing turns me on more than this, let me tell you!"

"Well, I sure as fuck ain't getting that rancid junk blasted all onto my face!" Ezekiel cringed.

Rufus thought back to what Aphrodite had told him about his friend's lackluster performance tonight. Why would he get to reap the benefits of all Rufus's hard work? He had been carried by Rufus throughout most of The Gauntlet. How is it fair that he gets a piece of her delectable pie? A black, poisonous cloud of hate continued to take residence around Rufus.

"I'll do it, chicken shit. Think you can manage to at least elbow-drop the dead bitch?" Rufus spat.

Ezekiel gulped in shame and nodded profusely. He knew his friend was getting exasperated with him, but Ezekiel didn't sign up for this kind of freakshow fucking! He would have rather just gone out into the fields and cornholed himself a cow than endure any more of these filthy fetishes. He was at a loss how someone as beautiful as Aphrodite would be so enamored by all this vulgarity. But Rufus was his best friend, and he was trying to help the best he could.

Aphrodite loved seeing the seeds of hate she had planted in Rufus's mind begin to slowly take hold in the simpleton's pea brain. She loved it when a well-made plan came together!

"All right, fellas, let's git along, little dogies and get to the cemetery. We got some munging to do!"

The walk to the boneyard was uneventful. Everyone was lost in their own thoughts as they trekked through the moonlit night. Aphrodite led the way by the light of her lantern. Rufus watched her supple rump undulate as the two shovels softly clanged together in the pack on his back. He couldn't wait to tongue her shit box and make her squeal like a pig! Besides his perverse, never-ending fantasies for the blonde goddess, a sinister vision began to gain traction in his mind. He didn't want Ezekiel to get a piece of the action. He didn't deserve it one bit! He had been goldbricking the entire time they played The Gauntlet. And he made Rufus have to eat his damned puke to boot!

Yessir, he doesn't deserve to touch her, Rufus thought darkly.

Rufus's stomach churned violently as his mind pictured how this would play out. He was a simple-minded feller, but he knew it would be gross! A week in the grave in this kind of heat? She was going to be mighty ripe! Shit, he could barely handle it when they had to dispose of dead cattle, so he wasn't sure how he was going to make it through the final leg of this gross game.

Rufus looked up and halted immediately, almost crashing into Aphrodite because he was lost in the thought of ravaging her beautiful body and hadn't noticed that they must have found the grave of the murdered whore. He unslung the two shovels they had grabbed before leaving the saloon and curtly handed one to Ezekiel.

"Here, make yourself useful and help me with unburying this dead tramp!" Rufus spat. "It's the least you can do!"

Ezekiel meekly took the rusty shovel and began to unearth the loose soil from underneath Jezebel's tombstone.

Aphrodite listened in rapt fascination to Rufus's brusque orders to his friend. It always amazed her how easy it was to mold a man's mind to her will. Just shake your ample cleavage at a man and suddenly the little head takes charge over the big head. She had effortlessly driven a wedge between the two friends with barely any effort on her part. She was curious how this new aspect of the game would play out for her.

The two cowboys dug in silence until the sound of the spades striking the coffin broke the quiet. They scraped off the remnants of dirt and slowly opened the creaking lid. Neither man was prepared for the putrid stench that wafted up and assaulted their nostrils. The smell was awful, but the sight of Jezebel was worse. Her bloated corpse was littered with heinous wounds from the maniac who raped and killed her. Brownish, watery fluid dribbled from countless atrocities littered across her lithe, prone form.

A large gash on her forehead exposed the gleaming white of her skull underneath her unzipped flesh. A writhing sea of larvae made her a literal maggot girl!

The grubs blanketed her carcass, feeding off the abundant, pestilent rot. Her skin had taken on a greenish hue and looked like it was sweating. Her face was bloated, and her sightless eyes had begun to pop out of her mangled skull. Her roach-coated tongue hung out of her mouth like a spent phallus. A centipede skittered out of her nostril, then quickly absconded into her ear canal. Ezekiel began to retch uncontrollably from the fetid stench of the corpse gas billowing up into his nauseated face.

"So help me God, if you throw up again I will fucking kill you!" Rufus raged.

"I can't help it. I ain't never smelt somethin' so foul!" Ezekiel whimpered.

"We are burning daylight, boys! Put the lid back on that stinky whore and get that coffin up here so we can finish The Gauntlet!" Aphrodite commanded.

The two men did as she ordered and began the arduous task of hefting the seeping casket out of the yawning grave. After a tumultuous time, both cowpokes tiredly plopped the coffin on the ground beside Jezebel's cheap gravestone.

"Fantastic, fellas! Get that rotten wretch outta that cheap pine box so we can get this show on the road. My pussy is getting all creamy in anticipation!"

To drive her point home, she spread her luscious labia apart and exposed the glistening fluids cascading down her shapely, muscular thighs. She dipped her pointer finger into her frothing honey pot and stuck her cum-covered digit out for Rufus to suck on, which he did with great gusto. He wished he could coat her copious cum onto everything from now on. It tasted finer than maple syrup!

Rufus felt like he was falling in love with this beauty. He had never felt this way before. She had a bewitching power over him. He felt beguiled by her charms and appearance. If she wasn't such a looker, he'd swear she was some kind of witch or somethin'!

Rufus felt energized from ingesting her vaginal fluids. He was ready to kill this task. And then he'd be ready to kill his pathetic pardner, Ezekiel!"

"C'mon, let's get this slaughtered slut out of her coffin and knock this munging business out," Rufus said.

Both men reached into the pauper's coffin and began to try and remove the disintegrating corpse. The minute they attempted to heft her out, their hands immediately began sinking into her malleable flesh almost at once. Rufus felt his fingers submerge into her rotting tissue. A bevy of gore-caked cockroaches emerged from the newly made cavity he had just created, and they quickly skittered down into the dark confines of the ground. Ezekiel had a similar experience—but with maggots—when he went to grab her legs. Her tenuous flesh crumbled apart in his hands, coating him in her putrid, rancid rot. Fat earthworms slithered languidly in the putrefying, decomposing pool of muck.

"I don't think I can do this!" Ezekiel wailed.

"If you fuck this up for me, you will be as dead as this moldering twat right here!" Rufus warned.

"You both are so close, don't give up now!" Aphrodite begged.

Rufus dutifully nodded, went back to the corpse, and stared at her for a moment. There had to be a smarter way to get her out of the box in one piece.

Then it hit him like a ton of bricks. They could just tip the coffin over gently and pour her onto the ground. He relayed the newly revised plan to Ezekiel and both young men capsized the coffin slowly and discharged Jezebel's blowfly-filled body onto the weed-strewn ground like a fully loaded omelet. Rufus then knelt between Jezebel's legs. He lifted her stained sundress and rested it on her swollen stomach. He stared in contempt at her devastated cunt. The killer really did a number on it. It looked like he had taken apart her tender lady parts with a pair of dull scissors. Ghastly gashes adorned her heinous, mistreated fuckhole. Most of her pussy lips and clitoral hood had been jaggedly cut off from her abused orifice. A cluster of starving maggots staunchly clung to her decomposing clitoris, consuming it with great passion.

"I'm ready, Ezekiel. Get on top of her tombstone and do an elbow drop on her gut so's I can ingest this putrid pussy-soup concoction!" Rufus said.

"And put some power into it, knucklehead! No half-assed shit, you hear? I want her to shoot out an anal blast of rotting rectal seepage to go with the vomitous vaginal discharge!" Aphrodite crooned.

Ezekiel took a deep breath, slowly climbed atop the tombstone, and looked down at the foul scene below him. This debasement of the poor dead woman was deplorable, but it felt like Aphrodite was doing the same thing to them. She had orchestrated this symphony of sickness for her own demented pleasure, and they were all just unimportant pawns in her wicked games. Ezekiel's simple mind couldn't fathom why, though. Where was all this heading? Rufus was a lost cause, of course. His head was inches away from this dead gal's obliterated, detestable pussy, expectantly waiting to sip her horrendous discharge at any moment. This highfalutin' uppity whore, Aphrodite, had him wrapped around her pinkie. After they won The Gauntlet, he would tell Rufus that she was all his. Ezekiel wanted nothing more to do with this awful woman. He would take his old mare and head back to their camp as soon as this horror show came to its conclusion. He would never look down on jerking off ever again. After this, he also didn't want to fuck a woman ever again!

Snap outta it, Ezekiel! Are we doing this or what?" Rufus hollered.

"Sorry, Rufus! Here goes nothing!"

Ezekiel took a deep breath, crouching down as low as possible on the tombstone before launching himself into the air like a hopping bullfrog. Time seemed to go nightmarishly slow as he soared into the air over Jezebel's bulbous gut. Rufus opened his mouth as widely as possible in anticipation of the oncoming explosion of sickening snatch sewage. Ezekiel slowly began the arc of descent, extended his elbow, and prepared to hit the bullseye. He scored a direct hit in the center of her belly with one hundred and eighty pounds of force.

The results were immediate and horrendous.

A purulent, pus-soaked, weeping paste poured from Jezebel's minced pussy. The mixture—which resembled crunchy peanut butter combined with strawberry jam—shotgunned into Rufus's salivating mouth like a speeding bullet from hell.

Rufus only had a brief amount of time to ingest the copious, vile concoction before Jezebel's maggot-filled asshole hemorrhaged a torrent of aged turds and stinking diarrhea water, as well as the aforementioned colony of feasting, burrowing maggots.

But that wasn't the foulest part! Not by a long shot!

The worst part was the release of the corpse gas that was allowed to ferment in her rotting carcass. It dispersed not only an unpleasant odor of decomposition but a fine mist spray of putrefying viscera that splattered into Rufus's eyes, nasal cavities, and mouth once again. He was forced to chomp mightily on the smorgasbord of smegma-infused stew that had been gestating in its rotting tomb for a week straight.

Ezekiel stood rooted in place, horrified by the nightmarish event unfolding in front of him. He tried not to vomit but the smell was too unrelenting to deny. He turned his head and hurled all over Jezebel's modest tombstone.

Aphrodite threw the delicate simpleton a sardonic glare that cut like a knife's blade.

What a miserable excuse for a man, she thought blackly.

She then turned her gaze back toward Rufus and was blown away by the young man's tenacity. She had to hand it to him, that boy wanted her succulent snatch BADLY! She was going to give it to him all right. Aphrodite watched with fascination as he finished consuming the gag-worthy buffet, seemingly hungry for more. She gawked in awe as he gave Jezebel's gangrenous, infected cunt a massive lapping before sticking his enormous tongue inside her vagina like a ladle extracting the last vestiges of maggots and other remaining waste stuffed deep within her moldering crevices. He then dropped down to her masticated sphincter and began imbibing the squalid feces from the dripping orifice with vehemence. Rufus licked her prurient, haggard holes like a dog lapping at its red rocket dick.

Rufus was amazed that he didn't throw up. Perhaps it was the prospect of being balls deep inside Aphrodite's majestic love canal? Regardless of the reason, he had done it! It was the most disgusting thing he had ever performed in his young life. But now he was about to be with the most beautiful woman on the planet, so it was worth all the short-term strife and misery.

"Wow, what a man! This is the most impressive display of devotion from a male I have ever seen since I started running this contest. Rest assured, my dear, sweet Rufus, I have such sights to show you very soon!"

That was all Rufus needed to hear to cement the next turn of events in his mind. Without saying another word, he arose from between Jezebel's newly-cleaned crotch and wiped away the excess rot residue from his glistening mouth and chin. Ezekiel began climbing down from his perch atop the tombstone to congratulate his friend on accomplishing The Gauntlet with such a flourish. As Rufus strode toward Ezekiel he picked up one of the cast-aside shovels like a javelin. Without saying a word, Rufus struck his ex-friend in the head, cleaving the top of his skull in half in one fell swoop as if he had been scalped by a Comanche warrior. Ezekiel briefly continued to walk in a clunky, jittering manner as his blood fountained down his face in torrents. He fell heavily onto his knees, first sloshing and then spilling his uncovered brains onto the cemetery floor. He crashed face-first onto the ground, instantly breaking the cartilage in his nose. Somehow, his cerebellum remained in its perch atop his exposed skull as the blood pooled around his face like a moat. If he wasn't dead already, his own crimson essence would have drowned him.

Aphrodite stared ravenously at Rufus. She couldn't wait to devour him. She was so hungry for his touch. It had been so long since she had found an appropriate mate.

"Come to me, Rufus. It is time to claim your rightful prize."

"Yessum, I want to be inside you so bad!"

"You will be, baby. You will be all the way inside me!"

As Rufus went to Aphrodite, he reveled in her perfect, bronzed form. Rufus instinctively started taking off his clothes as he walked toward her. He had removed the last stitch of clothing by the time he arrived next to her. His erection pressed urgently into her mons pubis. They began to French-kiss passionately. Their tongues snaked around each other as if they were dueling to the death. Their arms caressed one another seductively, their digits traced across their erogenous zones. All of a sudden and without warning, Aphrodite shoved Rufus heavily onto his rump, his penis smacking against his thigh from the sudden jostling. He momentarily looked alarmed until he eyed her face, revealing an impish leer.

She strolled over to him and straddled his groin before slowly dropping down and impaling herself on his pulsing cock. Both groaned huskily as she began to ride him ardently like one would ride a bucking bronco. Rufus had never felt such heat emanating between a woman's legs before. It felt volcanic. He was also shocked by how rigid her vagina felt around his prick. It was crazy but . . . she felt tighter than a virgin. It was impossible, of course, her being a painted lady and all, but he remained steadfast in his ludicrous belief. Everything about Aphrodite seemed like a walking contradiction to him all of a sudden.

As both bounded against one another's genitals, Aphrodite looked down and observed Rufus deep in the confines of ecstasy, his eyes closed tight in lust-filled concentration as their bodies slapped harshly into one another. *It's time for The Coupling,* she thought excitedly. It had been ten long years since she had found a worthy mate who was able to feed her the energy needed to complete the draining act of The Coupling, and now it was finally happening. Rufus could feel his semen building up in his balls. He knew he was about to fill her cunt with his virile load, but he desperately tried to stave off his orgasm for a wee bit longer. He tried to think of as many mundane things as possible and that worked for a bit longer . . . until it didn't. He was about to cum his brains out when he felt an immense pain emanating from his dick.

"What the fuck is happening???" Rufus screeched.

"It's what you wanted, baby. You said you wanted to be deep inside of me, and I'm gonna make that happen!"

Rufus's eyes bolted up at Aphrodite. Her voice had taken on a deep, demonic tone. Her eyes had turned to onyx and her teeth looked like angry daggers. Thick ropes of drool cascaded down her mouth and onto his upturned face. She pressed her clawed hands into Rufus's chest. Her spade-shaped talons easily sunk into him like he was made of quicksand. Rufus's flesh quickly began to meld with Aphrodite's as they slowly started to blend as one. The pain was all-encompassing. Rufus felt his dick melt inside of her fiery cunt. Liquid flesh poured from her twat momentarily before she sucked it back up inside of her with an atrocious slurping sound. The ogling Aphrodite-thing beamed with brilliant malice as her serpent tongue slithered out of her fanged maw and began to lap at Rufus's face, removing long strips of flesh like one might do when one peels an apple to its core. Rufus cried until his voice was raw and it felt like his vocal cords might shred in his throat.

"You have beautiful eyes! I wonder what they taste like." Aphrodite cackled.

She first sucked out Rufus's left eye, bursting it in her mouth and spraying optic juice all over his shrieking face. She then sent her tongue snaking through the newly made hole and sucked out his remaining orb from the back of his eye socket like a particularly well-done magic trick. One minute it was there, staring wildly, and the next, it was vacuumed from existence. Rufus tried to scramble out from under her body, but her strength was as immense as a grizzly bear. Her body felt vastly heavy to Rufus.

"It is time for The Coupling, boy!" The Aphrodite-thing chortled maniacally.

She wrapped her arms and legs around Rufus in an anaconda's death grip. His flesh began to effortlessly strip from his body in loud, painful rips, attaching to her epidermis momentarily before quickly dissolving into her flesh. Rufus's body began to melt at breakneck speed. The Aphrodite-thing lovingly placed her head against Rufus's bellowing face as her body absorbed his swollen and inflamed flesh. The minute their faces touched, Rufus's visage began to bubble and peel. His skin became degloved by Aphrodite's ravenous hunger until his face was merely a sightless, bloody, screaming skull. And still, she held Rufus in a massive bear hug. The cacophony of cracking bones easily eclipsed the screeching young man's death throes. She continued crushing his bones into pulverized dust as the remainder of his flesh slowly oozed from his body and became one with the jabbering creature. The last thing Rufus heard before he succumbed to his insurmountable agony was the Aphrodite-thing's callous laughter mocking him.

It was well past one a.m. when Aphrodite wandered back into the Spittoon Saloon. She was nude and covered in blood and flecks of partially absorbed pieces of Rufus's flesh. She even had bits of Rufus embedded in her crimson-coated pubic hair. John looked up from cleaning the last remaining beer mugs as he chuckled bemusedly at Aphrodite.

"Jesus, woman! You look like a damned murder victim!"

"I didn't kill anyone, John, I only did what that goofy kid told me he wanted!"

"I seriously doubt he wanted The Coupling, Aphrodite. He was dumb but not that dumb!" John quipped.

"No, silly! What he said was he wanted to be deep inside of me. It doesn't get any deeper than this!"

She rubbed her plump belly seductively and laughed harshly at her little joke. It wasn't a young woman's laugh; it was more akin to an old hag from a scary children's story. Aphrodite had been alive for a long time due to The Coupling. The number of men who were worthy and who could complete The Gauntlet had heavily waned, yes, but had not depleted entirely. She could last on a single Coupling for decades, so she wasn't worried in the slightest about wilting away to a shriveled old crone just yet.

"Well, good night, Aphrodite. I'm gonna hit the hay. I just waited up to make sure you arrived home all right."

"Same here, John. Good night. I just need to rinse all this spilt Rufus off of me, and I'll be hitting the hay as well."

John smiled at her and still felt amazed that a real, living succubus resided in his establishment even after all these years. She kept him and his property safe . . . and all he had to do was turn a blind eye to her more unsavory antics and occasionally get some dumb kids to partake in The Gauntlet. It was a win-win situation.

He tossed the dishrag onto the ornate mahogany bar and headed out the batwing doors to his rear bedroom.

Aphrodite effortlessly bounded up the stairs in a heartbeat. She was always full of vitality after The Coupling. She could kill ten men with her bare hands and not break a sweat if she wanted to, but she didn't. What she wanted to do was take a steaming hot bath, then crawl into her comfortable bed and play with herself. She had to admit, though, he had an impressive pecker for a human, and he had fucked her surprisingly well with it before it dissolved inside of her frothing cunny.

In hindsight, she wished she would have cut it off instead; that way she could masturbate herself to orgasm with his disembodied tool after her bath.

Oh well, I guess my hand will have to suffice, she thought to herself merrily as she made her way toward the bathtub, humming a jaunty tune.

***

Mique Watson claps Otis Bateman on the back, congratulating him on a gross-out well told. It's a tough act to follow, but I know Mique has the chops to pull it off. Especially when his scrap is revealed. It's a shimmering blade, which I immediately recognize as a scalpel.

Suddenly and deliberately, Mique cuts through the air, dividing the pillar of smoke that rises up from our fire . . .

Amateur Surgery

Mique Watson

Teddy Duncan scratched his head and squinted to make sense of the warped video. He swiped down the control center and raised the iPhone's brightness to have a clearer view of what was on the screen.

"Dude, nothing's happening . . . I don't get why we're watching this random kid at a gas station."

"Patience, my friend," Milton said.

"I don't get it, I—"

"*Shhh*, here's where the good stuff starts."

Sure enough, the *good stuff starts.*

A sudden surge of heat built at the base of Teddy's neck as a pulsing wave of anxiety tore through him. The little girl who they'd been watching for about five minutes being followed around the gas station was now seated in a filthy room, tied to a rusted metal water pipe. Her bruised eyes were swollen shut and looked like a couple of infected, gummy polyps. She was completely naked—her chest a tapestry of black and red welts, bruises, burns, and cuts. Both her nipples had been sliced off, and cigarette burns scarred her neck.

There was no shine in her eyes. Her gravelly breath made Teddy wince. A blackened, shattered stump completely caked with blood was once her nose. Her jaw hung limp with pink drool.

"All right, open your mouth for Daddy. Baby looks like she wants to be slutty. Do you want Daddy to play with that peachy pie between your legs again?" the man operating the camera asks.

He pried open her mouth with his thumb—fingernail caked with dried blood and gunk. Her molars were still mostly intact, yet there was nothing but open lacerations where her front teeth were supposed to be.

"Dyaww, now that pretty pink mouth matches that pretty pink cunt. I bet your mama's wondering where you are now, you little shit. I bet your daddy's scared too. That rat bastard son of a bitch owes me a fuckton of money, you know . . . but I'll take this instead."

The man behind the camera broke out in hysterical laughter that reminded Teddy of a hyena. He wondered if the child had been drugged. She was eerily subdued despite the horrific situation.

The camera panned around a filthy room. Walls stained a sickly yellow-brown and littered with pornographic pictures of women in compromising positions. The white-tiled floor was strewn with streaks of feces, blood, red clumps of meat, and teeth.

"I think this little cunt is hungry, don't you?"

The camera panned up toward another man in the room. He was dressed in black overalls and sported a clown mask. The camera panned down to his erect penis.

"Nah, I think she's just thirsty," the clown said, before placing the purple head of his penis in front of the girl's destroyed face. He let out a thick grunt as a torrent of piss jetted out of his cock's mushroom head. The stream poured out of him for so long you'd think he'd been saving it up the entire day. The only signs of life the little girl exhibited were brief coughs in response to the sudden splash of piss.

The hysterical laughter continued.

"I'm bored, let's finish it."

"Yeah, same."

The camera jerked downward as another man slapped several layers of duct tape to the girl's mouth. The footage cut out for a second before coming back to life. A dagger was buried deep in the little girl's gut. The man rapidly jerked the blade to one side, prying open her flesh as mauve and gray entrails seeped out. Still, she made no noise. The stab wound was a baby's toothless mouth spewing out a pink octopus of organs and blood. The video cut to black as Milton Russel locked the screen.

"Well?"

"Man, where do you find this stuff?"

"Cool, huh? I've got this guy in a chatroom I'm part of who sends me the sickest shit. Casual dark web stuff," Milton said.

"I . . . Yeah," was all Teddy could muster.

Teddy didn't think this was cool. Frankly, this debased state of humanity terrified him . . . but Milton was his only friend. He had no one else, and to make matters worse, he was often subject to the harshest verbal lashings at the hands of the school's jock, Robert Quinn. Teddy and Robert—who now went by Robbie—had been close friends in grade school, but once Robert became a jock, his friends encouraged him to bully "That fucking pussy faggotard, Teddy."

He was a fifteen-year-old lanky teen whose arms looked like they had the muscle mass of a toothpick, his stringy hair had all the appeal of sun-dried straw, and his complexion was akin to the greasy texture of today's cafeteria special: four-cheese pizza. Outside of his camaraderie with Milton, the *only* human interaction Teddy had was the violent taunting by Robbie and his gang, which included but was not limited to pushing, shoving, theft, verbal abuse, and the rumor that had spread like wildfire—that Teddy's dad left because Teddy stopped wanting to suck his dick.

The reality was that his father had vanished a few years ago after his mother, Nancy, grew chronically ill and had to drop out of work; she'd been bedridden ever since. Her movements were hampered by a colostomy bag sticking out of her abdomen. His mother was financially supported by his grandparents who lived about an hour away. They didn't have the closest relationship, but they weren't going to withhold aid from their youngest daughter in her time of need.

"Okay, I can tell that this one upset you, my bad."

"Mil, it's all good. I swear. I am intrigued by the depth and darkness of your mind to come up with something like this."

"Bullshit."

"No, I swear," Teddy said, forcing a smile.

"One time I saw this video of a guy shoving some sort of glass thing up his ass . . . you know, the kind we have in the science lab?"

"A beaker?"

"Yeah, that! Anyway, he shoved it up his ass while he was in this squatting position and cracked it inside of him."

"Bull. There's no fucking way that was real."

"Fuck you, man, you can't fake that shit! Like, I saw it go all the way in. It looked like he was shitting out those black jelly-like blood clots we saw when we dissected those pig hearts last week."

It took everything in Teddy to stifle his gag reflex.

"Yeah . . . Awesome."

"Yo, Ted. I've got some cool shit to show you. I don't have it with me now, but can I stop by your house later?"

"I don't know if I can have guests today."

"Come on, man, don't be such a fuckin' queer. It's Friday. It's so cool! You won't regret it, promise."

"Is this one of those eBay DVDs of gore movies so rare you can't even find them on torrenting sites? If you make me sit through another one of those *Faces of Death* things, I swear—"

"Nah, dude, this one's way cooler."

"What is it?"

"A video game."

"A what?

"Yeah, anyway. Gotta go. My dad needs me to help out at the shop today. Some shit about a 'Mother fuckin' labor shortage in this shitty Democrat-run economy.' Seeya!" Milton dashed off before Teddy could ask him anything else.

AMATEUR SURGERY

On the bus ride home, Teddy's excitement at getting to play a video game intermittently pulsed at the back of his mind. He liked having something to look forward to but knew better than to expect anything good to just be handed to him. He'd never owned a video game console. He'd grown up poor and had nothing but cable television, his imagination, and threadbare library books. While everyone was flaunting the new games they'd gotten on the Nintendo Switch, Teddy was sitting in the corner with whatever recent dystopian book the library got its hands on.

Teddy hopped off the bus and started down the gravel path on his usual route home. The last of the afternoon sun lay her gentle palm on his head. The golden rays ricocheted off the slate roofs and made way for the lavender twilight haze. Droplets of sweat dotted his cheek and forehead. It was the start of an Indian summer.

In front of him lay a vast, suburban stretch of unkempt lawns.

The sound of footsteps grated on the gravel.

Stepping into the light from nearby streetlamps was the silhouette of three men in red and blue jackets—the school's varsity colors. It was Robbie, flanked by his two lackeys, Brandon and Mikey.

"Hey, fag. You got our money?"

Teddy was able to avoid Robbie's torment outside the school's hallways, but today Robbie showed up on his route home.

"B-but I already gave you everything I had," Teddy muttered.

"Don't sass me, asshole. I know your sick, fucked-up mommy wouldn't notice if you took a bit more from her."

Teddy could handle verbal lashings on the daily, but what he refused to put up with was anyone insulting his mother. She did her best to provide for him; she made every birthday special even when she was working herself to death in the face of her deadbeat husband and his alcohol addiction. Now, she was so drained of life she couldn't do anything for herself.

"Fuck you," Teddy muttered under his breath.

"The hell did you say?" Robbie scoffed.

"I said fuck you! You leave my mom out of this.

"Or what?" Mikey said, stepping forward. Teddy had no answer. He turned around to find Robbie's silent companion, Brandon, lurking behind him. He was surrounded. Without having to look back, Teddy sensed Robbie's hulking presence standing behind him. "I said . . . Or. What?" Mikey glared down at him.

Teddy heard a loud thud, followed by a sharp, throbbing pain pounding behind his head. Landing on the asphalt, his face scraped the hot street beneath him. Kicks rained down and assaulted him from all directions. The soles of their feet hit his teeth, gut, and back. Brandon stomped on the side of his face, sandwiching his head between his foot and the ground as the other two continued to mercilessly decimate him. "Search him," Mikey yelled.

Their hands explored Teddy, violating his person and digging through all his pockets. The weight on his back got lighter as his backpack was torn off his shoulders.

Its contents were flung all around him. They took whatever spare change they could find and left everything else.

"Oooh, look what we have here."

Robbie held up a copy of Teddy's recent library rental. A copy of Suzanne Collins's *The Hunger Games*.

"No, please! Robbie!"

"Don't you dare say my name, fag."

"I'm sorry . . . I'll pay. Just. Don't."

"Oh right, all little Teddy boy has at home is a shitty box TV, his dumbass imagination, and his stupid bitch mom!"

Robbie let out a loud, obnoxious belly laugh, and the other two followed suit. Teddy's core burned with rage. He swore he'd one day get strong enough to make them pay. He'd make them beg for his forgiveness.

Amidst their laughter, Robbie tore pages out of the book and flung them in the air. Teddy watched as the billowing pages fluttered in the wind. The way the white pages caught the reflection of the setting sun made them look like crisp autumn leaves. He gritted his teeth as a bead of water welled up in the corner of his eye.

"You guys, I think Teddy here looks thirsty."

The abrasive noise of a zipper was followed by a stream of warm, foul liquid cascading over his face. Some of the amber-colored pee trickled into Teddy's mouth. Its taste was just as rancid as its smell.

"Man, that felt good," Mikey said.

"Bro, did you find anything on him?"

"Nah, just a couple of coins."

"This little piggy is going to have to turn into a fuckin' thief if he doesn't want this shit to ever happen to him again. Who knows, maybe next time we'll find something to shove up his ass."

"Hey bro, come on."

"What? Teddy boy might actually like that shit."

Teddy was left on the side of the street. He didn't bother wiping the liquid from his face. He just lay there and let the tears leak from his eyes. He wished he could do to Robbie and his friends what was done to the people in Milton's videos.

Teddy slapped the ground and hauled himself to his feet.

When he finally got home, he fixed his mother a bowl of tomato soup and crackers. She hadn't moved from her position since he'd last seen her. Her skin was a sheet of wet paper draped over her brittle skeleton. By the time he washed up, the sky outside had become an orange-lavender ombre.

"I love you, Mom," he said.

He planted a gentle kiss on her head.

She responded with a smile and a series of coughs.

"Do you need help? I . . . I can feed you."

"No, no. I can manage . . ." she rasped. "I think you should get started on your homework."

"I don't mind, Ma."

"Trust me, honey, I've got this."

"All right," he said, frowning.

Despite her current predicament, there was still a little spark in her eye that reminded him of the woman she had once been. The one who loved to sing and dance, the one who had all the energy in the world, the one who shot Nerf guns outside with him on the lawn.

He glanced around the living room and rested his woebegone gaze on the dirty clothes that hung from chairs and lay in piles along the floor. There were old boxes in the corner and a dusty wall shelf containing the knife collection his dad had left behind. All these things were bathed in the deep purple haze of the summer twilight.

In the one-bedroom bungalow they shared, his mother stayed in the living room—which also comprised the kitchen and storage area. He had planned on doing some spring cleaning but was utterly exhausted.

Suddenly, a knock.

"Hey, Tedd-o, open up, it's me!"

His heart leapt in his chest. He completely forgot about Milton saying he wanted to show him the so-called video game.

"Coming. One sec!"

"Yo, Ted, what's going on? You look more dead inside than usual," Milton said.

"I've just got a lot on my mind."

"You? A lot on your mind?"

"I . . . Uhhhh, school. Yeah, today's math homework is on a lesson I don't remember being taught."

"Man, who's got time for quadratic functions and shit, right? Fuck that. We aren't gonna need that useless crap in life."

Teddy caught Milton staring at the fresh cut above his lip; there was no doubt he was about to ask about it. He paused for a moment, thinking of how to swerve the conversation in another direction.

"Anyway, what's that video game you wanted to show me?"

"Oh right, check this out!"

AMATEUR SURGERY 283

Milton dug inside his backpack and pulled out a bulky headpiece. He reached in again and produced a couple of long wires and two black gloves.

"What is it?"

"Neat, huh? It's a VSS. A Virtual Surgery Simulator. It's sort of like a gaming console that you hook up to your head."

"And then what?"

"It makes the game all immersive and shit. There were a couple of other cool things I tested out last night that I wanted to show you."

"What cool things? Like porn or something?"

"Fuck yeah."

Teddy rolled his eyes.

"Okay, hear me out, Teddy. Remember the video I showed you a while ago? That little girl getting fucked up?"

A sharp chill ran up Teddy's spine at the sheer nonchalance in Milton's tone. Milton's look alone exemplified the kind of kid parents would forbid their child from associating with. Both his eyebrows were shaved, his hair was bleached white, and his eyes were two different colors. It wasn't natural heterochromia, of course; he just wore an ice-blue contact lens on the left eye. He was rail-thin and often wore T-shirts with metal bands on them. When the two had first met, Teddy told Milton about his love for YA dystopian books like *The Hunger Games, Divergent, and The Maze Runner*. The following day,

Milton introduced his favorite book to Teddy—it wasn't from the library, and he only showed it to him underneath the bleachers after school. It was a copy of *Michaël Borremans: Fire from the Sun.* It was a book that contained painted images of castrated toddlers being burned alive.

"Yeah, I remember the video," Teddy said distastefully.

"Well, with this device, you can do that shit too. Can you keep a secret?" "Yeah," Teddy said.

A huge part of him regretted even dignifying this abhorrent conversation with continued responses.

"This isn't a toy, ya know. I took it from my dad's office. Apparently, this thing isn't even sold here. You can't buy it here legally."

"What the hell, Mil?"

"Yo, my dad is into all this fucked up shit too. It's where I learned about all this stuff. I just had to show this to you."

"What does it do?"

"Okay, so it's this game called *Sicko Surgery*. You play as this surgeon, and you need to perform an operation on someone. The best part? The person is whoever you want it to be."

"Huh?"

"I mean, like, you can customize the person you're performing the surgery on. You can adjust even the slightest details to make your patient look like anyone you want. And the graphics are fuckin' insane, bro. I tried it last night, and it looked so real."

"Did you beat the game, Mil?"

"That's the cool thing. There is no *winning*. You just keep going until you get tired. And you can do whatever you want."

"I just don't see the point."

"That *is* the point! Having the ability to do *whatever* the fuck you want! And getting to do it to *whoever* the fuck you want!"

"I'm not into that."

"Look, *Teddy boy* . . ." Milton glared at him with calculated intent.

At that instant, Teddy's blood chilled. *How did Milton know Robbie's derogatory name for him?*

Milton continued, "This isn't about fun . . . it's about catharsis. Know what that word means, bud?"

Teddy didn't, so he stayed silent.

"Yeah, I guessed so. Let me put it this way: every one of us . . . every person on this planet has some kind of hatred in their heart. We all have this desire to cleanse ourselves of our sins and our depraved thoughts. Look at ancient history for a fuckton of evidence of people bearing witness to savage scenes to purge themselves of their immoral impulses, man. People love being bystanders—it gives them that same vengeful satisfaction without having to do the *bad thing* themselves—which, in their head, makes them feel like they're guilt-free."

"Bullshit."

"It isn't bullshit, dude. Those ancient Romans watched gladiators literally tear each other apart with their bare hands. Was it disgusting and barbaric? Fuck yeah! That was the point. It gave each person in the audience the chance to take every grievance they had and live vicariously through the gladiator ass-raping someone's corpse. With this device, you won't just watch, you'll get to do the damn thing yourself. You can fuckin' rape Robbie's ass with a chainsaw over and *over* again . . . and you won't go to jail. No cleanup necessary either, unless . . ."

Milton started to chuckle under his breath.

"Unless what, Mil?"

"Unless you have a bit too much fun and accidentally jizz your jeans." Teddy shoved Milton's shoulder, "You're a fucking sick piece of shit, you know?"

Milton laughed. "Ease up, man. I'm only laughing because it happened to me."

"You jizzed your jeans?"

"Sure did."

"Mil, who did you create in the game?"

"Mrs. Ramirez. Ya know. Your Spanish teacher with the huge knockers? I rubbed one out as I sliced off her tit with one hand. Came on the bloody stump too."

Teddy wanted to vomit. Before Milton, he'd never even seen a *Saw* movie. Now he had to force himself to maintain his composure almost every day as Milton showed him real gore videos. Snuff films. Teddy took a deep breath to still his beating heart.

"Y-you can do that?"

"You can do *anything*. And when you're done, I promise, it'll give your mind a sense of"—Milton paused— "let's call it peace."

The two boys nearly jumped out of their skins when a bell rang in the other room. "Shit! What the hell?"

"Sorry. It's my mom. She pushes this button that rings a bell all around the house whenever she needs help. I made some soup and crackers for her, and she said she could manage, but I think she needs me. She can barely move. I sometimes need to ask Mr. Kellerman next door to help move her around. Give me a few minutes. I think I've got to feed her."

It took his mother about an hour to finish the bowl of red soup. Her appetite slowly dwindled with each passing day. Her rapid weight loss scared Teddy—she didn't have much weight left to lose.

When Teddy returned to his room, Milton was gone. A *ping* sounded. There was a text message on his phone.

MILTON THE GREAT: *Hey Ted, I had to go. The 'rents wanted me back before dinner. They asked if I was staying at your place, but I didn't want to hassle you. Anyway, see ya Monday. I left a surprise for you. All you need to do is slip on the gloves, pop in the earbuds, and flip the switch next to your right ear. Have fun . . .*

"What the fuck, Mil?" Teddy said under his breath. Despite his fatigue, blind rage from this afternoon coated every muscle, tendon, and fiber in his loins. He picked up the device, strapped it onto his head, and flipped the switch.

The temperature in the room instantly dropped. His field of vision was reduced to nothing but pitch-black emptiness. It was as if he was lost, alone in a cave so dark he couldn't see his hand in front of his face. It was a darkness so uncompromising, one the human eye was incapable of adjusting to. Suddenly, a prompt appeared.

RAISE ANY HAND TO START.

Teddy complied. Two options flashed in the distance.

RANDOMIZE or CUSTOMIZE.

Robbie.

Teddy raised his right hand. In front of him was a sexless mannequin.

MALE or FEMALE.

He raised his left hand.

The nude mannequin opened his lifelike eyes. Teddy raised his right hand once again to open the menu of options: hairstyle, eye color, skin color, height, and body type. He worked for hours. The more Robbie began to materialize, the more rage ravaged Teddy's psyche like wildfire. Teddy was an omnipotent deity crafting the first man in the image of his choosing. The figure ceased to be a blank slate; this was Robbie through and through. Teddy edited the man's voice to resemble that of Robbie's in an effort to bring the most authentic, genuine reactions out of him. He wanted to make Robbie feel the pain of all the days of torment he'd lived through. Teddy wanted him to know the suffering that came with being made to feel like a worthless piece of shit. He wanted Robbie to be viciously tortured like one of the people in Milton's snuff films.

Teddy raised his hand, manipulated the drop-down menu, and selected **DONE**. The screen went black. Through the tarlike void, a light glowed in the distance. It floated toward Teddy. He walked in its direction until the light was so close it could almost be touched. The light turned into a face. The face of a young man.

Robbie.

The avatar's resemblance to the bane of Teddy's existence was spot-on. Looking down, Teddy saw that he was clothed in some sort of bloody butcher's apron. After an expectant beat, he glanced around. The scene was someone's basement. The walls surrounding him were concrete, mantled with blood and viscera. The putrid stench of piss, shit, and copper instantly violated his olfactory sense. Despite this, Teddy embraced how real everything felt.

Milton, what the fuck is this?

On a shelving unit located on the opposite side of the room rested a hunting knife collection, gardening shears, a claw hammer, and a chainsaw. In the corner of the room, Robbie—eyes closed, dressed in hospital scrubs—lay on his back atop a cold metal slab. On the filthy floor below him was a white Styrofoam box. Taped to a thin rope hanging from the ceiling above him, a small sheet of paper with these typewritten words.

KIDNEY TRANSPLANT

Fuck that. Teddy picked up the claw hammer and held it above Robbie.

"Wake up."

Nothing.

"I said, wake up, you son of a bitch!"

Robbie's right eye eased open. The rest of his body was sedated. It was as if someone had injected acid into the top of his spine, paralyzing him from the neck down.

"Teddy?" Robbie rasped.

The . . . *thing* . . . its voice sounded just like Robbie's. Teddy felt a sudden surge of excitement zing through him.

"Wh-what are you doing?"

"You told me we were best friends, Robbie. You lied to my face," Teddy hissed. "You piece of shit.

Do you know how many times I've cried over this? Over you? Do you know what it's like wishing your friendship with someone would last forever, only for them to throw you away like a used toy? Do you? Huh?" Teddy yelled.

He again hoisted the hammer above Robbie's face, cursing him. Robbie tried to say something, but Teddy couldn't hear him over the marching band from hell thrashing in his head.

"I trusted you. I loved you like a fucking brother, and this is how you choose to repay me? People like you fit in. People like you think you're above people like me just because you play sports and girls fawn over you. People like you get used to having their asses kissed, to being worshiped. All that crap goes to your head, you know? You're not better than me. You're not better than anybody else! Do you know how many times I've wanted to die? How many times I've thought about killing myself? How many times I've woken up crying because I was still alive?"

Robbie thrashed upward with arms outstretched but was met with the full force of Teddy's claw hammer. The collision struck Robbie right in the teeth. "Fuck! You!"

Again and again, Teddy struck Robbie in the mouth, the chest, and the shoulders. The thud of steel collided with enamel. Chipped tooth fragments slid down the back of Robbie's throat. His wailing sent a tingle up Teddy's legs. He wanted more. He wanted to squeeze every last bit of pain out of this bastard.

Teddy concentrated the blows on Robbie's joints. He struck him multiple times on both knees, elbows, and hips. Beyond the spasmodic twitch of his fingers and toes, he was now incapacitated. Still, Teddy wanted more. He paced around the room, opening drawers until he found something that caught his eye. He picked up a spoon.

He dug the curved edge of it into the base of Robbie's eyeball. His eyelid flicked rapidly, as if straining to keep the invasive object out of its crevice. The metal was cool to the touch and slicked with the tears welling up in protest to this sudden intrusion.

Robbie screamed and thrashed against the brutal penetration.

Frustrated, Teddy picked up the hammer and rained more blows down on Robbie's chest. He hit the clavicle three separate times in the same area until it responded with an unceremonious *crack!* He repeated that same process with Robbie's ribs—striking him over and over and *over*.

He then returned to Robbie's eye. Teddy nudged the metal into the wedge between the eyeball and the pink bed of muscle beneath it. He dug his index finger into the top crease of the socket as he nudged the rest up from below with the spoon, working in tandem to pry it loose. The spoon punctured the

AMATEUR SURGERY

eyeball like a knife cutting into the albumen of a hard-boiled egg. He forced the spoon in deeper, until a puddle of blood formed at the base of Robbie's skull. The spoon sunk further into the milky sphere as vitreous fluid oozed out onto Robbie's cheek. The tissue attached to the eye tore with a shredding sound.

Pop!

Robbie's skull was now relieved of his left eye, but it remained his—tethered to him by the length of a fragile red cord. Teddy almost repeated the same process with the other eye but decided against it. Instead, he pinched the top of the eyelid and sawed off the delicate flap of skin with a serrated knife. Robbie laboriously rasped with the anguish of knowing one's life was in peril. The eyelid ripped off like an elastic piece of rubber from a deflated balloon.

"There, now you won't be able to blink when I stare into your eyes as I fuck you in the ass with this knife."

Teddy bent down to retrieve his next instrument. A box cutter. Pinching Robbie's cheek, he dug the tip of the box cutter into the vulnerable patch of skin lining the jaw and sawed into it. The blade sliced through the thick flesh like a knife through lard. He sliced from the corner of Robbie's mouth to the back of his earlobe, yanking the skin free and cutting into the tissue and nerves under each layer of flesh.

As he flayed the skin completely from Robbie's face, he began to feel more pressure in his groin. A growing erection.

Teddy couldn't believe he almost passed up this opportunity. This. Felt. Fucking. Amazing.

"Now, now. Talk about a face only a mother could love."

Retrieving something from the shelving unit, Teddy returned to the table with a pair of garden shears.

"Bet I can fix that."

He clamped the shears around Robbie's nose and squeezed. The distinct crack of both nasal bones, followed by the squishy clicking sound of hyaline cartilage being snapped, made Teddy grin from ear to ear. He clamped the tool shut and violently yanked it back. All that remained was a gaping hole where a nose once was. The elixir of life generously oozed out of the meaty crater and stained the boy's entire torso red.

"On second thought, I don't see how a mother could love this face. But your dad might, which is why I created a new hole for him to fuck."

No screams came from the decimated boy. Gravelly sounds and the occasional rasp were all Teddy was afforded now.

"Hmmm, I wonder . . ."

Teddy moved toward Robbie's lower torso and yanked his boxers down, exposing him. Tears and bubbling blood came from the red, lumpy mass that was once Robbie's perfect face. He took the same box cutter that had sliced off Robbie's cheek and placed the sharp, glinting edge against the tip of Robbie's flaccid penis.

"I remember hearing you were going out with Suzy in math class. I wonder what she'd think of this."

"Ha . . . Hngg . . ."

"What's that?" Teddy asked derisively.

Before Robbie could protest any further, he gripped the boy's penis with his right hand and plunged the tip of the blade into his slit. A low, gurgling wail erupted from Robbie as Teddy wedged the sharp metal deep into the center of his glans. He forced the blade deeper inside the limp, gummy tissue of Robbie's urethra, all the way down to the bottom of the root. The more the metal dug into his penis, the more the blunt side protruded from Robbie's reddening stem. He didn't stop until the grit of Robbie's pubic bone scraped against the metal. His penis was now split in half—a snake's forked tongue shriveling into the teen's wiry pubic hair.

Robbie's screaming stopped. The momentary silence was punctuated with a gagging sound as Robbie purged himself of everything he'd eaten that day. The acrid smell of bile, vinegar, and blood wafted through the room as vomit gushed from Robbie's mouth.

"Tell me, Robbie, did you get to fuck Suzy with this little dick, huh? I wonder what she would think, seeing you like this. I bet she likes how nice and tall you are. I bet she . . ."

His voice trailed off as a thought entered his head.

"Say, who said someone this tall could exist in the eighth grade?"

Teddy's gaze landed on the chainsaw. He'd seen his father operate one before, so he did exactly as his father had once done. Placing the chainsaw on the ground, he made sure the bar was clear of obstacles, switched on the chain brake, and then engaged the safety switch while simultaneously pulling the trigger switch.

The chainsaw roared to life.

Robbie stared at him pleadingly, with one eye emerging through all the gore and viscera.

"Never again will you kick me while I'm down."

Wasting no time, Teddy lowered the revving machine and sunk the spinning, serrated blade into Robbie's upper thighs. Blood and viscera sprayed everywhere. A crimson cyclone of splattering meat flew up at Teddy's face. The act required more effort once the chainsaw hit bone. The eventual and oh-so-satisfying *crunch* came when the chainsaw sliced all the way through. Teddy repeated the same process on the other leg. Sweat dripped from Teddy's brow, across his cheeks, and down his lips. He

AMATEUR SURGERY

licked the savory taste of salt-fused iron from his lips and swallowed.

Teddy used the box cutter to sever the few remaining strands of muscle linking Robbie's legs to his torso. He shoved both off the surgical table and stood back to admire his creation. A masterpiece.

"Aww, poor *little* Robbie is what . . . three feet tall now? At most, I'd say you're about three and a half feet. Shame. You could've grown to six feet two had you not been a jerk."

No response.

All Robbie imparted were the faint wheezes involuntarily emitted during labored breathing. The sounds drew Teddy's attention to his mouth. Thick, black blood seeped out of the jellied lacerations where the majority of his teeth used to be. He used to have a perfect, straight set of white teeth, but now only the backmost molars remained intact.

As an avalanche of violent thoughts invaded Teddy's mind, his cock hardened even more.

"Fifteen years old, and you're already bragging about being the first one in the class to fuck a girl. They likely believe you, but me . . . not so much. I wonder, though, do you know what it feels like to *be* fucked?"

No response.

Fuck that.

"Allow me to be your first."

Teddy scooped up a handful of puke from Robbie's chest and rubbed it all over his mutilated penis.

"Look at you, all nice and wet for me now."

He picked up one of the hunting knives, held the tip of the blade along Robbie's crotch, and thrust forward. He gouged the weapon deep into the tender webbing of the young teen's ball sack. Another torrent of yellowish puke spewed out of his mouth and landed on his face. Some of the vomit ebbed back into his mouth, making him gag again. Blind rage completely enveloped Teddy's mind as he fucked Robbie's scrotal cavity with the knife. The jagged edge of the blade ruptured one of Robbie's testicles, and the blood that had accumulated—due to internal scrotal bleeding—now cascaded like a waterfall. The deeper the knife entered him, the more open his ball sack was torn. Teddy could now see the contents of his scrotum: two egg-shaped gray gonads oozing black sludge. As if on cue, blood squirted out of the center of his split penis where his urethra had once been intact.

"Now, cum for me," Teddy said, twisting the blade in Robbie's scrotal cavity. Blood gushed like a heavy torrent of water bursting through a newly broken dam.

Suddenly, a deafening noise shook the entire room. It was the sound of wood fracturing and rusty metal clanging.

AMATEUR SURGERY

"Stop! On the ground. Now!"

Teddy's head whipped around, but no one else was in the room with him. A blast of white light invaded his senses. The pressure around his head had suddenly abated, and the device was ripped from his skull.

He was now back in his one-bedroom bungalow, surrounded by a group of cops—their flashlights, the source of the white, invading lights. The rest of the room was dim and out of focus; the effect it had was disorienting.

"On the ground!"

A couple of large hands forced Teddy down. His knees buckled, then slammed onto the cold tile floor.

"Head on the ground, arms behind your neck," the cop yelled.

The barrel of a gun pressed on the back of his head, the sound of metal meeting metal behind him.

Click!

Handcuffed.

Why?

Humiliation stabbed Teddy's newfound inflated ego. The lights went on above him.

"Oh fuck. It's bad. It's really bad."

"Smith, what was that thing on his head?"

"I think it's one of those new, illegal machines that sick fucks use to enhance the experience of killing someone."

"What?!" the other cop exclaimed.

"Human trafficking rings have been smuggling in all sorts of people from third world countries and letting psychopaths rape and kill them. This thing was invented to put these bastards into some sorta virtual world where they can customize the person they're kill-fucking to look like anyone they want. I think the FBI's been trying to track down its origins—they found some leads in Japan and Russia—and I heard that it might've even been invented here."

"How the fuck did this kid get it?"

"We'll question him down at the station."

Teddy was frozen, paralyzed by fear at the implications of what he had just heard. He couldn't fathom the likelihood that he had just done something that would require the presence of policemen, yet here they were. Teddy couldn't talk.

"What have you done, young man?"

"I-I didn't . . ."

"You're coming down to the station. We have a lot of questions to ask."

"What did I do?" Teddy asked, his sobs breaking through.

The policeman hoisted him up. It took a moment for Teddy to register the scene in front of him. The shelving unit was emptied of his father's gardening tools. On the floor was everything missing. Covered in blood. Teddy looked down at his mother's bed. The thing on the bed wasn't his mother. It was a body—a corpse—desecrated far beyond recognition. Her legs sawed off, her breasts badly bruised, her genitals completely bloodied and defiled, and her face . . . was not a face. The *thing* on this bed didn't resemble anything remotely human.

Teddy's feet went out from under him as fire torched the back of his neck. He blinked in and out of vision as he was guided toward the dark rectangle.

A door. Rather, what used to be a door.

He hobbled toward the threshold, toward the red and blue neon lights made translucent behind the disorienting blur of his hot, watery gaze. Thrown into the back seat, his head slapped against the squad car window.

Looking back toward the house, a figure bathed in the light of a streetlamp materialized.

Milton.

In his hand was a camcorder. Whatever Teddy had done, he'd filmed it. Teddy and his mother were duped into starring in his original production of a snuff film.

Milton promised to be his friend after Teddy had undergone years of betrayal and pain. After trying so hard to be Milton's friend—desperately doing anything he could to be worthy of being called someone's friend—this was how Teddy was rewarded. He could've sworn Milton was smiling.

Milton disappeared into the unforgiving night sky as Teddy was propelled forward, screaming into the abyss.

***

Our next storyteller is Stephanie E Jensen. She waits until the dust has settled from Mique Watson's story before she embarks on her own.

She greets us all warmly with a chuckle. Then, she shows us that she's found a backpack. She unzips the bag and opens its mouth wide, as if she's cracking its jaw. Inside, is her story . . .

Putrefying Malediction

Stephanie E Jensen

Juliette struggles to move her little legs fast enough to keep up with her father. Dan is tugging his daughter's arm, stretching her skin out as if her arm was a Slinky. Juliette feels the sting of the stretch, the delicate skin on her wrist turning red as Dan's grip gets tighter. She wants to ask her father to let go, but Juliette thinks back to the menacing look in her father's eye when she asks him for anything. Instead, her little head looks upward at the big kids.

Her jade eyes follow every teenager. *What will life be like when I'm as big as Laurent, attending high school with other big kids? Will I go to football games like this one? Will I have a boyfriend and lots of friends?*

Juliette looks up at her daddy, whose slitted brown eyes also move with fervor.

Dan leans toward Juliette's older brother, Laurent. "Got some nice-looking ladies at this school." Dan tried to keep his voice down, but Juliette could still hear him.

A student is walking in front of them, and Juliette sees her father's head moving in her direction. Juliette has been watching her too. The student has long brown hair and bangs, like Juliette. But Juliette notices her dad's head is moving up and down the entire length of her body.

Laurent's pointed nose scrunches up, his lips forming a scowl. "Eh, the girls here look too basic. Not into the girl-next-door look, if you catch my drift."

"Let's sit at the top of the bleachers so we get the best view," Juliette's mother, Maggie, cuts in as the family approaches the bleachers.

The family makes their way up the stairs as Dan bends down and picks up Juliette. She rubs her tender wrist, feeling more comfortable in her father's arms.

Dan points to an empty section in the top row. A young woman sits by herself at the end of the row, her blonde hair glittering underneath the overhead lights.

"How about her? She's a real beauty. And there's an open seat next to her." Now Juliette can hear her dad more clearly.

Laurent scowls again. "Denise? She's weird. I don't want to sit next to her."

All Dan sees is her petite frame and perfect blonde hair. "Let's sit next to her anyway. Besides, that whole row is open. What do you think, Magdalene?"

Maggie frowns. On their first date, she told her husband she hates her full name and prefers being called Maggie. Dan never listened and always called her Magdalene.

"Sure," she responds in a quiet voice.

The family makes their way to the open row, Dan leading the way. "If you won't sit next to her, then I will," Dan tells his son as they approach the lone woman.

Denise looks over at the family approaching her. She rolls her eyes when she sees Laurent, that jackass in her English class. With his long hair and brown eyes, he should look like a hot surfer guy. But something about his face screams douchebag, perhaps his goatee.

Laurent has that snobby scowl plastered on his face, the way he always looks in class. But an older man, who Denise assumes is his father, advances toward her with a dimpled smile etched on his skin.

Dan sits next to her and says, "Hi." Denise looks back at her book, not wanting to make small talk with her classmate's father. She can feel his eyes on her, causing her to move closer to the chain-link fence.

"Do you like to read?" Dan asks Denise. From a distance, Dan only saw her sparkling blonde hair. Now that he's closer, he can see why Laurent thought she was weird. She's wearing an oversized T-shirt and jeans, not the tight crop tops, high-waisted skirts, and summer dresses that have brought life to Dan's crotch. She has also been hiding her radiant blue eyes in that book.

Denise looks back at Dan, ready to tell him to leave her alone. Instead, she sees a precious little girl in his lap. Denise feels soft inside after seeing her brown bangs framing her jeweled green eyes. The little girl waves at Denise. Denise can't help but smile and wave back.

"See, you look prettier when you smile."

Denise is now the one who scowls at Laurent's father. She turns back to her book, but her backpack draws her attention. Denise smiles again, putting her book down and opening up her backpack. She fishes inside and pulls out a baby doll.

Denise holds onto the flimsy plastic arms, staring into its beady blue eyes. She found it at a yard sale;

by its faded coloring and messy hair, she could tell another kid used and abused it. The doll is tiny, the same size as a real infant. Its small facial features look like they were drawn on by an amateur. But she chose this doll because you can feel its eyes invading your soul.

With the doll in hand, Denise turns back toward the little girl. "Hi, sweetie. I have a gift for you."

Denise hands Juliette the doll, and her eyes glow like emeralds. She gasps and reaches her little arms toward Denise, grabbing the doll. Juliette hugs the cheap baby doll to her chest and starts rocking it.

Denise looks up at the family. Dan's dark eyes and lips form small lines. Denise is sure he's bored by the interaction—all men are bored by women who don't act like sex objects. But Denise sees movement on the other side of the bench. She first sees a lock of long, dark brown hair followed by a lazy eye, the same brilliant shade of green as the little girl's eyes. Her full lips turn upward in a smile, but Denise senses the woman is holding back from showing too much gratitude.

"Thank you," is all she says in a soft voice.

Dan grunts as he sees Juliette walk into the kitchen, the doll in one hand. With her other hand, she rubs her little eyes as she yawns.

"Do you have to carry that thing around all the time?" he sneers.

"Dan . . ." Maggie says.

"Look at it! It's so creepy!" He points to Juliette and the baby doll flopping in her weak grip.

Juliette pouts as Maggie rushes over to her, wrapping her arms around Juliette's small frame. "It's okay, honey, you can take the doll wherever you go," she coos. "Daddy is having a rough morning."

Dan rolls his eyes and turns his attention back to his phone. He scrolls through Instagram, finding some of the girls that go to Laurent's school. Life enters his pants again. He stands up and rushes to the bathroom.

"Don't you want breakfast?" Maggie asks as her eyes follow Dan.

"In a little bit," Dan responds as he closes the bathroom door behind him.

Dan pulls down his pants and gasps as he sees his half-erect penis. His penis is bright red, like a fleshy fire hydrant. Dan pinches the skin with his fingers. The sensation on his tender skin makes him shudder.

I should stop fucking that intern. She gets around.

Dan bends down and grabs his pants but notices his legs are also bright red. He shrugs and pulls up his pants.

I can't miss the wife's breakfast and be late for work. But I have to tell the intern to get her pussy checked.

PUTREFYING MALEDICTION

Dan opens the front door. He rubs his arm and wipes sweat from his brow as he walks into the house. Dan confronted the intern, and he found out she had quit. Guess she couldn't handle being called a "slut."

The first thing Dan hears is the TV. *What the hell? That woman knows I demand lunch when I come home.*

Dan rounds the corner to the living room and sees the back of Laurent's head, his long brown hair bunched on the couch in tangles.

"Laurent? What are you doing home?"

Laurent looks back over the couch, a stupid grin plastering his face. "I'm sick."

Dan scoffs. "You don't look sick," he says as he unbuttons his work shirt.

"Am too! The nurse said I have a fever."

Maggie rushes into the room, panic sweeping over her face. "Hon, I forgot to call. I'm sorry. I've had to take care of Lau—"

"Jesus Christ! What is this? A sauna?" Dan takes off his shirt, fanning himself with the fabric.

"Hon, you might be sick too. Look at your arms! They're all red!"

Dan looks down at his arms. They have that same fire truck hue as his penis and legs.

Maggie walks toward the bathroom. "I'll take your temperature. Laurent's arms are also red."

"And my penis!" he calls after her.

"Watch your mouth!" Maggie calls from the bathroom.

She walks back into the living room. With the thermometer, she stands on her tiptoes to push the device under Dan's tongue.

Beep beep beep beep beep.

The thermometer makes a commotion as Maggie grabs it from Dan's mouth.

"One hundred and three degrees. I'm going to get you some Advil. You boys sit on the couch. Hon, I'll make you some chicken noodle soup. Laurent already had his. And no going back to work!"

Dan wakes up, choking on the sour bile caught in his throat. The vomit starts to dribble as it piles up in his esophagus. Dan runs to the bathroom, projectile vomiting. He misses the toilet, a splatter of brown and green covering the walls like paint. Dan looks up to see chunks of vegetables and noodles meshed with his stomach acids, causing the puke to escape his mouth in waves. The acrid smell of sour chicken fills his nostrils, and he gags out the rest of yesterday's soup. A tidal wave of vomit enters his esophagus, and he expels the sickening fluid into the toilet.

Thhhrrrrrpppppp.

Dan feels the weighted pool in his pants. He turns and places his butt on the toilet seat, the sight of the liquid diarrhea swimming in his pajamas causing more bile to fill his mouth. Dan grabs the trash can and vomits again, wretched goo flowing out both ends. The fluid burns his insides as he screams. Dan watches the vomit pool over the trash can, knowing it will overflow. Diarrhea starts to leak from his pants, muddy liquid and corn chunks spilling onto the floor.

Dan breathes a sigh of relief after the last of the thin stool escapes his anus. He looks down and notices diarrhea is already crusting the floor grout. He knows he needs to clean the floor but doesn't have the energy to get off the toilet. He sets the trash can down on the diarrhea-crusted grout, chunky vomit rivulets covering the black plastic bin. His bathroom reeks of pungent undigested food and shit. The scent blooms in his nostrils, and he starts breathing out of his mouth.

Dan looks up. He continues gasping for air, staring at the water stains on the ceiling to distract him from his misery. He sees movement out of the corner of his eye, realizing he never closed the bathroom door. He turns his head and sees Juliette standing in the corner of their bedroom.

"WHAT ARE YOU DOING IN HERE?" Dan yells.

Juliette sobs, and elephant tears fall down her chubby cheeks. She holds up her doll. "I . . . wanted . . . to . . . show . . . you . . . Catherine's . . . new . . . dress," she says in between sobs and sniffles.

Dan stares at the little doll. He feels its eyes on him, causing him to shiver all over. This time, Dan knows it's different than the other creepy dolls. There's something wrong with that fucking thing.

"Hmmm . . . this is very rare."

Dr. Fulton puts his gloved hand on Dan's arm, rotating it around. He winces in pain as the doctor squeezes his hand near the ulcers, green pus escaping like icing from a tube. The doctor lets go of Dan's arm and moves to Laurent.

"Have either of you gentlemen ever struggled with this?"

"No," both respond.

The doctor examines Laurent's arm. The pus escaping the ulcer is so vibrant, it glows under the fluorescent lights.

"Ow! Cut it out, dude!" Laurent retracts his arm after Dr. Fulton touches his reddened skin.

Dr. Fulton sighs as he writes something down on his clipboard. "*Epidermolysis bullosa*. A genetic skin condition. You both have a severe infection."

"But doctor, what about the nausea and diarrhea?" Maggie asks.

Dr. Fulton lowers his eyelids, staring hard at Maggie. "As I was about to say, nausea and diarrhea are symptoms of their infection."

The doctor wheels his chair back to his desk, taking out his prescription pad. He scribbles something on the paper and hands it to Maggie.

"Antibiotics. For both of them. That will address the infection. You'll have to clean and treat the skin. My assistant will come here and teach you how. You can get all cleansing and dressing materials at any pharmacy."

Dan feels a piece of his soul leave as he gazes upon his crumbling manhood. His penis, a larger-than-average member that satisfied many women behind his wife's back, now looks like a rotten hot dog. Even from his height, he can smell the putrid odor. It's worse than the diarrhea crud on the floor grout.

The antibiotics that Dr. Fulton prescribed for his ulcers never worked. The infection spread in his penis; at first, the mass was red, then it grew to a circular sore with an eyeball of green pus oozing in the middle.

Over the last few days, the pus eroded the surrounding skin. A bright green halo encompasses the ulcer, which is now as black as a pit. He might as well cut the thing off and display it as a Halloween decoration.

Dan touches his penis. His once firm member that could get hard with ease now burns in pain. He picks up the spray bottle on the counter and washes it. Dan winces as the soapy water sinks into the ooze, the suds gnawing at his rotten skin. The clean smell of soap mixes in with the dumpster stench of the ulcer.

He holds back puke as he washes his infected penis. What is left of his flesh now feels slimy, like the consistency of hair gel. At this point, he knows cleaning and dressing his ulcers don't do anything. But Dan knows he can't let what's left of his manhood go to waste.

Dan finishes cleaning the ulcer and wraps it up in gauze. He looks down at the rest of his body. Those same black-and-green ulcers cover his arms, legs, hands, feet, and all of his fingers and toes. The ulcers stare up at him, looking more like Halloween candy than infected pustules from a rare genetic skin condition.

One down, so many more to go.

He takes the same spray bottle and mists an ulcer on his leg. The liquid hits the black pus as Dan cries out in pain. He watches the bubbles foam into the rotted skin, moving as if it were a monster coming to life.

PUTREFYING MALEDICTION

"Daddy! Do you want to come out on a walk?"

Dan jumps as he was about to put a bandage over the ulcer. He looks over and shivers, catching the doll's sinister blue eyes.

"Juliette! You can't be in here!" Dan screams.

"Honey, leave Daddy alone. He's sick." Maggie appears in the bathroom doorframe. She looks over to Dan, her once-kind green eyes now turning the same frantic colors as the ulcers on his skin. "Julie, baby, go play with Catherine in the living room. Mommy needs to help Daddy."

She pushes Juliette out of the room and runs back to Dan.

"Hon! Dr. Fulton told me I had to do that. Look! The infection spread to your fingers." Maggie sighs as she holds up one of Dan's hands, each finger black and green like a moldy carrot. "I'll give Dr. Fulton a call after I clean and dress these ulcers."

"*Hrmmppppp* . . . this isn't good."

Dan looks the doctor square in the face. "No shit, this isn't good, Doc!"

He and Laurent undress their gauze, and that's the first response they receive? Some fucking doctor they chose.

"No sir, this *isn't good*. You have gangrene."

"Gan-huh?"

Laurent perks up. "Oh, Dad, it's gross. I saw it in a horror film once."

Dan grunts and looks over at his son. "This is reality, Laurent, not some fucking scary movie." Dan turns his attention back to the doctor. "What is this *gangrene*, and how did we get it?"

"It's a condition where certain areas of your body lose blood supply, causing the tissue to die. It can happen for different reasons, though I'm certain the infected ulcers caused your gangrene."

"WELL, DOCTOR! We did what we had been told! We took the antibiotics. Cleaned and dressed our ulcers. My wife had to start helping because my fingers are rotting away!" Dan lifts his fingers, which now look like wriggling black snakes. Tufts of green pus stick out from his cracked fingernails. Laurent holds up his digits, which also look like black worms wallowing in a grassy heap.

Dr. Fulton sighs. "Gentlemen, I have no other choice. We have to rush you both in for surgery. We'll start by amputating your fingers and toes. We'll continue the antibiotics, and I'll prescribe more aggressive medication to stop the infection."

Dan lifts his head toward the little string. He opens his mouth and grabs it with his teeth, feeling the soft threads wrapping around his molars. Dan closes his

PUTREFYING MALEDICTION

mouth and pulls on the string, ringing the bell. He moves his head up and down as if he were headbanging at a metal concert.

Dan lets go of the string as Maggie rushes into his room, a water bottle in her hand. She takes the empty bowl of porridge off his bedside tray, wiping the milky dribble away from his lips with the sleeve of her shirt. She opens the water bottle, pouring the liquid into Dan's mouth. Her hand shakes, and water drips down his chin.

"Oh, hon, I'm so sorry!" she exclaims as she wipes away the water with his blanket.

Dan no longer has the energy to say anything, let alone yell at his wife. He only has the energy to pull the bell string with his teeth.

"I have to clean you now, sweetie," Maggie says as she lifts the blanket, the bitter stench filling the bedroom in a powerful wave.

Dan sighs as he's reminded of his pathetic existence. The amputation didn't work. He watched his feet rot more every day. Maggie told him she would take him back to the doctor when his muscle meat became exposed, but Dan told her not to bother. He might as well let the infection reduce him to nothing.

Maggie grabs the spray bottle from his bedside tray, misting his limbs. Each spritz feels like a blaze of fire, but Dan is used to the pain by now.

The stump looks like fried bologna—the exposed muscle holds a red tint with speckled black rot. Maggie directs the spray bottle on the reddened muscle and around the fibula, which juts out of his calf like a turkey bone. The soapy water bites at the stumps that were his feet. Maggie applies fresh gauze to the stump and moves to the next stump.

Instead of watching his wife, Dan looks at what's left of his arms. Everything from the elbow down is gone. The gauze is entirely sanguine, though he will see the shredded remains of his biceps and triceps when Maggie removes the bandages. Even with the gauze still on, the harsh smell of decay invades his sinuses.

Dan mourns his penis the most. He tries not to look at it but always gets a glimpse when Maggie washes his legs. His once near ten inches is perhaps two inches at best. The rotting flesh withered, exposing the bulbospongiosus muscle underneath. When it happened, Dan would scream for days in agony as chunks of his penis wilted away like a dying flower.

Juliette stands in the doorway, Catherine still in her hands. "Hi, Daddy," she says as she waves.

All Dan can do is nod in acknowledgment.

"Go play with Catherine in the living room. Daddy needs a bath."

Juliette nods and shuffles down the hallway.

Sure, there has to be a medical explanation for what happened to Dan and Laurent. But deep down, Dan suspects that fucking doll had something to do with it. He and his son were completely normal and healthy before that little slut at the high school gave Juliette that doll.

Denise brushes the synthetic brown hair from the doll's face. Her blue eyes are the wildest of any she's ever seen—they're so big that they take up most of her plastic face. But unlike the sweet eyes of Precious Moments dolls, these are the eyes that will give anyone nightmares. *Any man nightmares*.

Under her breath, Denise starts chanting the curse. She runs her fingers over the doll's eyes, giving life to the painted blue orbs.

As she recites the incantation, she thinks back to the acidic memories of her father. How he made her touch his penis. First with her hands, then her mouth.

Denise puts down the doll and picks up the small box next to her on the table. She opens it, revealing a decayed penis. Denise picks it up, so small it can now fit in the palm of her hand. Instead of the smooth and veinous texture of her father's penis, what's left of the flesh is cold and lumpy.

She presses the wilted penis onto the doll's dress, ooze staining the pink fabric. She repeats the curse, this time with her eyes closed. Her mind enters the most depraved part of her memory when her father introduced her to sex toys.

Denise finishes the curse and places the doll in her backpack. She hopes her next victim will fall into her lap as easily as the last.

This reminds her—she hasn't seen Laurent in class for a long time.

●●●

A hush falls over our crowd. We have time, fortunately, for one more story.

The closer.

It's one I've told before, and probably one I'll tell again. Some folks love this disgusting tale, while others hate it.

The flames are diminished, glowing like cat eyes. I begin to tell my story, revealing a scrap I've carried with me for a long . . . . . . long time.

This scrap is a half-burned book called . . .

FETAL BACKWASH

A Novella by Judith Sonnet

ONE

Congratulations! It's a *Thing*!

She was sure it was a miscarriage with all the pain that ripped through her. It was like someone had taken a sword, plugged it up her tunnel, and was now trying to mix up the contents of her belly. Slicing the fetus into a little sushi roll. That macabre visual almost made her laugh before another belt of agony lashed her.

Clutching her swollen abdomen, she leaned forward and strained. She could feel the veins filling up on her brow and neck, like taut guitar strings, just waiting to be plucked. She clamped her teeth together.

She could hear the enamel *crack*.

Something *plopped* beneath her.

It wasn't the baby. Not yet. It was too early. The pain had only just started. It had to have been shit. She'd heard that whatever was in her bowels was gonna get pushed out one way or another during the birthing process.

Hank slammed his fist against the bathroom door. "Flo! Flo! You unlock this door right now!"

Flo ignored him. She wept loudly as she tried her best to shuttle the baby from her. She could hear sloppy fluids seeping out of her cunt. It dripped like an animal's slobber into the basin of the toilet.

"Flo! Flo! You goddamn bitch! Open this door!" Hank roared.

"Get the fuck outta here!" Flo shouted. She didn't want her lousy boyfriend anywhere near her. Yes, it was his seed that had produced the child, but he was no daddy. He was barely fit to even qualify as a proper man, far as Flo was concerned.

"Flo! I said I was kickin' you out an' I meant it!"

"Now ain't the time, asshole!" Flo shouted. "I'm having yer goddamn baby!"

God, she wished that things were different. Wished that she'd pursued college, hadn't fallen head over heels for dopes like Hank, and had quit smoking after she'd realized that she was preggers. But some things—like speeding cars—feel unstoppable. Especially for a woman like Flo.

She was only twenty-two, but she looked like she was in her forties. Fat, baggy, and sour-skinned. Her voice was a garbled rasp, and her hair was stringy. She pulled at it sometimes; just one of her many bad habits. When she went into town, she wore wigs to conceal the bald patches on her scalp where the hair wouldn't hurry up and grow back.

She had dropped out of school in the eighth grade when her nineteen-year-old cousin claimed to love her. He drove her out of town to live with him and his friends on a farm.

After a few weeks of being brutally raped by the scumbags, she'd come back home to find that her folks didn't care what had or what *would* happen to her.

She'd stopped going to school and no one said anything about it.

Hank had seemed like a good deal at first. He'd had a trailer, ran his own business mowing lawns for rich people, and he only drank on the weekends.

He was also an okay lay. Flo didn't mind riding his hog.

But what she found—after moving in—was that Hank had a short temper and angry fists.

Until this moment, as she was miscarrying into the greasy toilet that neither of them had ever been brave or motivated enough to clean, she'd thought the worst pain in the world was being hit by someone while they said they loved you.

Hank was a bastard.

Sullen, agitated, and mad at the world. Even though he had a few things that others would kill for, he wanted more and better.

He wanted to kick Flo out, simply because she'd gained weight.

"I'm pregnant," she'd told him in defense.

"So?" was his response.

He'd packed her bags for her and was gearing up to plant a boot on her ass—

—and then there was fire.

Fire that ran through her like piss from a racehorse.

Fire that burned even the marrow of her bones.

Fire that bugged her eyes and caused her to clench her hands into sealed fists.

She'd charged into the bathroom, yanked her skirt and undies down, and sat down hard on the toilet. And now, the screaming detonation persisted even though her brain was yowling for it to stop . . . stop . . . *STOP*!

"You really givin' birth in there?" Hank asked.

"Yes!" Flo shouted.

"Well, ain't that convenient timing?"

"You fucker!"

He smashed a fist against the door. "Listen, fuck-face, you don't talk to me like that in my house!"

She didn't care. His anger was nothing compared to the hell that was flaming through her.

Flo mumbled a quiet prayer, ignoring Hank's rant. She needed God. Needed Him to take all this hurting away from her and give it to someone else. Preferably a person that she didn't know. Someone different and distant.

"I hope you really are givin' birth in there!" Hank shouted. "Just so I can shove that brat back up yer loose fuckin' pussy!"

Don't listen to him. He'll see what's going on and he'll feel real sorry he ever said that.

Hank? Sorry?

Not on yer life!

She looked between her legs and into the bowl.

It was spattered with blood and strands of tissue. The bowl was also streaked with skid marks, which turned her stomach.

Christ. We really live like this?

She looked around the bathroom.

The mirror was smoky. The paint was peeling. There was a clump of toilet paper left on the corner, gathering mold. The ground itself was sticky.

She turned her head and saw the tub. It was lined with rust, and the showerhead was calcified. So much so that she thought stalactites were growing from its edges.

The drain was clogged with matted knots of brown and blond hair. They didn't need a stopper for the drain. When they showered, the bottom of the tub filled ankle-deep with water simply due to the blockage.

There was a hammock of spiderwebs in the corner. No one had bothered to take a broom to it.

We live in filth.

Redneck trash.

This baby is lucky it's bein' born dead.

Imagine growing up in a place like this. With a mom like me and a dad like Hank.

Christ.

Flo closed her eyes. She tried to retreat to her happy place . . . whatever or wherever that was.

As far as she knew, she'd never really been happy.

Flo Bailer had been born to trailer trash herself. Her dad was a heavy smoker. For her fourth birthday, he'd given her a pack of Marlboro cigarettes. It was the proudest he'd ever been of her, just to see her fumble with his lighter and try to spark her first smoke.

Her mother had been a former beauty queen. She still dressed up like royalty, even though they lived in a dump and her body was decomposing. She had spent much of Flo's childhood gossiping with her like they were gal pals instead of mother and daughter.

The old woman was always struggling to maintain her beauty. With thick makeup, hair extensions, and a constant change of outfits. Yet, the Bailers never seemed to have any money around when it came to caring for their little girl.

Flo remembered begging for a new pair of shoes when she was in the third grade.

"Mine's got holes in 'em. All the kids make fun of me!" Flo whined.

"You think money grows on trees, girl?" her mother had snapped. She'd been sitting in front of her vanity mirror, smacking her face with powder and struggling to keep her shaky hands under control so she could apply eyeliner.

"Don't we buy ya dinner an' stuff? You wanna skip meals to buy yerself a new pair of shoes, be my guest. Hell, you could stand to lose a few pounds, I reckon'!"

Flo had left her mother's "beauty room" in a huff. The child didn't even have her own bedroom. She slept on the living room sofa, which Dad had picked up from a curb. It was ratty, mushy, and the springs poked her back if she laid on it wrong.

She only had a sheet to sleep under. No blankets and no pillow.

Her dad was sitting on her bed. He farted loudly, not caring to hide it even though he knew his daughter was in the room with him.

"Daddy?" Flo asked, trying to put as much sweetness into her tone as possible.

"What's up, sugar lump?" Dad asked, putting a cancer stick into his chapped mouth.

His pot belly was sticking out beneath the torn hem of his wifebeater. The white material had faded into an ugly yellow. A combination of sweat, food stains, and smoke. Sometimes he dropped ashes on himself and didn't even bother to flick them off.

His narrow face reminded her of Frankenstein's monster. It was like the butt of a log, with a flattop and knobby ears that stuck out like bolts. He had a mossy beard and caterpillar eyebrows.

"Mama said I can't get new shoes, but I need 'em!"

"*Humph*." He farted again. The musky smell of it made Flo's eyes water. Evidently, he'd eaten his favorite bean and shredded beef burrito at the Maverik for lunch today.

Her folks existed on a diet of fast food and gas station snacks. For her fourth birthday—the very same one where she'd received her first pack of cigarettes—her cake had been a chocolate shake from McDonald's with a gritty candle stuck in the lid where the straw was supposed to go. Flo didn't much like the taste of stale leftover Taco Bell, or Popeye's chicken reheated in the microwave, or the spongy burgers and dry hot dogs Dad brought home every time he ran by the Maverik. But that was all she ever had to eat.

And her mother mocked her weight, but Flo didn't think she had much of a choice in the matter. Besides, she didn't purge after she ate like her mother did. She couldn't bring herself to, even when Mama was coaching her.

"Ya just gotta stick them wormy little fingers of yers as far down yer throat as ya can."

"I need new shoes, Dad!" Flo insisted.

Dad sucked at his cigarette and expelled a gassy cloud.

He followed it up with a hacking cough.

He decided he wasn't done and gave her another of his noxious farts.

"Nah," he said.

Flo felt her chin pull in and her eyes shimmer. "Why not, Daddy? I got holes in mine!" She was close to screaming.

He tossed his butt, picked out another smoke and lit it. "Ain't got the money for it."

Fuckers.

It was a word she'd been aware of, but this was the first time she'd used it—albeit internally.

Her parents, she decided, were fuckers.

She used duct tape to hold her shoes together. At school, her peers made fun of her. The nickname "Sticky Feet" stuck with her until her cousin drove her out of town and effectively ended her schooling.

No one even called the police when he took me away. When he and his friends kept me locked in their house. No one cared that the dumpy little redneck bitch was being raped. Only reason I got loose was because they got bored of me.

Pain.

It filled her like a flood.

Grinding her teeth together, she clenched her sphincter, then pushed her stomach muscles. Blood sloshed out of her and sputtered in a guttural wave. It sounded like a tire rolling in a mud puddle.

She parted her legs and looked again into the toilet, hoping that it was over but knowing she was nowhere close to having the baby squeezed out of her body.

Her pubic hair was a thick, black nest. It was soaked with bloody dewdrops. Her vaginal lips had peeled back, exposing the bumpy crown of her dead baby. It was coming through.

The bowl was a disaster. It looked as if someone had dropped a strawberry cake into the toilet.

Push.
Ya gotta push it out.
Push.

God, I wish I had a cigarette.

She'd picked up so many bad habits from her folks. She still ate like she did when she was a kid. Fast food and gas station garbage. She also smoked as often as her dad did. Sometimes, she wondered if she was trying to give herself cancer. Like an elaborate act of self-harm.

Push.

She held the walls of her protruding belly and shrieked. She could feel the baby shifting inside of her, traveling down her canal and out of her opening.

Hank battered the door. Pretty soon, he'd kick it down. He'd done so before. It wouldn't surprise her if he beat her black and blue just for inconveniencing him.

"Fat fucking whore!" he screamed.

Flo shrieked.

She watched as the baby's head stretched her hole, then flopped out of it. It dangled out of her like the base of a meaty dildo.

Its eyes were sealed shut. Its mouth was gummy.

Babies weren't supposed to have teeth, were they?

She hadn't done much reading during the duration of her pregnancy. In fact, she'd spent most of her time pretending she wasn't pregnant and wishing that she could afford to abort the little fuck.

She'd chain-smoked, binge drank, and continued eating like shit.

She shouldn't have been surprised that she was miscarrying Junior, but she was.

Why did God let me get preggers if He was just gonna kill the dang thing off?

No.

Babies weren't supposed to have teeth.

Not teeth . . . like *that*.

The baby's mouth was filled with them. Slants of bone that jutted out of its dripping lips. A dank shade of yellow, punctuated with serrated points. Fully developed but jagged with mistreatment and rot. Like the mouth of a crackhead. Or a demented horse.

That ain't right.

Smoking while pregnant shouldn't cause . . . that.

Sumthin's wrong.

Real wrong.

The baby began to cry.

It brayed loudly, catching Flo by total surprise.

All that pain and . . . and it was *alive*.

It unspooled from her and landed in the toilet with a dense *thunk*. It began to burble and thrash, whipping its squirmy body in her expulsions. She remained on the toilet, looking at the crusty fetus in the bowl. It was thin and wiry, with long legs and strange, deformed hands.

Hands like turkey legs.

With scales!

The scales were warty and beaded. They looked like a cluster of overgrown moles, and they stopped at the child's elbows. As if his original hands had been removed and replaced with these . . . monster limbs.

He had three fingers on each hand. They were tipped with black, slightly curved talons.

The baby spat, drowning in the bloody toilet water and the curdled shit she'd dropped. Its mouth gaped open, filling then expelling the viscid broth.

Lord.

Ain't it ugly?

Maybe I oughta let it drown.

She stood, leaving her panties and skirt around her ankles. Blood coursed down her thighs and stained her clothes. They'd have to be thrown out.

Or burned.

Her stomach and womb were still on fire. Tears stippled her shaking cheeks. She hunkered down, feeling more blood slip out of her.

Gingerly, she reached into the toilet. She cupped the baby's head and lifted it.

It wriggled like a freshly caught fish in her hands.

"*Shhh*. It's okay, Junior," she susurrated. "It's okay."

The baby coughed and burped. Its breath was rancid. As if it had compost in its guts.

Wrinkling her nose, she brought the child over to the sink. She bathed it cautiously, taking care to gather small handfuls and dribble the lukewarm water over its struggling form.

She didn't know what she was doing.

Could be making things worse.

Do doctors wash babies directly after they're born?

Do they use sink water or somethin' fancy?

God. I don't know.

She noticed more peculiarities about the child.

Its skin was deep red. It wasn't merely stained with her blood—that was its pigmentation! A harsh scarlet that reminded her of rashes and mortal injuries. A crimson that brought to mind the rarest of steaks.

Its long legs were just as strange as its birdlike claws. They ended in miniature cloven hooves.

She turned the child over and examined his hindside.

Yep.

He had a tail.

A stubby tail that ended in a black arrowhead. The tail flicked back and forth like a snake's tongue.

Lord.

But ain't that the weirdest thing my eyes ever done saw?

Juddering with fright, she used a washcloth to clean the rest of the crud off of her baby's body. Aside from his limbs, teeth, and tail . . . the little guy looked like a munchkin. Full cheeks. Seepy eyes. A button nose. His belly was fat and his—

Oh.

He didn't have a belly button.

There was nothing connecting mother to child.

This is . . . this can't be!

Flo Bailer had never been so confused before in her life.

She hobbled back to the toilet, leaving the baby in the basin, wrapped in the washcloth.

She sat down with a gust of exasperated air.

The pain was dissipating.

She was sure that wasn't right.

A birth this violent? It had felt like her pelvis had been split in two a moment ago. But now . . . aside from some soreness and a tear at the cleft of her pussy, she didn't feel that bad at all.

In seconds, even those discomforts were gone.

She held her belly and stared between her legs.

There was still a small current of blood, but it was decreasing.

It was almost as if she'd—

Regenerated?

But the evidence of the destructive birthing process was all around her. Blood inked the ground, splashed the walls, and led a trail from the toilet to the sink and back.

Her head felt clear. Her organs felt safe inside of her. And her heart was inflated with . . .

With what?

Love?

FETAL BACKWASH

Pride?

No. She looked over toward the sink. The child had stretched out one of his clawed hands. The talons looked like sickles.

How could she be proud of having delivered a child that looked like *that*?

But she was.

She wanted to swaddle it close and coo it to sleep.

Flo didn't want to rest until her baby was nurtured and content.

That was when the ax hit the door.

Flo yelped and held her hands over her mouth.

She'd been so distracted by her baby that she hadn't realized Hank had gone quiet for quite some time.

He'd left to get the ax from the back of his pickup truck. The one he used when clients wanted to get rid of pesky trees on their property.

The ax was wrenched away from the door and slammed back in. A slot of wood jutted out, followed by a grunting heave. The ax reeled back, then struck again.

He's gonna kill me with that thing!

No.

He's gonna kill the baby!

The second he spots it . . . he'll kill it.

Because it's different . . . and scary.

But it ain't fair!

Ain't the baby's fault it was born this way! Lookin' the way it does! It ain't the baby's fault!

She stood, rushed to the sink and gathered the child. It swiped at her with its claws, grumbling unhappily.

"Hank! Hank, I'll do what you asked! I'll leave!" Flo shouted. "I promise! I'll leave!"

"Too late, bitch! You done pissed me off fer the last time!" Hank growled as he chopped once more into the bathroom door. "I'm gonna cut off yer damn fool head and put it on the porch! Yer gonna be my jack-o'-lantern, cunt!"

She knew he'd do it.

Hank had been nothing but sadistic. He'd tricked her and love bombed her during their courtship, but once she'd moved into his double-wide, he'd shown her his true character.

Hank Cathcart was a degenerate.

He couldn't get off unless someone was hurting.

One time, he'd even brought the neighbor's dog into the bedroom, along with a jar of peanut butter. He'd forced Flo and the dog to congregate, lathering her cunt in peanut butter so the creature would be tempted to lap at her until she was given an unwanted orgasm. Then, he'd encouraged the dog to hump her between her legs while he took the animal from behind.

The pooch had whined and cried, obviously distressed by the intrusion and by the beating Hank gave its sides.

Afterward, he'd let the animal go.

It'd looked sulky and surly ever since. Eventually, their neighbor put it down.

Offhandedly, their neighbor said to them both, "Had about no choice. What's the use of a dog if every damn thing scares it? Couldn't guard shit."

Flo, sworn to secrecy through her own shame, had nodded. "Yes. Probably a good thing you put ol' Spud outta his misery."

That night, Hank had crooned with laughter, recalling what the man had told them. He reveled in the trauma he'd given the pet, and he was even happier that it had resulted in Spud's demise.

It became his obsession, fucking household pets. Especially dogs, but he wasn't picky. If there was an animal that someone loved, he made it his goal to get the critter and screw it senseless. He'd once even snuck into a little girl's room and masturbated into her hamster cage.

"I wonder," he'd said while fucking Flo's rear, "if she noticed how sticky its fur was the next day!"

Flo had wanted to leave him, but he was the breadwinner. He kept a roof over her head. And besides, he'd made it abundantly clear that he'd kill her if she left him.

So, when he'd told her she was too fat to turn him on and he wanted her gone . . . she'd put up the necessary fight but had been internally relieved.

Nervous . . . but relieved.

Her parents still lived in the trailer park. She was sure she could convince them to let her sleep on the couch until she figured out her plans.

But they'd probably charge her rent.

After the debacle with her cousin, they looked at her less like flesh and blood and more like a nuisance they were too lazy to kick away.

She'd been fretting over this when the pain had hit her.

And then she'd given birth.

And now . . . she was standing in the greasy shower, clutching the baby close to her while her maniacal boyfriend tore the door open with an ax.

He stepped through the splintered door, holding the ax just beneath its head. His mouth was frothy, and his eyes were stiff. Hank Cathcart looked like a mean sumbitch, with his hard face, grizzled beard, and tanned flesh.

He was wearing nothing but a pair of low hanging sweats. She could see his gnarled, girthy bulge imprinted against the frayed material.

He ain't just gonna kill me.
He'll rape me too.
He'll make it hurt.

And no matter how much I scream and cry . . . ain't nobody gonna call the fuzz.

Did I call the cops when May-Lou Rickets shot her husband, then sat on the porch with the gun in her hand and her eyes full of tears?

Nope.

I minded my own.

I waited for her to shoot herself 'fore I even considered calling the pigs.

That's what everyone else will do.

They'll wait till it's done . . . then they'll hide their meth pipes, tell their kids not to tell, and call a cop out to clean up the mess ol' Hank leaves behind.

Maybe they'll say I had it comin'.

Say it was no wonder he snapped, living with the whale.

A man has needs, after all.

Fuckers.

Fuckers.

FUCKERS!

"I was gonna be respectable to you, slut!" Hank declared, stepping over a puddle of blood. "I was gonna let you walk free. Now . . . no more Mr. Nice Guy!"

Quivering with fear, Flo tried to hold her baby close. It rattled in her arms, shaking like a windup toy. She tried to calm it, shushing weakly.

"That the little turd ya crapped out?" He indicated the bundle in her arms. "It just as ugly as you?"

"Please, Hank. Don't hurt the b-baby!" Flo wept. "I don't want you to hurt him! You can kill me all you like, but I swear ta God, if you hurt this baby—"

"Shut up, whore! I'll skin his botched ass and toss him in the oven 'fore I have my fun with you!"

"No!" Flo wailed. "Please, Hank! No!"

The baby was shaking in her hands like it was trying to escape. Like a child running after a ball that was rolling away from it. Like a dog after a stick.

She grappled with the kid, holding it in her pudgy hands and begging God that she wouldn't drop it and hurt it.

The child zipped out of her hands.

NO!

Hank held a bemused expression as he watched the child bolt across the air and fly toward him.

She heard him mutter a startled, "Huh?"

And then the baby was on his throat.

Hank backpedaled, grabbing at the newborn with one hand while the other tightened around the ax.

The child clung to him like a screeching bat, kicking its cloven hooves and skittering its claws against his flesh. She saw that the talons were razor sharp. They easily slid into his facial tissue and tore it away in fat gobs.

"No! No! Getitthefuckoffameyoubitchfuck!" Hank screamed. His pitch turned girlish as the beastly brat sank its teeth into his throat and tore it wide.

A gully of scarlet blood pumped from the wound, re-bathing the already-crimson child.

The child turned its head, showing its mother the proud clump of bearded meat it held in its vicious chompers.

This can't be happening.

It's just impossible.

But it had happened. The baby had leapt onto her man and was now ripping him to shreds.

She saw that its scrabbling claws had drawn deep trenches through Hank's cheeks. One of the talons had punctured his left eyeball. A gray gel oozed like squeezed toothpaste from the socket.

Blood was foaming around his lips, filling his mouth as it rushed out of his throat. He dropped his ax. The weapon landed on the soggy linoleum with an impotent *thud*.

Hank gurgled, like he was trying to swallow a mouthful of marbles. He tipped backward . . . and landed half in and half out of the door he'd broken through.

Splintered shafts of wood gouged his lower back and punched through his gut. Blood piped ferociously from the wounds.

Hank writhed in place, pinned between the child and his lower injuries. His left leg kicked wildly while his right fell limp.

Mutedly, Flo watched as her boyfriend died.

In no time at all, the blood flow turned into a gentle current, then a soft eddy, and then a coagulated drip. Then, his last raspy breath was nothing more than a memory.

Still, the devil-child worked on his face. Since that section of his body was outside of the bathroom, Flo could barely see what was happening. But she could hear it.

The creature was tearing his flesh like paper. It was also digging into him. The sound of its talons scrabbling inside Hank's cranium was enough to cause Flo to puke. She did so, not even bending over to facilitate the deluge. She just opened her mouth and allowed her half-digested McDonald's to travel back out the way it had come in.

If she'd thought the bathroom was a mess before, it was absolute hell now! A swampy, humid, iron-tasting cloud hung around the room. It prickled her nose, drew goose bumps along her arms, and made her stomach rumble.

Let's keep things in order, Flo.
Ya gave birth ta that thing. It came out like that.
It killed yer man.
Now . . . you should be in agony, but you feel good as new. Even though yer terrified, at least you don't feel like you just pushed a wrecking ball outta yer hoo-ha.
Does any of this make sense?
No.
But that ain't stopping it from happenin'!

Hank's corpse jittered around as the beast worked at it.

Flo swallowed.

Her throat burned with the acidity of her vomit.

"J-Junior?"

The stillness was abrupt.

The creature had heard her.

"You 'bout done?" she asked.

"Not yet. Still hungry," the creature croaked.

Flo fainted right there in the shower.

TWO

Mind-Blowing Sex

When Flo awoke, she was still in the tub. She'd knocked her head pretty badly, and it was thumping like her heart had relocated into her skull. She winced and inspected her noggin for bumps. She found a big one with a crusty gash along its swell.

Welp.
Might have a concussion.
Hey, maybe that shit was all a dream! I just slipped in the tub and had a nightmare.

One pull of air convinced her otherwise.

The atmosphere tasted salty with blood and gore.

She turned her head and saw Hank's corpse, laid out just as when she'd last seen it—halfway through the busted door, spiked with broken wood. His face was out of sight and for that, she was grateful.

She was also relieved to note that the demon was nowhere to be seen.

It spoke.
Newborns don't speak.
That's impossible too.

Add it to the list.

Shaking her head, Flo sat up. She was wearing nothing but her shirt. Her skirt and undies were so blood sodden that they blended in with the rest of the mess.

Gingerly, she turned on the shower and tried her best to wash the brittle blood away from her head wound. She also took care to clean up her nether parts, although they weren't torn up nearly as bad as they should've been.

Afterward, she looked around for a towel. They were bloodstained too.

Fuck it.

Flo peeled her wet shirt off and dabbed at her hair with it. Leaving the shirt behind, she tiptoed across the bathroom. She tried her best to step through the door and over Hank's corpse.

And although she didn't want to—

Flo saw his face.

It had been hollowed out.

Scooped out like a bowl of ice cream!

Just a red dish, devoid of features. Even the bones had been cracked and removed so the interior of the skull could be licked clean. What remained was just a cup of white rimmed with seared flesh.

It ate all of his face.
Just ate it right out.
Mmmmph.
Couldn't have happened to a nicer person.

Flo wondered if the dog Hank had abused was laughing up in Puppy Heaven.

She investigated the hallway, looking for signs of her child. There were bloody paint strokes and claw marks on the tacky walls. A few framed pictures had been knocked to the floor.

The living room was pretty messed up, she saw. Not as bad as the bathroom, of course.

It looked like a tornado made of mad cats had run through there.

The TV screen was shattered.

The sofa had been unstuffed, and its innards were strewn across the floor.

Deep gouges decorated the walls.

A standing lamp had been broken in two.

"Junior?" Flo called, both anticipating and dreading a response.

She walked into the kitchen, which had been a nightmare even before she'd birthed herself a demon.

The dishes were stacked high with fruit flies aswirl. The sink had gotten clogged up and no one cared to fix it, so their plates were left to stagnate in the gunky water below.

The fridge was open and most of the food was on the floor. But that food was old news. Flo and Hank tended to just get burgers when they were hungry, leaving their groceries to rot.

She saw rancid, moldy cheese . . . clumps of sour chicken . . . and curdled milk.

Great.

My demon son will eat out a man's face . . . but is too good for home cookin'.

Hardy-har.

"Junior? You hangin' out in here?" Flo asked with a gulp.

"Why do you call me that?"

She whirled, gasping with shock.

The demon was standing behind her.

He'd grown.

Now he was a man. Full chested, strong-armed, and with a cock like a hammer dangling between his legs.

His skin was still a tart shade of red and his mouth was filled with shattered-glass teeth. His eyes were also clearer to her now than they'd been before. They were a sickly olive green.

"Oh Lord!" Flo put a hand against her chest. "You scared me!"

The demon tilted his head curiously. "Why do you call me Junior? That isn't my name."

"Well . . . it's what Hank and I were planning on namin' ya. Hank Jr."

"Why were you going to name me?" the demon asked, genuinely flummoxed.

"You . . . you were going to be our son. You *are* our son," Flo explained.

This interaction was just baffling. She glanced furtively, as if looking for an escape route.

The demon chuckled. Despite his nasty appearance, his voice was calming. "Oh, I see! No. I'm not your son. I *ate* your son!"

Flo's face fell.

"Excuse me?"

"Sorry. I was hungry. And I still am." He flashed a wicked smile.

She noticed chunks of Hank were lodged between his crooked teeth.

"W-Well . . . if'n yer gonna eat me—"

"Not that type of hungry." The demon laughed. "Not yet."

He swept toward her, moving like an animal. Flo backed away, her feet squishing a pack of gooey bologna.

"Wait! Wait!" she cried.

The demon grabbed her by the cheeks and pulled her toward his mouth.

His tongue snaked out of his gullet—

—and slipped into hers.

She struggled and moaned, pushing against the demon as it pulled her into his hard embrace.

When would the pain start?

Would he eat her face the exact same way he had Hank?

She wished he'd get it over with.

His tongue was like a bulbous worm. It slathered her cheeks and clogged her throat. She retched against it, feeling her esophagus balloon as it crept down her windpipe and toward her guts.

It's getting longer.

And inflating.

And it ain't the only thing!

She could feel his naked cock rubbing her cumbersome belly. Drifting toward her deep, dust-filled navel.

She tried pushing him away again, but he pushed back.

They fell down onto the food.

She felt a hard-boiled egg detonate against her ass, releasing its curdled insides.

They struggled together, writhing in the debris.

She could feel the tongue working its way down her body. Pretty soon, it'd be lodged in her stomach.

It flexed, inflating and deflating in a strange rhythm.

He parted her legs and drove his prick between her thighs. The gruesome penis was ridged and bumpy, as if it was covered in the same scales that decorated his arms and clawed hands.

He began to buck in and out, plunging the depths he'd only hours ago been born from.

Jesus Christ!

I'm being fucked by a demon!

A demon . . . I GAVE BIRTH TO!

Of all the impossibilities that had occurred, this was most definitely the weirdest of them all.

And she could taste the blood dribbling out of his mouth.

Hank's blood.

Hank wasn't her husband . . . but he may as well have been. For one reason or another, Flo had stuck to him like glue.

The tongue vibrated like a full-body sex toy. She felt something wet trickle from her pussy, helping the cock to glide in and out of her.

She reached around his hips, grabbed his pig tail . . . and pulled.

She saw the demon's eyes glaze with pleasure.

The tongue retracted, and as it did, she could feel him spurting deep inside of her.

She couldn't help it.

She was cumming as well.

The demon pulled its rod out of her. She saw a sticky, green gel dribble from its inflamed cockhead. The slit pulsed like a winking eye.

Panting heavily, Flo tried to rationalize what had just occurred.

There was no rationale.

This wasn't just a nightmare anymore. It was now a perverse, incestuous, violent, horrendous, demon sex fantasy.

And she'd *loved* it.

So far . . . this has been nothing but a bed of roses for me.

He killed my bastard man . . . then laid pipe like a pro!

Lord!

Was she going crazy?

Would she wake up and find herself in a straitjacket at the funny farm?

She almost hoped so, if only to better explain what the fuck was going on.

The demon picked up a head of raw lettuce and wiped at his leaking, deflating manhood with it. He tossed the vegetable aside, then glared down at her.

"What's your name?"

"Flo."

"I'm Caim," he spoke offhandedly, as if they'd just met at a party. "Lord of Murder and Madness. One of the Seven Princes of Hell."

"Nice ta meetcha."

"I am sorry about the mess. I needed to break things," Caim stated. "Being trapped inside you for so long . . . it felt good to stretch my limbs."

"No. It was honestly a mess 'fore ya even got here." Flo tried to laugh. The noise was awkward. "You really done ate my baby?"

"Yes," Caim said. He drew a talon up to his mouth and picked at his teeth. "Does this sadden you?"

"I reckon not. I was tryin' ta kill the little bastard myself. Smoked and drank through the entire pregnancy."

"Yes. It added quite the flavor."

"I also tried provoking my man, Hank. He's the fella whose face you ate."

"He was delicious."

"Well, I kept hoping he'd lay a fist on my gut, and I'd just squirt his little spawn outta me. Never did, though. He beat me plenty, but not in ways that'd hurt the child. He probably woulda done terrible things to that kid if you hadn't eaten him. Oughta be thanking ya."

Caim laid a hand between Flo's breasts. She shuddered at his raspy touch. The lumps all felt like pebbles superglued to his hands. And his claws were cool to the touch.

One swipe with those and it's goodbye, Flo!
He could kill me any time he pleases.
Why don't he?

She felt his penis inflate once again. He was ready for round two.

"W-wait," Flo started.

He dug his claws into her haunches. She felt blood slip out of her and grease his palms. His eyes took on a sinister glint. That rapist glint, which Flo knew all too well.

"Wait!" she protested.

"I don't want to," he said.

She felt his cock worm its way into her tunnel. It pulsed rhythmically, tickling her nervous system.

"No! I ain't tryna say I won't fuck ya. I just wanna ask ya something first!" Flo shouted.

Caim froze mid-pump. "Ask me what?"

"Ain't you demons supposed to cut deals fer folks?"

Caim screwed his face up. "If you want riches or need to learn how to play the guitar, you have to go to the crossroads for that."

"No. Nothing like that. I just—" she whimpered. Boy, did his dick feel damned good inside of her! It seemed to radiate an electric current that made her pelvis feel hollow and full in rapid intervals, even when it wasn't moving.

"I just wanted to . . . see if we could come to an understanding 'fore we continued."

Caim shook his head. "There is no understanding. I'm going to fuck you and then I'm going to slaughter you and then I'm going to eat you. Then . . . I'll find another pregnant bitch to feed off of."

Flo shook her head, frightened and repulsed despite the good feelings in her groin. "It don't gotta be like that."

"And why not?"

"Because . . . I can feed ya more."

Caim gripped her haunches tighter. His talons were gouging her doughy flesh. The pain was intense, but it only served to complement the pleasure.

"I can feed ya better than you have ever been fed! Better than just a shrimpy little baby and a dirtbag like Hank! Better than me!" Flo jeered.

He was like a piston now. He swerved his hips, making sure his organ touched every part of her wet cavity. She could feel his previous deposit *squelching* against the friction.

"What do you mean?" Caim asked.

Flo shook beneath him.

Her breasts jiggled on her chest.

Her face was sheened with anticipatory sweat.

Her eyes were puffy with rapture.

Oh, God. If yer real—

Forgive me.

"I . . . got . . . people . . . I . . ." Her panting was out of control. She wanted to bite down on her lower lip until she drew blood. "I got people I want dead!" she shrieked as her orgasm put a fist through her womb.

THREE

God Don't Like Sinners

Caim didn't respond to her offer. Instead, he flipped her over and stuffed himself into the fissure between her buns. She was slick with fetid fecal material from her mid-birth bowel movement. She could smell her own musk as his dick swept in and out of her anal cavern.

He took the back of her head and crammed it onto the messy floor. She inhaled the scent of rotten tomatoes and spilled milk. It was a rancid odor that clouded her head and fizzed her eyes with tears.

When he came, it was like he'd poured hot sauce into her tube. She squirmed against him, cringing as fire raced through her.

Caim unearthed himself from her. Flo felt jellied shit steam out of her hole and frost her thighs. The color of iced tea and laced with solid scraps.

Caim breathed a sigh of relief and squeezed out the last bits of green cum from his hose. He sat down on his rump, legs spread and clawed hands working over his armor-plated prick.

Flo turned onto her back, spread her arms and legs, and panted like she'd just run a marathon.

The linoleum was so shit-stained it would have to be removed and burned.

Probably be best if the whole trailer was set ablaze.

She looked over her mounded breasts toward her offspring. Caim was lost in a haze of ejaculatory euphoria. His demonic spunk drooled out of him in congealed ropes. It reminded her of pond scum.

Wonder if he's diseased.

Probably got a hellish STD out of this.

Lord!

Once a month . . . I might start pissing actual razor blades! Or I'll get crabs the size of actual crabs! Or my teeth will fall out and be replaced by wiggling little tentacles! Or . . .

What if I get pregnant?

Again.

Probably won't live long enough to see any of the side effects of this here rendezvous.

He seemed to have his heart set on killin' me and eatin' me up.

Wish he'd get it over with.

No, I don't.

He fucks too good for me to want this ta be all said an' done.

I bet that's why I healed up. Just so he'd have something good to fuck after he finished eating.

"You were serious?" Caim asked.

"Yup." Flo nodded. "I got people I wanna see dead. I figure . . . you'd be better at it than me. I ain't never killed nobody 'fore."

Caim sneered. "You should've killed that louse you were with. Hank. I could hear him sometimes through the walls of your womb. I was usually too distracted to focus on it. Your baby was a tasty morsel. But Hank . . . he was a bastard, wasn't he?"

"He was one of many," Flo countered. "I got a whole list of people that deserve to have their insides pulled out."

Caim continued to tug at his cock, even though it was as limp as a spaghetti noodle. More beads of ectoplasmic sperm dropped out of the slit and comingled with the shit heap she'd left on the floor.

"How about my mom and dad?" Flo sat up. She felt pieces of mushed hard-boiled egg slide around beneath her. "They're real motherfuckers! Neglectful and . . . and they didn't care when my cousin abducted me! Didn't even call the police. And then there's my cousin. He *groomed* me, then took off with me when I was just a child. He and his buddies gang-raped me for weeks! And the things they made me do— You wouldn't believe it!"

"Shut up," Caim said.

Flo did as instructed.

"God hates sinners. The Devil loves them."

Her eyes fell down.

"Lucifer would hate to see me remove such animals from the planet. He needs them here . . . to corrupt. To defile. To fuck up God's 'perfect' creation."

Flo shook her head. She didn't want to cry, but she was angry. Would she be punished while pieces of shit like her folks and her cousin got to live long and happy lives?

"B-but you killed my husband," Flo said.

"I was hungry. He was in my way." Caim shrugged. "There was no purpose to it. I killed him because he was meat on the table. If I'm going to target people . . . they need to be innocents."

"B-but—"

"Unless . . . we make a deal."

Flo's eyes brightened.

"For every person I kill for you . . . you must take an innocent life for me."

Flo swallowed. Her tongue felt like a sponge. Her eyes were dry and irritated. Her skin burned.

"W-well . . . why don't I just kill these fuckers myself then?"

"Because if you and I don't have a deal. I'll fuck you and then I'll kill you and then I'll—"

"Yeah, yeah. Then you'll eat me. I get the picture." Flo frowned.

Caim tilted his head and gave her a smile. "Besides, if you killed them yourself, how would you do it?"

Flo shook her head. "I dunno. I never really thought 'bout killin' folk before."

"I'd make them suffer. I'd make their last moments . . . agonizing. And that's *actually* what you want, isn't it? Not just momentary pain and then nonexistence. You want these . . . *fuckers* . . . to suffer. Don't you?"

Flo felt her guts churn.

Yes. That was what she wanted.

She wanted her parents to cry and scream, regretting that they'd been so shitty to her all their lives.

She wanted her cousin and his goonish pals to experience pain worse than what she'd endured in their company.

"Who I gotta kill to make this happen?" Flo asked.

"It'll be easy. All I'll ask is that you perform one itsy-bitsy little act of violence. Just to shock and horrify and convince people that there is no goodness left in the world. After you're done, commit suicide . . . and I'll see to it that you are rewarded in Hell."

"Wh-what do you mean?" Flo asked.

"Hell wants children. Tomorrow, you are going to kill an equal amount of children for the lives I take for you tonight."

Children?

She pictured herself performing the deed.

Would they be lined up execution style, waiting for her to end their lives? Or would she have to find them and kill them one by one, picking and choosing who lived and who died herself?

There's a bus stop where all the kids from the trailer park wait every morning.

Innocent children, all with budding futures and happy hearts. Each one guaranteed to be faultless—their worst crimes being light shoplifting and obstinance toward their parents.

She imagined pulling a trigger and firing into their herd, popping their heads like zits and tearing their chests open with lead slugs.

Innocent children.

But she'd been innocent before. It hadn't gotten her very far in life.

She'd innocently believed her parents would care for her, her cousin loved her, and that Hank was a decent man.

Maybe she'd be doing these snot-nosed brats a favor by ending their life before they grew up.

Could she do it?

Could she actually kill *children*?

Maybe not right this second . . . but after tonight, she theorized that she'd be desensitized to blood, guts, and killing.

"You got yerself a deal, son," Flo stated.

"Excellent!" Caim beamed.

Then—and this fiercely surprised Flo—he got on his hands and knees and scuttled toward her.

She instinctually spread her legs, thinking that Caim was aiming for another round of hide the salami.

To her shock, he dived toward her cunt headfirst.

And as he went, his skull contorted, shrinking down with a series of sparky cracks! The bones dipped in, the eyelids puckered, and then folded, drawing the eyes back into their sockets. His mouth hung open. Wet foam fell in seeping waves between his teeth, lubricating his skull in a quick sheet.

What's goin'—

Flo shrieked as his head fell into her vagina and began to burrow. He twisted and writhed, his shoulders snapping backward and his arms drawing up to his chest. He heaved forward, propelling his narrowing body inside of her. Like a battering ram through a delicate gate.

There was a rush of hot pain.

Oh Lord Jesus!
HE'S GOIN' BACK IN!

FOUR

In the Cuck Chair

Windi Bailer preened in front of her vanity mirror. She was fighting a losing battle, but she wasn't going to go out without a pretty smile.

She combed her hair, tugging at the few knots and tangles she found until her scalp burned. Then, she applied makeup. She wore makeup all the time. Even to bed.

Beneath her makeup, her skin was crinkled, dry, and rusty. She had zits like a teenager and bags beneath her eyes that were as big as coat pockets. But she fought against all of the obvious and natural signs of aging with tenacious ferocity.

Not that there was anyone around who appreciated her efforts. Her fat-ass daughter never gave Windi the devotion she'd craved. Her husband, Larry, was about as useful as a dildo in a nunnery. He sat around, soaking in his own farts and sweat, while she toiled away at her appearance.

Last week, she'd asked him if he didn't mind opening their relationship up to a third party. Someone who'd give her the attention she so desperately desired.

He'd responded with a chuffed laugh. "Yeah. You jus' try an' find someone willin' ta fuck yer wrinkly ass. You do that . . . and I'll sit in my chair and applaud when yer done!"

She'd taken the challenge seriously.

Windi started by hanging around the local tavern, which sat on the outskirts of their ratty trailer park. Men who smelled like fish and engine oil came there to douse their sorrows in alcohol and play pool until their arms hurt. Although a lot of them were bent out of shape about the lack of cooze, none of them had been jumping to bed her. Even though hardly any of those gents were lookers themselves!

Well, that had soured her ego, but it was worse coming home with a vacant pussy to her stupid husband. Larry would laugh at her, telling her she couldn't even get laid if she was offering her ass out for charity.

Then she approached Dustin.

Dustin was . . . not all there.

He was something of a village idiot, although no one had seen fit to give him a proper diagnosis. The truth was, he'd been born to dumb parents who'd seen no cause to give him any schooling. He'd retained his childlike aversion to baths, proper hygiene, and learnin' long past the age when he should have grown out of such behavior.

He worked at the bait shop, selling nightcrawlers to fishermen in a pinch and chatting with the locals who swung by for sixers. Most folks had to breathe through their mouths around him, but he wasn't any more or less stinky than men like Larry. In fact, the two oafs had a lot in common. They farted pure methane and they didn't take showers.

When Windi had come into the bait shop that evening, she'd been wearing a tight white skirt that exposed the flabby cleft of her rear and a tube top seemingly fighting to grope her loose, deflated tits. She had enough makeup caked on her face to look like a circus clown, and her hair was in a tightly wound bun that reminded her of a coiled snake. She thought she looked pretty good, but Larry sniggered at her appearance before saying, "You ain't getting laid like that! You look like a damned cartoon!"

Well, she was confident she'd show her husband what was what! And Dustin was just the man for the job.

She'd approached him at the cash register, where he was reading a Superman comic and chewing on a toothpick.

Dustin Rittman was a chunky guy with greasy black hair, cowlike eyes, and poor posture. He often seemed to push his gut out and curve his back—like he was stooping into a Hobbit house.

His fingernails were long and caked in dirt and his teeth were moldy with yellow fuzz. Dustin's folks had left him to his own devices, so there was no one at home to properly tend to his wants and needs.

FETAL BACKWASH

Dustin stank too. Like he'd been out in the sun all day. A ripe smell, which Windi had to pretend was a strange perfume.

"Hello, Dusty!" Windi said. "Hey! Windi and Dusty! We make us quite a pair, don' we?"

"Shore. I guess," Dustin muttered, keeping his eyes on his comic.

"Hey!" Windi leaned over the counter, hoping to give him a peek at her dangling boobs. "Hey, you wanna talk ta me, Dusty?"

He looked up at her, red-faced. As if she'd just caught him picking his nose.

"You ever been laid, Dusty?"

He shook his head. "I dunno."

"You don't know? Dusty. You'd know if you'd been laid or not."

"Whaddya mean?"

"I mean . . . ya ever make it with a pretty young thang like me?" She twirled around. She could feel her skirt riding up her rump. "Pretty" and "young" were both words that were hard to attribute to Windi Bailer, but she was convinced that was how she looked. And to Dustin, she figured she was the best he'd ever get.

"Whaddya mean?" Dustin repeated, earnestly confused.

"I'm talkin' 'bout sex, Dusty! Ya ever had sex?"

"Sex?"

"Yeah."

"Nah. Ain't done that." He scratched his belly. "I been meaning to, but . . . I jus' ain't had the time. Ya know? What with work an' all." His face turned even redder.

"I'm sure! Yer a busy man, Dusty." She hoped using his name would facilitate things. She knew some guys got turned up to eleven just by hearing a sexy gal say their name.

Dustin grinned, showing his chompers. He had bits of beef jerky stuck between his blockish teeth. "Yeah. I work hard, ma'am. Every day."

"Well, I think a hardworkin' man deserves hisself a re-ward, don't you?"

"Shore. Boss said he'd frame my picture—make me employee of the month!"

"I'm talkin' a better re-ward than *that*!"

Dustin tilted his head, totally flummoxed.

"I'm talkin' about givin' you a little pussy!"

He frowned. "I can't take in no stray cats, ma'am. I got my hands full as it is—"

"Not kitty cats, Dusty. Don't you know what I mean when I say 'pussy'?"

He shook his head. "Like vaginers?"

"Yes."

Dustin's mouth dropped open. He glanced around the store. "Whose vaginer?"

"Mine!" She was becoming exasperated.

"Yours?" Dustin gawped.

"Yes, Dustin," she huffed. "I want you to lay pipe."

"I ain't a plumber. I don't know tha first thing 'bout pipes."

"Jesus Christ, you idiot! I want you to *fuck* me!"

A cloying silence fell on the bait shop. Above them, the fluorescent light buzzed achingly. From outside, country music played from a truck's speaker. Tinny and distant.

"Oh," Dustin said.

"Well?" Windi tried to reclaim her flirty tone, but it was now laced with frustration and desperation. "You wanna do me or not?"

"I mean . . . ain't you a little—"

"If you say old then I'm gonna claw yer goddamn eyes out."

Dustin swallowed.

He stepped around the desk, undoing his belt.

"Not here, Goddamnit! Yer coming back with me to my trailer once yer done with yer shift!" Windi said.

"Oh," he said. "But won't your husband be there?"

Windi nodded. "He's gonna watch."

"Like some sorta *cuck*?"

Great. He didn't know what "pussy" or "laying pipe" meant, but "cuck" was an easy part of his vernacular. That made perfect sense, Windi thought.

"Yes. He's gonna sit there and watch while I take your big, manly dick. That sound hot to you?"

"I mean, I reckon. But ain't it a little gay? Fuckin' while a feller watches?"

"What's gay about that?"

"I mean. He'll see my peter an' all."

"He ain't gonna touch you."

"You sure?"

"My husband ain't no homo-sex-u-all." She flipped a lock of hair over her shoulder. "After all, he's married to a fine piece of ass like me."

"I guess yer right. Still seems a bit queer to me."

"You wanna get laid or don't you?"

Dustin sighed. As if he really didn't, but he didn't see a better alternative. It wasn't like he was an eligible bachelor. "Yes, ma'am."

"Good. You know where I live?"

"Sure. I walked by there a time or two. Ain't far."

"You finish your shift . . . you come on over. I'll show you a real good time." Windi smiled. She wouldn't realize until later that she had a green smudge of lettuce stuck between her front teeth.

When she returned home, Larry sat up on his musty couch and sneered at her. "Home already? And empty-handed? I told you, girl, ain't no one fuckin' you! Even if their dick was on fire and yer pussy was drippin' wet!"

"Oh, lay off!" Windi frowned. "I got a date comin' over soon as he's finished workin'. Unlike *you*, he's em-ployed!"

"Oh! A company man, huh? Where's he work? Wells Fargo? Goldman Sachs?"

"He works at the bait shop, if you must know." Windi walked over to the fridge and popped it open. Her stomach was empty. She tried her best not to eat when she was hungry—lest she wound up looking like her bloated whale of a daughter—but she was sure that humping would work the calories off. She took out a mozzarella stick and unsheathed it.

Larry hooted with laughter. "Only man I know who works at the bait shop is that damned retard, Dustin. You ain't bringin' an invalid home to fuck, are ya?"

Windi shuddered.

"I knew it! I knew it!" Larry slapped his knee. "Oh, I'm definitely watching! This'll be better than anything on the TV!"

"He ain't no retard. He just ain't ed-u-cated."

"You know, Willis caught him masser-bating? He came into the bait shop on a slow day and caught Dustin givin' himself a hummer with half a peach! Dustin stood upright and tried hiding his hog, but it was too late. He'd already cummed on the damned thing! Willis asked him where the other half of the peach went and Dustin got all red-faced before sayin', 'I ate it.' That cracker is dumb and horny and desperate enough to put his thing in fruit while he's clocked in. What makes pullin' him impressive, Windi? You ain't proving shit to me! Except that yer just as sad and pathetic as he is!"

"Well, what about you, huh? You ain't no stud. Yer nuthin' but a goddamned couch potato!"

"Yer right. I am. I'm a lazy bum. I smell like shit, and I got dick cheese as thick as that mozzarella yer munchin' on. I also got me a goiter, pimples, and bunions on my feet. You know what else I am, Windi? I'm old. I'm old white trash. So are you. You jus' won't admit it."

"Fuck you!" Windi threw her half-eaten cheese stick. It smacked Larry's head. He chortled.

"Nah. I ain't the one gettin' fucked tonight! You are!"

Windi stormed off.

She did her hair and makeup, fighting back tears as she worked. By the time she was done, Dustin was knocking at the door. She raced out of her room but was too late. Larry had beaten her to the door. It was the first time he'd removed himself from his seat to do anything other than piss or wander down to the Maverik to pick up burritos and cigarettes.

Dustin had a backpack over his shoulder. He clutched the strap tightly.

"Hey, Dusty, ol' boy! Welcome in! Welcome in! You make it all right? Wasn't too tough of a walk, was it? Hey, you looking forward to fuckin' my wife?" Larry clapped Dustin on the back.

Fidgeting, the bigger man looked around their trailer. "I reckon so."

"You know, she did used ta be beautiful . . . 'fore she got old." Larry shot a glare toward his wife. "Hey, you got any particular fetishes you wanna horse around with? Whips? Chains? Pissin' an' shittin'? How about fruit play?"

Dustin went red.

"Leave the poor boy alone!" Windi squawked.

"I just wanna make sure our guest is treated well. Don't want him tellin' folks we's bad hosts!" Larry defended with mock sincerity.

"It's okay, Windi. I'm used ta bein' ribbed on," Dustin said. "Guys come in the bait shop all the time jus' ta rib on me."

Windi shook her head, as if she actually cared about what people said to Dustin. Hell, she said worse to her own daughter and didn't give a shit about that! In Windi's eyes, some people needed a little bullying, just so they could get their life on track. If Flo had taken some of Windi's harsh words to heart . . . maybe she'd be better off.

Skinnier.

"C'mon, Dusty!" Windi took his hand. It was grubby with sweat. She felt as if she was holding a pile of worms. "Let's get you ta bed!"

She walked him down the hall and toward the bedroom. Dustin's face grew hot, and his hands oozed. He gripped her tight enough to hurt, but Windi didn't complain.

"Hey, Duster! You wanna beer first?" Larry shouted.

Dustin nodded.

"Comin' right up!"

Larry brought two Blue Moons with him into the bedroom. Windi was disappointed he hadn't grabbed one for her, but she wanted to pretend Larry wasn't even there, so she didn't acknowledge his slight.

She watched Dustin guzzle his drink. Each gulp was noisy, and they were followed with hiccups.

"Yeah, boy!" Larry hollered. "Yer gonna need ta get good and drunk to fuck this slut! Lemme tell you . . . she looks like roast beef and smells like moldy tuna under all them clothes!"

"Oh, shut up, Larry!"

"Hol' up. Lemme get my chair!" Larry opened the closet and rummaged around. He came back with a folding lawn chair that was missing its arms. He sat down on the rickety chair and stretched his legs. Sipping his beer, he indicated that the two should go on ahead. He was ready to watch the show.

Dustin downed his beer and set the bottle on the nightstand. He didn't remove his backpack. She wondered if he was hanging onto it for security, like a little kid clutching his teddy bear during a thunderstorm.

Tentatively, Dustin waited for Windi to make the first move.

"You don't need ta listen ta that old coot. I got the finest boobies in all of Dade County, Dustin. Your first time is gonna be yer best time! I can promise you that!" Windi moaned.

She pulled her top away and tossed it aside.

She expected Dustin to start slobbering.

In Windi's mind, her breasts were perky globes topped with springy nipples.

In reality, they looked like deflated balloons, and there were ingrown hairs circling each turgid teat. Creamy pus deposits hung like milky dewdrops around the areolas.

Dustin looked at her ta-tas with a mixture of fear, confusion, and repulsion.

"Ain't these just 'bout the finest titties you ever did see?" Windi pressed her boobs together. Her pasty white flesh looked like stale turkey leftovers. "And just wait till you get a look at my pussy! I'm as tight as a virgin, believe it or not!"

Larry stifled a giggle. Dustin nodded. It looked like he didn't believe it.

"You know she prolapsed givin' birth to our daughter?" Larry cut in.

"You shut up or I'll make you leave the room, and you won't see nuthin'!" Windi sniped.

Larry mimed sealing his lips.

"You wanna help me outta my panties, Dusty?" Windi asked, trying to sound girlish.

"Uhm . . . sure," Dustin said.

He stepped over, watching as she pulled her skirt up so he could see her underwear. He tugged her panties down quickly—not even a hint of eroticism in his touch. He let out a soft moan when he saw what lay beneath them.

She looked like a butcher's shop. Red, raw, tube-thick strands of meat hung between her legs. Like stuff was falling out of her and no one had the courage to push it back in. Her pubic hair was tangled, knotted, and sticky. It smelled like spilled milk and rank fish. A green streak stained her taint, connecting her unwiped asshole to her diseased pussy.

Her underwear had skid marks.

Unexpectedly, he seemed to like this detail. When Windi stepped out of her panties, he held them up to his face and took a quick, nervous whiff.

"Pretty, ain't it?" Windi beamed.

Larry was doing his best to hold his laughter in.

Not wanting to be rude, Dustin tried to smile up at her. "Prettiest beaver I ever did see!" He stowed her underwear into his back pocket.

"Don't it smell just right? Like fruit an' honey!"

"Sure."

She swayed her hips, hoping to provide a sexy dance for her lover. Instead, the motion seemed to make her vagina *squirm*.

"Now, you get yer drawers off so I can see what I'm workin' with!" Windi said as she secured the hem of her skirt above her hips.

"Okay," Dustin said, unbuckling his belt and yanking down his trousers.

His penis was gnarled. It looked like a tree root.

The uncircumcised flesh was peeling. A heavy curd dripped from its end. Smegma, cheese, and dick-snot coagulated together to make a putrid stew.

He really had no room to judge her with a *thing* like that.

His pelvis was dotted with acne. Flakes of dried spunk clung to his happy trail. He had a habit of masturbating toward his belly button, then forgetting to scoop the cum out when he was done. The glaze of crinkled sperm seemed to shimmer in the poor lighting.

"Oh Jesus, boy! You ever wash yer ass?" Larry pinched his nose. Sitting behind Dustin, he could see every boil, wart, and stain left on the man's massive posterior.

Dustin whimpered.

"Don't listen to him!" Windi laid back on her bed and spread her legs. It looked like she'd been chopped with an ax between her thighs. "You jus' show me what you got, Dusty!"

Dustin shook his head. "B-but I ain't hard."

"You must be nervous! I get it! Layin' a gal as fine and fancy as me? Well, shoot. Even Hugh Hefner would have a little performance anxiety, wouldn't he?"

"You keep tellin' yerself that, hon!" Larry clapped his hands.

"What do you like? Huh? Want me to suck yer dick? Or do you got somethin' special in mind?" Windi bit her lower lip.

"Well . . ." Dustin hesitated.

"Go on. No need to be embarrassed."

"Well, I saw me a video on the inner-net the other day that turnt me on real good!" Dustin said.

"Yeah? What was it?"

Dustin looked toward the door, as if he worried someone was eavesdropping.

"I got it here in my backpack," he said. "It's a little weird . . . but I think it'd give me jus' about the biggest woody you ever done saw!"

He shuffled around, then unzipped his bag.

Windi felt her guts churn when she saw what he'd been carrying with him.

From his chair, Larry said, "Oh my fuckin' God."

FIVE

Fart Machine

Flo stumbled toward her parents' trailer, clutching her belly. It burned. Like someone had turned her upside down, stuck a funnel in her crotch, and poured hot wax into her.

This better be worth it, she thought.

It will be. You saw what Caim did to ol' Hank's face! Tore it up and scooped it clean!

He's gonna do that to everyone that fucked with you.

Good. She was happy to think that. These fuckers all deserved to hurt. Her parents especially. They'd neglected her throughout her childhood, then abandoned her after her cousin had violated her. Even now, they rarely called. They treated her like an inconvenience whenever she came around, as if she was just a pest. Like she didn't fuckin' matter.

Well, I do matter. I mattered enough to make a deal with the Devil! They'll rue the day they birthed me!

These thoughts eased the pain in her middle. Slightly, only slightly, but enough to press her forward and toward the door to her parents' double-wide trailer.

They were located toward the edge of the park, and the trailers beside them were both vacant. A lucky happenstance.

You can make 'em scream a little.

Not for too long . . . but long enough.

Shoot, even if both trailers were occupied, no one would call the pigs. My neighbors sure didn't!

Maybe we should kill them too . . . for ignoring my cries.

Nope. Stay on track.

Mom, Dad, and Cousin Frankie.

Get the fuckers who hurt ya personally.

She stumbled up against the door, her swollen belly touching it. She could feel the demon, Caim, writhing inside her. Like a bushel of centipedes. Like a nest of snakes. Like an orgy of tentacles.

She knocked.

No answer.

She pressed her ear against the door. She could hear the TV blaring, but that meant nothing. Whenever Dad left to get bean burritos and booze, he sometimes left the television playing. He seemed to figure that it'd just be turned on again when he got back.

Flo stepped back, frowning.

Overhead, lightning crackled. The rain was coming and going. It'd be a downpour before long, she knew. She didn't want to be caught in it, although it might have done her sweat, sex, rotten food, and bloodstained body good.

After Caim had reentered her womb, Flo had put on sweats and a baggy T-shirt from Hank's closet. She figured she'd have to change wardrobes several times before the night was over.

Flo knocked again. It was almost eleven at night. Her folks *never* stayed out late.

Maybe they're fuckin'?

Nah. They don't even hate-fuck.

She knew that because her mom was always griping about Larry's lack of enthusiasm whenever she and her daughter did talk. Apparently, Larry wasn't at all interested in Windi's stale pussy.

She wouldn't be surprised if her folks were getting off with other people. As disgusting and as hateful as they were, there were folks just desperate enough to share some loving with them.

Flo shuddered at the thought.

She knocked again.

No response.

She stepped back and looked at the welcome mat. It was faded with age. The words *Home Sweet Home* could barely be read. They were ghostly.

She stooped over, groaning at the cramps in her womb, and swept the mat aside.

There was a spare key.

Smiling like a fool, Flo picked up the key and fit it into the knob. The door stuck, but a grunting pull popped it outward.

Flo stepped into the trailer.

The place stank of smoke, sweat, and must.

Dad's couch was as repugnant as it'd been when Flo last laid eyes on it. Her father's scummy imprint was like the shadow left behind by a nuclear blast.

The whole trailer smelled like a wet fart.

It made Flo and Hank's place look like the Taj Mahal.

Holding her bulbous belly, Flo waddled around the living room. She wished that she could talk to Caim, let him know exactly what she was seeing and experiencing.

Maybe he's got extra senses. Maybe he can see through my womb and into my environment.

Maybe.

Maybe not.

She heard a shout from the back of the trailer. From her parents' bedroom.

Scowling, she walked down the hall toward it.

They got all this space in this big ol' trailer, and all they do is lay around. If I had this much room, I'd—

She shook her head. No use in being jealous.

Flo wondered if she would have inherited the double-wide after her mother and father passed. But she wouldn't have any use for it now that she had an appointment with Hell to keep.

FETAL BACKWASH

Can I do it?

Go to the bus stop and kill a bunch of innocent kiddies?

I think I can . . . if I turn my brain off. Treat it like a weird dream. Or a video game.

Thankfully, I won't have to live with myself afterward. And Caim said I'd be rewarded in Hell.

Wonder what that'll be like.

Will they turn me into a demon?

Will I get a pitchfork and a set of horns?

Or will they just leave me alone? I'll receive a "Get Out Of Torture Free" card and then I can just wander through Hell and watch while all the suckers get burned and boiled!

I'd rather be a demon.

It'd be fun to torture sinners.

Flo heard another exclamation from the bedroom.

Were they doing it?

It'd be the first time in years! Maybe her folks had rekindled the spark in their relationship!

Too little . . . too late.

Grinning, Flo marched toward the bedroom door. She planted her ear against it and listened. She expected to hear slapping meat and giggles. Instead, she heard something . . .

Foul.

A long, echoey detonation of gas, followed by a simpering moan of pleasure.

"Jesus Christ, boy!" Larry said. "This is about the sickest thing I ever did see!"

What's going on?

Flo took the knob and began to slowly turn it.

"Wait . . . I got another 'un!" Windi said.

She farted. It sounded like tearing fabric.

What the hell?

Flo pushed the door open and gasped at what she saw.

Her mother was stripped naked. Her skeletal body reminded Flo of a corpse. And she was so white she was almost translucent. Her dark veins seemed clogged just beneath the pasty surface of her flesh.

She was on all fours, her butt in the air. A funnel was affixed to her rear, wrapped around with silver tape. Secured tight so that she was farting directly down its spout and into the bowl.

A long hose was attached to the funnel's end—again, with duct tape. The hose led to the head of the bed, where a nude man was reclined. It was sealed against his face . . . with a gas mask! An old relic, which Flo imagined had been made for soldiers in the Second World War. It had mosquito eyes and a nozzled snout. It was Army green and cinched tight to the man's lumpy skull.

Windi relaxed her face as she expelled another long fart. From behind the gas mask, the stranger snuffled like a truffle pig. He was inhaling nothing but Windi's guttural bottom burps.

And he was LOVING it.

His prick was standing up like a water tower between his greasy, hairy thighs.

Who was that? Flo squinted, but she couldn't make out his frame and figure, and his head was obscured behind his gas mask—his *literal* gas mask.

"Oh cripes!" Her father stood up. He'd been sitting in a folding chair in the corner, watching while this stranger inhaled his wife's gurgling farts.

"What's the matter now, Larry?" Her mother rolled her head around, then caught sight of the intruder.

The stranger looked over as well.

All three of the deviants stared at Flo, who was slack-jawed and dumbfounded.

"Mama?" Flo asked, after swallowing a lump. "What are ya doin'?"

"It ain't what it looks like!" Windi remained on the bed, on her hands and knees, her butt held up above her. "We were gonna fuck regular, I swear, but Dusty couldn't get it up unless we did—"

"Dusty?" She looked toward the man. "That you under there?"

The gas mask joggled, and he replied, but his voice was muffled by the hose and the duct tape.

"You get off on sniffin' old lady poots?" Flo cackled. "Oh! That's rich! That's about the funniest damn thing I've ever done heard! You— Oh God!"

Flo bent over, clutching her bulging belly. It felt as if Caim was breakdancing inside of her. She clenched her teeth and squeezed her eyes closed.

He's gonna come out.

"Flo, I'm glad yer here ta see this!" Larry crossed his arms. "I'm glad that our daughter gets to witness her own mother's ultimate humiliation! I'm pleased as fuckin' punch!"

Flo shuffled her sweats down, baring her ass and her hairy crotch.

"Oh shit! Flo! I don't want you joinin' in!" Windi sneered. "I ain't into that mother-daughter shit!"

"I am!" Dustin cried, still muffled but clear enough for all to hear.

Flo squatted, holding her legs as far apart as they'd go. She strained and grunted.

"Flo? What're you doing, girl?" Larry asked. More repulsed than concerned.

"Oh! Lookit! Her belly's all squirmy!" Windi pointed. "She's givin' birth!"

"Not in *my* house, you don't!" Larry marched toward her.

"This's the best day of my life!" Dustin cried through his mask.

Flo felt her "baby" slough out of her. It came out of her pussy like a turd dropping from a wet asshole. It landed on the carpet with a spluttery splat. She felt more liquids pour out of her. Some as thin as paper, others thicker than syrup.

"Oh! Oh! She dropped it!" Windi shouted. "Ugh! It's ugly! Get it outta here, Larry!"

"Teach you ta give birth in my house!" Larry stooped over and took the baby-sized demon by the ankles. He stood and swung it over his head, spraying a halo of blood and womb juice around the room.

"Larry! Yer makin' more of a mess than she is!"

Flo landed on her rump, keeping her legs open. The pain from her vagina was like salt poured into a widened wound.

Caim made no sound as he was rotated in the air above Larry's head.

If that was a real baby, Larry'd be murderin' him!

He definitely deserves to die . . . and he oughta die BAD!

Flo smirked, watching as Larry heaved the baby away from him and toward the wall. He probably imagined the fragile little body would break apart like a pomegranate beneath a mallet. Instead, Caim hit the wall . . . and BOUNCED!

Larry's face fell as the baby-demon soared through the air and landed on his chest.

"Ouch! Jesus! Ouch!" Larry leapt back, swatting at the little creature. Caim had dug his claws through Larry's shirt and into his flesh. Blood spurted from the slash marks.

"What's happenin'?" Windi asked.

"Little fucker's got me!" Larry grabbed the baby by the head and tried to peel him away. "Jesus! It's got nails like . . . like *nails*!"

Flo cackled from the floor, watching as Caim climbed up Larry's chest and bit into his throat. Hot blood painted the demon's face and filled its gory mouth.

Larry unleashed a high-pitched and girlish scream. He punched down into the demon's head, hoping to blow Caim away.

Flo could see—almost in slow motion—Larry's hand crack apart. Like he'd punched a concrete wall. His hand seemed to split down the middle, sending shards of busted bone through his flesh. Blood piped from the fissure, further coating Caim's demonic body.

Caim leapt away like a cat from a high shelf.

Larry clutched his broken flesh and yowled, ignoring the sheets of blood pouring from his chewed throat.

"Yes!" Flo jeered. "Yes! Suffer and fuckin' die!"

Caim hit the ground—

—and grew.

It happened in the blink of an eye. All of a sudden, he was the tall, naked man who'd ravaged her in the kitchen atop a pile of moldy food.

"Oh Christ!" Windi shouted.

"Fuck!" Dustin cried. He was bracing himself against the headboard of the bed, watching everything from behind his fart helmet.

The demon stretched his arm. His hanging cock grew into a hard, granite finger.

"Ah, yes. My favorite sound!" Caim grinned while Larry blubbered.

Her father hit the ground, striking his knees hard. He groaned through a mouthful of blood, his eyes wide and weepy, his teeth bared.

Caim approached, taking Larry's head in his three-fingered paws.

"Any last words?" Caim asked.

"Guuuuuugh!" Larry shouted.

"You're a scholar!" Caim sneered.

The demon gripped the fluffy circlet of hair on Larry's head, holding it steady. Then he seized the shaft of his angry cock with the other hand.

He leaned in, pulling Larry toward his pelvis. The head of Caim's penis pushed against Larry's eye. He closed the lid, but that offered no protection. The cock drove *through* the lid. Breaking it like a seal.

There was a gush of white liquid.

Larry cried.

"Oh God! Oh Jesus! Oh Christ!" Windi screamed from the bed, still in her farting pose. "You get yer hands offa him! That's my husband, you bastard! Leave him 'lone!"

Ignoring her, Caim pumped his hips, filling Larry's orbital socket with his pulsating meat-rocket.

"Quit skull fuckin' him!" Windi screeched.

Caim didn't heed her request. He pulled back, slicking his dick in more fluids, then pumped again—harder this time.

Larry's breathing had deteriorated into a raspy sizzle. His remaining eye had turned bloodred. His mouth hung open and his tongue lolled.

Caim began to jackhammer, pulling and pushing Larry's head in rapid motions. The effect pulverized the inside of his skull. Flo could hear the sloppy sound of the penis spearing her father's brain and mashing it.

Caim laughed gaily as he boned Larry's stupid skull into smithereens.

Flo cheered.

Like last time, her body was healing rapidly after Caim's sudden expulsion. She could feel her vaginal tissue adhering back together, her womb repairing from the claw marks he'd left inside of her, and her organs settling down.

All better.

Caim rocked himself into Larry.

Her father's arms fell limp and his shoulders slumped. She heard something crunch inside his dome.

When Caim extracted himself, he came away with a gushing *slurp.* Green semen and red gore flowed out of Larry's head like water from a tap.

Caim released him.

Larry landed on the floor.

Dead.

"Oh Lord! Larry! Larry! Wake up! Oh God! I'm sorry, Larry! I'm sorry we was always fighting and shit! Please! Wake up!" Windi said, crawling toward the end of the bed and pouting at her husband's corpse. The movement pulled Dustin's head, still attached to his hose.

Caim stood back, watching Windi mourn with fascination.

"It's too late now, bitch!" Flo shouted from the floor. "Caim's gonna make you *both* pay! For treating me like trash all my life! For refusing to love me! For being so self-centered and lazy that you couldn't even take care of your own flesh and blood! He's gonna make you hurt!"

Windi looked up with sad eyes. "W-why? I always tried my best to love you!"

"Yer best? Ha! If that was yer best, I'd hate ta see ya at yer worst!" Flo laughed. She hauled herself up and walked away, leaving her sweats behind.

Caim stepped to the bed, glaring down at Windi. "It really is nothing personal, ma'am. But a deal's a deal."

Windi looked at his blood-glazed cock.

"Y-you gonna do me like ya did Larry? You gonna fu-fuck me to death?"

"No," Caim responded.

There was momentary relief.

"I'm going to *squeeze* you to death."

Windi's eyes widened. Her chin crinkled and a line of snot climbed out of her nose. "You d-don't mean it!"

"I always mean what I say, and I always say what I mean!" Caim jumped onto the bed.

"Stay back! Stay away from *me*!"

Dustin shook his head and mumbled beneath his mask.

"Take him!" Windi pointed. "Yeah! You can have him! He's a gross-ass cracker anyway! Can only get off on farts an' shit! You can have him!"

"I don't *want* him. I want you!"

"No! Please!" Windi cried.

Caim leapt onto her. He wrapped his muscled arms and legs around her. He rolled like a crocodile, tossing sheets and spinning Windi so she was facing the ceiling.

"No! No! *No*!"

"Yes! Yes! *Yes*!"

Caim tightened his hold, squeezing her belly.

Dustin groped his mask. It was locked around his head. His grubby fingers were too panicked to unclasp its straps. He screamed inside his gassy prison.

"No!" Windi wailed.

Flo heard her mother's belly implode.

Red blood sluiced up the hose and into the mask.

Dustin sputtered, trying his best to fight the rush of shit and blood away from him.

Windi moaned like a rabbit in a trap. A long, high-pitched squeal that fell into a distempered grumble.

Caim squeezed her like a tube of toothpaste.

Flo watched as her mother's belly caved into her core. Watched as shredded organs left her ass and traveled up the hose like a creamy, crimson slushy.

Like human bisque.

Dustin was drowning in Windi's internal slop. Blood crawled out of the sides of his mask, trickling in wavy strands down his cheeks and cloaking his hairy shoulders. His erection had died.

"Squeeze 'er out, Caim! Squeeze 'er out!" Flo shouted.

Caim was like a vise.

Windi was like a rotten pumpkin.

He squeezed again . . . and she broke.

SIX
Let's Do It on All These Dead People

Flo came over to the bed and investigated what was left of her mother. At the headboard, Dustin's body reclined. The eyes of his mask were bright red. More blood leaked from the sides of the apparatus.

He'd choked on Windi's insides.

What a way to go.

He ain't done nuthin' too awful.

Least not to me.

But hey . . . wrong place . . . wrong time!

It boded well for her that she didn't feel bad about Dustin. Didn't feel like she'd done something wrong by allowing an innocent life to be taken in the middle of her vengeance mission.

It meant she'd probably be fine killing all those kids when this was all said and done.

Just think of them all as little Dustins.

Little fart sniffers.

Wrong place . . . wrong time.

Caim stood in the middle of the bed, gazing from one corpse to the other.

"That was mighty good," Flo said. "You really showed 'em!"

Caim shrugged. "I'll make the next ones worse."

FETAL BACKWASH

"I'm counting on it. Next up is a real piece of shit. My cousin! Frankie Brentford!" Even saying his name aloud caused her to shudder.

"Yes. And his pals."

"If they're still living with him, and I'd wager they are."

Caim sat on her mother's bloody remains. Criss-cross applesauce. He planted his claws on his knees. His dick stuck up from his pelvis like a curved sword.

He's a handsome devil, ain't he?

Ha!

And he can maintain an erection longer than any man I ever did meet!

"You want to head right over?" Caim asked.

"No . . . not yet." Flo climbed onto the bed, mashing her mother's frozen face beneath a knee.

"You want to do something else here?"

"Yes. I wanna fuck." Flo pouted. "If yer up for it."

Caim grinned, showing his jagged, broken, blood-stained chompers. "Put your mouth on my staff. I'll tell you a story while you work."

Flo opened her mouth and dived down. His penis was still iced in her father's blood, and lumps of broken brain clung to his head.

It's so hard.

Literally feels like solid stone!

No wonder it did all that damage on ol' Pa!

Jesus. One hard thrust and he could puncture the roof of my mouth and scramble my *brain!*

"They call me the Lord of Murder and Madness," Caim said, tilting back and sighing deeply. "It was I who whispered to Cain that he should kill his brother."

"Abel?" Flo asked around her mouthful.

"You paid attention in Sunday school. Good. Although . . . the truth is darker than the retelling will permit."

"What—*gulpugh*—happened?"

"After Adam and Eve were kicked from the Garden of Eden, they fucked like rabbits. They had three sons. Cain, Abel, and Elliph."

She'd never heard of that third one.

"They were all incredibly devout to God because back then . . . God was to be feared. He'd appear in their camp often to rape Eve and force Adam to watch, as punishment for the original sin. He used her and abused her so often, she could barely walk, and she only spoke in cries." Caim smiled, as if recalling a *good m*emory. "They were all terrified of God, and so they sacrificed to Him. They gave unto Him their finest livestock, their best crops, and their own blood, which they poured onto their fires with split palms."

She tongued his slit. It tasted salty. A relief from the hot iron taste of her father's fluids.

"Hold my balls," Caim commanded.

She followed his instructions. It was like gripping a leathery coin purse.

"Elliph was the most devout, and he was also Adam's favorite. He was the only one of the three who tended to their broken mother. He'd use his tongue to clean her wounded cunt, slurping out God's cum and spitting it into a bowl, which he'd then carry into the canyon and dispose of. He also prayed the most. Even in sleep, he would mutter prayers under his breath.

"The other two children were jealous of him. And it was Abel who decided that if Elliph was the best of them, then it was Elliph who ought to be sacrificed. But this was not murder. When the notion was revealed, Elliph was glad to be sacrificed. He said that it was only fair.

"And so, they tied him to a tree and lit it aflame. He didn't even scream as the flesh was seared from his bones.

"And God was pleased. He vowed to leave their mother alone for thirty days since they had done well to sacrifice their most devout brother to him."

Flo slid her finger into Caim's asshole. It puckered and tightened, closing around her digit like a slick, sweaty fist.

"Oh. That's good, Flo," Caim confirmed with a moan. "Very good."

"Whu-happen'-nex?" Flo asked in gulps as she fellated Caim's monolithic prick.

"Next? Oh, thirty days went by. God kept His promise. He always does. But then, He returned.

And it was worse than ever for Eve. She suffered so. While she screamed and cried in her tent, Cain stewed. He hated God, but he didn't want to offend Him. And now that Elliph was gone, Cain realized that his brother, Abel, was now the favorite of Adam's offspring.

"This, dear Flo, is when I came in. I snuck stealthily into Cain's tent, sat on his shoulder, and whispered into his ear. I told him that if he sacrificed Abel, then not only would he be the favorite child, but he'd then be the Father of Man. He'd be allowed to fuck Eve, and together they'd produce enough babies to start a colony!

"He listened close and well. He agreed with me. And so, the next day, he lured Abel out into the field, convincing him that the crops were showing signs of sickness. Abel was quick to follow, unaware that his last moments were near.

"Cain picked up a stone and used it on his brother. The sound of rock striking skull was like a thunderclap, which was heard through all of Heaven and Hell.

"It was no sacrifice. Abel, stunned and injured, fought back. Cain smashed his brother onto the ground and gouged the rock into his face, tearing his cheek away and exposing his molars. Blood seeped into the crops, staining their roots. Feeding them on filth.

"Cain sent the rock into Abel again. This blow was the killing one. It put a dent in the center of Abel's forehead, like a gory, crimson third eye. The rock dived in and out, followed by a thick rope of blood. Blood that I nipped from the air and swirled in my mouth. Blood that tasted as sweet as honey."

Caim shuddered. Flo felt his cock pulse. She closed her eyes, expecting a fat load of cum to fill her oral cavity. But Caim slowed his pumping and withheld his orgasm.

"Cain then dragged his brother's body away and left it for the vultures to peck. Then he went back to his camp and raped his mother. As I foretold, this produced the first of their children. It was certainly not the last."

Caim coughed and shot a cannonball of jizz into Flo's waiting mouth. The creamy, green custard rushed through her throat, then exploded from her nose. She felt her cheeks expand, then shrink as she swallowed.

Magnificently, the rapturous orgasm didn't diminish Caim's cock. It still stood tall and firm.

"Turn over. I want to fuck you on top of your dead mother. Then . . . we'll seek vengeance against your cousin," Caim said.

"Yessir!"

Flo presented her ass and Caim was quick to plunder it.

SCRAPS

SEVEN

Slacktivists

Frankie had changed a lot.

In his late teens, he was the sort of man who said whatever he felt, no matter whose feelings he hurt.

Now, he was socially aware and conscious. Most of his best conversations began with "Something must be done with what's happened in the Middle East" or "None of us are free until all of us are free."

He'd just come back home from a workers' rights protest, and he was dead tired. Being a caring, generous, thoughtful person was a lot of work.

He often felt strained from all the sympathy he had for the sufferings of his fellow men and women.

I just have too big of a heart, he thought as he shed his jacket and stamped toward the fridge.

Frankie Brentford was tall, chiseled, healthy, and handsome. His blond hair was combed back, his face was smooth, and he followed a strict health regime. He was as strong as an ox and ate just as many greens.

He was trying to look much younger than he was, and he was succeeding.

Part of that was because he was a vegetarian.

The suffering of animals was a cause just as important as the suffering of human beings, he felt. Especially since there was a testing facility located only one town over! He spent many days with his friends picketing the laboratory. He even had a sign he reused every time. On it was a picture of a chopped-up monkey, with the slogan *Do I Not Also Have A Soul??*

Yes. Frankie was a good person.

He cared about all of Earth's creatures.

He was a registered Democrat.

He wrote poetry and attended art shows on his days off.

He was an activist. A champion for the downtrodden.

He was also a rapist.

He'd started with his cousin. She was so gullible and vulnerable back then. He'd taken her under his wing, convinced her that he was more than a friendly relative, and then he'd taken her home with him, and he and his buddies had taken turns pounding her ass and pussy until she bled.

But he felt that his karma was aligned.

He did so many good things . . . there was no way he'd be punished for *one* little vice.

Right?

He'd raped a few others. One was a vagrant woman he'd given a ride on a rainy night. She'd been filthy and smelly, but he'd fucked her against her will regardless. He didn't mind a little stink now and then, especially when it wasn't *really* about sex or attraction. It was about power.

After raping her in the back of his environmentally-friendly car, he'd punched her face until he heard her nose shatter. Then he'd put his hands around her throat and squeezed, telling her, "If you tell anyone about this shit . . . I'll fuckin' kill you, slut!"

And he would.

Although he hadn't had cause to kill before, he knew he was capable of it.

He often fantasized about killing the imperialist capitalist pigs he railed against in protests and organized marches. He dreamed about tying them up, driving them to a secluded place, and taking his time.

He thought about their begging, and it made him hard.

Frankie dug out a salad bowl, popped its plastic top, and walked over to the living room. He ate with his fingers, not minding the dressing that ran down his arm. He was too beat to care.

"Hey? That you, Frankie?" A groaning voice slipped down the stairs.

Frankie turned his head. He lived in a two-story house with other activists and longtime friends. They all cared passionately about the same causes and were often linked arm in arm together at events for social justice.

Taggart McCannon came down the steps, rubbing his eyes. He'd had the flu for the last few days, so Frankie was happy to see him up and about. If Frankie was a stud, Taggart was a hunk. He was beefy, sandy-haired, and his chin jutted out like an open desk drawer. He wore a shirt that said *Equality! NOW! NOT TOMMOROW!* in bright red and a pair of gym shorts. He was a barbarian and the only one from their group who hadn't been around when Cousin Flo was fucked. Not that he was ignorant of the crimes. They did have them on videotape, after all.

What was the use of committing a crime if it wasn't on record?

Even the rape of the hitchhiker had been captured on his dashcam. He'd shared the video with his pals, and they'd all engaged in a spat of group masturbation to the footage.

Taggart sat down on the love seat across from Frankie. He snuffled weakly, rubbing his nose with the heel of his palm.

"Feeling better?" Frankie asked.

"Yeah. Much. Still snorting curds, but I'm better."

"Good. We'll really need you at the vigil next week."

"Yeah."

"Numbers matter. Enough of us show up in one place then maybe our government will actually do something about—"

"I said I'd be there."

Frankie held up a salad-coated hand. "Hey, don't snap at me."

"I'm not. I'm sorry. Ugh. Listen, something has been on my mind lately and I think we need to talk about it."

Frankie set his food on the coffee table. When someone had something important to say, he fuckin' listened.

"What's on your mind, bud?" Frankie asked.

Taggart sighed. "So, yesterday I was feeling really bad. And Willis came in and told me to Uber whatever would make me feel better and put it on his account."

"That was nice of him."

"Yeah. It was. But then, well, I saw his previous orders."

Frankie lifted a brow.

"I wasn't snooping. They were just on there," Taggart said with little conviction.

"What'd you see?"

"He's been eating meat."

Frankie felt his heart drop.

Taggart continued, "Processed meat. From all sorts of terrible places. Taco Bell, McDonald's, Burger King—"

"They all have vegetarian options, though, don't they?" Frankie countered.

"Yeah. But that wasn't what he was ordering. I saw, Frankie. Hamburgers. Double meat burritos. The meat from Subway . . . it was like the Holocaust in a bun!"

"Did you confront him?"

"No. I just ordered my smoothie, said thank you, and sat on it until you got here."

"Good. I'm glad. Because we need to confront him together." Frankie shook his head. "Meat is more than just a defilement of nature. It's an addiction. We need to hold an intervention."

Taggart shuddered. "But what if we just convince him to keep it better hidden? What if we can't change him back?"

"Listen. I know Willis Windum. He's been a pal since I was in grade school. He can change."

"I'm not sure. He sometimes— Well. I shouldn't say."

"This is a safe space, Tagg. You can tell me whatever you want."

Taggart swallowed. "He sometimes acts like he's in charge. Like he's the leader."

That hurt to hear. It was an unspoken rule that if any one of their ranks was in charge, it was Frankie. Willis was second-in-command. And Taggart was the one with something to prove. He was new to their group ever since Patrick Lorde had blown his brains out, leaving behind a note that said *We are all guilty.* Whatever that meant.

Willis was maybe in need of a reality check.

Frankie nodded. "Okay, Taggart. What do you think we should do about it?"

Taggart brightened up. "I think we should hit him where it hurts. Make it clear that he needs to step in line or step out."

"What are you proposing."

"I think we should break the agreement."

Frankie felt the air vanish from the room.

A few months back, Willis's sister, Daisy, had needed a place to stay after their closed-minded folks had booted her out for being gay. Before she'd moved in, Willis had sat the boys down and sternly forbade them from touching his kin.

"Dude, why would we? She's gay," Taggart had said.

"I just want it to be clear. We ain't treating her the way we treated Frankie's cousin. We ain't treating her like every other woman that comes in."

"Because . . . we'd be homophobic if we did," Frankie had said.

When she'd come in, Taggart had instantly been smitten with her, despite her identity. She was a beautiful lady. That was for sure. Tall, slender, purple-haired, and bubbly. She was now sleeping in the guest bedroom, which she'd decorated with posters of old movies from the sixties.

"Taggart, are you lying to me?" Frankie asked, drawing himself back to the present, and to the current issue.

Taggart looked mortified. "A-about Willis? No. No. I wouldn't lie. Not to you, boss."

"Is this just an excuse to get in that young woman's panties?"

"No. I mean it. I saw that shit on Willis's phone! He's eatin' meat!"

Frankie looked him up and down. "Okay, pal. I believe you. But if we do this and Willis proves you were a liar, it ain't gonna be the both of us that get punished for it. It'll *just* be you."

Taggart swallowed.

"Where is Willis now?"

"He went out for beer. Should be back in an hour."

"Well. We better not waste any more time."

EIGHT

Blue Lives Splatter

Flo had never been fucked so well in her life. She almost popped another orgasm when Caim slithered back into her cooch and nestled into her womb. Pleasant tingles rushed through her flesh in electric pulses. She felt as if she had two vibrators in every orifice!

She almost didn't hear the knock at the door, she was so lost in her own ecstasy.

The second round of knocks startled her into a sitting position. She was still on the bed, her mother's flattened body beside her, Dustin's drowned corpse leaning against the headboard, and her dad on the floor.

Who the fuck is that? she wondered.

She received an immediate answer.

"Police! Open up!"

Police?

Jesus!

Flo felt her high dissipate and her bowels tremble.

No! Not the cops!

We ain't done yet!

We still gotta kill Frankie!
I can't be locked up!

She grabbed her belly and whispered toward it, "Caim! Come out! We got more work to do!"

Her stomach shuddered, but Caim didn't explode out of her.

She was alone. Stuck in a double-wide with three goddamned dead fuckin' bodies! And who would they blame for this atrocity? Well, who else? Besides, her sticky DNA was all over her mother. She may as well have slapped the cuffs on her wrists herself!

"Police! Responding to a noise complaint! C'mon! Open up!"

A noise complaint?

Where were these fuckers when Hank was beatin' down my bathroom door with an ax?

Jumpin' Jesus!

"Come out, Caim! Come out and help me!" she screeched, much too loud.

"I can hear you, ma'am! Listen, we just need you to open the door and talk to us. Ain't nobody need ta go to the slammer tonight. Just come on over to the door and we'll talk this through."

Swallowing bile, she looked around the room. Her clothes were blood-coated. And would she fit in any of her mama's tight-fitting slutwear?

She couldn't open the door, naked and gore greased, and expect a quick conversation and a snappy goodbye.

Her vagina released a raspy expulsion of air. She watched as a red bubble grew and popped. This queef was followed by a warbled voice.

Caim was speaking through her cunt, "Do it."

"Do what?" she whispered, panicked.

"Open the door. As you are. I'll handle it from there."

"Really?"

"Really."

"Okay. If you say so."

Flo heaved herself off of the bed and waddled toward the bedroom door.

She took one last look at her father's body.

Fucker.

She grabbed the knob and threw the door open, calling out, "Okay! I'm comin'! Shit!"

The cop stopped knocking.

She walked down the hall, leaving bloody footprints on the tattered carpet.

In the living room, the TV was still playing. She took a second to flick it off, then went to the front door. Taking a deep breath, she pulled it open.

The cop standing on the porch was a tall, handsome young guy. He had a mustache, a bald head, and strong arms. He looked like the sort of dude who could kick a horse in half but was too polite to do so. A ways away, his partner was standing by the patrol car with a flashlight. She was a lady cop with thick hips and a butch haircut.

Flo was surprised that he didn't immediately yank his sidearm and shout at her to put her bloody hands on her head.

"Evening, ma'am. I'm Officer Renton, and back there's my partner, Lydia. You know what brought us out here tonight?"

Flo shook her head.

"Welp, you got a neighbor two houses down that says you and your buddies have been having too much fun."

"Oh," Flo muttered. "That so?"

"Yep. Shouting, screamin' . . . Listen, I'm all for a good old-fashioned orgy, myself, but we can't be interrupting the whole block's sleep, can we?" He winked.

"Well, I'm awful sorry,"—Flo started to close the door— "we'll keep it down."

Renton put his boot in the door's way. Startled, Flo allowed it to swing back open.

"Listen, ma'am. We heard this call and, well, we got a little question for ya."

Flo's eyes widened and her teeth chomped down on her wiggling tongue.

"Got room for two more?"

She was stunned.

Did this happen in real life? Did cops actually come to people's houses where suspected hedonistic orgies were taking place . . . and *ask to join in?* It sounded like the plot of an uncreative porno.

And couldn't he see all the blood?

Flo looked toward Lydia. The female cop was grinning like a well-fed cat. She swiveled her hips and bit her lower lip.

Oh my God.

They're for real.

What the fuck?

"Well? How about it?" Renton showed his teeth. "Or . . . would you rather talk about this back at the station?"

Now he's leveraging a potential arrest.

Does he think there's a crowd of fun-lovin', free-wheeling swingers hiding behind me?

What a night!

"Well," Flo said, "so long as you wear a rubber!"

"I always got one on me!" Renton patted his breast pocket.

Lydia came up the porch. She was already undoing her shirt.

"Where are all the bodies?" the lady cop asked.

The question made Flo's face go red.

"In . . . in the back."

"We ain't been fuckin' nobody but each other this last month!" Renton admitted. "We've been looking for an opportunity like this."

Flo looked from one cop to the other. "Are y'all, like, married or somethin'?"

"Married? No." Renton snickered. "Lydia's just . . . Well. We all use her when we got the urge."

"It's great stress relief!" Lydia piped in.

Inside, the cops stepped out of their clothes.

They were both gorgeous, Flo realized. Renton's abs were like granite, and his erect prick was like a hoof behind his white undies. Lydia was sexy too. Her body was curvy, her breasts shook like Jell-O, and she was wearing a constrictive thong that bared the humps of her rear.

Flo walked them down the hall.

Renton's foot squelched into a bloody pile that had been left by Flo.

"Whoa! Someone spilled some lube here!" Renton cawed. "You know what I always say. Reduce! Recycle! Reuse!"

"Oh, gross!"

"What?" Renton asked his partner. "It's all going in the same place!" He scooped up the blood, lowered his underwear, and slathered his cock in it.

"Hey, what type of folks you got here?" Lydia asked. "Any lookers?"

Flo paused. "It's . . . a slow night. We got two hunks and a slut. And they love a good fuckin'."

"Ass and pussy city!" Renton hooted.

"Lemme go in first. Just to warn them they've got newcomers."

"Got any bud?" Lydia asked.

"Huh?"

"Grass?"

"Oh. No. Sorry. Ran out."

"I always got a dime," Renton added. "Lemme run back to the living room and dig it outta my pockets."

"Okay," Flo said, opening the bedroom door and stepping in.

She looked around the room and was surprised.

A sparkly-eyed nymphet with red hair and a puffy pussy was lying on the bed, her breasts full and firm on her chest.

On both sides of her stood two of the prettiest men Flo had ever seen. A Greek god with a thick beard and a girthy cock was porking the babe in the mouth.

Between her legs, gobbling her pussy like it was going out of style, was a slim guy with cherry-red cheeks and black locks.

Flo about screamed.

Who were these people?

What had happened to her folks and Dustin?

She shook her head, not believing what she was seeing.

The room was spotless. Clean enough to smell sterile.

Flo looked down at herself.

She was wearing a leather corset, which confined her body like a stout hug.

"This is what they see," Caim spoke through her vibrating cunt. "Welcome to Xanadu!"

Flo almost shrieked with mad laughter. She held her pregnant belly and spoke aloud, "Caim, I think I love you."

She could feel his laughter tickle her clit.

Flo opened the door.

Lydia rushed in, moon-eyed. "And who are these studs!"

"That's Dustin and Larry! You'll like 'em a lot."

"And the babe?" Lydia's mouth watered.

"That's only the prettiest gal in town. Windi! You ain't never seen her before?"

Lydia's mouth was popped open. She waved lightly. "Hi, boys."

Reality and fantasy flipped back and forth, allowing Flo to experience both at once.

This demon shit is pretty wild!

"Hi, darling!" Larry cooed from between Windi's spread legs.

"Hey, you wanna ride this?" Dustin asked, clenching his rock-hard cock in his fist. It was oozing with saliva and pre-ejaculate.

"You bet!" Lydia almost cheered.

She rushed over and turned around. She pried her slick thong away from her crack, then sat down with a squishy *splat.*

Flo watched as she grinded her ass against Dustin's blood, shit, and piss-creamed pelvis. She moved violently, imagining she'd been penetrated by an exciting lover. Behind her, Dustin's carcass wobbled in place. Blood slipped out from his overfilled gas mask and dribbled down her back.

"Oh God! Ain't you a good 'un!" Lydia shouted.

"Don't start without me!" Renton pounded into the room, his weed abandoned.

He froze by the bed, looking down at Windi's crumpled corpse. "My God! And how old are you, ma'am? Sheeeiiittt! You better not tell nobody!"

He moved between her legs, rubbed his already bloodied prick into a full erection, then drove it into her slit.

His eyes rolled back with sudden pleasure. As if he wasn't cramming his cork into a mashed and squishy mess of flappy flesh. He was picturing the tightest, wettest, softest pussy on the planet.

"Lord! I'm about ta blow! I swear, ma'am, I don't tend to go this fast but— Goddamn!"

He pulled out and sprayed pearls onto Windi's belly.

The young version of Windi rubbed the semen into her stomach, giggling happily as she played with her lover's sperm.

"You liked that, huh? Well, let's try something you might like more!"

He knelt between her legs and began to lick.

From her vantage point, Flo could see him moving his tongue over thick, bulbous, deer tick-sized moles, curdled clumps of discharge, and coagulated blood, locked in knots of musky-smelling pussy fur.

Lydia was screaming now, content with the fucking she thought she was getting.

"Oh Lord! Oh, I'm gonna BUST!" Lydia shouted, then squirted. A thick line of water jumped out of her and splattered against the floor.

Looking from one to the other, Flo was genuinely struggling to hold back laughter. If these dumb cops only knew who—and what—they were boning!

"You like that?" Renton asked from between Windi's legs. His mustache was stained cherry-red. Lines of bloody drool fell from his lips. "You like that?"

Renton set his hand against Windi's stomach and pushed.

A sloppy explosion of gory fluids blew out of her pussy and against his face. He blinked happily. "We got a squirter! Just like you, Lydia!"

Flo stepped out the door and closed it. This had been fun, but she needed to get back to business. Frankie wasn't going to kill himself!

"I'm gonna snap them out of it as soon as we're on our way," Caim said. "First, get the keys from that cop's pants. We're taking their ride!"

"What's going to happen when they realize what they've done?" Flo asked, as she made her way to the pile of clothes. "Think they'll freak?"

"I think they'll kill themselves," Caim said. "Wouldn't you?"

Flo chuckled. "I hope so. I hope they blow their own brains out!"

"You'll get along very well in Hell after all of this is said and done."

"You think so?"

"Yes. You're demented, Flo. And you wish the worst for humanity. Satan will be pleased to shake your hand."

NINE

A Violation of Trust

Frankie knocked on Daisy's door. He could hear her radio playing. He didn't recognize the song. It was some hippie tune—folk mixed with pop. He liked it, but he didn't think he'd get a chance to ask her who the artist was. Not with what he and Taggart were planning on doing to her.

He knocked again, which roused her.

"Coming!" Daisy shouted cheerily. He could hear her walking toward the door, her footsteps light and *swishing*.

She's throwing a robe on.
She's probably naked under there.
What was she doing?
Flicking the bean?

Frankie licked his lips.

When the door opened, his theory was confirmed. Her chest and collar were flushed, and her hair was sweaty.

Yes. She'd been masturbating.

Are we your dream come true? Or are we your worst nightmare?

She was confused to see Frankie and Taggart looking at her like she was prey. She instantly cinched her robe tighter.

"What's up, guys?"

Frankie pushed her into her own room. His hard shove knocked the wind out of her and sent her back onto the bed. She flopped down with her legs open.

Frankie stomped in. Taggart followed.

"What're you doin'?" Daisy cried through gasps. "What the fuck? When my brother hears about this—"

Taggart snapped the door shut.

He locked it.

All the fight seemed to leave Daisy. She tried to draw her robe closed, but her fear was paralyzing.

"Wh-what do you want?" she asked.

"We want you to pay your dues. Simple as that," Frankie said.

Daisy gulped. "I . . . I don't understand. Willis said I didn't need to pay anythin' until I got a job. If you wanted me to pay rent you shoulda told me—"

"You actually gay?" Taggart asked. "Or are you pretending for attention?"

This question shocked her as much as the shove had. "I'm . . . I'm gay."

"Yeah? How many girls you fucked?"

"That's personal."

"How many guys?" Frankie asked, stepping over to the radio and turning it off.

"Listen. Just leave. Leave my room and I won't tell Willis about any of this. I won't tell anyone. I swear."

Taggart opened her top drawer and began to rifle through her underwear.

"Hey! Stop it!" Daisy mewled.

"Look! I knew she wasn't gay!" Taggart pulled a pink dildo from the bottom of the drawer.

"Put that back! That's private!"

"You like fake cocks, huh? Have you ever tried a real one?" Frankie asked.

"It was a gift from my girlfriend! It's just a toy! Put it back!"

"How often do you use this thing?" Taggart asked, waggling it like an accusatory finger. "Nightly?"

"That's none of your business! And using a dildo doesn't make me any less gay, you bastard!"

"How many guys have you slept with?" Frankie asked, approaching the bed like a stealthy cheetah.

Daisy shook her head. "I don't owe you shit. Get out of my room."

"Hey. We just wanna know!" Frankie said. "We're curious. How about this? You tell us . . . and we'll leave."

"You're just saying that."

"Maybe. But I could be telling the truth. So what's the harm? Just answer the question."

Daisy looked toward the floor. She held the edges of her robe, clinging to the garment as if it were the only thing keeping her on the ground.

"Two," she admitted.

"Well, now yer gonna fuck two more!" Taggart laughed.

"No!" Daisy panicked, looking from face to face. "I thought you guys were— I thought you were feminists!"

"We are. We love women!" Frankie showed his teeth. "We love fucking women too. You and I have that in common, Daisy." He reached out and cupped her cheek.

Daisy reacted as if she'd been struck by lightning.

"Two guys, huh?" Taggart whistled. "Did they know you were pretending to be gay?"

"I'm not pretending!" Daisy whined.

"Well, how about we prove it? If you like what we do . . . then that means you're as straight as an arrow. If you don't like it . . . you'll thank us! Because you'll never have to question your own sexuality *ever again*."

Taggart sat down on the bed. He reached out and traced the dildo across her lips. She scampered back, pressing herself into the corner where her bed met the wall.

"Please!" she cried. "I don't want to!"

Frankie peeled his pants away.

Taggart tossed the dildo aside and followed suit.

"Just spread 'em, close your eyes, and this'll all be over in no time." Frankie snickered.

Outside, a siren whooped.

Frankie felt his heart stop. His penis wilted.

Taggart spun around, looking toward the window.

Blue and red lights were flashing.

"Fuck!" Taggart proclaimed.

"Fuck!" Frankie yanked his pants back up his legs.

Daisy rushed past them and scrambled toward the door. She beat her body against it, forgetting it had been locked.

Before Frankie or Taggart could catch her, Daisy was clawing the lock and spinning the knob. She hit the hallway and ran toward the living room, breathless, terrified, and scared that one wrong move would result in her rape.

Those bastards!

Acting so high and mighty! Like they're progressive! Like they're allies! If people knew what they were really like—

She rushed out the door and onto the porch, screaming, "Help! Help me!"

Daisy was blinded by the swirling lights.

She held a hand over her eyes and dashed toward the cop car.

By the time she reached it, she realized that the woman standing outside of it was no police officer.

She was a big, naked lady with sad eyes and—

FETAL BACKWASH

Holy shit.

Was that . . .

BLOOD?

Daisy froze in space. Her scream was cut short.

The lady was pregnant, too, she noted.

"Wh-what?" Daisy asked.

The woman smiled. "Did those boys try and hurt you?"

Daisy looked over her shoulder at the house. Her tormentors hadn't pursued her.

"Yes," Daisy admitted. "They were going to—"

The lady took a jaunty step toward her. Her smile didn't waver.

It was creeping Daisy out, especially in combination with the blood.

"Don't worry, darling. *We'll* take care of it." The crazy woman chuckled. "Keys are in the car. Why don't you drive somewhere safe and call the cops tomorrow?"

"Tomorrow?" Daisy whimpered.

"Yes. Because tonight . . . we've got a lot of work to do."

The woman started to walk toward the house.

Daisy watched her for a second, then scuttled into the cop car and drove off. She figured that her girlfriend wouldn't mind seeing her, although it was late in the night.

TEN

Vengeance

Flo was surprised by how little Frankie's house had changed. It was a two-story building located on a patch of rustic farmland. Behind it stood a row of towering trees, and around its sides and front were grassy knolls, mounds, and curvy hills. There really was no worry of their screams being heard by neighbors.

They had no neighbors.

Flo's grin split her head open.

She tramped up the stairs, ambled toward the screen door, and swung it open.

"Frankie, you miserable shit!" Flo jeered. "I'm *back!*"

Ker-CLACK.

BOOM!

The sound of the gun detonating was as loud as a thunderclap.

Flo's face fell right before it was blown through her skull and out the back of her head. Blood and brain splattered across the porch and crashed down the steps.

Flo wavered on her feet, trying to see who'd shot her, even though her eyes had been punched into the red cavity that had replaced her visage.

Flo stumbled around, struggling to maintain her footing.

I was too confident.

Well, how could I be any less confident?

Frankie was always talking about how all firearms should be removed from gun owners.

I shouldn't be surprised that he's a hypocrite on that front too.

Another gunshot ripped through her. She felt her sternum crack open. A gust of heavy blood spewed out of her as she spun, then toppled.

ELEVEN

Who Is That Bitch?

Frankie had been holding his hands over his ears. The gun belonged to Taggart, and before now, Frankie had been trying to figure out a way to get the ugly thing out of his house. But Taggart was sure Frankie was happy it had been here. The weapon had proved its usefulness.

Taggart expelled the casings, replaced the shells, and racked the shotgun.

"Where you think Daisy ran off to?" Taggart asked.

"I don't know. I honestly haven't been thinking about her much since we saw this bitch coming up. Who is she?"

"I dunno. She knew your name but— I don't know. I didn't see her face before I blew it off her skull," Taggart relished this. It'd been like killing a zombie in *The Walking Dead*!

"We'll be in trouble if we don't catch up with her ass," Frankie muttered. "Christ. What a clusterfuck! One dead bitch, one crying cunt . . . God. I'll say it, I fucking hate women."

The corpse jostled around, startling both men.

They stared down at the body as it struggled to climb back to its feet.

"CHRIST! JESUS! SHOOT IT! FUCKIN' SHOOT IT!"

Taggart yelped and rushed over to the corpse. He crammed the end of his gun into her mushed face, tilted it down, then yanked the trigger. The blast tore her neck to smithereens, then sent shards of hot fire down into her core.

Blood gurgled from the hole in the center of her head. Burping, gulping, slobbery waves of blood fell from the tatters that ringed her shredded throat.

She was still moving.

Just like a zombie!

But yer supposed to shoot a zombie in the brain!

I took that brain right outta her God blasted motherfuckin' skull!

Taggart knocked the second hammer back and fired again. This blow sent a patch of flesh and her wriggling spinal cord out of her back. The white rope dangled out of her like a misplaced tail.

He pulled the gun away. Drooling strands of blood clung to it.

Still, the corpse attempted to stand.

"No!" Taggart shouted. "No! No! No! NO!"

One of her gnarled hands lashed out and grabbed him between his legs. The thin gym shorts offered no protection.

Taggart seized up. The pain was automatic. She'd grabbed a handful of his balls *and* the limp shaft of his dick. She wrenched her hand, digging into his groin as if she was trying to get her digits underneath its surface.

"Taggart!" Frankie screamed. "Taggart! Watch out!"

Taggart squealed and writhed in place.

"Please! Lemme go! Lemme go! Oh good God, lemme go!"

A nasty voice came slurping up from the human debris that was clinging to Taggart's favorite body part.

"I'm your god, fucker!"

The zombie yanked down, crushing both of Taggart's testicles and spearing his pipe. Blood rushed over his thighs and wet the floor beneath him.

The hand relinquished its grasp, but the damage was done. His left nut was flattened like a stomped olive. His right dangled by a strand of exposed tubes.

Taggart dropped his gun and landed on his knees. He clutched his decimated cock and howled in pain.

"You bitch. You bitch. Oh God. You bitch. You got my goddamn boys. You fuckin' motherfuckin' stupid fuckin' evil fuckin' goddamn fuckin' asshole fuckin' no-good fuckin' absolute fuckin' total fuckin' Christ fuckin' holy Jesus cunt fuckin' BITCH!"

Something burst out of the woman's carcass, shedding it like a winter coat.

FETAL BACKWASH

It was red, muscled, and the size of a full-grown adult.

Entranced and terrified, Frankie pissed his pants as he took in the demonic creature.

"Yer here for Frankie, aintcha?" Taggart muttered, his hands quilted in syrupy blood. "Well, fuckin' have him! Just leave me alone!"

Frankie took a hurried step back. His heart yipped like a kicked puppy.

The demon took Taggart's head in his clawed hands. "Silly child, I'm here for *all* of you."

"No! No! No!" Taggart screamed.

The demon spoke in Daisy's voice, "When my brother hears about this—"

He racked Taggart's head back. A shard of bone protruded from his neck, spraying blood.

The demon wrenched the head around, then pulled it loose with a successive cacophony of snaps.

Blood flew into the air in bright streams.

The body tipped over and hit the ground.

Sneering, the demon held Taggart's head out for Frankie to observe.

"It'll be worse for you . . . *cousin raper!*"

Flo.

The body had been Flo's.

Frankie whirled around and smashed his feet against the steps. His heart slammed against the sides of his rib cage.

Demon.
It's a demon.
Can't be real.
No such thing.
Oh God. It killed Taggart!
Ripped his head off his shoulders!
Oh God!
Demons are real!

Frankie couldn't process all of this at once. It was tearing his mind to pieces just thinking about it.

He needed to rely on his survival instincts.

Had to move as fast as he could.

Get to his room, lock the door—

Then what?

Call the police?

Hey. My cousin Flo, who I raped, summoned a demon to punish me. Yeah. It's a really bad one too. Pulled my housemate's head right off. *Like it was nothing!*

Sure.

They'd buy that.

Frankie looked over his shoulder.

The demon was in hot pursuit.

It was crawling up the stairs after him on its hands and feet, like a massive, evil spider.

It was naked and it had the biggest penis he'd ever seen in his life. It immediately emasculated him, just watching that organ bob between the beast's legs.

"Leave me alone!" Frankie shouted as he hit the top of the stairs and scrambled toward his bedroom.

"No!" The creature shouted in Flo's voice, "Stop! I don't want it in me, Frankie! It feels bad! It feels *bad*."

Frankie crashed through his door and slammed it shut behind him. He gripped the knob and braced himself against it.

His room smelled like weed and sperm. It was littered with soiled clothes, old videotapes, and signs he'd made for protests and marches.

The slogans swirled around him, mocking him.

From the other side of the door, he heard Flo's voice again.

"I thought you were a good person, Frankie. But yer bad. Yer *real* bad."

Frankie swallowed a rising tide of vomit.

He'd never felt bad about what he'd done to Flo.

Not until now.

Now that he'd been caught.

"I trusted you," Flo said. "I thought you loved me. Then you raped me. You raped me, and your friends joined in. I know that one of them died. He killed himself because he was guilty. Why didn't you kill yerself, Frankie? Didn't you know the wrong you did?"

Frankie clamped his teeth together. "Shut up!"

"I trusted you. You abused me. You were going to abuse that other girl, weren't you? Going to put her through what you did to me. Maybe worse. Well, I won't stand for it. You're a *fucker*, Frankie. Jus' like my mom and dad. Just like Hank. Yer just a no-good, dirty fucker!"

He heard the demon step close to the door.

"And you aren't a rare breed, Frankie." The demon's voice was in charge now. Guttural, raspy, and dark. "You think you'd belong in Satan's ranks? No. You aren't even half as depraved as we are."

Frankie heard something rustle behind him.

He spun around.

He shrieked.

The demon was in the room with him. It'd teleported in and was towering over him, like a figment from a nightmare.

It leapt toward him, slashing its claws at his screaming face.

TWELVE

Tongue Punch

Frankie blinked awake.

He was tied to a kitchen chair. The demon had used bungee cords to secure him in place and zip ties to hold his hands behind his back.

He was in the living room. All the furniture had been removed.

Except for the TV.

On the screen, the fuzzy videotape of one of Flo's many rapes was playing.

Frankie looked wearily to his side.

Willis was trapped next to him, tied in a similar fashion.

Willis was skinny, pale, and his black hair fell down his shoulders. He wasn't very handsome, which was why he had gone all in on Frankie's escapades. He'd even once said, "Hey, a lay is a lay. Don't matter whether or not it's given or taken."

On the screen, Willis was cheesing it up for the camera while he violated young Flo.

We're pathetic.
Old men living like teenagers.
Fuckin' people without their permission.

Filming it.

Pathetic losers.

"Willis? You okay?" Frankie asked.

"Don't talk ta me," Willis snapped. "That fucker that tied us up told me what you were trying to do to Daisy."

Frankie's balls tightened.

He realized he was naked.

His cock looked like freeze-dried shrimp.

"We can talk about that later, can't we? We gotta figure out how to get out of this!"

Willis shook his head. "I ain't helping you. I just hope he kills you first!"

Frankie gritted his teeth together and pinched his eyes shut. He tried to think through this.

Could a demon be bartered with?

Could he make a deal?

He doubted it. The fiend had seemed intent on giving Flo the vengeance she was owed.

He looked back at the screen and felt a crushing wave of guilt.

We should've killed her so she couldn't tell nobody about what we done.

Should've killed her.

The demon walked in front of him. His sudden, naked appearance startled Frankie, causing him to gasp loudly.

The demon held one of the beers that Willis had come back home with. He punctured it with a thick talon, then caught the fizzing spray in his mouth. He drained the can, then crunched it against his thick brow.

"That's good," the demon said in its nasty voice. "You have taste, Willis."

Willis nodded. "Hey. I know you gotta kill the both of us for what we done, but can you kill Frankie first? I'd like to fuckin' watch!"

The demon snickered. "No. Unfortunately for you, Flo was very specific. She wanted me to save Frankie for last. Besides, you are not innocent. You will suffer, die, and find no reward afterward. They will feed your soul to The Pit."

Willis gulped. "The Pit?"

"You'll see when you get there." He then addressed both men, "Do you know who I am?"

They shook their heads.

"I'm Caim. Godhead of Depravity. Lord of Murder and Madness. President of Hell. It was I who spoke into Cain's ear and convinced him to slaughter Abel. It was I who sat on John Wilkes Booth's shoulder and commanded him to pull the trigger. It was I who dwelled beneath the crawl space in John Wayne Gacy's home, feeding on the boy corpses he buried there. In Amityville, I convinced Ronald DeFeo Jr. to butcher his whole family. Did you know this?"

Frankie felt his bowels squirm. He was close to shitting himself.

"Every murder that has ever been committed on your dismal, rancid planet . . . I was *there*." Caim squatted down, leering at Frankie. "And now . . . I'm *here*."

Frankie shook his head. "I don't believe you."

"You don't want to believe. But you do. I'm as real as that wilted thing between your legs. I'm as real as the air you breathe. The tears in your eyes. The *feces* in your bowels."

It was like he'd spoken a magic word that triggered a bodily reaction. Frankie felt a wave of warm shit stream out of his ass and inflate beneath him. It was like he'd sat down on a mushy plate of pumpkin pie that smelled like compost and roadkill.

"Aw, Frankie! That's foul!" Caim chortled as he pinched his nose.

Frankie dipped his head and held his tongue. He wanted to shout at Caim. Wanted to tell the demon that his days were numbered.

But it would have been fruitless bravado.

"You really shit yerself?" Willis asked. "Oh God! That smells bad! What've you been e*atin'*, Frankie?"

"Do you feel violated, Frankie? That's how Flo felt. Humiliated. Shamed. You did that to her. And then . . . you had her killed." Caim curled his lips, exposing his broken teeth. "She was going to die anyway. She'd pledged to do so. But you killed her before she could watch you suffer. You took her innocence, then you took her vengeance. I'm going to give it back to her, Frankie. I'm going to give it back."

Caim's own belly rumbled thickly. He released a gassy string of farts, which were noxious to the noses of his victims.

Willis began to cough, then puke. Piss-yellow vomit streamed out of his mouth and spattered the floor.

The demon squatted, maintaining eye contact with Frankie.

He began to push something out of his ass.

It peeked from his anus like a periscope's eye, then sloughed out in a wet wave.

It was, Frankie saw, a baby.

A baby coated in shit, oil, and wet strands of gore.

It landed on the ground with a wail.

Caim stepped aside, allowing both men to take in the sight of the child.

It was growing, as if its development was under the control of a TV remote. Fast-forwarding through all stages of life until it was a large woman lying on the floor in a fetal ball, covered in Caim's gory backwash.

Flo came to with a gasp.

"Oh God, no!" Frankie's eyes were prickled with tears. "No! It ain't *possible*."

Caim helped her to her feet. She was naked, hairless, and oozing. She smacked her lips and rolled her eyes.

"My love," Caim said.

"Darling. I was almost sad to leave Hell!"

"It's a beautiful place, isn't it?"

"Yes," Flo confirmed.

"Look what I got for you!" Caim indicated the crying victims. "A rebirthing present!"

Frankie pulled on his binds and screamed.

Willis rocked crazily back and forth, continuing to heave even though he'd expelled all of his available fluids.

Flo showed her teeth. "Oh, you shouldn't have!"

"Only the best for you," Caim said into her ear. "Come on. Let's take them where they belong."

Flo stumbled toward Willis, struggling to figure out how her legs worked. Like a colt.

"No! Oh God! Please, Flo! I'm sorry! I didn't even want ta do it! I just . . . It was peer pressure, Flo! You understand? I didn't *wanna*!"

Flo grabbed his lower jaw and pulled it down with a grunt. Willis could see the edges of his friend's lips part open. A flood of blood spilled from the cracks and leaked down his jouncing jowls.

Willis cried, but the vents in his flesh made it look like he was wearing a crimson clown's smile.

She rocked his jaw down again, exposing the insides of his mouth.

His tongue waggled around like a flopping fish.

Flo leaned in, opening her own oral cavity for a gruesome kiss.

"Willis! I'm sorry!" Frankie cried. "I'm sorry!"

Flo's slimy tongue leapt out of her mouth and invaded Willis's. He *hrrrrk*ed loudly, then shut his eyes.

"This is what it means . . . to be filled against your wishes!" Caim laughed.

Flo's tongue seemed to be growing. Like an absorbent sponge.

Willis shook in his seat. His naked body was sheened in sweat and his prick was pissing like a split firehose. His toes curled, digging into the floorboards.

Frankie could hear his toenails crinkle, bind, then break.

"Oh God! No! Leave him alone! Please!" Frankie railed.

Willis's tongue grew like a condom being filled with ejaculate. It expanded and inflated and *ballooned.* He could no longer scream. The tongue was like a stopper in his throat. It sealed all of his sounds and caused his gullet to bulge.

Willis began to seize like he'd been poked in the gonads with a cattle prod. He clamped his teeth down over the invading organ, but the tongue was made of stronger stuff than pink muscle. It flexed, and in that single motion the vicious tongue broke *all of his teeth*. They fell like white pebbles, followed by streams of red.

"No! Oh God, no! Yer hurtin' him, Flo! Yer killin' him!" Frankie wept.

On the TV, a younger Flo said almost the exact same line, "No! Cousin! No! Yer hurtin' me!"

When Frankie tried looking away from Willis, he was confronted with his own crimes. With the vile actions that brought him to this. They blared on the TV like a disturbing sports event. One boy after another, taking their turn with the young woman they'd separated from society for their own sick desires. They were beating her, taking turns slapping her face until it was as crimson as the blood pouring out of Willis's fractured gums.

Frankie looked back at Willis.

He was trying to breathe, but the pressure in his head was overloading his nose with melted-hot-adhesive-textured snot. Green ooze poured out of his nostrils and coated his rumpled upper lip.

His eyes had rolled back into their sockets. Blood vessels broke in the white orbs, staining them scarlet.

"Oh, Willis," Frankie said, hoping to calm his panicking friend down. "I'm sorry. This is all my fault."

"No, it isn't," Caim snarled. "Both of you are sinners."

The tongue punched into Willis's center. Frankie could see his stomach distending, growing pregnant. More piss spritzed from his cock. This fluid was tinted a rusty red.

She's fucking up his insides.
Rearranging them with her tongue.
Like an elephant trunk plunging into him!
Dear God!
Dear Lord!

Frankie mewled like a child with a missing dolly. He rocked against his binds, not caring that the zip ties were searing into his flesh and drawing blood. Not even minding the scratchy rope burn left by the taut bungee cords.

He wished he'd been a better person.
He wished he'd practiced what he'd preached.

Willis groaned. His belly grew, bursting at the seams. Fissures ripped along the sides of his swelling middle, raining blood on the already soused floor. His thighs jangled and his fists clenched so hard he buried his nails into his palms.

"Leave him alone! He's hurt enough!"

Flo grabbed Willis by the shoulders. More of her impossible tongue seemed to roll out of her and fill his orifice, to travel down his throat and further inflate his beach-ball-sized belly.

All the while, Caim stood nearby, stroking his heavy hog and grinning madly. Enthused by the pain and torment that Flo was causing Willis.

His stomach burst. It popped like a water balloon.

Gore spilled out in a frantic rush.

It dribbled, slopped, sloughed, raced, spattered, splattered, smattered, and sprayed.

It was like a wax candle melting all at once.

"Willis, no!" Frankie brayed.

Tongues began to fall out of Willis's open abdomen. They leapt out after the blood trail like frogs from a draining pond. Thick, pink, wriggling worms severed from their host.

Flo stepped back, her own tongue receding back into her mouth like a chameleon's, leaving the parasitic muscles to ravage Willis's dying body.

His jaw was busted open. It swiveled below his shuddering head. His eyes refused to turn over, so he was blind.

But Frankie was willing to bet a million bucks that Willis was capable of *feeling* what was happening to him.

The wave of tongues fell out like tokens from a winning slot machine. They slapped the floor wetly, then flopped around like dying birds. Flipping over from one side to the other.

Willis reclined, tipping his head back. He made a snuffling, groaning sound.

"You fuckers!" Frankie cried. "Oh God! He didn't deserve that!"

"Compared to what we're going to do to you," Flo said as she wiped the slobber from her smiling lips, "that was only a *tongue lashing*."

Caim honked with laughter. "Good one, darling!"

The two demons showed their teeth proudly.

Willis croaked with a heaving gasp. His body had gone snow-white from blood loss, and his organs were spooling out of him now that the tongues had voided his innards. They'd effectively mashed his insides into a pasty, pink pulp.

"You didn't— I woulda said 'Sorry' for all that stuff we did to you. You didn't gotta *kill* us," Frankie moaned.

Flo cackled. "No, you wouldn't. You've never been sorry a day in yer miserable life."

THIRTEEN

Raped with Fire

Frankie was left alone.

He had no idea where Flo and Caim had gone off to.

He'd blacked out shortly after Willis had stopped breathing.

Now conscious, he wished he'd stayed in the ink-dark netherworld, where all of reality was a dream.

He could smell Willis. Even when he wasn't looking at him, he was reminded that the corpse was there.

The floor was crowded with tongues. They'd eventually died. Exposure seemed to be the cause. Instead of jumping and drooling, they wilted, curled, and dried. Like oversized rose petals.

The TV was still playing. It seemed to be caught in a loop, showing Flo's abuse again and again. Forcing Frankie to feel guilty and angry all at once.

Should've killed ya.

Should've killed every bitch I ever fucked.

He pulled at his restraints. It was a fruitless and painful maneuver.

Patrick was lucky he killed himself.

Maybe he knew what was coming.
Maybe I'll see him in Hell.

He truly believed in the place. How could he not? He'd met a demon and watched as another was born.

Born right outta his ass. Dropped Flo like a fat turd.

Frankie held his breath and squeezed his eyes shut.

Maybe he could suffocate himself to death before his tormentors came back.

Right when he felt he was getting somewhere, he heard the back door swing open and shut.

Caim and Flo came into the room together.

"Miss us?" Flo asked, scrunching her brow. "It's almost daytime. You slept a good while . . . but yer up now. That means we gotta get to work."

Flo stepped in front of him and showed what she and her hideous lover had left to retrieve.

"Know what this is?" Flo asked.

Although he did know, Frankie shook his head.

"It's called a sounding rod. Just picked it up at an all-night magazine shop. You know the place? And no, they didn't see all this blood an' shit on us."

It was a stainless steel rod comprised of rounded metal balls affixed in a straight line. Its end included a small handle that looked like a metal piercing, which ended in two delicately crafted bulbs.

He knew this instrument was used to pleasure men, but he was sure Flo had found a way around that intended purpose.

"How about this?" she set the rod on the floor by his clenched feet. When she stood, she opened her hand and presented another toy, which had materialized like magic.

This was the pink dildo they'd handled in Daisy's room.

He felt sudden shame.

"You don't gotta do this," Frankie muttered.

Flo set the dildo down, then presented another item—again, via magic that would have been an easy sleight of hand if she wasn't nude.

A pincushion that looked like a hedgehog; the quills on its back were silver quilter's pins, each one topped with a yellow plastic bead.

Caim stood behind her, arms crossed, observing.

"I was around thirteen when you stole me away and raped me. I think thirteen is your unlucky number." She let him look at the pins, counting all of them.

"I don't wanna die."

"You'll change yer tune after you start hurting," Flo said, extracting the first needle. "Now hold still. We're gonna start easy, then work our way up to the big stuff."

Caim slithered over and took Frankie's head. He held it steady despite Frankie's vocal protests.

"Just a little prick, cousin. You won't feel a thing," Flo promised, leaning in, filling Frankie's vision with her hairless dome and lumpy body.

He squirmed, writhed, and pleaded, but it was all for naught.

The first needle slid just beside his left eye and above his orbital bone, spearing his tear duct and sliding coolly against the edge of his vision. His eye turned blurry but didn't go blind. She hadn't punctured the orb itself.

Blood trickled out like fresh tears.

Frankie roared and bucked, but Caim's clawed hands held him still.

"*Shhh*. You're doing so well, Frankie!" Flo smiled.

"Please! Fuck you, cunt! Please! Fuck both of you! Please!" Frankie couldn't decide whether he wanted to be mad or pleading. Neither had any effect on the demons.

Flo extracted another pin from the cushion. She almost sat on his lap, compressing him into his chair.

The second needle went into the opposite eye socket. Identical to the first, it turned his vision fuzzy but didn't erase it.

Frankie opened his mouth to scream.

Caim clamped his jaw apart and held it wide.

He was sure there'd be tongues filling his oral cavity, just like Willis, but instead, a third pin was pushed into the tip of his tongue and buried into its middle. It held the tongue stiff and filled his maw with tangy blood.

Frankie tried to speak, but his words weren't intelligible.

The next pin—number four—was pushed into the gums, just between his front upper teeth. She prodded and worked, ensuring that the pin scraped against his nasal cavity *through* his mouth.

The pins burned and itched.

The fifth quilter's pin was inserted into his left eyelid, peeling it up and securing it in place so he couldn't blink without tearing the flesh.

The sixth needle went into the opposite eyelid. Now there was no dark sanctuary for him to escape to. He'd have to watch everything that occurred to him.

He was almost thankful his vision was blurred.

"The easy part is over, Frankie. And you did so well! But life ain't cupcakes and rainbows. Every person gotta face their challenges head-on! And it's about to get really challenging for you."

Frankie whimpered. Six pins had been inserted into him, and despite his fear and anxiety, none of the pain had been numbed. His eyes were drying out since he couldn't blink, and every involuntary movement of his tongue sent sparks through him.

"First, I'm givin' you a break from the pins. We're gonna use the rod to get this procedure going." Flo hunkered down.

FETAL BACKWASH

"Pleath-I-thorry-pleath!" Frankie mouthed around his oral injuries.

"Hon, would you mind heating this up for me?" Flo asked.

"With pleasure," Caim replied.

He took the rod from her hand, put it in his mouth, and licked it. The effects of his demonic saliva were instant. It was as if the rod had been put over an open flame.

He handed it to Flo. Frankie was surprised that she didn't flinch when she touched it, but then again . . . she wasn't exactly *human* anymore.

Flo took Frankie's cock, rolling his foreskin down to expose the stern bulb of his head. He pissed with fright, spritzing her face and chest. She didn't react.

"You penetrated me, Frankie."

He begged with his eyes.

"And it . . . burned."

She slid the rod into his urethra.

The burning sensation was much worse than Frankie had anticipated—and he'd been expecting it to hurt like hell.

His thighs tensed, his toes curled, he dug his fingers into his palms, and he brayed like a dying pig.

She twisted the rod like a corkscrew as it smoldered its way down the length of his aching shaft. With her hand, she squeezed the organ, ensuring that its innards wouldn't escape the burning.

"You like that? You like being *raped with fire*?" Flo laughed.

Frankie responded with guttural moans.

He could feel the tissue inside his dick bubbling.

She ruined me!

I'll never fuck again!

Frankie fidgeted, trying his best to free himself from this trap.

Caim stepped behind him once more and secured him in place with a headlock. The demon's flesh was warty and scaly all at once. Its touch sickened and disturbed him.

Flo released him. His prick hung like a duffle bag from his pelvis. Red, blistered, and sizzling. Smoke leaked from his slit in gray strings. Blood leaked from the hole as well.

Frankie had never bled from his dick before.

Even with all the women he'd raped, he'd never caught anything. He'd kept himself clean.

Now, he was ruined. His favorite part of his anatomy was destroyed.

Frankie passed out, closing his eyes and tearing the lids in half.

FOURTEEN

Paid in Full

When he woke up, Flo had put the rest of the quilter's pins into his testicles. His ball sack was seeping blood and gray fluid. A long stream of wormy tissue squeezed its way out of a hole in his scrotum. It puddled onto the shit-coated chair like a patch of musty spaghetti.

Frankie whimpered.

His eyelids had been ripped apart. Blinking them seemed to furl the flesh like a watery, soggy scroll. His vision was muddled, but he caught glimpses of his surroundings.

"Oh, you're up. Like what we did with the place?"

He looked around.

The walls had been painted with Willis's blood.

Pentagrams, demon faces, snarling mouths, spurting cocks, and weeping cunts surrounded him. It looked as if he'd stumbled into a bloodred porno theater.

The details were incredible. Even in his state, and with his vision turned blurry, Frankie could admire how Caim and Flo had used Willis's fluids to paint a picture of an eight-armed monster with ram horns fisting a crying girl whose own arms had been detached from their sockets.

There was also a painting of a dog eating a wailing baby. One of a man with spiders coming out of his empty eye sockets. Another showed vultures pecking at the corpse of a young girl.

"Murder is an art," Caim said. "Ever since I created it, I've said that. So look at our gallery and weep."

Frankie lowered his head, then flinched when he got an eyeful of his ruined groin. He turned his face away from the atrocity, then saw Willis's hollowed-out cadaver. He tried to seek something safe and peaceful, but wherever his broken, blistered, blurry eyes went . . . he saw agony. His own. His victims. His friends.

Perpetual and unending agony.

Frankie wanted to close his eyes for good. He actually wanted to die.

"We're almost done," Flo said.

Thank God.

On the TV, Flo's younger self was begging for mercy.

Frankie rasped and grumbled.

"What's the matter? Can't say what's on yer mind?"

Frankie shook and trembled. He felt hot and cold all at once.

"Get his hands loose," Flo commanded.

Caim worked for her like a servant. Using his claws, he cut the zip ties.

There was no relief in freedom. Frankie's hands felt limp.

When they were brought around, he saw why.

They were as purple as plums, and the flesh around his wrists had been gouged by the plastic. He was lucky he hadn't nicked an artery.

Actually, that would've been for the better.
I'd be dead already if I had.

Flo investigated his face, gently touching the ends of the pins she'd put through him. The two by each eye, the three in his mouth.

"You look like something out of a fetish magazine!" she giddily declared.

"Ff-yuck yew." Frankie coughed.

"Put your hands together as if yer prayin'. You ever pray before? I mean, honestly pray. Like, talked to God and shit. Not closed yer eyes at the dinner table or bowed yer head during the national anthem. I mean, have you ever prayed?"

He shook his head. What was the point of lying?

"Did you wish to God that you wouldn't get caught for all them nasty things you was doing?"

Frankie froze.

"Yeah. Bet you believed in God every time you almost got caught. Bet you promised Him that you'd reform just as long as he didn't let the cops look yer way. Just as long as no one spoke up 'bout what you done. Hell, God's just as bad as you, ya know? He'd actually have made a good pal for you. Too bad you ain't going to Heaven. Because when all is said and done . . . yer comin' back with *me*!"

Frankie lifted his arms. His hands hung from them like blood bags.

He couldn't fight.

Couldn't run.

There was no hope for him.

He put his hands together, mashing his purple and blue fingers into knots.

Frankie bowed his head.

Flo picked up the pink dildo.

When Taggart had pulled the toy out of Daisy's drawer, Frankie had hoped they'd use it on her. He'd hoped they could take something that was intended for pleasure and mutate it into an object that only inspired pain and shame.

He wriggled in his seat. The muddy shit glued him to the chair. It had turned crusty and itchy, further irritating his already breaking body. He felt like he was sitting on stinging nettles.

Caim was behind him. He grabbed Frankie's hair and pulled his head back.

Sitting upright, his hands planted together in deformed supplication, Frankie watched as Flo swallowed the dildo with her cunt. It glided into her easily, like it belonged there.

She pulled it in and out, slathering it in her vaginal juices.

Then, between pumps, another fluid joined in on the fun. Instead of a clear mucus, something green and noxious began to emit from Flo's vagina. The color of flu snot and the consistency of egg yolks. The mushy fluid smacked like macaroni as her speed increased.

Flo spread her legs and squatted, muttering to herself as she fucked her sex. With her other hand, she squeezed one of her huge breasts, twisting and twirling the nipple like a spigot.

Frankie shook his head, wanting to look away, even though there was nowhere else to look. Nothing left to see.

Caim leaned in and whispered in his ear, "You made her taste you. You made her hurt. You brought her pain and misery. For that, I'm thankful. You made Flo hate the world. You made her . . . perfect."

The juxtaposition of Caim's words with the actions they'd taken on Frankie and his friends—

His stomach lurched like a fussy chainsaw. His cock was lit with newfound pain. His tongue writhed, shredding itself against the pin lodged into it.

Flo extracted the dildo. It was sizzling. Gobs of green goo clung to its rubber shaft and oversized head.

She held it out and gave it a tight squeeze, draining her fluids onto Frankie's face like the greasiest cum shot in the world.

The burning began instantly.

It was as if he'd gotten a face full of acid rain.

As if he'd had bleach poured into his pores.

The green fluids melted through him. He felt as if his skull was crumbling beneath his flesh. He chittered, brayed, and then outright cried.

Bloody snot dribbled down his cheeks and splattered against the chair.

Caim released him and stepped back.

Frankie shuddered, shook, then began to bounce up and down as if he were riding an untrained steed. His legs opened and closed rapidly, further pulverizing his cock and pushing the pins deeper into his wrinkled ball bag.

"NOOOOOOOO!" Frankie shouted.

The liquids crawled *through* his cheeks and into his mouth. His tongue felt like a strip of bacon on a greasy skillet.

He could hear his flesh popping and sputtering as it fell away from his facial muscles.

Frankie jittered in place, wishing he could run upstairs and stand under the hot spray of his shower. As if that could stop this hellish fluid from corroding and melting him.

"I'm soooooorry! PLEEEEEEEEEASE!" Frankie roared.

FETAL BACKWASH

The cunt nectar found its way into his eyes.

It was like they'd been injected with hot tar.

The darkness didn't consume his eyes. It outright flattened them.

He could hear them melting in their sockets. Sizzling like eggs left on the stove, abandoned by an overworked cook. Blistering, bubbling, farting, crackling, smacking, sizzling!

The metal pins curved and bent, then seeped into his skull, liquified by Flo's toxic waste.

This is a dream.

A horrible dream.

If this was happening in real life—

It couldn't happen in real life.

Women don't cum hot lava!

They can't fill people with so many tongues that their stomachs burst open!

They can't rip heads off of bodies!

They can't stand up after being shot!

They can't! They can't! They can't! Oh my God! THEY CAN'T!

He felt his nose slide off his face. It plopped onto the floor, a gooey lump of pink and bloody tissue. Made formless and syrupy. Like a jellyfish washed ashore.

He felt his tongue turn into pulpy, chunky soup. It filled the bowl of his throat until he was forced to swallow.

His cheeks were stripped away, baring every tooth for the world to see.

Then those began to crumble as well. Decomposing at a fast pace into depreciated shards. His mouth looked like a shattered clay vase.

They can't! They can't! They can't! They can—

His head fell into itself like a rotten pumpkin, terminating his thoughts.

FIFTEEN

My Love, Forever

Flo relished the process. Watching Frankie's face fall away from his skull, then watching the skull suck itself *into* his head? Holy God. It was about the best thing she'd ever witnessed during her short life and short period as a demon.

When Frankie was done, his head was completely gone. It was a sloppy puddle that dribbled down the back of his chair. A blackened cave had grown between his shoulders, chewing into the meat of his sturdy torso.

His body was unrecognizable. She'd reduced it to scrap parts.

Caim stepped beside her.

"Impressive. You've taken to this well, my love."

They kissed.

Their tongues fought.

He held her rump.

She clutched the fleshy coin purse between his legs.

"I can't wait to spend eternity in Hell with you," Flo said. "I never thought I'd be lucky to find myself a man quite so perfect!"

Caim showed all of his rancid teeth. "I can't wait either, Flo. I mean that. But first . . . there's another order of business you must take care of."

"There is?" She scrunched up her face.

"A deal's a deal."

Her eyes brightened.

"Oh yeah! I 'bout forgot! Think that shotgun they had would do the trick?"

"Flo. How disappointing. I figured after *this*"—Caim indicated the corpses—"you'd come up with something a bit more creative!"

Flo frowned. She thought a moment, pursing her lips and knitting her hairless brows. Then a wicked smile slashed across her face.

"Oh, don't underestimate little ol' me, Caim. You oughta know . . . I'm fulla surprises!"

●●●

With all of our stories told—and recorded by Danielle Yeager, who sits by my side—we slither back into the shadows. Flinchingly and painfully, we vanish. Like ghosts through walls. The smell and heat of our stories linger in the air, coiling around The Scrapyard like venomous snakes.

Some people can handle living here . . . others can't.

We've tested you tonight. Our guest. You sat with us and listened to our tales.

Next time, you need to participate.

Next time . . . you must find a scrap of your own . . . and you must tell us a story . . .

ABOUT THE WRITERS

Judith Sonnet is a very sad girl. She writes gross and disturbing horror books, and she collects old paperbacks as well as '70s action movies. She grew up in Missouri, but now she lives in Utah. She's trans, asexual, and is an abuse and suicide survivor. If you want to know more about her, check her out on Facebook... or contact her through your nearest Ouija board.

She is the author of *No One Rides for Free*, *Beast of Burden*, and *Low Blasphemy*. *Scraps* is her first curated anthology. She plans on doing a few more.

Harrison Phillips is an English author of extreme horror and splatterpunk fiction. His literary influences range from Clive Barker and Stephen King to Jack Ketchum and Edward Lee. He was born and raised in Birmingham, England, where he still resides with his long-suffering wife, their two daughters, and a schnauzer named Minnie. He is the author of *Shotgun Nun, Night of the Freaks,* and *Field Trip.*

Twitter: www.twitter.com/harrisonhorror
TikTok: www.tiktok.com/@harrisonphillipshorror
vestigialpress@hotmail.com

Cassandra Daucus is inspired by HP Lovecraft, MR James, Shirley Jackson, Robert Aickman, and a ton of fan fiction. Cassandra Daucus (she/her) writes soft horror (mostly). She is intrigued by how the human mind responds to the unknown and also enjoys a good gross-out. She has stories in *Ooze: Little Bursts of Body Horror*, *October Screams*, *Mouthfeel Fiction*, and *Witch House*, and forthcoming from Hungry Shadow Press, From Beyond Press, and others. Cassandra lives outside of Philadelphia with her family and three cats, where she ponders the medieval and lovingly caresses dead skin while working as a curator of rare books.

Her social media and website can be found at https://residualdreaming.com.

Stephanie E. Jensen is the author of the *Dissecting House* series and *The Howling of the Dead*. She received a Bachelor of Arts degree in English from the University of South Florida in 2014. She's a full-time professional writer and a music journalist. Stephanie lives in Tampa, Florida, and travels frequently.

RE Shambrook writes horror smut, or what he likes to call GORErotica. He prefers to be called Bob, but he can't figure out how anyone decided that Bob could be derived from Robert. He can understand Rob or Robbie, but Bob? In fact, his family still calls him Bobby, but I digress. He writes the *Graves* series. It's full of good stuff! If you like demons and snuff films, explicit sex and gore, and small-town cannibalism and satanic cults, then he invites you to Graves, Illinois, where devil worship, burgers, and violent sexual activity are all the rage.

Jayson Dawn is modern horror's answer to "What's that smell?" Quickly rising in the ranks as a name to watch, he uses his distinct descriptive ability for evil. Well-versed in many forms of horror, his stories defy genre stereotypes and offer passage into terrors only the most deranged can fathom. An eccentric lifetime lover of horror, he's honored to be welcomed into the world of splatterpunk and the extreme and hopes to push readers to their darkest, most suppressed limits. Jayson Dawn is currently sleep-deprived in a lightless dungeon somewhere near Orlando, Florida, likely with a cat on his lap.

He is the author of *Bloodbag: A Floridian Love Story*.

Ruth Anna Evans is a horror writer, anthologist, and cover designer who lives in the heart of all that is sinister: the American Midwest. She has self-published the horror collection *No One Can Help You: Tales of Lost Children and Other Nightmares*, along with novellas, novelettes, and several short stories. She is the editor of *Ooze: Little Bursts of Body Horror.* She also has work appearing in several recent anthologies, including *The First Five Minutes of the Apocalypse* from Hungry Shadow Press. She is the author of *What Did Not Die,* published by PsychoToxin Press, and the novella *Do Not Go In That House* from Gloom House Publishing. Most recently, she edited the anthology *Dark Blooms: Girls' Coming-of-Age Horrors*, featuring sixteen women writers telling stories of the death of girlhood.

Follow Ruth Anna on Twitter @ruthannaevans and on Facebook at Ruth Anna Evans. Contact Ruth Anna Evans at authorruthannaevans@gmail.com.

Chaz Williams is a horror author, poet, and reviewer, and blogger for Uncomfortably Dark. He's been published in multiple anthologies and his debut novella *Family Til' It Can't Be, Gang Til' It Ain't* released this year. He lives in Southern California with his family.

Brian G Berry is a writer who specializes in bringing the golden era of slasher, action, and sci-fi trash films to book form. He has written over fifty books, including *Snow Shark* and *Fragments,* and is featured in eight anthologies. He started Slaughterhouse Press in November 2023 and is currently writing his next book.

Otis Bateman lives in Missouri, where he writes his sick and depraved stories in his dilapidated trailer home. He is creepy and disturbing. When he is not writing, he enjoys slasher, gore, and snuff films, especially snuff films. He also enjoys watching random people sleep through their bedroom windows late at night, while tapping on the glass softly. He is the author of *My Vice is Your Unfathomable Agony.*

Mique Watson is the author of *Them*, *Broken Dolls*, and *Broken Dolls: Deliverance*. He is a red flag who makes money off his trauma. When he's not thinking of ways to ruin your day and defile a human body, he is . . . Actually, I don't know what else he does with his time. Steer clear of this one.

A very special thank you to Judith Sonnet's Patreon members!
Mandee Kelly
Ashley Chmielewski
Carli Love
Shannon Bradner
Sam Wehry
PRC
Kris Bentley
Don Taylor
Mary Curran
Marc Scharbach (A Podcast on Elm Street)
Damaris Quinones
Carrie Shields

Milton Keynes UK
Ingram Content Group UK Ltd.
UKHW032043180324
439698UK00001B/48